MIRRORS

MIRRORS

PHILLIP A. WEAVER

proving
press

Book Design & Production: Columbus Publishing Lab
www.ColumbusPublishingLab.com

Paperback ISBN: 978-1-63337-315-0
E-Book ISBN: 978-1-63337-316-7

Printed in the United States of America

Dedicated to my family, with a special thank you to Tracy Dils and those who encouraged my writing journey.

PROLOGUE

The year was 1931. Two businessmen were in their office in a heated argument. Blows were exchanged, the fever of the fight grew; rage took over, and with the crack of a single shot the fight was done. A spray of blood jetted through the air and across the very first mirror their father had made in this factory, a large rectangular masterpiece which had hung from the wall behind his desk their whole lives. Thus the disagreement was ended and all fell silent.

The Depression was in full swing; times were tough and looking only to get worse for the future. The men were more than just partners in a mirror business. They were brothers, best friends, and also about to be broke. Thomas and Richard Walton were twenty-two and twenty-five, respectively. Young, but men by the times. Their father had come to this country before they were born, crossing the Atlantic with little more than hope in his heart and lint in his pockets. Taking an American wife, he found a home, made a family, built a business and made it work—America by example, the dream lived.

In the old country he had worked in a glass factory. He was not highly educated, but was a smart man, dedicated to quality and craftsmanship. With a loan from his bride's family, he opened the doors to a glass and mirror factory. In twenty-seven years he built a solid business, employed hundreds, and made a quality product for a reasonable price. His competitors respected him, his customers appreciated him, and his employees saw him as an honorable man. He was not greedy and paid his employees well. Deals were done with a handshake and credit was given to all.

Their father's death was sudden. Thomas and Richard were now equal partners, and it couldn't have come at a worse time. Economic conditions were almost medieval. Costs were up, the value of a dollar was thin, and they had hundreds of people counting on them. As with many brothers, they were often on opposite sides, and the question of what to do with the factory was no different. Debts were overdue, payments were late, payroll was vapor and stress was overflowing.

MIRRORS

Thomas Walton wanted to liquidate the business, sell off what they could while they could, take the money and run. Thomas had gone off to university, learned business and accounting; he could see the Depression for what it was. He could see only a black future for all if they didn't cut loose now. The bleeding of what funds they'd had was over and the money was gone. They had made cuts where they could, but quality was suffering. He could foresee a slow and ugly death for the business, leaving him and his brother with nothing, or even worse, debt.

Richard Walton had his father's hope and dedication. He never went off to school. Instead, he stayed and learned the business from the bottom to the top. He was the eldest and felt his obligation to the workers they had employed for years. Selling off the company was not an option, in debt or not. He had cut his own wages to as low as those of the boy they paid to sweep up. He had sold his car and a number of items from his own home to make the payroll. He had learned from his father and wanted to keep his workers working.

With such ideals and characters, with so much hanging in the balance, the debate went back and forth. Words aren't always enough in an argument, and this particular one was no different. Harsh words and deep feelings led to pushes and shoves, which evolved into a punch, and the brothers dispensed with conversation. They wrestled from the desks to the floor and around the office they had played in as children, in the very room where they had sat upon their father's lap behind his desk and learned to be men. They now each fought for their ideal of what was right, and their futures.

Every problem was solved in the fight. No way around it, no way to avoid the inevitable. The stronger the ideal or principle, the greater the man's willingness to see his way forward. Blood may be thicker than water, but it spills the very same, and has stained the world in its journey toward a believed sense of righteousness since Cain and Abel.

The year was 1938. Through a beautiful stained glass and oak front door entered a not-so-notorious gangster, closing the door behind him. His fedora and overcoat were the uniform of his profession as a thug, a gangster, a bootlegger; living high on the hog with blood money, uncaring of the destruction in his wake. He whistled a tune of the day as he removed his hat and coat and placed them on the rack just inside the door. Pulling off his suit jacket, he revealed the tools of his labor: a forty-five caliber automatic hanging under each arm.

What a dapper fellow, he thought as he pushed back his slick hair, looking into the large and very decorative mirror that hung in his hallway. He cracked a smirk, pleased with his life and feeling swell with his status. He was a made man, wealthy, with his pick of women—voluntarily or not. Women never turned him down. His smile grew as he thought of other people, poor, out of work, weak, standing in lines and sweating for pennies. Suckers—he knew a chump at a glance. They were his prey, and anyone else who might stand in his way.

He squinted at his reflection, thinking of the reputation he had cultivated: cold-blooded, ruthless, hard. Such a rep was a benefit in his work, and he made the effort to ensure he had a story to match. When the bosses needed a job done, they called him. His ambition was not lost in his own gaze; he could see the want, the need for power, money, all the things he ever wanted. He knew in time he would have it all, for he would take it. Taking what he wanted was the core of who he was and the basis for what he did.

A knock at the door took his attention away from his reflection. He approached the door with a cocky strut, seeing two of his fellow thugs through the stained glass. He let them in, giving a grin to his friends, thinking the boss must have another job to be done, a call for his skills as a badass. For such a man it should not have been such a surprise to find gun barrels awaiting him on the other side of the door. But it was.

The gangster had no time to react. Standing there holding the door, he felt the heat as the barrels spat fire. Thunder followed as the flames continued to burp forth from each gun, a slight delay in sight and sound, flash then crack. His body caught shell after shell, and he could feel the flesh being pushed through his body. He felt a searing heat and could taste copper. He tried to close the door, as if there was some protection to be had behind it. The stained glass shattered, raining down in colorful shards onto the hardwood floor.

He found himself on his fancy carpet, flat on his back. The shooting had stopped and his ears rang, but he could hear one man laugh, footfalls on the steps, the sound of a dog bark in the distance, the beat of his own heart. At some point he had stopped feeling the penetration of the lead, though ten bullet holes flowed with blood. He couldn't feel or move his legs, he could taste the metal in his mouth and spat blood. He screamed and cursed his killers, spewing blood from his lips with every word. "God damn you!"

He looked around, hoping for help but knowing better. His beautiful door was closed. The stained glass was gone, and he could see into the night. His hat hung from its hook above his coat and his jacket lay on the floor. His eyes moved along the wall. He needed to reach the telephone, to call for help. Part of him actually hoped the police had been watching and would rush in to save him. His eyes were drawn to the fancy mirror upon his wall; the image was not right. In the reflection, there was not the same ceiling he could see above him. It was dirty, and the paint was chipped and peeling. The reflection was darker, ominous.

So, this is death, he thought. Thoughts of his deeds and his life flooding him, until the mirror rippled like a pond, drawing his focus. The glass of the mirror began to extend. A head came out of the reflection. As it turned and looked at him, lying helpless on the floor, he recognized familiar features. The Roman nose, the black slicked-back hair, those eyes of a true killer...

He blinked. It was his face, but very, very different. There was no color to it—it was grey and pasty, like the day-old dead. He felt fear in his heart as the image and his eyes locked. The expression on its face was one he had never seen before: not angry or mad, but its eyes were filled with pure hate. Vicious, savage, primal. The face was thin, the bones predominant with gaunt cheeks and sunken eyes, dark circles under them. As the torso emerged from the mirror, he saw that it was unclothed.

The gangster's mind raced. He must be dead already and hell had come to claim him. Yet, as he lay there wide-eyed and terrified, he could feel the beat of his heart in his throat. He was still alive. It pounded, racing faster as the blood flowed from his wounds in a steady stream. There was no way this was real.

It emerged from the mirror and landed on the walnut floor with a thud. It—for though it looked like him, like a man, it was not.

It moved quickly, but in a jerky manner, like a foal on fresh legs. It was bony, starved, and the fingers were long and strange-looking. From the fingertips grew long, thick nails that were bloody at the quicks. Claw-like and dirty, the nails extended at least three or four inches. Within a blink it stood over him, squatting over his chest, face to face. Its mouth opened and a foul smell fell upon the gangster's nose. Blackened and broken teeth, sharp edges and a stench of decay, but no sound came from the beast. Horror gripped the gangster, as he gasped to scream out, but his lungs had long been emptied of air by the bullets.

The gangster looked into the face of the mirror image, the creature that looked like him, had him. Its bony hands gripped his neck, the claw-like fingers wrapping all the way around. His throat felt as if it was in a vise, and the pressure made it feel as if his spine would snap. The monster stood and jerked him up by his head, lifting him clean off the wood floor with one hand. His feet dangled.

The gangster could feel darkness taking over. The creature bent at the knees and lunged toward the mirror, taking him back where it had come from.

With a final wave in the glass, both were gone. Only a broken stained-glass door, a few bullet holes, and the bloodstains on the hardwood floor were left to show they were ever there.

The year was 1941. December 7, 1941, to be exact. Hawaii: paradise to most, and up until moments ago, paradise for the young Navy lad who now found himself on a stretcher. He had been on leave, enjoying the beautiful island. He was sleeping off a hangover when he awoke to the sounds of war.

He ran out to see what the commotion was and was hit in a strafing run by a Japanese Zero. He was alive, but from the waist down he was riddled with large-caliber bullet wounds. He had lay there in the grass for what seemed like forever, listening to the sounds of bullets and bombs, the planes flying overhead. They were under attack.

Finally, a few men arrived and began to pick up the wounded. He was the fifth to be taken into the house for cover. His pain finally overcame his fear and he passed out. When he came to, he had no idea how long he had been unconscious. Now there were about twenty men in the room with him. Some of the men were shot like he was, some burned, but all were in bad shape. The moans and cries were just terrible; his own agony seemed only to echo back at him.

He could hear people yelling outside and moving about the home. Men would come in and set another man onto the living room floor, then rush out again. A young woman checked on him, gave him water and looked at his legs. In the distance, he could still hear the sounds of war, explosions and sirens, a sound he had hoped to never know. It was now all too clear.

A scream from one of the other men brought his attention back. The man was burned black, the flesh pulled away from his bones. He had jumped ship, seeking the safety of the water: a mistake. Fuel and oil from the sinking ships floated on the water and caught fire; there was no escape. Stay aboard the ship and get shot, blown up, burned alive, or sink and drown. Flee to the water and get shot, burn alive with oil sticking right to you or drown trying to stay under water and away from the flames.

This guy had jumped, and what a horror. His pain had to be unimaginable. You could hear it in his screams, his moans. The oil baked to his skin, and it was pink and red beneath. Only sections where some of his clothes had covered him and were wet had escaped somewhat—those were blistered and red. It wasn't a question of whether he was going to die or not, only a matter of when. He wasn't alone in his torture; most of the men looked as he did. Their screams were a choir of agony, singing a song of the living dead.

The young navy lad could only think to pray. He closed his eyes and began. "The Lord is my shepherd, I shall not want." Other voices joined him, weak and frightened: "Though I walk through the valley of…" It was not an "Amen" that stopped this prayer but a very different kind of scream: a scream of terror. He opened his eyes and scanned the room. Other men also searched for the source of such fear. The sound came from the lips of the woman who had given him the water.

He looked her up and down. Her mouth was open, her face drained of color, frozen like a stone. She didn't appear to be injured, but her eyes were locked on something behind him, and filled with terror. His stomach knotted: had the enemy somehow invaded the room? He followed her gaze to the back wall, but there was nothing there. Only a mirror that hung from the wall. Could she see a reflection of something?

Then he saw. He couldn't believe his own eyes; he rubbed at them, trying to clear away what he was seeing. Men were crawling out from the glass. He looked over their faces. Their stares were not of this world. Evil lay within each of their eyes. That was when he saw what looked to be a twin of himself stand from the floor after birthing from the mirror. He had no brother, but this naked thing looked exactly like him, except for its color and the fact that he could see its ribs. The damn thing looked like it had never known the sun.

With grotesque motions, each creature moved quickly toward a man. His own familiar came to him. The woman's screams never stopped, but were only joined by many of the other men. He couldn't scream, he couldn't talk and he couldn't take his eyes from his own face. Even as the creature picked him up off the stretcher with one hand clinched around his throat, fear turned him mute.

From the corner of his eye, he could see that other men were also being abducted. These creatures moved with such speed and strength, but also in such a twisted manner. Trying to turn his head and follow one of the other injured men, he watched as the kidnapper leaped at the mirror upon the wall with his victim in his arms, and disappeared.

Fear or not, he began to struggle against the stranglehold of this man-beast, but to no avail. The bony fingers only gripped tighter. The navy lad could no longer catch a breath. With a bounce he was airborne, coming parallel to the floor. He could still hear the screaming woman who had watched the whole thing. Then he was gone.

The year was 1956. A man stood shirtless in a bathroom, his slicked-back hair in exact position. A handsome and well-built man of only twenty, strong and fit, rebellious in nature but solid in convictions. A greaser or hood by current terms, yet not so different from anyone else. He brushed lather on his face and began to shave with a long stroke. The reflection revealed a smooth face and strong chin.

As he ran the razor over his upper lip, he nicked himself, not terribly but deep enough to bleed. He wiped away the blood with his finger and continued. Finished, he splashed water onto his face. A small trail of blood streamed down from his upper lip, over his mouth and down his chin. He splashed his face again, washing away the blood, then moved closer to inspect himself. "God knows, you are one good-looking man."

His expression changed from confident to questioning. His gaze into the mirror showed the walls behind him turning dingy and grey. The tiles cracked and the mortar blackened, looking aged and overused. He returned to his own image, the handsome man of whom he was so proud. His reflection grew pale, the veins in his face becoming apparent. He looked sick and weak, ugly. The man before him wasn't correct. The reflection was a lie.

He turned to the room, seeing it as it had always been: clean and white and new, all the tiles complete, the caulk fresh as the day it was installed. He returned to the mirror, now a total contrast to his world. The image before him was a recognizable stranger. He drew closer to explore the phenomenon, this odd twist in reality. He raised an eyebrow; the image echoed it in return. He smiled at the distorted reflection and it smiled back, with black gums and jagged teeth. Then the image cocked its head, though he had not.

He pulled back in pure surprise, but it was too late. From the mirror leapt two hands, gripping his fresh face on either side. The hands jerked him into the dark world and he was gone.

The clean white bathroom was quiet and empty, the reflection in the mirror gone. The only color was a single drop of red blood running down the porcelain sink toward the drain.

The year was 1967. A voluptuous woman in a white robe entered her bathroom and got supplies from the medicine cabinet behind the mirror. She sat on the lid of the toilet and lifted a lovely leg up, resting it on the side of the tub. Her beehive hairdo, large and well sprayed, was almost solid. She hummed a little tune as she rubbed lotion up and down her leg.

She thought of the night ahead as she shaved her long legs. She knew she was a sexy woman, that her legs drew a lot of attention from men. Many men had complimented her; these legs were her best feature. Rubbing the soft. smooth skin, she shaved high up her thigh. Tonight was going to be a very good night, she thought.

She switched legs, rubbing lotion on; with long strokes, she removed the coarse hairs. Perhaps thinking of her plans for the evening or the short miniskirt she was going to wear, she lost focus and gashed her shin. A deep cut, very painful. "God damn it!" she yelled, from the shock of pain and the sight of the cut. It wasn't exactly lady-like language, but she knew that would leave a scar.

Stepping into the tub and turning on the water, she splashed cold water down her leg, rinsing the cut. The blood mixed with the water as it ran down the drain. She examined the wound, not pleased with this turn of events. She had taken a chunk of meat from the top of her leg. In her preoccupation, she never even realized she wasn't alone…not until it was too late.

The creature that came from the mirror did so in complete silence. Her darkest self took hold of that large cone atop her head. It began dragging her backward by her hair. The leggy woman kicked and screamed, helpless to stop her mirror image, hopeless in the effort. The naked beast sprang into the mirror, the beehive in its grip, towing the screaming woman along by the hair. With a ripple in the glass, they were gone. The only sound was the running water into the tub and the resonance of terror.

The year was 1975. A young woman, not even in her twenties, stood naked in a tub full of hot water. The steam lifted as she sat down, the water flowing over the rim of the tub and onto the floor. She leaned back and closed her eyes. She was beautiful. Built like a brick shithouse, or so she had been told. The face of an angel, with a body able to tempt any man. Large, firm breasts, perky and round—more than a mouthful. Long straight hair, like the black of a raven's wing. Her skin was flawless, soft and smooth; her ass was round and taut. She truly was a vision of youth and beauty.

How could something so perfect on the outside be so broken on the inside? The girl's eyes filled with tears as her delicate fingers slid the razor blade from the edge of the sink. She took a few deep breaths as she looked at her wrist, wet and dripping. The purple-blue of her veins lay just underneath her creamy white skin. Taking the razor in her left hand, holding up her right wrist, she focused and eased the edge across.

The pain was slow in coming because the blade was so very sharp. Her tears gave way to sobs as she realized that she had not cut deep enough. She must try again. Hesitation marks: that was what she had heard them called. The real skinny was the fear and the pain, but also the remaining doubt. Suicide was rarely a quick decision, not a spur-of-the-moment thing. The choice to end your own life had to build, develop; the act was no different. She switched hands and gave a true and deep cut to the other one, a solid swipe. She felt her pulse.

She tried to do the other wrist, but the tendons were cut and her hand wouldn't work. She put the razor blade into her mouth and with a quick motion, ran her wrist across the edge. The hot water was now a ruby red. She spat the razor into the water and laid her head back on the edge of the bathtub. Looking up at the ceiling, she said, "No one cares. No one loves me. Even God hates me."

She caught movement out of the corner of her eye and looked over her shoulder. She could not believe what she was seeing. A naked alter-image, crawling through the mirror. Hands on the sink, half of its body was still unrevealed. Long fingers gripped the porcelain, like claws. She sat up with a jerk, frightened, sliding to the other end of the tub to gain as much distance as possible. Her movement pushed a wave of bloody water over the side and onto the floor.

The figure's hair was dirty, stringy, hanging over its face. It moved swiftly but as if on broken legs. It was at the edge of the tub reaching out for the girl. She put up her hands to try and defend herself, but a number of her fingers were floppy and useless. Attempting to keep the creature at bay, fighting to stay away from it, she pushed herself into the corner of the bathtub. Blood ran down her arms, dripping from her elbow into the steaming water. Her bloody slashed wrists pumped out the life she now fought so hard to hang onto.

The girl extended her hands to try and keep the pale thing away, but her wounds made her hands useless. The creature knocked the girl's arms out of the way and extended its own bony arm. The long fingers opened; with a quick movement, the monster's palm punched into the girl's mouth and nose with incredible force. She felt the bony hand wrap around her skull and take hold. The grip was crushingly strong. Holding out its arm straight, the creature pulled back and stood erect, dangling the naked girl above the hot water. Blood dripped from her toes back into the tub.

Through the gaps in the fingers, the two exchanged a look, meeting eye to eye for just a moment. Bloodshot and colorless, the creature's eyes weren't blue or brown or green, just grey with crooked lines; the veins in the whites vivid like a road map of evil. The creature's eyes only held dark intentions, creating such fear in the girl she began to urinate.

It turned, pulling her away from the tub and out over the floor. With one leap the two passed through the mirror. With a final ripple in the glass, they were gone.

Slowly, the reflection of the dark world returned to our own and the gateway closed. The dripping of the bloody water from the tub echoed in the silence.

The year was 1989. A group of young urban professionals were gathered to celebrate the holidays, seated around a coffee table, drinking, smoking pot, and doing lines of cocaine. The conversation was lively and all were of good cheer. One of the women mentioned to the owner of the apartment what a beautiful coffee table he had, then proceeded to snort another large line of powder off of the glass table. Talking a mile a minute, the owner of the apartment explained how he found the large round mirror at a yard sale in New England, and bragged how he had haggled down the price. He had the stand built especially for it.

He went on about how it was one of a kind, a classic, what with the quality and thickness of the glass, the clarity of the reflection. He cut himself a number of thick and very long rails and began to sing: "I'm dreaming of a white Christmas." He stopped to inhale a healthy amount of coke. "Oh, yeah." His eyes bulged and he gave a heavy snort, swallowing the drainage. Running his index finger over where the line had been and rubbing it across his upper gum line, he said, "That's good shit."

Then he sprang to his feet. "Drinks, drinks?" he asked, pointing from person to person, his mind rushing with a fresh dose of energy. As he skirted the coffee table and headed for his kitchen, one of the women moved into his spot and prepared a line for herself. She chopped at the powder with a gold razor blade, then drew the edge down the mirror to reveal a straight line of white. Laying the razor on the table, she picked up the hundred-dollar bill and snorted half of the line into one nostril.

She put the tube up to her other nostril to finish her line, but her nose began to bleed, dripping down onto the coffee table and into the coke. "Damn it!" she said, as the blood really began to flow.

"Move! You stupid bitch! You're getting blood in the shit!" The owner rushed back to save the drug.

"Hold your head back," one of the other women instructed the bleeding woman.

Trying to scrape the pile of coke away from the blood, the owner continued to lash out in a hateful tone. "You dumb bitch! What in the fuck! Messing up the party. Don't you know what you're doing?"

"God, I am so sorry; you and your precious cocaine. I'm fucking bleeding here." She held her head back, pinching her nostrils together.

As the owner continued to scrape and move the pile with the gold-colored razor, he saw the drops of blood begin to soak into the glass. Leaning back and shaking his head in confusion, he blinked, attempting to refocus. He watched the blood continue to simply melt right into the table. Not truly believing his own eyes, he said, "Wow, that is really good shit." He looked around at the other items on the table: all of them were sinking into the glass. Beer bottles, the hundred-dollar bill, the razor, but to his horror, also the coke, each slowly sinking into their own reflection.

As he watched this incredible sight, he realized something wasn't melting into the glass but beginning to emerge from it. It was a head and then shoulders; topless and skinny, the spitting image of the bloody-nosed girl. The owner took a number of steps back, saying, "What the fuck!"

The other guests also began to create distance between themselves and the coffee table. The bloody-nosed girl pushed herself back against the sofa and looked up at the figure towering over her.

One of the women, now fleeing toward the kitchen, screamed, "Where are its legs?"

The owner could see the naked figure from the edge of the couch where he had now moved. Leaning over, he could see the thighs and knees, pasty white or almost grey, but they stopped at the surface of the mirror. He moved his head further to see under the table. The naked creature was not standing on the floor or the table. It was standing inside the glass.

The creature's shoulders slanted and its gaze traveled the room, finally focusing on the girl with the bloody nose sitting feebly on the sofa. Its arms raised and its hands extended as the back arched. It looked like a snake trying to slither. Then, like a coiled rattler, it struck, pouncing forward, embracing the coked-up girl. She freaked, kicking, screaming and flailing.

The owner grabbed a beer bottle and threw it at the naked creature, but watched as the bottle bounced off its head and smashed against the wall. This gained the attention of the creature. Its black eyes turned on the man. "Leave her alone!" he screamed. The naked she-beast threw the bloody-nosed girl against the wall, knocking an audible grunt from her. In a flash, the creature took hold of the girl's hair. Pushing her head out to face the man, as if displaying it, the creature spoke.

".enim si ehS" it growled, in a raspy and gargled, strained voice.

Its eyes were trained on the owner. The creature then threw the girl by the hair toward the coffee table. The owner winced at the sight of this woman being flipped head-first toward the glass. He expected to hear it shatter, but it didn't. As had been the case with the creature's legs, the bloody-nosed girl didn't break the coffee table, didn't hit the floor; she had been thrown into the mirror. In a blur, the creature followed right behind her, diving headlong into the coffee table. Ripples in the glass were all that were left, like a calm pond with a single stone thrown in it.

The year was 1996. A family gathered around a large dining table to celebrate Thanksgiving. Parents and children, aunts and uncles, grandchildren, all at their proper seats. The whole room was filled with smells that moistened the palate. Mashed potatoes with gravy, creamed corn, noodles, turkey and stuffing, fresh bread and all the trimmings; the food was steaming hot and visually magnificent. Mother entered with the fixture of the occasion on a large platter: a large golden roasted turkey.

Father took a large carving knife and began to sharpen the blade, down one side and then the other. The sound of metal on metal quieted the room. He took a towel and wiped the blade clean, then picked up a large fork. He penetrated the golden skin of the turkey. Juice flowed down onto the plate. "Juicy," Father said. The meat was white and moist as father lays slice after slice upon a serving dish.

Moving one of the legs toward the dish, he nodded his approval to the rest of the family. As he again sliced the bird, the blade slipped and struck Father on the first knuckle of his left hand. He put down his utensils and stepped away from the table, wanting not to bleed on anything or disturb anyone's appetite. Taking a towel, he dabbed at the cut; deep, but not so terrible. He wrapped up his hand. Mother was now by his side to play nurse. Father insisted all be seated so they could continue. Then he asked all to join in the grace.

As they finished and their heads raised, eyes were opened and smiles shared all around. That was when Father saw a figure standing on the serving table at the side of the room, just below their large mirror. A large, bald and portly man, a naked man; a man who looked—well, it looked just like him. Father pushed back from the table and stood.

The figure leapt to the center of the table. Everyone jumped with a start. Gravy spilled; the fat, grey man stood in the sweet potatoes. The family fled the table. There was a commotion of screams and children crying, chairs being knocked over. But not Father: he stood his ground, reaching down and picking up the carving knife.

The creature moved directly for Father, stomping the festive meal as he approached. Father took a step back and raised the large blade, pulling it back. With a striking blow he drove the large carving knife deep into the chest of the fat, bold figure. There was no sign of pain, no blood, not even a look of discomfort—only a glance down at the weapon embedded in its chest.

The creature crouched, scooped, and reached out under Father's arms and lifted the hefty man like a feather, then tossed the two-hundred-plus-pound man over its shoulder like a bag of dog food. Father began to kick and yell, struggling to come loose of the creature's grasp. He fought with everything he had, but to no avail. With a turn in the stuffing, the creature kicked the turkey to the floor and started back down the long dining table.

With an effortless hop, the creature and its bounty return to the serving table below the mirror. Father's eyes scanned his family, a look of terror exchanged between each member. As quickly as it had begun, it was over. As if disappearing behind a waterfall, the mirror absorbed the two, and they were gone. Sobs and fear were left in their wake as the monarch of the family had been stolen away, taken, right before their eyes.

CHAPTER 1

The year was 1996. The Mason family had planned an overdue vacation: a road trip across the country. Time to bond as a family and see the sights; no rush or hurry, no one to visit or destination to arrive at, no schedules, no agenda. Just drive, view the countryside, take pictures, stay at motels, relax and enjoy each other's company.

The Mason family arrived at the Star Bird Inn only a little after three in the afternoon. Even though they had no real schedule, their normal time for stopping for the night was closer to seven. The Star Bird was also a little higher price range than they had averaged, but the night before had been crazy, so Cole had decided to upgrade so they could get some rest.

The previous night, the Mason family had stopped at one of those chain motels, a thirty-bucks-a-night type place. It was clean and all had seemed normal enough, so the family had gone to bed with no worries. At two thirty in the morning, all kinds of bells and whistles sounded, commotion and people yelling and running about. Someone had pulled the fire alarm.

Cole had put on his jeans and shoes, wanting to investigate. He stepped out onto the walkway—they were on the second floor—but didn't smell any smoke or see any flames. Back in the room, Cole told Molly, his wife, to stay in here with their son, Johnny. He would go check things out and make sure everything was all right. Grabbing a shirt, Cole closed the door behind him and headed downstairs. A crowd had begun to gather, so he approached to gain information.

The alarm was still sounding loudly and it was difficult to hear people just a few feet away. People were pointing, and he could make out a few phrases. Cole mused to himself that not all people knew the difference between white smoke and black. He noticed a number of biker types, their leather vests with fancy skulls and snakes on the back a dead giveaway. They were now pointing up at the motel. Turning to see what had caught the rough crowd's interest, Cole saw his wife standing at the railing. Apparently, he had been gone too long; Molly was out waving at him, trying to get his attention over the sound of the alarm.

Molly had gotten his attention now, along with an entire bike gang. She was in her nightgown, totally unaware that there was a large emergency floodlight on the wall right behind her. The white cotton nightgown was almost transparent, and the silhouette of her figure was gaining hoots and whistles from the bikers.

Molly looked at him as he tried to yell over the alarm. He waved at her to go back inside, but she didn't understand his flailing. "Is there a fire?" she mouthed from the banister. The hoots and catcalls grew. Cole realized he needed to get her back inside their room.

Dashing up the stairs, he pulled his wife from the spotlight, to the chagrin of the biker fans she had begun to assemble. He explained as he led her back to the room. Cole watched his wife turn three shades of red in embarrassment. Needless to say, they got no sleep that night. The alarm wasn't turned off until the fire department arrived and assessed the situation, well after three in the morning. The flashing of the firetruck lights went on until after four.

So an early stop, at a nice hotel, just seemed like the thing to do. A treat for all on their vacation. The Star Bird was a five-story behemoth with classical styling and atmosphere. There was a restaurant, a bar, a spa and an indoor pool. Old as it was, it had class and style, an obvious remodel at some point. The main desk was large and made of oak, with key slots on the wall behind it, like in the old movies. The light fixtures were classic-style but new with a pewter finish. The carpet too was lush, but recently purchased.

Little Johnny was excited about the pool; even as they rode the elevator up to the fourth floor, he hadn't stopped asking to go swimming. As they started down the long corridor, Molly told Johnny he could swim before dinner. Cole noticed how quiet and plush the hotel was. The carpet thick and new, the numbers and knobs on the doors were all brass, with fresh polish. Light fixtures lined the hallway, also in shiny brass. The molding at the baseboards and along the ceiling were all oak. Yet the most predominant feature was the large decorative mirrors that alternated left and then right on the walls between each room.

Johnny bounced down the hallway, this side and that, trotting along and jumping to catch his reflection. "Here it is, Dad!" Johnny yelled from halfway down the corridor. Cole trudged along with the luggage, and gave the boy a smile. The concierge had offered to help, explaining the bellboy had not shown up for work, but Cole had declined. The man was old, and alone at the front desk. He just looked old, frail, and weak; it was probably a task for the man to just round the desk. Still, the old bird had spunk, even to offer.

Molly had the key; she stepped around her husband and opened the door for him. The room was very nice, with the same care and detail as the rest of the hotel. *This remodel must have cost a fortune*, Cole thought. The brass numbers on the door read Room 411. The numbers were so shiny, Cole saw his reflection as he entered the room. Two queen-sized beds took up most of the room. There was also a table and chairs by the window, a dresser on the right side, an easy chair in the corner, and a nightstand between the beds, with a phone on top of it.

Above each bed hung paintings, the type of cheap art you purchase at a Holiday Inn over a weekend, those manufactured pieces they churn out for just this type of theater. Tired travelers would look over the painting once before putting it out of their minds forever. The color choice of the bedspreads and curtains was a touch odd to Cole: a thick blood-red, dark but not dark enough for his taste.

Johnny was already bouncing on one of the beds as Cole set down the bags. Molly had gone straight to the bathroom and closed the door, then yelled for Cole to pull out Johnny's swimming trunks. Cole walked over to the bed and sat down with a plop. Laying back, he felt the softness of the bed, and his whole body relaxed.

Molly threw open the door. "You have got to see this bathroom, it's beautiful. What are you doing? Did you find the trunks?"

Cole furrowed his brow. He had found a comfortable spot and did not want to move. Pushing up from the bed with a groan, he said, "I didn't know what bag it was in."

"Well, go look at that bathroom. That's what I want for the house if we win the lottery."

Cole went to the door of the bathroom and looked inside. It was very nice indeed, posh even. The tiles on the wall had golden birds in a white background; the birds fanned out and kind of looked like a star. *Star Bird Inn*, he thought.

There was another large mirror over the sink; *this place must have gotten some kind of deal on huge-ass mirrors*, he thought. The sink was large, with brass-colored fittings. The spout was wide and open at the tap. He turned the handle and water ran out like a waterfall over the edge of the spigot. "Never seen that before," Cole said to the empty room. In the reflection, he saw that the tub was gigantic, at least a two-seater, more probably a three or four, if they were little. There was a vanity and another mirror, a shower, and a window with smoked glass. It was very, very nice. Even the toilet was fancy: a throne, to be sure. The tank had a gold line in it and the lid of the commode had a golden bird fanned out.

Molly came in and ran a hand around Cole's midsection. "I need to get my suit on. Could you help Johnny with his? Are you coming swimming with us?"

"Hell, he could swim laps in that damn tub. Bet that thing holds a hundred gallons of water."

"Maybe we can take a late-night swim of our own, after Johnny goes to bed," she said with a naughty smile as she pushed Cole from the bathroom.

Johnny was already in his suit and raring to go. "Are you coming swimming with us, Dad?" the boy asked with enthusiasm.

"No, I don't think so, buddy. You and your mom can," Cole told his son.

Molly opened the bathroom door and Cole's mouth actually dropped open. "Like my new suit?" She smiled and gave a wink. It was a black two-piece, and it just barely covered her. She grabbed a couple towels off the bathroom rack and strutted out with attitude. "Honey, your trunks are on backward. Did your father not help you? The pocket goes in the back."

Johnny dropped his suit and flipped it around quick as you please.

Cole was checking out the back of his wife's new swimsuit. "You going down to the pool like that?" he had to ask.

Molly bent over and began to dig in one of the bags. "Thought I packed a wrap, to cover up with. Mind your eyes there sir, I'm a married woman," she said, as she squatted.

"There are robes in the closet, Mommy," Johnny said.

When did my son look in the closet? Cole wondered.

"Oh, I am taking this home," Molly announced as she produced a white terrycloth robe with a little golden bird on the upper breast. She slipped into it.

"This is so soft and fluffy. I'll bet they have to get these dry cleaned."

"Come on, MOM! Let's go already!" Johnny whined.

"I had better walk you down; don't want you running into any more bikers," Cole joked.

Molly opened the robe and shook her breasts at her husband. "They seemed to have enjoyed the show." She laughed.

She picked up the towels and Cole pocketed the room key. Johnny flew out the door and ran ahead of them down the hall. The family entered the elevator; even it was rather classy. It had a small sofa, which Johnny jumped right onto. Someone paid attention to the details. The elevator walls were like mirrors, but were actually some kind of polished brass or aluminum. You could see your reflection, but it was cloudy. The buttons were in an old-style font, and the indicator above the doors was the old-fashioned arm type that moved from number to number. He could see why the place had cost a little more.

CHAPTER 2

Walking through the lobby, Cole noticed many more things than he had upon entering. The columns, the crown molding, the chair rail, the fabric of the chairs, and the quality of wood on the tables; the whole hotel was full of expensive details. He gave the old man at the desk a wave as he and his little family followed the signs to the pool. Even the directional signage was upper scale: large brass engraved with large print.

He noticed one sign pointing the direction to the restaurant and bar, and one pointing the way to the pool.

"Going for a swim then, are you?" the old man asked from behind the desk.

"It's open, isn't it?" Molly asked in return.

"Absolutely. Just be careful: no lifeguards or anything. I'll have more towels brought up to your room for you. Anything you need, I am here."

The family found their way to a large door with the word *pool* painted on it in blue letters. It was like opening a door back in time; the pool was beautiful. The water was calm and blue, and the pool was very large, in an "L" shape. Large lions' heads made from brass lined the pool, spouting water from their open mouths. There were lounge chairs scattered about and a number of sun lamps on the far side. There was a large whirlpool and even a sauna.

A row of full-length windows covered the back wall. The whole place was empty. The only sound was the streams of water from the lion heads surrounding the pool. The sound made Cole need to pee.

"Oh my god, honey, this is so nice. I'm glad we stopped here. Guess it was worth a peep show for the bikers in order to stay here." Molly smiled a wicked smile as she peeled off the terrycloth robe. "I may have to get me some sun," she said, pointing at the sun lamps.

A scream drew their attention; Johnny was running and jumping into the pool. He splashed, happy, screaming just to hear the echo of the room.

"Sure you don't want to join us? That whirlpool would really relax you," Molly suggested.

"Maybe we will after dinner. Burn some of that energy out of the boy. Right now, I want to check out the bar," Cole said.

He headed back the way they had come. The restaurant and the bar had separate doors, one right next to the other. Pulling the bar door open, he saw that the room was dimly lit; his eyes quickly adjusted. There was a long bar that ran the length of the wall, with all the bottles up on the wall. There were tables scattered about and a piano toward the back. It was as he had expected: classy, and the attention to detail had not been spared.

The well-polished brass foot rail, the crystal-clear mirror behind the bottles of liquor, even the grandfather clock that stood in the corner: all perfect. The bartender wiping the bar said, "Good day to you, sir. And what can I do you for?"

Cole slid onto the stool, which was leather and soft. "Johnnie Walker, neat." The barkeep got right on the job, setting the glass on the bar and pouring a very healthy amount into the glass.

Cole flicked the glass with his finger and listened to the ring. "Crystal?"

"Of course, sir. Treat your guests well and they will always return," the barman said.

Cole sipped his drink. "That's a good motto. Do you have an ashtray?"

The bartender pulled an ashtray from behind the bar and wiped it clean before setting it down. There was a golden star bird in the bottom.

Cole had the bar to himself, and he enjoyed the quiet. The bartender kept busy dusting the bottles and wiping areas of the bar, and was quick to arrive as soon as Cole had emptied his glass. After three, he could feel a good buzz beginning and settled up the bill. Walking out of the bar and its quiet and darkened environment, Cole realized it was still pretty early. He rode up in the elevator, thinking of a cat nap.

The dial reached four with a dinging sound. The doors parted and Cole stepped into the corridor. Feeling the effects of the scotch, he smiled and headed toward his room. Suddenly, Cole Mason heard screaming—a bloody scream, horrific in nature. Worse, it sounded like his wife, and it was coming from their room.

Breaking into a run, he dashed toward the door to 411. Digging the key from his pocket, he threw open the door. The scream, no longer suppressed by the door, was loud, and coming from the bathroom. The bathroom door was ajar. Cole shouldered into it, expecting any kind of emergency. What he found made him just stop and question.

Molly was on her knees in the center of the large, fancy bathroom, screaming at the top of her lungs. Her hands were stretched out and her eyes were trained on the large mirror over the sink. She paused, took a deep breath, then screamed again.

Cole looked wildly around. There was a towel with blood on it next to the tub. He looked back into the room; Johnny was nowhere to be seen. Approaching his wife and trying to pick her up from her knees, he asked, "Molly, what the hell? Where is Johnny? Why are you screaming?" He purposefully kept his tone calm, seeing pure fear and panic in his wife's eyes. Her glazed expression began to change, her eyes filling with tears, but her focus remained on the mirror. "Molly, what is going on?" Cole began to shake her, trying to pry her from her condition.

She jerked away from him and rushed to the mirror, pawing at it, running her hands over the glass and the reflection. She began screaming again, digging at the glass with her fingernails.

Grabbing her by the arm, Cole pulled her away. Her eyes were no longer filled with fear: now they were determined and angry, angry that he had grabbed her. The screaming never stopped. She jerked free of his grasp and returned to the mirror.

Cole took hold of his wife again, and stepped between her and the mirror. "MOLLY! Stop this. You need to tell me what's going on!"

Her screaming stopped. She was breathing heavily, then she rushed at him, flailing and yelling, fighting like a lioness. Her hands slapped and her nails flew, as if he were an enemy. He felt her nails scrape across his face like claws in one good swipe.

Pushing her back with his left hand, he slapped her across the face, sending her to the floor in a lump.

Cole had never struck his wife, not ever. Looking down at her in her new bikini and feeling the pain in his face, he had no idea what in the hell was going on.

"It took him," Molly sobbed. Her whole body shaking and quivering as she hunkered on the floor.

"What?"

"IT TOOK HIM!" She screamed and her arm extended, her finger pointing.

Cole followed his wife's finger and turned to look. There was his reflection with three bloody lines down the left side of his face. He turned his head to get a better look and saw his wife rise up behind him.

"NO!! Don't get near the mirror!" she screamed again, grabbing him and trying to drag him out of the bathroom. He looked at his wife; he had never seen her like this before. He had never seen anyone like this before. She was out of her mind.

"What the hell is wrong with you?" Cole asked.

She grabbed his hand again and tugged at him, dragging him from the bathroom. As soon as he had stepped past the doorway, Molly rushed back into the bathroom and slammed the door, locking it.

"Molly, open the door; open it right now," Cole commanded. He was somewhat surprised as the door did open. Molly went right past him, to the baggage, throwing things about, then turned back around with his shaving kit in her hand. Running by him, back into the bathroom, she again slammed the door and locked it tight behind her.

"What the hell are you doing?" he demanded, but no answer came. Cole took a step back and delivered a full-force front kick. The door flew open. He couldn't believe his eyes: his wife was running his razor across the palm of her hand. She looked at her hand, then extended it over the sink and touched the mirror.

Cole dashed in, picked her up, and carried her from the bathroom, the sound of her bloody hand streaking across the glass as they went. She screamed and convulsed, fighting to free herself, her hands outstretched and reaching for the mirror. "I have to get him, put me down. I have to go after him," she said with urgency in her voice.

Flopping her down onto the bed, he stepped back and said, "Honey, you have to tell me what happened. You have to tell me, right now. What happened to Johnny?"

Molly put her head in her hands and cried for a minute. Then, pushing back her hair, she looked up at her husband. She had blood on her face and in her hair, her bottom lip quivered, and tears rolled down her cheeks.

Cole ran to the bathroom and grabbed a towel, bringing it back. Kneeling in front of his wife, he wrapped her cut with the towel.

"We were swimming, having fun. Johnny got out of the pool, to jump in and make a splash. He was running and fell down; cut his knee." Molly's voice was almost a whisper. "Wasn't a bad cut. But it was bleeding, so we got a key from the desk and some antiseptic, a band-aid, and came back to the room. Something came out of the mirror and took him. Took my baby!" she broke into tears again.

Cole didn't know what to think. "Something came out of the mirror?" he questioned. "Someone? What did they look like? Who came out of the mirror?"

Molly had broken down; tears flowed like streams from her eyes.

Cole marched back into the bathroom and examined the mirror. There was nothing strange about it. Finally, he pulled it from the wall with a powerful jerk, caulk and plaster falling into the sink. Only solid wall was behind it, the bare brick of the exterior wall, four floors up. He went to the other mirror and looked behind it, but there was nothing there either.

Molly stood at the door in shock and sadness, a glazed look upon her face.

"We have to call the police." Cole stepped past his wife. Pulling her by her uncut hand, he sat her on the bed and went to the phone. Cole picked up the receiver and punched nine, to get an outside line; then nine-one-one.

He explained to the operator that their son was missing. He gave the name of the hotel and the room number. The operator wanted him to remain on the line, but Cole needed more information from his wife so he hung up.

"Police are on the way; they will find him. Honey, tell me again, what happened? Every detail, everything. Tell me the truth." Cole kept his voice calm.

Molly was dazed, expressionless, glazed over. "I had him on the side of the tub, putting on the antiseptic. He complained that it burned. And then this thing, a creature, jumped out of the mirror and grabbed him."

"Creature? What did the man look like?" Cole asked.

"It. It, it, it looked like… It looked like Johnny; it looked like our son," she said, pure terror in her words. "But it wasn't. It was small like him, but looked dead. Naked and grey, bloodless. Little skinny body with ribs showing." She stared off into her memory. Molly's hands touched her own face in some sort of delirium. Then she looked at him. "What happened to your face?" she asked her husband.

Cole took a deep breath and stood there, looking down at his wife as she sat on the bed. Her mind so overtaken, he almost couldn't recognize her.

Then he looked up to see two police officers walk into the room, guns drawn.

Cole put up his palms. "I called, our son has gone missing."

CHAPTER 3

P lease step away from the woman; allow us to clear the scene, sir," one of the cops ordered.

Cole stepped aside and toward the officers, his hands still raised. "No problem. I don't know what the hell is going on here, guys, but our eight-year-old son is gone."

"Are there any weapons in the room, sir?" the officer asked.

"No, nothing like that."

One officer stayed by the door while the other took a quick look at Molly and then into the bathroom. He yelled out, "Clear," to the other officer.

The cop standing by the door lowered his weapon. "You left your key in the door there, sir. Now, why don't you tell me what's the problem?"

"My son is missing!"

The other officer came from the bathroom. "We have blood. Signs of a struggle," he said to his partner.

"Sir, why don't we step out in the hall here and you can tell me what happened?" the officer asked.

"Look, my son is missing! I asked my wife what happened, and what she said doesn't really make any sense. We need to search the hotel. Now!"

"Sir, I detect the smell of alcohol. Have you been drinking today?" the officer asked.

"I had a couple drinks at the bar. We need to find my son!" Cole reached for his wallet.

The cop reacted and started to raise his gun. "Watch what you are doing, sir. Hands where I can see them," the cop ordered.

"I was getting a picture of my son. So you know what he looks like." Cole again showed his palms.

"Get some detectives down here," the officer said to his partner, who began talking into his walkie talkie. "Those are some pretty serious scratches on your face. How did that happen?"

Cole was not liking the vibe that these two cops were dishing out; it was accusatory, and the tone was full of doubt. He had enough of his own questions, he didn't need some beat cop who wrote tickets for a living giving him shit. He needed action, but knew that he had to be careful. "Look, let's get the detective down here, but can we start looking for my son?"

"Sir, detectives are on the way. Where did you last see your son?"

"My wife said they were in the bathroom together," Cole started, but the officer interrupted.

"When and where did *you* last see your son? We will ask your wife what she knows here in a second. I want to know about when you last saw him," the officer said, matter-of-factly.

"The woman is injured. She is bleeding," the other officer stated from across the room. "Said it was his razor that cut her."

Cole saw the officer again talking into his radio. Then he stepped closer to Cole. "Sir, at this time, for your protection and mine, I am going to take you into custody. We will get this sorted out, but right now, I want for you to place your hands on top of your head and turn around. If you would, please go to your knees and allow me to place my handcuffs on you, for everyone's peace of mind." The officer ordered all of this in a very polite manner.

Even so, Cole knew it was not a request. This was going to happen regardless. Exhaling a long breath and rolling his eyes, he said, "Just hurry up and find my son." He placed his hands on his head, turned, and knelt to the floor.

He felt the pinch of the cuffs as he heard the clicks. The steel was cold on his wrists. Cole was fighting hard within himself to maintain calm, telling himself that these beat cops didn't know what the situation was or what was happening. Of course, he didn't know what was happening either. Cole knew they had to be involved, and he would need their help.

"Okay, sir, let me help you up. I want you to have a seat on the edge of the bed." The officer directed him, guiding Cole by the bicep to the soft bed.

Cole listened as the other officer tried to question Molly. All she kept saying was, "It took him."

The officer who had just cuffed him said, "You want to tell me your side of what happened?"

Before he could answer, more police arrived, along with paramedics, who began bandaging Molly's hand. The cop who had cuffed him spoke to the other officers: "We have a missing boy." He turned to Cole, clearly realizing he hadn't gotten any real information.

"He is eight years old and his name is John Mason. Johnny. I have a current picture in my wallet, in my back pocket. Someone has taken our son. Please find him!" Cole told the whole room.

"We need to get this woman to the hospital. She's in shock and shutting down," the paramedic told the police.

A gurney was wheeled in from the hallway, and Molly was strapped to it. They rolled her right past Cole; he could see her lips moving. "It took him," she said in a doped-up voice. They must have given her something.

"Where are you taking my wife?" Cole demanded.

"County hospital," one of the paramedics said as they wheeled her out the door. Then they were gone.

Two plain-clothed cops walked in and inspected the scene from the door. "That the woman? Injured?" the older one questioned.

Cole watched as the two detectives made quick inspections of the bed area and the bathroom. Then they pulled the two responding beat cops to the hallway. A few minutes passed as Cole sat there on the bed in handcuffs. He tried to calm his thinking, to ponder what his wife had said. None of it made any sense. The more he thought about it and replayed his search, the more he knew no one could have come through the mirror.

The older and fatter detective entered the hotel room carrying Cole's wallet, looking through it as if a clue might fall out. His partner followed, a tall, large man, not fat. He was almost as wide as he was tall, and he ducked coming through the door.

"I am Detective Jones and this is Detective Jerkowski," the older detective introduced.

"Find my son!" Cole shouted.

The older detective nodded and stepped up in front of Cole, angling the picture of Johnny so he could see it. "Your boy? Mr. Mason, we have officers all over the hotel, patrolling the neighborhood, and have issued an Amber Alert. We will find your son. I do need to ask you a few questions to help us figure out what all went on here, where best to look. Everything. Why don't you go ahead and tell me what you know. Give us a breakdown of events."

"My son wanted to go swimming so my wife took him to the pool. She said that he slipped and fell, cut his knee. She went to the front desk and asked for a first aid kit. Band-aid, something like that, and the room key. She said they went into the bathroom and something came in and took my son. She said something about going into the mirror and that's why I took it down. She must have been in shock. She said the person left through the mirror, or something. That's all I know," Cole told Detective Jones.

"Okay, and how did you get the scratches on your face?" Detective Jones asked.

"I heard my wife screaming, I ran in; she was on her knees freaked out. She was going on and on about the mirror. I went to the mirror and she flipped out, clawed me in the face."

"Your wife on any kind of drugs or medication?" Jones continued his questioning.

"No," Cole answered flatly.

"She ever act like this before?"

"No."

"Officer says you've been drinking," Detective Jerkowski stated.

Cole left it hang. The man wasn't asking a question, he was making a statement and it was a leading one. "Look, you have me sitting here in handcuffs, for everyone's safety. I do believe you are all armed and I am just a guy. Now we can go on about whatever, but my son is missing and I want to be looking for him. So, whatever you need to do, let's get on with the looking. I called you people. Whether I had a drink as a grown-ass man is irrelevant. Find my fucking son, let me out of these fucking cuffs, and stop asking me stupid fucking questions." Cole knew he sounded aggravated. He had tried to hold his patience, but it had reached its limits.

"Sir, you need to calm down. We are searching for your son. We need your help to figure out what actually happened here," Jerkowski said.

"I don't know what actually happened. I wasn't here when all went down." Cole emphasized the word "actually," pushing back the suggestive tone with a bit of irritation and attitude.

The older detective sat down on the bed next to Cole and let out a long breath. "Look here, Mr. Mason—what's your first name?"

"Detective, find my son. My first name isn't important. I don't want to be your friend. We aren't going fishing when this is all said and done. We can't dispense with the goddamn good cop, buddy-buddy bullshit. Find my son!"

"You been in trouble with the law before, Mr. Mason?" Jerkowski asked.

"FIND MY SON! I don't have him, I don't know what happened. My wife said someone took him. Do you understand? Do I have to speak any slower or clearer? It doesn't matter that I had a drink in the bar. Do your job. My first name, whether I have had trouble with the law—are you two kidding me? I didn't hide my son from myself! He's not under the bed; or is he, have you looked? Find my son! Do I really have to say it again?"

"Mr. Mason, I think we will finish this conversation downtown. Allow the forensic team to come in and see what they can tell us. Okay?" Jones said with a gesture toward the hotel room door.

"You're fuckin' arresting me?" Cole countered in disbelief. "You need to find my son. NOW!"

"Mr. Mason, you need to calm down. You aren't under arrest; we are simply going to ask some questions and allow our crime scene unit in here to collect evidence. That's all. Now, if you resist, we will be forced to restrain you and protect ourselves and those around us," Detective Jerkowski said with a shitty smile.

"If I am not under arrest, then take these damn cuffs off of me. I'm not going anywhere until we find my son," Cole demanded as he stood.

The young detective stepped toward Cole. The man had a good five or six inches over Cole and probably well over sixty pounds, a mountain of a man. Cole's temper grew as he could see the cop wanted a confrontation. This giant idiot walking around with a badge and a gun had only caused him to think he was some kind of tough guy. Cole had seen the type before and was in no mood to deal with a power-drunk cop.

The big detective reached out and grabbed Cole by the collar of his shirt, clenching it into his fist. "You're comin' with us, like it or not. Know this: if I find out you did something to that little boy, you'll answer to me," Jerkowski said, coming face to face with Cole.

"Oh, yeah," Cole answered, and brought his knee up hard, driving it into the man's nuts. The big man expelled the air from his lungs and dropped to his knees. Cole took a full step back, eyeing his target. Taking a step forward and using a front kick, he drove the sole of his shoe right into the large man's nose. The giant fell back flat on the floor, blood pouring from both nostrils. Cole turned and ran from the room, yelling for his son. "Johnny! Johnny!

Son, please! Son, where are you?"

Cole was tackled onto the thick carpet of the hallway by one of the uniformed police. He felt liquid on his face and instantly couldn't breathe. He tried to keep yelling for his son, but the spray had taken his air and all he could do was cough and try to breathe. Cole's eyes burned and his face felt like it was on fire, he was coughing so strong that he began to vomit. Then everything went black, but he could hear the older detective's voice: "Put that sicko away. Take him to the station and someone look under the goddamn bed. Jerk, get off the floor and go clean up your face. No, not in the fucking crime scene bathroom, you dumb ox."

Cole tried to open his eyes but the burning and throbbing of his head was too great. By the time he could somewhat open his eyes, the thick carpet felt like a field of manufactured grass. He felt someone pulling at the cuffs, lifting his arms up behind him; it was very painful. Whoever pulled him to his feet, it felt like they were going to dislocate his shoulders.

"Get up," a voice commanded.

Climbing to his feet, Cole felt a push in the back, moving him forward. He yelled out for his son again. "Johnny! Son! You have to find my son!"

Another push in the back, and the cop behind him told him to shut up and keep walking. The tug on his arms was the signal to stop as they reached the elevator. The cop stepped around Cole without letting go of his cuffed arms. Cole heard the ding of arrival. Through blurry, burning eyesight, he watched the doors of the lift open. The Mace was really burning in his lungs at this point, and his head ached like someone had it in a vise.

CHAPTER 4

D own they went and out into the lobby. Cole took a mental note of the police speaking with the man at the desk. He also noticed his reflection in one of the big mirrors, how chemically damaged he appeared. The cop led him outside. The sun was setting, and the brightness hurt his eyes. His face felt like it was ablaze and his lungs sizzled with man-made brimstone. In college, he had once been in a crowd protesting something or another, and the police broke out the pepper cans. It was something he had never wanted to experience ever again.

Keeping his eyes mostly shut, he heard the sound of a car door open. He squinted at the open rear door of the patrol car. "Watch your head," the cop guiding him instructed. Cole felt a hand on his head, pushing him down and into the car.

Falling into his seat, he lay down, exhausted. "Sit up, got to buckle you in. Rules," the cop ordered. He pulled on Cole's shirt to get him upright and buckled the safety belt across his body. Cole blinked numerous times, trying to clear his eyes and vision. It was no use; he needed to rinse them, and that wasn't going to happen anytime soon, so he closed his eyes and just waited.

He felt the car start and shift into gear, and then it began to move. Cole's heart ached as they pulled away, as the thoughts of what had gone on began to sink in. His son was missing, his wife was in some state, and he was all fucked up in the back of a police car. He was also very angry with himself for striking that officer. That was stupid, and it didn't help his cause.

The ride didn't take very long. Cole's eyes were swelling and still burning, his vision blurry and sensitive. Most of all, he was pissed, irritated with himself and the situation. The car stopped, and someone pulled him from the seat. "Step inside," a voice instructed. "Put your hands through the slot and I will uncuff you." The voice went on, "You can get that crap off of you." It almost sounded compassionate.

Cole stepped into a small holding cell, still squinting to see. The door closed behind him, and he turned to see a rectangular opening in it. Backing up to the slot, he squatted down and pushed his hands through. He felt someone uncuff him. One wrist, then the other, and he was free—or at least his hands were. Cole was glad to be rid of the pinching metal bracelets and to finally have a chance to clean up.

Through his blurry vision, he could see a square room with nothing in it but a metal object at the far end: a steel toilet with a sink built into the top. He stumbled over to it, happy to see the sink at least. He longed to get this chemical weapon off his face, out of his eyes. He pushed the button for the sink. There was a sound of function, but nothing happened. He depressed the button again. Once again, sound without action. There was another button, so Cole pushed it, and the toilet flushed. The flush was aggressive, like a powerful vacuum, sucking the water from the bowl with great force. He pushed the first button again, but still nothing happened. He hoped to jar the mechanism loose by banging on the button, but no water.

"Damn it, damn it, DAMN IT!" Cole said out loud, the words echoing in the small space. The cinderblock walls allowed his irritation to reverberate. He pushed the button for the toilet, flushing it again, watching the force of its power. A strong whoosh and some gurgling sounded as the vacuum emptied the silver bowl and then began to refill. Cole fell to his knees in front of the institutional toilet. He needed to get this chemical crap out of his eyes. He rationalized: water was water, the bowl was just a bowl. Surely it had been sanitized at some point.

Then he thought of some of the abuse this particular bowl had probably faced, and what a nasty situation this was.

Then he acknowledged that the bowl wasn't going to get any cleaner, and what needed to be done was going to need to get done.

He pushed the button to flush one more time, then tried the water button once more, hoping against hope he would not have to do the nasty. Nope. "Damn it." Cupping his hands, he plunged them into the bowl. The water was extremely cold, and Cole was thankful for small blessings. He was trying not to think of how many asses had wrecked this commode, how many drunks or junkies had barfed into it. He shook his head, attempting to shake the thoughts from his mind, but he still felt a quiver run down his spine.

He threw cold water onto his face. At first, the splash felt so relieving. Yet the Mace fought with the water, causing a burning. His scalp even seemed to ignite from the chemicals. He plunged his hands in again and again, washing the evil substance from his head. Finally, the heat began to diminish, but even as the burning dwindled, Cole continued to dowse his head with the funky toilet bowl water. He could feel the chemical mixed with the water running down his back, headed for the crack of his ass. Peeling off his shirt, Cole wiped the water from his body. Flushing the bowl once more for some nonpolluted water, he washed his shirt in the fresh liquid.

Falling back, sitting on the concrete floor, Cole wiped at his eyes. Still blinking and trying to see, he saw halos around the fluorescent lights at the top of the cell. Rubbing both eyes with his palms, he looked around the room. It was a typical holding cell. A big steel door with a slot cut into it with a trap door, so they could access the cell to cuff and feed you, or dispense more of that evil gas. A narrow wood bench along the wall, not wide enough to lie on or even sit comfortably. Those buzzing-ass fluorescent lights and the fucking blue hue they gave to everything. Not to mention the nasty-ass toilet which he had stuck his face in.

He noticed a metal mirror over the sink, riveted to the wall. Grabbing hold of the edge of the toilet bowl, Cole pulled himself up. He looked down at the place where he had just gotten his water and could see scum lining the entire bowl. Some green growing fungus ringed the waterline. The shiver ran down his spine again and he shook one more time, trying not to hurl. He looked into the warped metal mirror. His eyes were red and irritated, swollen, puffy. The skin on his face was red, like burned, and he had streaks on his chest where the chemical and water had run down.

"Sons of bitches," Cole said to the warped reflection. He took a deep breath, wincing from the damage the spray had done to his lungs. He walked over to the bench and tried to lie down, using his wet shirt as a soggy pillow. That's when he noticed the goose-egg-sized bump on the back of his head. "What the hell." He rubbed at it; it was tender to the touch. The realization brought back the splitting headache. Turning onto his side so as not to press on the lump, Cole closed his eyes for what seemed like just a second.

The sound of the big steel door unlocking and opening pulled Cole from his respite. The older, rounder detective stood next to a uniformed officer. "You calmed down yet, Mr. Mason?" the detective asked.

"Did you find my son?"

"I'm going to ask those questions now, if that's all right. Think you can keep your head and manners so we don't have to hit you with the spray again?" the detective said.

"You hit me with more than just the spray, you son of a bitch."

"Are we going to have to put the cuffs back on, or will you keep your hands to yourself?"

"Did you find my son?" Cole asked again.

The detective settled himself, like he had to ready his dopey body to answer. "No sir, not yet."

Cole met the man's eyes and squinted slightly, giving him a hard look. "You had best see to finding him. I have told you all I know."

"Well, let's see about that. You may know something that is valuable and not even realize. Come on," the detective ordered. Cole stepped out of the holding cell bare-chested, carrying his T-shirt in his hand.

Officers moved about, giving him looks as he followed the detective, who led them behind a counter and down a long hall to a door marked *interview*. The little plastic sign was red with white letters, and it should have read *interrogation*. There was a metal table with two metal chairs on each side, a camera hung from the corner of the room, and there was a smell. Cole couldn't identify the scent, but he knew it was from the nervous people who had been pressed in that room, like guilty grapes.

"Take a seat." The detective motioned to the other side of the table. The chair facing the camera, Cole noticed.

Cole took the seat and put his shirt on the table. As he settled, the door opened. The big, younger detective walked in, wearing a large bandage over his nose. The older detective pulled out the chair and sat across from Cole. Cole couldn't help but give a little grin. The big cop looked ridiculous.

"Something fucking funny?" the large man asked, anger in his voice.

"Nope. You're just better looking than I remember," Cole said with a smile.

The big guy started to move around the table after Cole. Sliding the chair back, Cole figured it wasn't over, and prepared for whatever the big guy might bring.

"Mr. Mason, nobody likes a smart-ass," the older detective said. "Sit down, Jerk," he told his younger partner.

"Mac, this son of a bitch broke my nose. Now he wants to crack wise.

He is asking for it," the cop argued.

"Yeah, well, the guy is kind of right; it did improve your looks. You are one ugly S.O.B. At least with the bandage, there's less to see. Sit down."

"Why aren't you looking for my son?" Cole asked.

"Mr. Mason, like I tried to tell you at the hotel, we are detectives. This is an investigation. We have to know what happened and then we go from there. We have officers still looking, don't worry. We will find your son."

Cole noticed the time on the cop's wristwatch, going on eight in the evening. "Eight o'clock; what the hell!"

"You were asleep," the younger cop said. "You know, that is how you can tell if you have the right one. Put three men accused of murder in a cell. The one who falls asleep, that's your man. They are caught and can finally relax. How did you sleep, Mr. Mason? Not so worried about your son so as not to catch a few winks in the drunk tank?"

Cole looked at the two cops and released a long breath. He could see the accusation in both men's eyes. He could see this had taken a very wrong turn from the start. "Am I under arrest?"

"You assaulted a detective, fucko. You are done. You are in for the long stay," the younger cop said with satisfaction.

"Is that the formal charge? If so, I want to speak with your captain and have pictures taken of my face and the lump on my head. I want to be taken to the hospital. I want to file formal charges against your big ass. You put your hands on me first. I'll wager a bet this won't be the first time for you," Cole said.

"Look, Mr. Mason, why don't we try and start over here. I am Detective Jones and this is my partner, Detective Jerkowski. We are looking for your son. We spoke to the desk clerk and the bartender, and we tried to speak with your wife. The doctor gave her something to calm her down and wouldn't allow us an audience. She was pretty out of it. We want to help here. Detective Jerkowski certainly may have been a little out of line, but you did assault him. You, in turn, got a few lumps for the trouble. Granted, you are upset. Why don't we start fresh?"

"This asshole breaks my nose and you want to call it even? No harm done? Look at my face. You are kidding, right?" Jerkowski asked his partner.

"No, Travis, I am not kidding, and you did grab him first. Cop up or go become a fireman," Jones said with irritation.

"Shirley, that's crap. Give me ten minutes alone and we will know where the kid is, and I'll settle up with this cocksucker," Jerkowski countered.

The older detective turned to his partner with a very pissed-off face. "I told you never to call me that. No one calls me Shirley. Say it again and I will rearrange your face. Do you understand? Nod, and sit there. Besides, you didn't do so well when this guy was in cuffs. You in a room alone with him—you might not want to see the results." Jones waited for his partner to nod before turning back to Cole.

"There is something off here. None of this makes sense. Either this is some really twisted shit, or I am missing something," he said to Cole.

"So, we call this a push, give each other a pass then? No assault on an officer?" Cole asked.

"I'll make you a deal: answer my questions, convince me and no bull-shit, and you have a pass," Jones said.

"Deal. Ask away."

"Okay. I'll tell you what we know, you fill in the blanks. You and your family, Molly and Johnny, check into the Star Bird Inn at 3:08 p.m. Why did you stop here? And why so early?" Jones began.

Cole explained about the night before: the fire alarm, the bike gang, everything.

"The desk clerk said you asked about the pool soon after arrival, and confirmed that your wife and the boy got the room key and some first aid supplies for the boy's cut. Bartender confirmed your attendance at the bar and that you had three Johnnie Walker Black Label scotches. The desk clerk estimated that he last saw your son at about quarter till, or ten till four. You left the bar just after four; the bartender charged your room for the drinks. The 911 call came in at 4:33 p.m., so what happened in that half hour?"

"You guys saw the condition my wife was in," Cole said. "I heard her screaming from the hall, so I rushed in. I tried to get her to tell me what hap-pened. She kept saying, 'It took him.' Not he or they but it: 'It took him.' She flipped out. Scratched me when I tried to take her from the bathroom. By the way, the Mace in the cuts was an especially stinging pleasure, asshole. Not pleasant. I thought I had her out of the bathroom when she got my shaving kit, ran back in, and locked the door behind her. By the time I kicked it in, she had cut her hand and was smearing it all over the mirror. I dragged her out and made her tell me what had happened. What she said, as you said, made no sense."

"Well, what did she say?" Jones asked.

"She said, she said something came out of the mirror. A creature. It took Johnny. She must have been in shock; I don't know. That's why I pulled the mirror off the wall. See if there was something behind it, a passageway or something."

"Was there?"

Cole shook his head. "Then, then I called you lovely people, and I am sitting here shirtless and pissed off. I called you people for help and you Maced me for it. You have been anything but helpful."

"What kind of fairytale bullshit is this?" Jerkowski asked. "You couldn't think up anything better than that? The fucking boogieman did it? Surprised a dingo didn't eat your baby. Jeez. Maybe a one-armed man will work his way into the story."

"Look, you guys wanted to know what happened. Play these good-cop, bad-cop games, whatever. You wanted to know, that's what I know. Don't know how any of it brings us any closer to finding my son, but you were all insistent. So, now can we go and look for my son?"

"Did she give any description of this thing, this creature?" Jones asked.

"No, no she did not. I even asked. She was in a real state of shock."

Jerkowski leaned forward on the metal table. "You an expert on shock?" he asked, suspiciously.

"Mr. Mason, can you try and look at this from our point of view? We get a call of a missing child. There are signs of a struggle—broken door, mirror off the wall, scratches. Your wife is cut and you've been drinking. We have your son's blood in the bathroom, the door you kicked off. Your wife's blood in the bathroom. Not to mention, Mr. Mason, you have been somewhat combative." Detective Jones eyed his partner's nose. "So, you can kind of see why we have a few questions."

"I am the one who called you," Cole countered.

"Trying to cover your ass, moment of remorse, a moment of sanity. We've seen it before. Woman drowned her own kids; called the police. Said a black guy did it," Jerkowski stated with disgust.

"We are wasting time here. I didn't hurt my wife, and I didn't hurt my son. My son is missing. WE need to find him," Cole demanded.

"Okay, so you didn't; how about your wife?" Jones questioned with a raised eyebrow. "She seems pretty out of it. People just snap sometimes. She's seeing creatures and whatnot. You're on vacation, the boy was getting on her nerves?"

"NO!" Cole said emphatically. "I get that you guys don't know what happened. I get that you have to look at the parents. You don't know us. So, I get it; I understand. But you don't know Molly. She would never. No way she would do something to our son. She is a great mother."

"That's part of the problem as well, Mr. Mason," Jones said. "No one around here knows you. You and your family check in to our hotel and next thing, I have men pulling overtime, we have a statewide alert for your son, we have an officer with an injury, and you are being somewhat difficult. Not to mention the story is a bit heavy to swallow."

"Sounds like a load of shit to me," Jerkowski said.

"You don't know me. Okay. This all sounds crazy, okay. Here's the thing, though: we need to find my son. Regardless of my standing in the community, this is your job. At this point, you better have figured out I didn't take my son. So, let's get on with this, shall we? I have told you what I know. I didn't try to hide the crazy-sounding story my wife told me, didn't shy away from the scratches on my face. I called you. If I was really trying to get away with anything, I wouldn't have called. I don't have a lawyer sitting here, even though you are treating me like a suspect. You figure out whatever you need to so we can get on with the search."

"Still sounds fishy," Jerkowski said.

"Shut up, Jerk," Jones told his partner.

Cole leaned forward on the table, the temperature of the room giving him gooseflesh. "You want to give me a lie detector test? Well, come on with it. We need to be looking for my son."

"What, you think you can beat the machine?" Jerkowski asked. "Won't do you no good in court. We can use them or not; that's the great thing about a lie detector. Inadmissible." Detective Jerkowski wore a shitty smile.

"Why would I be worried about court? I need to find my son. Apparently, this isn't going to happen until you two geniuses get the picture that I had nothing to do with my son's disappearance. So, if a lie detector is what you need, whatever," Cole said, irritated.

"Okay, Mr. Mason," Jones said, "I'll see if our guy is still here. Give you that test. Understand, we have to be cautious, thorough, cover all the bases and dot all the i's. To say we are a little apprehensive at a story such as the one you just told would be an understatement. If your wife really told you some kind of creature took your son, don't you have a few questions about that? Maybe a couple of reasonable doubts? That's your wife, but if it was me, I would have a few questions. Plus, you are the guy who fought with police and broke my partner's nose. So me being a little skeptical of your truthfulness is just my jaded way."

"I get it. You have a place I can wash up? Didn't really like having to use the scummy toilet to wash that fucking Mace off."

"Sure. Jerk, take Mr. Mason to the bathroom. I'll try and find you a shirt. Anything else?"

"Coffee and some smokes?"

"I'll see what I can do." Jones slid his chair back.

CHAPTER 5

The two detectives stood. Jones pulled Jerkowski to the side, speaking low. Cole strained to hear but couldn't make out what was said. Jones opened the door and exited the interrogation room. The big cop waved Cole to follow: "Come on." Detective Jerkowski led Cole to the men's room and held the door for him to enter. Cole wasn't stupid; after breaking the man's nose, he was reasonably leery of the large detective.

Cole picked up his speed as he passed the man and entered the restroom. He waited until he was fully in the room to turn and face the detective. Each man met the other's eyes. Cole could tell the big guy was still stewing. "This going to be a thing we need to settle, or what?" Cole asked.

"My partner said he would give you a pass. Well, the way I see it, I still owe you." Jerkowski had rage behind his eyes.

"Yeah, well, just you and me in here. Hope you are man enough to live with whatever the result may be. Don't go crying foul when you get put down."

"Oh, we will settle up later. You caught me, I'll catch you. You suckered me, and turnabout is fair play. I'll settle up when you least expect it," the detective said with a shitty grin.

Cole squinted at the cop and shook his head. "We were face to face. You put your hands on me and got what you had coming. I never sucker-punched you. I was handcuffed, you stupid asshole. I see the truth of you: great big guy with the heart of a mouse. You ain't a pig, you ain't a rat; you are a mouse."

Cole threw his shirt on the sink and walked to the urinal, taking a piss. He could see the big detective was eating his lip, clearly furious. The man's body language spoke volumes. Jaw clenched, rocking slightly side to side, eyes squinted and fixed on Cole's back. After washing his hands, Cole plunged his shirt in the sink and washed it. As he splashed cold water on his face and torso, Cole kept a watchful eye on the man.

He knew the detective was no pussy or coward; he also figured the older, senior detective had told the big goof to cool it. Cole also figured the big idiot would only restrain himself for so long. He sensed the movement before he ever saw it in the reflection of the bathroom mirror. The big dumb-ass was taking his shot.

Cole ducked forward, causing the punch to only be a glancing blow. Continuing with his motion, Cole spun away from the sink and back into the middle of the room. He wanted to have as much room as he could to deal with this big heavy detective. His size and weight mattered; he had surely been trained in some form of self-defense to be a cop. Cole didn't want this man grabbing hold of him.

The two men squared off, facing one another. Cole could see the rage in the bloodshot eyes on either side of the white bandages. "Swing and a miss, cocksucker. Now you are fucked," Cole egged on the larger man.

"I am going to kick your ass."

"You want to kiss my ass. See, I kind of figured that about you. Got me in the men's room and now you are propositioning me. You are a fucking fag." Cole continued to poke at his adversary.

The bathroom door opened and the older detective stepped in. "Can't leave the two of you alone for a second, can I?"

The big man's face changed from anger to that of a child who had just broken something or a dog that just shat on the carpet. "He, he, he broke my nose, Mac. Damn it! He has an ass-beating coming. He knows it. Just getting it out of the way."

"Jerk, get out of here right now. What the hell are you thinking?" Detective Jones demanded. Stopping his partner before he left the bathroom, the older man spoke in a softer tone. "You will make a good detective someday, but you have to put this physical part of yourself behind you. Start using your head. Just a thought: what if he had nothing to do with any of this? What if he is just an upset father? Imagine how crazy you might be." Jones patted the large man on the shoulder.

Turning his attention to Cole, Jones said, "Go ahead and finish up in here. We will be outside. The machine is up and ready." The older detective stepped forward and allowed the door to close behind him. He spoke softly, meeting Cole's eyes. "I have a sneaking suspicion you will pass this thing. There is something going on here; something rotten in Denmark. None of this is making any sense, and I don't believe you know either. There is one thing you should know about me: I am like a dog with a bone; I just don't let things go. I have three open cases, three, in a career of over twenty-five years. I solve shit, and I will solve this."

Cole looked into the man's eyes. With firm concentration as well as serious intent, he said, "You need to find my son. Nothing else matters in this world."

Jones gave a slight nod and turned for the door. "Pass the machine and you'll be free to go."

Cole could see past Jones. He looked at Jerkowski's face and the irritation it held with the man's last comment. A progression of irritation, surprise, shock, bewilderment, and finally plain disgust. "Gonna just cut him loose then? Are you fucking kidding me? Some bullshit."

The bathroom door closed and Cole returned to the sink. As he began to wash up without the threat of attack, he could feel the emotions swell. It was finally hitting him; this moment of privacy unlocked his awareness and the seriousness of his state. His son was lost, missing; his wife was in a condition of hysteria like he had never seen. It struck his heart like an anvil and rang so painful as to bring tears to his eyes.

Cupping his hands, Cole brought the cool water to his face again, bending at the waist over the sink. He allowed the moment of weakness to release, hiding his shame in the dripping water and the bloodshot eyes of post-macing. Washing the tears away before they could ever touch his cheeks, he questioned the bravado he had maintained his whole life and what good it served him now. He closed his eyes, not wanting to see the image of himself in the reflection, not wanting to witness his own pain, his own tears for his son.

Cole gathered himself and rubbed his face, wiping at his eyes. Some learn that showing one's emotions is healthy. Modern men, not afraid to express their emotions and feelings. For some it would be understandable, acceptable, reasonable; but he had not been raised that way. Cole gave another splash of water and took a few deep breaths, looking at his image in the mirror. *Now is not the time; toughen up,* he thought. The man looking back at him was tired, heavy-hearted and worried. Cole leaned in close to look himself in the eye. "Find your son," he told himself.

The man in the mirror changed, becoming serious and concentrated. His jaw flexed and his eyes sharpened. Wringing out his shirt, Cole gave a final look and saw that determination had replaced the worry. "No matter what," he told the image.

Jerkowski was waiting outside the door. "You got lucky," he said as they started down the hallway.

Cole stopped and turned to face the man. Stepping close, so close as to make the detective take a step back, he said, "When all this is over, you and I can settle up. Now don't go getting bent out of shape when I kick your ass and make you apologize to my son. You think the nose hurt? That ain't nothing compared to your pride."

He turned then, so quickly that the detective flinched. Jones was waiting at the door of the interrogation room. Cole could see from the doorway another man in a shirt and tie, and a machine on the table. The man at the table was a wiry, rat-looking man with a balding patch on his head, and glasses. "Have a seat, sir. I'll get you hooked up," he said as Cole entered the room.

Cole sat, and the man moved to attach him to the machine. Clips on his fingers, a wire wrapped around his chest, and a blood pressure cuff on his arm. "You done a lot of these?" Cole asked.

"A few. This isn't going to hurt. Just a few questions to get a baseline, and then we will get the questions out of the way. Just stay as calm as you can and answer honestly."

The man moved back across the table and took his seat. Cole could see the needles on the machine begin to move. The rat-like man turned a few knobs and twisted the dials before saying, "One-one-eight Secluded Falls."

"Is that part of the test?" Cole asked.

"No, I was reading your address." The man lifted a copy of Cole's driver's license.

Cole nodded and shifted in his seat, watching the needle move in a wavy motion along the paper.

"Have you lived there long?" the man asked.

"A short while."

The man used a pen to mark the paper of the machine. "Is your name Cole Mason?"

"Is this part of the test?"

"Yes. Please just answer yes or no to my questions, okay? Good, let's begin. Is your name Cole Mason?"

"Yes."

The man made another mark. "Are you married?"

"Yes, my wife Molly."

The man let out a sigh. "Just yes or no. Are you married?"

"Yes."

Another mark on the machine. "Are you an astronaut?"

"No."

"Okay, sir, I would like for you to pick one of these cards." The ratty man fanned out a number of cards. "Pick the one you want, look at it, and put it into your memory. You don't need to touch it or anything more than decide. You choose, and I will draw it from you. Have you decided?" The man waited for his nod. "Good. Now all I ask is that you say yes to the following five questions."

Five times the man asked Cole if the card was his, and five times Cole said that it was. The man marked the paper at the beginning of each question and watched the needle as he answered.

"Okay, now I have five different cards. Again, pick one, and this time simply tell me no each time I ask."

Cole did as instructed. Again, the rat man watched the machine. At the end of his questions he reviewed the lines on the paper and eyed Cole cautiously.

"You had the five of hearts and the jack of spades. I needed to create a baseline and see your rate at deception. Now you can't lie to me."

The two detectives stood at the doorway watching the whole process. The older, fatter detective handed the lie-detector operator a piece of paper. Cole figured they were the questions they wanted answers to.

"Okay, ready to begin. Remember, yes or no answers only. Try and stay calm and don't become agitated. Do not delay in your answer, just answer normally and honestly. You want this to go well. Now, your name is Cole Mason?"

"Yes."

"Do you know where your son is?"

"No."

"Did you have anything to do with your son's disappearance?"

"No."

"Your wife's name is Molly Mason?"

"Yes."

The man marked the paper before every question as before, and continued. "Does your wife take drugs?"

"No."

"Is your wife mentally ill?"

"No," Cole answered, but wondered whether the machine would pick up his doubt on that matter. He was worried over her state and the things she had been saying. Not to mention the fact that she had cut herself.

"Do you think your wife is mentally ill?"

"No."

"Do you love your son?"

"YES!" Cole found the question irritating and emphasized his response.

"Please remain calm. Do you believe your wife's explanation about what took your son?"

Cole paused, pondering what to say.

"Please answer without delay. Do you believe the explanation your wife gave about your son's abduction?"

"Yes," Cole said with conviction, if only in his tone.

"Are you an astronaut?"

"No."

The man marked the paper with a line, then allowed the paper to run before clicking it off and getting up to remove the clamps and wires from Cole. Moving back to the machine, the man tore the paper off and began to leave the room. "I'll review these results and confer with my fellow detectives. Just relax and we will return shortly."

———— CHAPTER 6 ————

Detective Jones stepped into the room to allow the lie detector operator to step out. Looking Cole in the eye, he gave a nod. "Detective Jerkowski will take you for a cup of coffee and that smoke you asked for. Then we will go over the test. Have a little talk about things." The man looked over at his partner. "Jerk, don't be messing with Mr. Mason. Get him a coffee and a smoke. Leave him be. Got it?"

"Yeah, I got it," the big man said begrudgingly.

Jerkowski led the way to a coffee pot where Cole filled a plastic cup full. No cream, no sugar: black, just the way he liked it. The swill was putrid, but it was hot and it helped to warm Cole. The big guy went to a desk and pulled out a pack of cigarettes: Pall Mall, no filters. Handing them over, he said, "Come on, got to go outside. No smoking in the building."

The night air was cool. Cole pulled on his wet T-shirt, then fired up the smoke. "Want one?" he asked Jerkowski.

"No, I quit."

"Nobody likes a quitter. 'Course, that does explain a lot," Cole said.

The large man met Cole's eyes. "You want to know something? I don't like you."

Cole smiled widely. "Yeah, oh well. I don't imagine you like very many people. I got to figure even less like you. I get the impression that you are one of those people that other people just have to put up with. Your neighbors, co-workers; you probably don't date much. You are big and that intimidates most folks, but down deep, you are very small. Petty. Probably can't keep a woman. You're like a skunk: don't mind your own smell, but you can't understand why everyone runs away from you."

Cole puffed his cigarette and inhaled deeply. The warm smoke in his lungs gave him a relaxed sense and he enjoyed the moment. He also enjoyed watching the big cop try and think of some retort to his verbal jab.

"That's deep; any further insights? Asshole. If I want your opinion, I'll beat it out of you. You don't know me, so just keep your comments to yourself. You are a suspect, this ain't therapy, and what you think or have to say don't mean shit-all to me. Got it? Smoke your smoke and keep your fuckin' mouth shut. Prick." The large detective was visibly angry.

Cole took a long drag and smiled as he blew the smoke from his lungs. He could still feel the damage from the pepper spray, but he really needed the break. Besides, it felt good to be outside, a little closer to freedom and all this being over, or so it felt.

"Strike a nerve?" Cole asked, lifting an eyebrow.

The sound of a throat clearing drew both men's attention. Detective Jones was standing at the entrance to the building. He waved them inside and waited.

Cole took a last drag and flipped the butt out into the night air, pocketing the pack of Pall Malls. "A chord struck rings true, Jerk. Perhaps you should give a little thought to therapy. Stop being pissed off at the world long enough to fix that shitty attitude of yours."

Detective Jerkowski stepped behind Cole and shoved him in the back. "Shut your hole."

"See what I mean?"

The lie detector was gone from the interrogation room, as was the ratlike man. Jones sat in his seat and Cole rounded the table to his own. The older detective had a file in front of him and seriousness upon his face. "Are you ready to talk?" the man asked. "Seems there are some inconclusive answers on your test. Discrepancies." Jones's voice was laced with suspicion.

Cole exhaled, shaking his head. "Okay, you got me, I really am an astronaut."

Jerkowski stood in the doorway. "Is this fuckin' funny?"

"I took your stupid test. Your guy said I couldn't lie to him. So. It's simple. I told the truth and you know that. All this is just cop shit, you playing games to stress a motherfucker into saying something to help you from doing your fucking job. Find my son. What's fucking funny is you two fuckin' jokers. Ass clowns. What the fuck? Either charge me or I am done here. If you aren't going to find my son, I will. But we are done," Cole said emphatically.

"You're right, we had a deal. The only question which spiked was whether you believed your wife's explanation. Guess it's a little hard for even you to swallow. Machine says you lied. I said you had to be honest. Now, would you like to explain?" Jones asked.

"Okay. My wife wasn't making any sense. How could I believe her, when her story wasn't complete and she was hysterical? I don't know what happened and I don't know if she does either. I will tell you this: I don't want the two of you, fucking Keystone Kops, questioning her without a lawyer. Is that clear enough?"

"You don't dictate to us," Jerkowski countered.

"After the way you have treated me, I think I will dictate the terms for my wife. You will not speak to her without myself or a lawyer I choose being there. Do you both understand?" Cole asked with the most serious of tones.

"Okay, Mr. Mason," Jones said. "Tell you what: we are going to process you out. Get your fingerprints and a photo, some DNA. Then you can go."

"No, I don't think so. You said I was here for questioning. You didn't arrest me. You said if I answered your questions I could go. No prints, no samples, nothing else. I am leaving, right now. You going to give me a ride to my wife, or should I call a cab?"

"Detective Jerkowski will retrieve your property and return it to you. Follow me and I will show you to a phone. I would advise your wife to get a good lawyer, Mr. Mason. I have some very serious questions which are going to need answers. I can only hope she can come up with something convincing," Detective Jones added with a shrug.

He led Cole to a bank of phones on the wall. "Pick it up and tell the desk officer the number you want. Local cabs are five, five, five, five, five, five, five."

Cole picked up the phone and nodded to the uniformed officer behind the desk. The man pounded in the repetitive number. As he spoke to the cab company, Jerkowski came up behind the desk with a large Manila envelope. The big detective slapped the envelope onto the counter and glared at Cole.

Cole hung up and moved to the desk. "You really get your jollies off having that little bit of authority. Cops are all the same. Can be the only man in a room with a gun and still be the most scared to death."

"Here is your shit. You can go."

Cole made his way outside and fired up another Pall Mall. The smoke filled his lungs and gave his brain a slight spin. He couldn't help but think that was far too easy. Cops never just let you go. The night had been long and rough; the older detective was no dummy, and wouldn't have just let him walk. Cole surveyed the street, paying close attention to the cars parked along the curb. They were all empty, but he couldn't shake the feeling of being watched.

He finished the cigarette and flipped the butt at the building in a small act of defiance. In a few more minutes, a yellow cab pulled up and Cole got in. He told the cabby he needed the local hospital, and the man nodded. Pulling down the arm on the meter, he logged the ride and pulled away from the station. Cole watched as a car pulled out behind them, following. He figured it had to be Jerkowski.

CHAPTER 7

A few twists and turns and twelve-fifty later, the cabby pulled into the local hospital. The car trailing them pulled into the lot too and parked. Cole went inside and stopped at the information desk, where he was directed to his wife.

Molly was still in the emergency room area. Cole followed the signs. To his surprise, a familiar man stood at the end of Molly's bed: Detective Jones. As Cole moved closer, he could see that Molly was asleep, but he glared at the detective nonetheless. "Can I help you?" Cole asked.

"Nope, just checking on my investigation," Jones returned.

Cole shook his head. "You might want to have a talk with your partner on tailing people. He is piss-poor at it. Now, what did I say about my wife?"

"I am simply checking on her well-being. Concern is all."

A man in scrubs walked up. "Can I help you gentlemen?"

"This is my wife. How is she?" Cole asked.

The man in scrubs nodded. "We stitched up her wound and treated her for shock. She is under sedation to calm her and allow her some rest."

"Is she going to be all right?"

"Physically, she should be just fine. I suspect that whatever trauma she suffered will have effects longer term. The ways people handle high-stress events is as diverse as we all are. Some people can deal with things, while others have to process."

The young doctor stepped up to Molly and gave a glance at the monitor. "The sedative will have her knocked out the rest of the night. We will keep her under observation and monitor her. We have a psych on call, but he will be in tomorrow morning. I would suggest a consultation." The young man gave a closer look at Cole. "Looks like you could use some rest as well. Those scratches on your face... and your eyes are a bloody mess." He came face to face with Cole, turning his head to the side.

"Yeah, Doc, it's been a rough night," Cole said. The man's name tag read 'Mann'.

Dr. Mann pulled Cole by the elbow toward an open bed. "Come over here and let me take a look at you." Then he turned to the detective. "And who are you?"

"I'm Detective Jones. Here's my card; when the woman is awake, call me. I need to ask her a few questions."

"I told you not to bother my wife," Cole said. "You don't talk to her without myself or a lawyer being present."

The doctor moved between the two men and handed the detective back his card. "Detective, I am not a secretary. You can call the information desk like everyone else. I don't believe you have any other business here, so if you don't mind, I need to examine my patient."

Jones didn't like the doctor's answer and it showed on his face. He snatched back his card and walked off in a huff.

"Cops think they run the world. Everyone is supposed to bow to their badge," Dr. Mann said with a grunt.

"Yes, they do." Cole laughed.

Cole sat on the hospital bed and allowed the doctor to examine him. "Mace. A chemical weapon. Funny, the United States signed a document saying they would never use chemical weapons. Guess that doesn't apply to their own people or if the police are the ones using them."

"Clubbed me in the head too," Cole told him.

Dr. Mann rubbed the tender knot on Cole's head. "Any vomiting, blurry vision, dizziness?"

"Nope," Cole said, shaking his head.

The doctor cleaned the scratches on Cole's face, flushed out his eyes, and gave him some Extra Strength Tylenol for his head. He repeated that Molly would be out for the rest of the night and that Cole should try to get some rest.

Cole needed answers, not rest, and he wasn't going to find them watching Molly sleep. He thanked the doctor and asked him to look after his wife. He told the man he would be back in a few hours and headed for a pay phone. Once again, he called the Yellow Cab company and headed outside, firing up a Pall Mall while he waited.

Cole could still see Molly in his thoughts, sleeping peacefully as he kissed her forehead. He was glad she was going to be all right. She had been so frightened and hysterical before. Cole racked his brain, trying to think of what could have scared Molly so badly. She was strong and never easily frightened. He had never seen her like that. Such a reaction was just so far out of character for her, it was hard for him to imagine what or why. He was tired; his mind and body felt the weight of the day.

CHAPTER 8

The same cab as before pulled up. Cole gave the man a nod as he flipped his cigarette butt out into the road.

"Star Bird Inn," Cole told the driver.

"Having one of those nights?" the cabby said, making conversation.

Cole gave the man a look in the review mirror. With a slight shrug, he said, "Why you ask that?"

"Well, buddy, picked you up at the cop shop, then a hospital, now you're headed to a hotel. You look like hammered shit, if you don't mind me saying. If you aren't having a rough night, I don't know who is." The cabby dropped the arm on the meter and pulled away from the hospital.

The rest of the ride was quiet. Cole noticed that his tail was back but much more discreet. The older detective must have taken over the wheel. After pulling up to the Star Bird, the cabby swiped Cole's credit card and thanked him for the tip.

Cole stepped out onto the curb and looked up and down the street, taking notice of the unmarked police car pulling in just down the street. He pocketed his credit card and headed into the hotel.

He felt strange walking into the hotel. An eerie feeling came over him. The old man was still at the desk. The rest of the lobby was empty and quiet. For whatever reason, Cole had figured there would be more activity, that people would be searching for his son. "Working late?" he asked. "Seems a little slow. Where is everyone? Cops leave or what?"

"Any word on your son?" the old man asked in return.

Cole gave a glance at the front door and saw the big detective lurking in front of the hotel. He stepped up to the desk, where he could see the concern in the old man's eyes. "I am sorry, I don't remember your name."

"That's fine, Mr. Mason. My name is Ernest Weber. I own the hotel. The wife and I, God rest her soul. Sunk our life savings into the place. Been twenty years ago now. Lots of slow nights, and that is why I am sitting at the desk. Trying to keep the old boat afloat."

Cole extended his hand and gave a firm shake. "Pleasure to meet you, Mr. Weber."

"Please, call me Ernest. I am so sorry about everything. Is there anything I can do? The police didn't really tell me what happened. Something about your boy being taken, but they didn't go into much detail."

"My wife said someone, something, came out of the mirror. Anything like that ever happen before?" Cole asked.

"No, sir. Only person we have ever lost here was the night my wife died in the kitchen. I have to admit that this concerns me a great deal. For your son, of course, but such news gets out and I'll have to close the doors." There was a look of true dismay on his face.

Cole nodded in understanding. "The police didn't seem to really have any ideas, beyond me or my wife. Not the brightest bunch; don't take much to be a cop."

"Yeah, they didn't seem to have any real good direction, at least not from the questions they asked me," Ernest confessed.

Cole furrowed his brow. "Why, what did they ask you?"

"Lots of questions about you and your wife. I told them you seemed to be a very happy family. Your boy cut his knee in the pool, I was worried about that. Then all this business happened. Your wife was caring and concerned, a very nice woman. Polite."

"She is a great lady, Ernest, but this whole thing has her really messed up. She tried to tell me what happened but—I don't know. She was pretty upset."

"Mr. Mason, they have your room closed, for their investigation. You look tired. Allow me to get you another room. No charge, of course. Sort all this out on fresh legs."

"Did they search the whole hotel?"

"Yes, sir. I escorted them everywhere, even unlocked doors in the basement no one has been in for years. I looked too, Mr. Mason."

"Call me Cole. Is the kitchen still open?"

The old man nodded. "Anything you want, on the house."

"Not a good way to stay afloat, giving things away. But I appreciate it, and I do recognize the gesture. Can you send up a sandwich and a Coke? Lunch meat of some kind is great."

"Certainly," Ernest said, pulling a key from the boxes on the wall.

"A room close to my old one, I may have to get in there and take a look around."

"Police taped it up," Ernest said, shaking his head. "Crime scene and all that. They will know if anyone goes in there. Do you still have your key or do you need another?"

"I have mine. Doesn't seem like the police are looking very hard for my son. I will have to find him for myself."

"Anything you need, Mr. Mason. Ask and I will do my best. Here is the room across the hall." He handed over the key with a weak smile.

Cole glanced toward the front entrance and Jerkowski standing outside. Then he made his way past all the large mirrors to the elevators. The doors opened and a bell rang as he pushed the button to go up. Pushing number four on the console, Cole plopped down on the little sofa in the back of the elevator and waited for the doors to close. He was exhausted and his bones ached. Closing his eyes just for a second, he felt the elevator begin to move, lifting him up to his floor. The box bobbed and the bell rang as he opened his eyes and watched the doors open. He pulled himself up from the little couch, gripping the frame of the elevator doors to steady himself.

As he walked down the corridor, Cole caught his reflection in the mirrors positioned down the hallway. He did look pretty rough. He stopped and looked down: the stain was right where they had Maced him in front of his room. He could only shake his head at the day he was having. He'd had bad days, but this was the worst. He was missing his son, and the cops were useless. Yellow police tape with the words CRIME SCENE covered the door to room 411, and a notice of legality was stuck over the jamb and the door, with a sticker showing the scene had been breached.

Looking into the polished numbers on the door, his bloodshot eyes reflected back at him, he read the notice. "Attention, crime scene, violators will be prosecuted," blah, blah, blah. He pulled the keys from his pocket and selected the one engraved with 411. Cole inserted the key and turned the lock, then pushed the door and broke the seal. He gave a glance up and down the hall, even as he reflected that the most instinctual thing to do when breaking rules was to see if anyone was looking.

Eyeing the room from the hallway, Cole pulled the yellow tape down and stepped into the room. The luggage was still open on the floor where it had been when Molly pulled out Johnny's swimming suit. The lights were still on, and even the impression on the bed was still there from where he had sat down. Yet there was something very off-feeling about the room. There was an absence, as well as a residue of something bad happening. Some places carry such feelings, like a graveyard or battlefield. Cole did not like what he felt, but he needed to investigate further.

A creepy feeling running through him gave him gooseflesh on his arms, and he felt the hair on the back of his neck stand on end. Cole looked around the room as he stepped past the bags on the floor. He hesitated at the bathroom door, gazing inside. The feeling of unease was thundering in his heart. The mirror and the sink had been dusted for fingerprints; the residue from the dusting powder was still visible. The bloody towel and his razor were gone—evidence, Cole assumed.

Stepping all the way into the bathroom, Cole turned in a circle. "I am missing something," he said aloud. "There has to be something." Walking back to the doorway, he imagined what would have taken place, what could have happened. He looked at the open door to the room, wondering whether Molly had closed the door of the room when she entered. Johnny was hurt; she could have just forgotten. Someone could have followed her to the room, or perhaps someone was in the room already, robbing them. All Cole could do was theorize. Perhaps the would-be robber hid in the bathroom, startled Molly, grabbed Johnny and ran away.

Cole turned back into the bathroom and picked up the big mirror which he had pulled from the wall. Startled or not, hysterical or not, Molly had said what she said, and she was so convinced. Cole leaned the mirror forward and inspected it carefully. He ran his hand over the surface, the frame, and the back. He inspected the wall and where he had smashed it. Leaning the mirror against the sink, he stepped back and looked at his reflection. He could hear his wife's words, that 'it' had come from the mirror. That 'it' looked like Johnny. "What am I missing? What happened here?"

"What?" a voice came from the doorway.

"AH!" Cole jumped and shouted involuntarily.

The owner of the hotel yelped too, and dropped the tray he was holding.

"Holy shit, you scared me half to death," Cole confessed.

Ernest looked frightened as well; the blood had drained from his cheeks.

Bending over to pick up the tray, he said, "I am so sorry. I didn't mean... I'll have to get you another..." he stuttered.

"No, no, that's fine. I was just... I'm a little jumpy is all, tired."

"The door was open. I just came in."

"Come on, let's go to the other room," Cole said, taking the tray from the hotel owner.

He closed the door behind them and pulled the key for room 410 from his pocket. The room was exactly like the other, only in reverse: the bed was on the left, not the right; the bathroom on the left, not the right. Even the bedspreads were the same. Cole sat the tray on the bed and uncovered a sandwich.

"Ham and cheese," Ernest said.

"Perfect. Thank you."

The old owner looked carefully at Cole. "What was that you said over there? About missing something?"

"I can't get over what my wife said. It doesn't make any sense." Cole took a bite of the sandwich, then opened the can of soda. The beverage began to fizz, and he slurped at the top to keep it from overflowing. "I am struggling with the day, Ernest."

"Talk it out. Maybe I could help, or hearing it aloud might make it clearer," Ernest suggested.

"Who is watching the desk? What if you get a customer?"

The old man shrugged and gave a tilt of the head. "This is more important."

Cole nodded and looked the man in the eye. "I appreciate that. How long was it between when my wife got the first aid kit and I left the bar?"

"She got the first aid kit about ten till four, but I didn't see you leave the bar."

Cole thought a moment. "It was just after four, so, about fifteen minutes. Give or take. Have you had any break-ins or thefts, any kind of vandalism?"

"Had some things come up missing a few years ago, but the thief was a maid and we fired her. I think she overdosed, or went to jail," Ernest said. "You should get some rest. You look worn thin." The old man stood and gripped Cole on the shoulder. "Everything looks clearer in the light of day."

Cole watched as the man moved for the door. "It came from the mirror."

"What?"

"That's what Molly said, that it came from the mirror. I can't make sense of it."

"That is strange. Get some rest, Mr. Mason," Ernest said, and closed the door to the hotel room behind him.

Cole needed a shower. Then he would need a change of clothes, and his clothes were across the hall. Moving to the door and pulling out the key, Cole looked both ways before crossing the hall. The corridor was empty. Reentering their old room again felt eerie. He went into the bathroom, just to look again. "There is nowhere to hide in here," he said to the empty bathroom. "It came from the mirror," he repeated.

He knew his wife. He knew she would never allow someone to take their son, not without fighting tooth and nail. Molly was a momma grizzly. Strong of heart, strong of mind, she would never have become so unraveled from a man trying to take their son. There was something missing. Cole again looked into the mirror at the scratches on his face. He had never seen her so desperate, so berserk, so unhinged. He leaned in close and looked at the reflection, then focused on the glass itself. *It came from the mirror*.

CHAPTER 9

The phone rang. It gave Cole a start; he had never been so jumpy, and felt almost foolish. "Got the damn willies," he said to himself in the mirror before walking out and answering the phone.

"Cops are on their way up," Ernest said. "I tried your other room, figured you might be over there."

Cole nodded. "Thanks for the heads-up."

"Mr. Mason, when you have the opportunity, could you come down? I would like a word."

"Did you remember something?" Cole asked, feeling new urgency.

"No. Well, I don't know really. Just when you can come down. I recalled a story from a few years ago, that's all. I will see if I can remember all the details. They should almost be there, the police."

Cole hung up and began to collect some clothes. The door was still ajar. He picked up clean jeans and a fresh T-shirt, socks and a pair of boxer shorts, then felt the presence of the police without having to actually see them. The swoosh of the door over the thick carpet only confirmed his feeling.

"This is a crime scene," Detective Jones said from the doorway.

"Don't they call this returning to the scene of the crime?" Jerkowski asked smugly.

Cole gave an impatient look at the big guy. "I need some clothes. Don't you have to take some kind of test to be a detective? 'Cause you are dumb as shit."

"Nobody likes a smartass, Mr. Mason," Detective Jones said as he entered the hotel room.

Cole gave the big detective a look. "Yeah, so how many times did you have to take it, big man?" He gave a wink and a smile.

"Fuck this guy, Mac, let's just bust him and head home. Crossing that police tape is enough to hold him. Tampering with evidence, disrupting an active crime scene. We got this son of a bitch."

Jones turned, stopping the approach of his partner. "Relax, Jerk. The man is getting some clothes is all. He keeps pushing your buttons because you keep letting him."

"Fuck this guy," Jerkowski said again. "I am about to push his button with a pound of hurt, and Shirley, I am getting really tired of you defending him. Fuck this guy!"

The older detective reached out and took hold of his partner's broken nose with two fingers. "Listen very carefully." Jones allowed for a moment of pain to subside before he continued. "First, I told you never to call me Shirley. You must have thought I was joking around, and now I hope you know different. Second, I am not defending this man. He is the one who broke this ugly beak of yours. Now, take your dumb ass to the car and wait. Think me up a really good and sincere apology. Do you understand?"

The big cop nodded and grabbed at his nose as Jones released him.

"I am going to hear you say it. 'Cause if you ever use my first name again, I am going to hurt you very bad, but not like your nose here. Nothing so gentle."

"I get it."

"Good, so go. Mr. Mason and I are going to have a little talk."

Both men watched as Detective Jerkowski limped from the hotel room holding his broken nose.

"Commissioner's stepson. He had to take the detective test six times before he passed. He isn't a bad kid, just thick is all," Jones explained to Cole.

"Saw a new side to you there, Detective. A little sensitive about the name, but I have to admit, I like the fire," Cole said.

The older detective gave him a sideways look. "I know you are a wise-ass, but give it a rest. I am in no fucking mood. Get what you need and let's go. You know tomorrow your wife is going to have to answer some difficult questions. She had better make sense of all this. You need to help me with that. You son is missing, and I know you don't want to think your wife may have done something, but you had better really think about it. I have seen some really messed-up shit on this job. You don't really know what people are capable of until they have done it."

Cole still held his clothes. "Yeah, we are both looking to figure this out and find my son. The difference is, you are just doing your job. This is my boy. Do you get that? Your partner couldn't find his way out of a Walmart, so you can understand my lack of confidence."

Detective Jones moved past the luggage and over to the bathroom doorway, looking inside. "The last place your son was seen. Did you find or remember anything?"

"No."

"Well, we printed the room. Granted, usually when we print a motel room it's like counting the stars. Oddly enough, this room was relatively clean. Nothing popped on the database, no criminals." Jones still looked into the bathroom.

"So, what's next?"

The detective turned and looked Cole in the eye. "Mr. Mason, this is the beginning. I know you don't want to think about that, and I know you aren't really prepared for what is likely to come, but this is square one. We will go through the computer, look for predators, similar MOs. This is now a process."

"My son just vanished, into thin air. How is that possible?"

Jones raised an eyebrow. "It's not. I am not looking to hurt your wife, but she was here. I need answers to do my job—leads, evidence, a direction to go by. I need the truth from her and I think you do too."

"Yeah, but you look at us as suspects," Cole challenged.

"Am I not supposed to?"

Cole squinting at him. "So all that happened to me, the Mace and the threats. Is that supposed to happen too?"

"My partner has been out of line, no doubt about that. However, you did break his nose. You aren't supposed to get away with that, but…" The detective allowed the thought to trail off. After a moment, the detective continued. "Come morning, this is all going to change. The press is going to be all over this, I'll have to call the FBI, and my bosses are going to want answers. I'll tell you, statistically, the parents are usually involved in child abductions. The Feds are by the book, statistics-driven police work, logic and experience. They don't think outside the box, they *made* the box. Your wife's story, her hysteria, the wounds on your face—that's a list of bad that only will get worse. No compassion, no understanding, just the facts, ma'am, and more time will pass with your boy missing."

"So… What am I to do?"

"Help me. They are going to look close at your wife. She was the last to see the boy alive. He was hurt. The Feds will interrogate her and, in her condition..."

Cole let his head fall backward, closing his eyes and thinking. "And I suppose you have a suggestion."

"Let me talk with her. I get that there is something strange, but it could just be her shock. I might be able to decipher what she really means."

Cole brought his head forward and met the man's eyes again. "Look around, Detective. Something is amiss. I didn't pass anyone on the way to my room, and no one saw anyone leaving. Your men searched. Something is off. You are the pro; doesn't something feel off? Figure this out for me."

Detective Jones met his gaze and nodded slightly. "Mr. Mason, it's not so much what I see as what I don't see. If this was a robbery or a burglary gone wrong, they didn't take anything. Well, except for your son. If this was a kidnapping, no one has called, no ransom. Plus, as you said, how did they get the kid out? Unseen, unheard, no evidence. Vanished into thin air."

"See, that's what I am saying. Something is off here."

The detective furrowed his brow and sighed. "Mr. Mason, this situation doesn't leave very many possibilities. Your son was taken, by someone who doesn't seem to want anything from you or your wife. A predator. You people are on vacation and this was not a scheduled stop, so this isn't a personal type of thing. Another option: something happened, maybe an accident, your wife lost her temper, whatever; and now she is covering it up."

Cole nodded. "Okay, let's go further. Accident, but where is Johnny? Your people searched. My wife doesn't know some secret fucking hiding spot. She was right here, in that condition. Which doesn't make sense either, because Molly is strong. She would fight for our son, she loves Johnny. She loves him so much. Something weird happened here, and the longer I think about things, the more convinced I get. Something messed my wife up. I have never seen her so afraid. Something scared her."

Detective Jones looked puzzled. "Something?"

Cole tucked his clothes under his arm and headed for the door. "I'll be at the hospital in the morning. Come by and we will talk with my wife. And leave your dumbass partner somewhere else."

"I can do that."

"We didn't do this. You need to find Johnny. Nothing else matters."

Jones moved toward the door with him. "We have an Amber Alert active and every cop in the state has his picture. We have faxed pictures to hospitals and children's services. We are looking. So, till tomorrow then."

Cole stepped into the corridor. The long hallway was empty, but with all the mirrors along the walls it just seemed longer, and as if occupied, somehow. He crossed to his new room as the detective closed the door of his old room. The older man gave a wave over his shoulder as he headed toward the elevator.

Cole entered his room, moved to the bed, and set down his clean clothes. He picked up the sandwich and took a healthy bite, then washed it down with some half-flat soda. After a few more bites, Cole began to undress.

In the bathroom, he turned on the shower and checked the temperature with his hand, then stepped into the steaming shower. He allowed the hot water to soak him and relax his muscles a little bit.

It felt good to wash the grime and funk from jail off his shoulders. He used the tiny shampoo bottle, washing up, allowing the day to come to a conclusion. After stepping out of the shower and toweling himself dry, he wiped a streak across the mirror and eyed his reflection. His emotions were coming and he wanted to cry, but he had been taught that real men don't cry, that it served no good to anyone. Still, his want for a good family vacation had turned so horribly wrong. Everything had come apart and he didn't know how to fix things. Another lesson he had learned: that Dad is supposed to protect and fix the problems.

Cole thought about what the detective had said: that there was no ransom demand, nothing else was taken, and no one saw or heard anything. He thought about how scared Molly had been, how she still wasn't herself. "It took him," she had said. What the hell could 'it' be? Cole wondered. Molly wasn't the type to just break down or make up some crazy story. Cole believed his wife, and that was the most troubling part.

CHAPTER 10

The night was restless, Cole's mind a tumble of thoughts. He had brief moments of slumber, but the dreams threw him from his sleep as quickly as he could enter. He didn't want to get up, but just lying there wasn't doing anyone any good. He needed to find Johnny, to get him home. Pushing the covers down, Cole sat with his legs over the edge, rubbing his eyes. Then he stood, stretched, and headed for the bathroom.

The reflection seemed to greet him as he entered, and the feeling gave him gooseflesh down the back of his neck. Cole eyed the beautiful mirror and pondered once again the words of his wife.

Then the phone rang in the bedroom. After picking up his watch from the nightstand, he answered the phone.

"Mr. Mason, this is Ernest."

Cole rubbed his face. "Is everything all right?"

"Yes. I saw the older detective leave and then the big one. I remembered a story I heard and think you might want to hear it. Can you come down?"

Cole yawned. "Is there coffee?"

"Of course, I just brewed a fresh pot."

"Let me get dressed and brush my teeth. I'll be down in a sec."

Cole hung up the phone and slipped into his Levi's. Firing up a Pall Mall, he inhaled deeply and allowed the day to begin. He wondered what the story could be, and why the man was calling at quarter to five in the morning. He checked the pockets of his other pants, transferring his wallet, change and cash, then dropped his cigarette into the flat can of soda and headed for the door.

As he exited the room, Cole glanced at room 411, feeling the goosebumps return. His life had taken such a turn; Johnny missing, Molly in the hospital, the police looking at him and Molly. He wasn't doing enough. As he walked down the hallway, passing the doors and the mirrors, Cole struggled to not be overcome by despair. He knew he needed to be strong, he needed to be active.

MIRRORS

He pushed the elevator button. Was going down to drink coffee and listen to some old man's story a good use of his time? Cole's mind was spinning, and the questions and stress only seemed to build. He felt helpless, that his actions or the lack thereof were inadequate.

In the plush elevator, Cole looked at the mirrors—even here. He shook his head at himself and pushed the button for the lobby. Cole rolled his head on his shoulders. He could feel the stress, but he was glad he had taken the shower and gotten at least some sleep. There was wind in his sails; he knew he would need everything he had today. His son could not be gone one more day.

The bell dinged and the doors opened to the lobby. Cole marched forward. He had to stay focused, positive. The key to finding his son was not aimlessly looking but figuring out what had happened. Now all he needed was a direction. The old man's story might just be the beginning.

Behind the large wooden desk, Ernest was on the phone. He covered the mouthpiece and said, "Coffee is back here. Pour a cup and have a seat. I'll just be a second."

Cole rounded the end of the desk. The pot wasn't finished brewing yet. As he sat in a nice leather chair, Cole waited to see which would finish first, the owner or the coffee. The percolating machine dripped a last drop. Cole stood up and went over to it. The old man watched Cole as he spoke on the phone. It kind of made him uncomfortable. He poured a cup, then gestured as if to ask if Ernest would like one too. The man nodded.

Ernest finally hung up. The look on his face was serious, stern. "Thank you for coming down," he said, taking the cup of hot coffee. He pulled his seat closer to Cole's chair, blew on the beverage, and looked the younger man in the eye. "What you said upstairs, what your wife had said. It got me thinking. *It came from the mirror;* that's just not something you hear. To have heard it before made it even more strange."

"What do you mean, you heard it before?" Cole sat up a little straighter.

"Well, to tell the truth, I thought it was just one of those Halloween type stories or some kind of ghost story. Like I saw a UFO or Bigfoot, some craziness like that. Guys talk bullshit all the time, so something coming out of a mirror—I never gave it another thought. Until you said what your wife said."

"And?"

"That was the guy who told me on the phone. He wasn't too happy with the hour, but I explained about your son and wife saying what she said."

"And?" Cole asked with growing impatience.

Ernest took a sip of his coffee and set the cup on the counter. "It was a few years ago now, I guess. A family was having Thanksgiving dinner. As they said grace, something came from the mirror. A creature appeared from nowhere. What my friend said was that the creature looked just like the father, but ghostlike or monstrous somehow. Far as the story goes, it took him, took him into the big mirror they had hanging on the wall. *It came from the mirror*. The man vanished without a trace, was never heard from again. Taken right in front of his whole family, but the police obviously dismissed the claim."

"Is this some sort of joke?"

The hotel owner shook his head as he took another sip. "No. That's why I called the guy, to find out where he heard this story. He used to live in Straightsville, and he read it in the paper. I guess it happened just a few towns over. The police never closed the case."

"So, you're saying this happened before?"

Ernest tilted his head. "No, what I am saying is that I remembered hearing a similar story. So I called the guy who told me, and he remembers reading it in the paper. Like I said, I thought it was some kind of spooky story, but now I don't know what to think. Every legend has some thread of truth, I suspect. Some event people add to, distort, exaggerate, or magnify to make the story more than it really is. There may be something to your wife's story."

Cole drank his coffee and pondered this. "So, what: am I to go to the police with a ghost story and expect them to believe such a thing?"

The older man set his cup on the counter. "Mr. Mason, I don't know what you are supposed to do. I don't know what the police will do. You need to find your son. He went missing in my hotel, so I feel partly to blame and want to help. I remembered the story, and it seems to fit your wife's account. I can't pretend to know the workings of the world or that I know everything in it. Are there monsters? People sure have been talking about them a long time."

"I am sorry, Ernest, I'm just tired and really confused. Tell me again, a family was having Christmas dinner…"

"Thanksgiving," Ernest corrected.

"And some creature came out of the mirror and snatched someone?"

Ernest picked up his cup and took a drink, nodding. "That's what the man said."

"So, there was a room full of witnesses, and the police did nothing?"

The older man shrugged. "I don't know what the police did or didn't do."

"What did you say the name of the town was? Where is it?" Cole asked.

"Straightsville. It is in the hills there, not very big."

Cole stood and twisted his neck, trying to relieve some of the tightness. "I'll have to check this out for myself. See what I can find out. Ernest, thank you, truly. Don't feel guilty: we will find Johnny."

"I am not a religious man, but I have lived long enough to know that some things, sometimes, are just not explainable. My missus was a strict Catholic and believed truly in the God Almighty. Mrs. Weber also spoke of the Devil and his deeds, that evil lives and walks among us. I never fell into the whole thing, and she never forced me to go to church with her. I have always viewed faith and belief as very strange things, which I never had time to ponder. You trust and love your wife; then you should believe her when she says something took your boy. Imagine how Joseph felt with Mary, pregnant by God? Did he doubt, question? To be true and strong even in the very worst of times: this is what makes you a good husband."

Cole shifted in his chair, pondering what the old man was saying. "I believe Molly. I just wonder if she knows what she is saying. If she isn't confused."

"Love is not an abstract thing, it is real. Love drives us, gives us strength and passion. Dive into the depths of love and have faith. Love takes us beyond the physical and the logical. With faith and love, you will find your son."

Cole realized that his opinion of the man had changed. When they'd checked in yesterday, he'd thought he was just some old man working the front desk. Probably some retired old geezer supplementing his Social Security. Nameless and faceless. Ernest Weber was no longer nameless or faceless; he was a good man with a kind heart and a loving spirit.

"I have to go to the hospital and see Molly," Cole said. "She should be up and better, having had time to rest. The cops want to talk with her, and I want to be there first. But then I'm going to have to check out that story. If it was in the paper, then there will be evidence of it. I have to do something. I am all coiled up inside. I feel like I should be doing more. I need to find Johnny."

"I can see the stress in your face. I don't know if my story helped, but I hope it gave some direction. I have to admit it seems a little out there, but I can't pretend to know every damn thing."

"Yeah. Some creature took my son—it's not the most reasonable of stories to tell. Might as well say the boogieman snatched him and they ran off with Peter Pan. Have to admit I am struggling with the aspect of the supernatural. Ghosts or whatever else, might as well believe in the Easter Bunny. There is just no such thing. There can't be."

The two men sat in silence for a long moment before Cole got up and rounded the counter. "Thank you, Ernest. I am going to get some fresh clothes for Molly and head over there. Then I'll try and find out what I can about that story."

The hotel owner nodded and Cole headed for the elevator, his mind flooded with more questions than ever. The second wind he had felt was already gone. The weight of the previous day had landed, and it was crushing. He felt out of gas. He pushed the button and leaned on the wall. In a few moments he was on the fourth floor. The elevator doors opened to an empty corridor, matching the way Cole felt inside: vacant.

He walked down the hallway, the mirrors looking at him. The quiet was everywhere. Not even his steps made a sound on the plush carpet. He passed by himself over and over, the continuous reminder of the mirrors. At room 411, Cole pulled the key from his pocket and entered. The polished numbers shone.

CHAPTER 11

In the bathroom, Cole looked at the bloody handprint from his wife still on the mirror. He thought of the story, how absurd it had sounded, but he looked at the reflection very differently now. What Ernest had said stuck in his mind: Cole did trust his wife, he did believe her. Something had happened, and it involved this mirror. Something had frightened her into hysterics.

Cole took the mirror from where he had set it against the wall on the counter next to the sink, and leaned it against the tub. Taking a seat on the toilet, he looked at the sheet of reflective glass and strained to comprehend a creature emerging from nothing. The mirror was attached to the wall, an exterior wall, and they were four floors up. Some kind of creature, a ghost, or whatever? The thoughts had him thinking he was going crazy.

He picked up the mirror and set back on the counter next to the sink. He didn't like the fact that he was even considering ideas so far-fetched. Johnny didn't need ghost stories; he needed his father to save him. Cole looked at himself in the mirror. "This isn't some kind of movie, where ghosts come out of the walls," he said. "Come get me if you're in there. Give me back my son."

Part of him felt like smashing the mirror, punching right through it, but he restrained himself. He left the bathroom and then the hotel room, slamming the door behind him in frustration. He was angry; his emotions were beginning to unravel him.

Cole made himself calm down and take a few deep breaths. He told himself that this day would bring clarity to the confusion of yesterday. He would find his son, he would discover the truth of what Molly was trying to say, and they would leave this place as a family. This was the test of a lifetime, and Cole knew he had to come through. His family needed him and he had to deliver.

He collected a few things and heading back downstairs. He stopped at the front desk and told Ernest, "Going over to see Molly."

"Here, I poured you a cup for the road and wrote down the directions to the Straightsville library. Figured you could find the paper or some information there."

"Thank you, Ernest."

"Mr. Mason, I do feel somewhat responsible. You and your family came to my hotel and expected to be safe, and you lost your son. I will do whatever I can to help you. Anything you need, anything."

Cole reached across the desk and gripped the man's shoulder. He could feel the frailness of the old body beneath his shirt, and it struck him as sad. The two men shared a silent exchange and a nod.

Cole headed out the front entrance, searching the dark street for signs of life. No one was out, no traffic, no people, not even the big dumb cop. At the rental car, Cole pulled out the keys and got in.

As he drove to the hospital, Cole's mind raced. He had so many questions, worries, and doubts. He knew the detectives would be arriving early, but not this early. They had questions Molly was going to have difficulty answering. Questions he wanted to hear the answers to first.

When he pulled into the hospital parking lot, the streetlights were bright and gave off a slight humming sound. He walked toward the building, surprised at how nervous he felt, the butterflies in his stomach taking flight. He could see the glow of sunrise off in the distance; the day was coming on strong. Women in white moved about, and a few patients wandered the halls, but for the most part everything was slow and quiet. He stopped at a bank of phones and called the information desk of the hospital, asking for visiting hours and Molly's room number.

Cole made his way to Molly's room, where they had moved her to from the ER, and quietly entered. She was still asleep. He was a little surprised that no one had paid him much mind; he doubted anyone even noticed him come in. He touched his wife's hand and leaned in, kissing her on the cheek. Molly stirred and opened her eyes.

"Where is Johnny?" she asked.

Cole shook his head but said nothing.

"Where am I?"

"You are in the hospital, my love. You're going to be all right. Can you tell me what you remember?" Cole asked her.

Molly's eyes were clearer now, not the glazed-over look from last night.

She looked alert and serious. "It took him."

Cole tilted his head and squinted an eye. "Who took him?"

"That thing took him into the mirror. Did you get him? Did you get our Johnny back?"

"No, not yet. Things have been—complicated. We kind of lost you there for a while, baby. I had to call the police, and they haven't been much help. They're going to be in to ask you some questions soon, this morning. They didn't understand about the mirror. Honestly, I'm not sure I do either."

Molly sat up in bed and looked deep into her husband's eyes. "We have to find Johnny. He needs us to go and get him. That thing took him. We have to get him."

Cole could see his wife growing more frantic with each word. Urgency grew in her voice. "Honey, we will. First, we have to deal with the police. I have a lead on the mirror, but we can't sound crazy to the authorities. They aren't going to grasp that something coming out of the mirror."

"But that thing took him. They should do something about a creature like that. They are supposed to protect us."

"I need for you to just stay calm and try to... I don't know."

Molly reached out and touched Cole's face. "I am so sorry. I freaked out, didn't I? I tried to hang on to him. That thing, it was so strong. Honey, it looked like our baby. It looked like Johnny, but it didn't. At first, I didn't even realize what was happening—that thing, that creature, it pushed me aside. It was so strong, it was like I wasn't even there."

Molly stopped and looked past Cole. He turned to see what had drawn her attention.

It was Detective Jones.

"Mrs. Mason, glad to see you are up and talking. I am a little surprised to see you here this early, Mr. Mason. I must say, you look better than you did last night. Seem a little calmer." He turned to Molly. "My name is Detective Jones, and I would like to ask you a few questions, if that would be all right." The detective moved to the end of the bed.

Cole patted Molly's hand and got to his feet. "It's okay, sweetheart. Will you excuse us for just a second?" Cole motioned to Jones to step into the hallway.

As the door shut on the hospital room, Cole turned to face the older man. "Okay, Mac, I know you have some questions and you don't want her and me to go over things before you have had a chance to question us both. Don't want us getting some kind of agreed-upon cover story. I get it. Still, I would like to get her back to the hotel and cleaned up. What do you say you go ahead and ask a few key questions, then let me take her back and get her a shower and clean clothes, and *then* we will come down and talk with you. Give a full statement. Hook her up to your lie detector."

"You seem much more cooperative this morning," Jones said. "Any particular reason?"

"We need to find my son, and we need your help to do so. The quicker you rule us out and get on with things, the quicker we will find him. Ask your questions, but listen to what she says, no matter how far-fetched."

"All right."

Cole led them back into the hospital room, moved to the side of his wife's bed, and kissed her on the forehead. "Honey, the detective here is going to ask you some questions. Just tell him what happened. The truth can be stranger than fiction; just tell the truth and we will go from there. I am going to get the paperwork started to get you out of here."

As he left, he gave a purposeful look and nod to the detective. Cole walked to the nurse's station, feeling a measure of relief. Molly was back and clear-headed, not the hysterical mess she was last night. He was still uneasy that her story had not changed—creatures and the like—but what could he do? There were no such things as monsters. And what if there were? Jones would still never believe her. Part of him didn't even believe her, so how could he expect anyone else to?

The nurse arrived and Cole explained they were ready to go. The nurse told him to wait, explaining that a doctor would have to release Molly, because of the self-inflicted wounds. Cole kept a watchful eye toward the hospital room where his wife was being interrogated. The nurse interrupted his thoughts to tell him that it would be a few minutes before the doctor would be available.

Cole nodded and headed back toward the room. As he drew close, the door opened and Detective Jones exited. "Are you kidding me?" Jones asked as the door closed behind him.

"What?"

Jones tilted his head and raised an eyebrow. "Do you know what she said?"

"Yeah, I suspect I do."

"You expect me to believe that? You want me to file a report with that being her statement?"

"Whether you file it or not, I don't really care. Do I expect you to believe it? Well, I don't really care if you do or not. I know how it sounds. I don't know what it means, but that's what Molly said happened. It is the exact same thing as what she said last night. She isn't crazy." Cole allowed a moment to pass, looking the older man in the eyes. "You are the detective: investigate. Prove her wrong."

"Your kid was pulled into a mirror, by a monster that looked like him? Prove her *wrong*? Common sense tells any sane person she's batty. You think if she told me Bigfoot took the kid, I would search out the local woods?"

Cole paused, sighed, and folded his arms. "This is why I said we would come down and give an official statement. You can check it on your machine, see if she is lying or telling the truth. Then we can go from there."

"Well, how can I search a mirror? The thing is solid, made of glass. Why are you pushing for a later meeting? Why you want to go back to the hotel so bad?" Jones pressed.

"I'm hoping that by seeing the place, it may jar her memory. Rattle something loose—other than a monster. I am trying to make sense of all this too, Detective. I know there are no such things as monsters, ghosts, or creatures of the night. Right?" Cole eyed the man.

"I don't think it's a good idea for me to allow the two main suspects in a child's disappearance to leave unescorted and return to the crime scene, after giving no statement of events beyond some very questionable and unbeliev- able accounting. I would be derelict in my duties."

Before Cole could answer, a doctor approached. "Is Mrs. Mason looking to leave?" the man in the white coat asked.

"If you say so, Doc," Cole said.

"Doctor, is there any sign of mental disorder or trauma here?" Jones asked.

The doctor gave the detective a strange look, furrowing his brow. "I am not at liberty to discuss a patient's condition with anyone other than the patient," he stated firmly.

"It's okay, Doctor," Molly said; appearing in the open doorway.

"The chart says Mrs. Mason had a laceration and suffered from shock. The wound is stitched and she seems to be responding normally. I would think even the simplest of minds would assume a level of mental trauma with the events that have transpired. A missing child is unimaginable." The doctor said in a monotone.

"She isn't crazy, Detective," Cole said. "Just because she said something that doesn't make sense to you, doesn't make her crazy."

Detective Jones shook his head and shrugged. "I will expect you no later than nine this morning. One minute past and a warrant will be put out for the both of you. Clear?"

"We will be there," Cole promised.

Detective Jones gave a sideways look at Cole and then, with a nod, he moved on down the hallway.

Cole rejoined his wife and the doctor in the hospital room and listened as the doctor explained about the stitches and changing of bandages.

"You take good care of the little lady," he told Cole.

"I absolutely will," Cole said. The doctor signed the chart.

The exit process involved a lot of paperwork and insurance information. It took thirty minutes before they were finally released and headed to the car, but they still had enough time before nine o'clock to head to the hotel.

"Baby, I am sorry. I should have kept hold of our boy," Molly said as she stared out the passenger window.

"Sweetheart, it doesn't sound like there was much you could do. We will figure this all out and get Johnny back."

"I know how it sounds. I don't know."

"I believe you." Cole took Molly's hand. "I believe you."

CHAPTER 12

C ole pulled into the same parking place he'd used earlier at the hotel. He helped Molly out of the car, and they walked into the plush establishment. The old owner perked right up at the sight of them.

"Mr. and Mrs. Mason, I am so glad to see you," Ernest said with a smile.

"Just back to clean up a bit and then head over to that Straightsville you were telling me about," Cole told him.

Molly gave him a strange look; he had not told her about the other incident. Cole paused at the desk. "The police will be calling eventually, that detective most likely. Tell them we were in and specifically told you we would be back. Don't tell them about Straightsville."

"Will do. Is there trouble?"

"They want an official statement from Mrs. Mason, and what she has to say is, well, let's just say it's hard to fathom."

The older man nodded, picked up a cup of coffee, and took a sip.

Cole and Molly headed to the elevator and journeyed upstairs. As they walked down the mirrored hallway, Cole could see the alarm in her eyes. "I got us the room across from the old one," he told her. "We'll get you a shower and change of clothes. Then we can head out."

"Where?" Molly asked.

Cole unlocked the door and allowed his wife to enter. Molly went right into the bathroom and closed the door. Then he stood, nervously waiting. He heard the shower start up and went to sit on the bed, figuring it would be a little while.

After a few minutes, though, Cole felt increasingly alarmed. Molly was alone in a bathroom just like the one where she had lost her child and cut herself. Moving to the door, Cole knocked lightly. "Honey, you all right?" He heard the water stop and the shower curtain pull back. The door opened, and there stood his wife with a towel in her hand, soaking wet.

"How are you going to get our son back?" she asked.

He took her in his arms. "I don't know yet, but I am working on it." He pushed back and held Molly at arm's length. "We have to get to this place called Straightsville. It's near here. Something like this happened there." He could see the questioning look in Molly's eyes.

"This has happened before?"

Cole stepped back while she dried herself. "About ten years ago or so, I guess," he said, moving back into the room. "The old man at the desk was telling me about it. He is the owner, name's Ernest."

"Ten years?" Molly asked. "Why haven't I heard of this type of thing before?"

"I don't know, baby, but we need to go. That detective will be expecting us, and I wouldn't put it past him to send that big dumb jerk over to check on us. I love you."

"I love you too."

Molly got dressed, and they headed back down the corridor of mirrors and into the elevator. Ernest looked tired as Cole paused to confirm his instructions.

"I am sure the detective will call, and will probably come around. Like I said, we told you we would be back. You have no idea where we went."

"No problem. Anything I can do. Mrs. Mason, anything you need," the old man said with real concern in his voice.

Molly reached out and patted the back of his hand. "Thank you," she whispered.

A tear rolled down his face as he nodded, then wiped it away.

Cole took his wife's hand and led her to the entrance of the hotel. Looking outside for any sign of the police, he saw Jerkowski parked down the street. "Jones didn't trust us," he said. Considering they were not heading to the police station, the distrust was well placed, Cole thought.

He wasn't sure how he was going to lose the guy, but he was going to have to try. He drove nice and slow, allowing Jerkowski to follow along. Cole pulled up to the police station, then watched as Jerkowski pulled past them.

"I thought we were going to check out that other story?" Molly said.

"We are. Had to get rid of the tail Jones had on us." Cole watched Jerkowski pull into the side lot of the police station. Then he made a U-turn and accelerated, speeding away; he turned the next corner squealing his tires.

"By the time they figure out we aren't coming, we will be out of the area," Cole assured his wife. Ernest had drawn him a map to Straightsville; it was four towns over. Cole worried how long it would take Jones to put out a warrant for them. He knew he was risking a lot of complications with such a move, but no way Jerkowski and Jones were going to check out some kind of urban legend.

Straightsville was not a large town; in fact, Cole was surprised that it would have a newspaper. He followed Ernest's directions to the library and parked the rental car out front.

"They have mirrors at the library?" Molly asked.

Cole smiled and shook his head. "No. The man Ernest talked to said he had read it in the paper. We need to find the story and get the details. Something black and white we can hand over to those Keystone Kops."

They walked hand in hand up the steps, but the large wooden doors were locked. Tugging harder, Cole let out a slight grunt. "Damn it."

Molly looked at the sign posted next to the big doors. "Doesn't open until nine."

"It is nine," Cole pointed out sharply.

A voice came from behind them. "Hold your horses."

An older woman with thin grey hair, carrying a canvas bag, was beginning her climb up the steps. "Kind of anxious to check out a book, are we?" she said with a smile, pulling out some keys.

"Glad to see you. On time and everything. Been having a rough couple of days and we need to get in here and check something out. You have back issues of the local paper, don't you?" Cole asked.

"Since the first issue in 1799. Those are on microfiche. We will get you set up; just let me get in here and turn on some lights." She inserted the key and opened the doors.

Cole held the door for both women, then followed them inside.

"Don't usually have people here so early, especially waiting for the doors to open. Haven't seen you folks around before, are you new to the area?"

As she turned on the lights, the beauty and historic feel of the building was revealed. It was an old-style library, with large shelves filled with books, high ceilings and pillars, oak reading tables and a large main desk.

"My name is Doris Lamb. I have been the librarian here for twenty-two years. I love the books. You name it, and I'll tell you if we have it and where to find it," Doris said proudly.

"Thank you, Doris, this is a lovely library," Molly said.

The librarian led them to her large desk and walked behind it. "Oh yes, it was built in 1809. It's the second oldest building in town. Courthouse was finished in 1808."

Cole looked around. The age of the building showed in the craftsmanship. The structure was well built; details like moldings and wood were part of the aesthetic. Such work, if done today, would have cost a fortune—that is, if you could even find anyone to do such work.

"So, you say you do have back issues of the newspaper?" Cole asked.

"Do you have a particular date in mind?" Doris Lamb asked.

"I am not sure of the exact year, but it was over ten years ago. It happened in November," he told her.

Molly put both arms on the main desk and leaned forward. "Doris, do you have internet access?"

"Yes, we do."

Molly whispered to Cole, "I'll do some research, see if this has happened elsewhere. You check the papers."

"That's good thinking, baby. You had me a little worried, but now you're back, huh?" Cole gave her a wink and a smile.

Molly gave Cole a kiss on the cheek and a little shrug.

He could still see the worry in her eyes, but he could tell she was feeling better and there was hope growing inside of her.

"Let's get you set up with the microfiche. Have you used it before?" Doris asked Cole.

"Not since I was in school, but I am familiar."

"Still the same. Follow me." The old librarian led Cole to the box-like viewing stations and the small drawers filled with the tiny films. "Okay. Now, how far back are you looking to go?"

"Let's start at ten years ago and just work back from there."

Doris moved to the wooden drawers and pulled out a box with a roll of film in it. "Now, all the boxes are marked with the years. Scroll through to the month and seek out the days. Here, let me set up the first one and show you, then you can take it from there." She inserted the negative and scrolled through the first few pages. "If you find something and want to make a copy, just press this button here."

"Great, thank you very much."

Doris left him and went back to Molly. "If you'll come with me, I'll show you the computer room."

The two women went to a door and disappeared into the computer room.

Cole wondered if the older cop was flipping out yet. He was certain the big detective had told him they had arrived. They had probably waited, but by now they had to know something was off. Cole knew that by leaving, Jones would truly believe they'd had something to do with Johnny's disappearance. He needed some kind of evidence, or at least a lead, or Jones was going to look no further than them.

The quiet of the library loomed around him as he searched the dates at the top of each page. The buzz of the machine seemed to wander down the rows of books and scurry around the ends. Cole heard a door close in the distance of the large building; it made him uneasy. He had never liked big old buildings, they were always scary to him as a child, as if haunted. He had watched all the old classic movies where there were always big old scary buildings or houses.

He looked around, but he was alone. Surrounded by bricks of words, all aligned neatly on the shelves, stories and tales, all the knowledge of mankind in a room. Even as a grown man, he felt strange. Try as he might to dismiss his feelings and encourage his manliest of emotions, he could not help but shake a shiver from his spine before continuing.

Cole scanned through the last Friday of the month of November, then that Saturday, but nothing. Changing the reel to the next year back, he continued his search. Again, he checked the last Friday and Saturday of the month. He figured a story of a disappearing man would have at least made the paper. Most of the stories were of what to do with leftovers and how to deal with relatives for the holidays.

"Everything all right?" The voice and presence of Doris Lamb about made Cole come out of his skin. She had totally surprised him; he jerked visibly. "I'm sorry," she said. "These old buildings can really get your imagination working. Many have said they hear things, that the old library is haunted." She smiled.

Cole's heart thumped vigorously, but he had to smile back at the old woman. She had scared him, and he recognized the humor in that. She had gotten him good. "It's been a strange couple of days, I'm kind of on edge. I never liked these types of places, spooky. Especially in here all alone."

Doris nodded. "If you need me, I will be back at the desk or in the rows putting away books."

Cole smiled and nodded. "Thank you for all the help." He returned to the machine. Inserting the next year, thirteen years ago, he flipped to the last Friday and read the local headline. "Missing Man" it said in bold print. He began to read the article. This must be what he was looking for.

A man named Paul Baker had disappeared during Thanksgiving dinner, according to the article. The family reported that a creature resembling Mr. Baker abducted him and carried him into the mirror located in the family dining room. The police were investigating, but had no leads or suspects. An anonymous source with the police suggested the Baker family had started drinking early, or that this was some kind of prank. They also suggested a batch of bad moonshine may have caused the hallucinations. The article made light in the end, reminding the reader that this was Thanksgiving, not Halloween.

The article was short, and Cole's mind began to spin. He moved on, looking for more. On December 29, a headline read, "Case of Missing Man Remains Open." His attention was focused as he read. The police were shelving the case, saying that they had exhausted all leads. Police had questioned the family, who all had spoken of some sort of creature. However, the authorities had no evidence of such a presence, and again they suggested that poisoning had caused hallucinations, this time bad oysters in the stuffing.

The official police position was that Paul Baker was classified as missing. There had been no credit card activity or access to his bank accounts, and no ransom demands. The case would remain open; if any new evidence came about, the police would follow it aggressively. They requested anyone with any information to come forward. A small reward was being offered.

"Oh my god," Cole muttered.

"What's that?" he heard.

Cole came to his feet in a start, knocking the chair over behind him. "Holy shit!"

There stood Doris Lamb, pushing a book onto a shelf. She stammered back at him, "I am so sorry. I didn't mean to scare you again."

"No, no; I am sorry. Wow, you are a very quiet lady. You scared the crap out of me."

"The restrooms are over there," Doris pointed out.

Cole smiled as he picked up the overturned chair and released a long breath. The old librarian moved down the row, inserting a book here and there. She paused at the end of the row and gave him a curious look before rounding the end and disappearing.

"Put a bell on that woman," Cole said to himself. Returning to his seat and the article, he reread the words, then printed out the page. He removed the reel and replaced it. Collecting his printout, he headed for the front desk. Doris Lamb was sitting quietly checking the cards inside the books, removing ones that were full.

"Mrs. Lamb?" Cole asked.

"You can call me Doris."

"Okay, Doris. I am Cole. I put the boxes back the way they were. I was real careful to have the dates in the right order. You seem to run a real tight ship here."

"Thank you, Cole. Are you named after the famous outlaw?"

"I don't think so."

She nodded and smiled. "Did you find what you were looking for?"

"Yes. Do you know the Bakers? A Paul Baker in particular?" he asked.

Doris's face changed, expressing sadness and concern. "Oh yes. Such a terrible shame. People talk, you know. I am not one to spread gossip. Still, whatever happened to that man is unknown to me."

"Do they still live in town?"

"I believe so. Can't say I've seen them in here in a long while. I think I saw Jackie Baker, the poor man's wife, at the grocery not too long ago."

"Would you happen to have their address?" Cole asked.

Doris smiled. "I don't have it, but I am sure it is listed in the directory." She pulled a phone book from behind the desk. Flipping through the pages, she mumbled to herself as her finger moved down the page. "Here we are. Baker; Oak Street." She turned the book facing him.

"Can I borrow a pen?"

Doris slid it across her desk to him.

He wrote down the name, address and phone number of the Baker residence on the back of the article he had printed out, then slid the pen back to Doris. "Thanks. I have one more question: where is my wife?"

Doris Lamb smiled and rounded the desk. "I am here to help. She is over here."

"You read a lot, don't you, Doris?"

"My fair share, I suppose. Truth be told, I love to read. All we know is from reading."

"You read a variety or stick to your favorites?" he asked as he followed her to the computer room.

"Well, I think a librarian should be well read on just about everything. Not that I can read everything. Why?"

She stopped at a door and looked Cole in the eyes. He handed her the articles he had printed. "What if the family was telling the truth?"

"Why would you look this up? Telling the truth about what?" Doris asked.

"My wife, Molly, our son and I were on vacation. We stopped for the night at the Star Bird Inn."

"I have stayed there."

"Yes, well, last night, this happened to us," Cole said, pointing at the article. "Our son Johnny was taken. I know that sounds crazy. I thought it was crazy, but now, after reading that—I want to know if you have read about anything else even similar. Has this happened anywhere else?"

Doris looked around the empty library. "You say this happened to you?"

"She witnessed the whole thing." Cole nodded toward the door where Molly was. "What she told me matches that almost verbatim. There is no way she knew this story."

"Well, there are plenty of stories of people vanishing. The Devil's Triangle, dimensional theories, alien abductions. People have all kinds of strange stories to tell. Can't really say I recall a creature from a mirror. There are those movies, *Bloody Mary* and *Candyman*, but people had to invoke the spirit by saying the name three times. Your son didn't do that, did he?" Doris asked.

Cole opened the computer room door. Molly's attention was fixed on the computer screen; she didn't even turn at the sound of the door opening. "It's happened before," he told her.

Cole and Doris stepped into the room as Molly finally turned from the screen. "I know," she said, in the gravest of tones. "I ran a search. Found two other stories that match what happened to Johnny. One was at Pearl Harbor during the war. A nurse was hospitalized, put into a mental hospital because she said she witnessed creatures come from a mirror and take wounded men away. The military called it shell shock from the Japanese attack. Said the woman was suffering from hysterical hallucinations. The soldiers she said were taken remain missing in action. They assume their bodies were lost during the bombing. Blown to smithereens."

Molly punched a key on the computer. "Here, look at this. Some people were having a party and a woman was taken. All the guests said she was pulled into the coffee table. A coffee table which was a *mirror*. Police found drugs at the scene and dismissed it as drug-induced hallucinations. The girl was never seen or heard from again. What did you find?"

Cole handed over the articles.

"Three different events in very different areas and times," Molly said. "With our Johnny, that makes four. God only knows how many times this has really happened. How many people have been taken."

Cole could hear the anxiety in his wife's voice. "Molly, you need to tell me exactly what happened, again. Every word, every detail, no matter how insignificant."

Doris Lamb moved next to Molly and looked at the computer screen, reading the information for herself.

"I brought Johnny in, had him sit on the edge of the tub, so I could put the disinfectant on his knee," Molly began. "He complained that it stung, then that thing appeared." Distress showed on her face.

"What did he say? His complaint, what did he say exactly?" Cole asked.

Molly thought for a moment before answering. "He said, 'Mommy, that burns. God, that stings, ouch.' I think that was it, or something like that. I can't remember his exact words."

"What did the creature look like?" Doris asked, leaning back from the screen.

Molly adjusted her posture, looking uneasy. "It looked like my son. But it wasn't Johnny. This thing was pale and sickly looking. It was evil." She shuddered. Her face grew pale; she shrank a bit.

Doris Lamb cleared her throat. "This is difficult to process. However, the amount we don't know about the universe and the supernatural far exceeds what we do know. I would only be guessing to propose a theory as to what or why such a thing might happen." The librarian leaned back toward the computer. "You say the creature took your son back into the mirror?" Molly nodded. "And the mirror was impenetrable right after that?"

"Solid," Molly said.

Doris moved away from the computer and bobbed her head back and forth. "Sounds like a parallel universe, another dimension. Some scientists have speculated that we don't live in a universe but a multiverse. Time and space are not constants; there are many planes of existence. Somehow, these mirrors are portals to that dimension. The being that lives there comes and claims its parallel self from this world."

"Why?" Cole asked. "Why did it only take Johnny and not Molly?"

Doris squinted at him. "I don't know. I am purely speculating about the dimensionary possibility. Seems that in each case, witnesses were left. The person matching the creature is the only one claimed. There must be a trigger, a key, causing the creature to come forth, and to claim just the individual who opened the portal."

"I thought it might have been the blood," Molly said, holding up her hands and showing her bandaged wounds.

"Blood has been used in multiple occult and historical rituals," Doris said. "Voodoo comes to mind. So, your son cut his knee, and you cut yourself?"

"She was rubbing it on the mirror when I came in," Cole said, earning a hard look from his wife. Shrugging, he went on, "Nothing happened, thank god. No one would have known what happened."

Doris shook her head and furrowed her brow. "This is all a little hard to take in. Let me go and see what I can find on the subject. We could run searches on dimensions and portals, even the occult."

Molly sat back down in front of the computer and began to type. "I'll run the searches and see what else I can find. Doris, if you could see what books you have on those subjects, maybe we can make sense of all this."

"I'm only guessing," Doris said, "but the fact there were witnesses seems troubling. I mean, it doesn't seem like this monster is trying to hide."

Cole said, "I wonder how many times this has happened and no one actually knew? People just vanish all the time. Here one minute, gone the next.

This could answer a lot of missing persons cases. People aren't missing; they were taken."

Doris moved to the door, then paused. "We need to find the trigger, the key that opens the portal, and not be taken ourselves. Opening the gate is only the beginning of the problem."

"What do you mean?" Molly asked.

"Getting him back. If it's a whole different plane of existence, he may not be in the place he was. The door may not open the same way from the other side. You may get in and not be able to get out. So many factors to consider. I realize you want to rush to your son, but the danger is extreme." Doris Lamb lowered her head and stepped through the door. "I'll see what I can find."

"Honey, I have these Baker people's address. I am going over there, see if I can find out what happened. See if they can tell us anything. Do you want to come, or keep searching?"

Molly tilted her head. "I think I had better keep looking, find what I can, while I can. The more we know and can show, it certainly will help us when we have to go back and talk with that detective. Here, take these printouts and show the Bakers. They may be more receptive to help, seeing that this has happened elsewhere."

Cole took the pieces of paper and kissed his wife softly on the lips. "I love you. We will get him back." He walked out of the computer room and called out into the empty building, "Doris." He heard a faint answer through the stacks of books and followed the sound. Eyeing the shelves and holding a number of volumes already, Doris turned her attention to Cole.

"Found a few on the multiverse and an old text on voodoo. I don't know how much this stuff is really going to help. I am sure that there are those who know a great deal upon the subject. Whether they wrote about it is another story."

Cole nodded. "I am going to the Bakers'. Can you tell me how to get to Oak Street?"

Doris gave him directions, along with a serious look. "I am real sorry about your son. I really don't know what to say. This is hard to believe, and certainly not what I expected for today. I want to help. We will find what there is to be found."

"We appreciate it, Doris. Our son Johnny needs us, and any help is welcome. If you would, keep an eye on Molly. I'll be back in a little while."

CHAPTER 13

Cole trotted out of the library and down the steps, jogging to their rented car. He got in and set the pages on the passenger seat, fired up the engine, and pulled away from the curb. He followed Doris's direction to Oak Street and checked the house numbers. He saw a mailbox that read "Baker", and pulled into the driveway. As he grabbed the papers and got out of the car, he wondered what to say to these people. This had happened to them over a decade ago, and now some stranger was knocking on their door first thing in the morning.

He pressed the button and heard the doorbell ring inside the house. He heard stirrings and then the unlocking of the door. The front door opened, and there stood a young man in a tank top and shorts. He had to be in his mid-teens and was at least six feet tall, but skinny. Cole could not help but picture his own son growing up to be a teen; he feared Johnny might not experience it. He mentally pushed the thought from his mind and focused. "Hello, my name is Cole Mason and I would like to speak with a Jackie Baker. Does she live here?"

"That's my mom. Yeah, she's here. Come on in." The young man stepped back and walked into the house, his bare feet padding on the hardwood floor. Cole realized how early it still was. "Sorry to come by so early, but it is really important." Cole closed the front door behind him and followed the young man into the living room.

"I'll get my mom," the young man said, and waved at the sofa. Cole thought about it, but just stood by the couch and explored the home with his eyes. He could see what he thought must be the dining room. Where the man was taken.

A woman in her late forties or early fifties came in, wearing a puzzled expression. "Good morning."

"I am very sorry to disturb you so early and I know that you don't know me. My name is Cole Mason. I really need to talk with you." Cole took a seat on the sofa.

"I am not interested in buying anything," the woman said flatly.

"Oh, I am not a salesman. You may want to sit down."

"What's this about?"

"You are Jackie Baker?" he asked, and she nodded. "My wife, son and I are on vacation, and what happened to your husband has happened to our son. Our Johnny was taken." He watched her expression of puzzlement change to irritation, so he went on. "I came here to ask for your help, to see if you could give me any information."

Her face drained, becoming pale. She plopped down in an easy chair as if her knees had suddenly gone out. Mrs. Baker's focus seemed to elude her, lost somewhere in the space between them.

"I truly hate to bring this up and disturb you in your home," Cole said. "I can see I have upset you, but this is important. I have to get my son back. I read about what happened, but I need to know everything. I need to figure this out." Cole handed over the articles.

Jackie Baker looked at the printouts and shook her head. "No one believed us. The whole room full of people saw it happen and the police dismissed it all. The press made it a joke. Insurance company investigated harder than the police, 'cause they didn't want to pay. We almost lost everything." She read the articles and shook her head. "It happened before, and now it has happened again." She looked up at the ceiling.

Cole could see she was back in that moment in her mind. He could imagine the thoughts going through her brain. "Can you tell me what happened?"

Mrs. Baker sat silent for a few moments, wiping away a tear. "What is all this? You come here and bring this up. We have put that behind us. He is gone. He isn't coming home." Her voice was almost a monotone.

"My son was taken, just like your husband. I need your help to get him back."

"You didn't see it, did you?" she asked.

"No. My wife did."

"Had you seen it, you would know." Her tone had turned bitter, and her eyes had grown cold and distant.

"Know what?"

"They aren't coming back," she said flatly.

Cole stood and moved over to the window, gathering himself. The woman had given up and time had taken its toll. "I can't believe that. I won't. I need you to tell me what happened."

"What good will it do? You don't want to know. You certainly don't want to see it for yourself."

Cole turned from the window and locked eyes with the woman. "It was Thanksgiving?" he encouraged her.

She started talking, her voice dull. "I brought out the turkey. Everyone was happy and seated around the table. Paul started to carve up the bird but cut his finger. He wrapped it up and we said grace. That's when it jumped into the middle of the meal. Paul fought with it, even stabbed it with the carving knife. It snatched him and leapt back into that damn mirror. Gone."

Cole ran it over in his mind. "He cut himself, your husband?"

"Yeah, but it wasn't bad."

"Did the creature look like him?" Cole asked.

"Yes, but no. That creature was naked and white as a sheet, ghostly. Had long nasty fingernails. It may have looked like Paul, with similar features, size and shape, but it was not him. You would know the difference."

"I am truly sorry to be bringing all this up for you. I can see it is difficult for you. I am just trying to figure all of this out. Police have been no help at all. We are left to do this on our own."

"I told you what happened. Truth is, I tried to figure it out too. You'll find out, you'll learn. Your son is gone, just like my husband, and that is that."

"Mrs. Baker, not to be a pest, but it has to be more than just the blood. Can you recall what your husband said? There has to be something more."

She stood. "Brandon!" she yelled.

The kid in the tank top and shorts reappeared. "What, Mom?"

She looked Cole in the eye and in almost a shrill tone she said, "Mister, you want to figure it out, you go right ahead. I've told you all that I can. I am sorry for your loss, but you will come to grips with that in your own time. The quicker the better, if you ask me."

She turned to her son. "Take him to the attic and show him the mirror." Then she marched to the cabinet along the wall and took a bottle of liquor from the shelf. She gave Cole a look and then walked into the other room.

"Come on, mister," the kid said, and started up the stairs.

"Were you here at that Thanksgiving?"

"Yeah. I was only four years old. Don't really remember much. Know that Dad was gone and Mom started drinking." The young man shrugged. "Sorry about her mood, it's a rough subject."

Brandon led them to the middle of the hallway and reached up for a rope hanging from the ceiling. Pulling it, he revealed a hatch and a ladder to the attic. The kid made his way up the narrow, steep wooden steps, and Cole followed.

He pulled a string and a naked bulb illuminated the space. "Be careful, there is a lot of junk up here."

Cole could see the entire attic was a storage space for the family, with boxes and random items everywhere. "Crazy, all the stuff we just keep."

"This is where we keep all Dad's stuff. Mom put the mirror up here after it happened. Don't know why she kept the damn thing." Brandon walked to the far end of the attic. "She insists we keep it covered. OUCH!" The young man recoiled his foot from the floor and took hold of it.

"What did you do?" Cole asked.

Brandon pointed at a large rectangular object covered by a quilt. "That's it over there. I stepped on a damn nail." He hopped over to a wooden rocking chair and sat down.

Cole moved past the boy to the object of his interest and pulled back the quilt, exposing the wooden frame and reflective glass. He could see Brandon begin to remove his shoe. Cole ran his hand over the glass, feeling the smooth texture of the surface. Giving a tap, he made certain the glass was solid. He bent down and leaned the mirror forward to look at the back. There on the back of the mirror was a familiar symbol, a company mark.

"My toe is bleeding," Brandon said.

Cole looked over at the kid sitting in the rocking chair, holding his foot, a red spot on his sock. "What did you say?" Cole asked.

"My toe is bleeding." He gave Cole a look of irritation; pulling his sock off his foot.

Cole's stomach dropped and his whole body tensed with alarm. "Don't move, don't talk!" he commanded the young man. Leaning the mirror back as it was, he tapped the glass one more time to confirm its solidity. Grabbing for the blanket to cover the mirror, he could see Brandon fidgeting in the reflection.

"Goddamn nail in the floor," the kid said.

He felt his spirit drain from him and shot the kid a look. "Don't talk. Just go, go now!" Cole ordered. He turned back to the mirror, readying to cover it, but he could see something was happening.

"Hey, what did you do to the mirror?" Brandon asked.

Cole looked in the reflection and then scanned the attic with his own eyes. The two images were not the same. "RUN!" he yelled. He could see the glass of the mirror extending, stretching outward like a bubble being blown. A head and a face formed, emerging from the mirror as if being born. As Cole stood there in dumbfounded amazement, he could see that the thing coming from the mirror did look like Brandon Baker, but monstrous.

"What the hell is that? What the hell is that?" the young man yelled.

Cole threw the quilt over the mirror and moved toward the kid. "You have to go. Now!" He took Brandon by the arm.

The young man had dropped the shoe he held in his hand and was pointing behind Cole. The quilt only outlined the body, creating a ghostlike appearance. As it moved toward them, the quilt fell away and revealed the creature. Pale face, bloodshot eyes, naked with long and blackened fingernails.

"Go, I'll try and hold it off," Cole ordered the kid.

Cole turned on the creature and took a step toward it, putting himself between predator and prey. It stood erect but seemed shaky, until it took a step forward, and then another. It moved quick but had a jerky manner. Cole couldn't believe his eyes.

"Is that me?" the kid asked from behind him.

"I said run. GO! Now!"

Cole glanced over his shoulder to see the kid finally heading for the trap door down into the house. "Damn kid." He squared up to the beast. As mind-boggling as this was, Cole knew this creature was what had taken his son. In that moment, rage overtook him. Charging the creature at full speed, he was determined to find out everything it knew.

One swipe of its arm tossed Cole across the room. Effortlessly, the creature had sent him flying, smashing into boxes and things stacked up along the wall of the attic. Cole was surprised by the strength of the creature; he was a six-foot three-inch man with a weight of over two hundred pounds. Being flung like a bag of flour shouldn't happen. He saw the kid climbing down the ladder, but the creature moved so fast, it had him by the hair and jerked him up from the opening. With one hand it held the teenager above the floor, turning back toward the mirror with its prize.

Cole knew he had to act and act fast. He searched around him and found a set of golf clubs against the wall. Pulling an iron and stepping in front of the creature, Cole swung the club as hard as he could. The club snapped over the thing's head but never fazed the beast; it didn't even blink. Looking at the broken club in his hand, Cole plunged the metal rod into the creature's stomach. It never made a sound, just looked at him with those bloodshot eyes, emotionless.

Cole looked at the teenager struggling to get free from the grasp of the monster that looked like him, but to no avail. The panic in the boy's eyes struck Cole deep, imagining his own son's fear.

Taking a step back, he saw the creature pull back its left hand. He knew a blow was coming, but the thing moved so fast, there was nothing he could do. With a swipe of its claw it sent Cole flying again. Right back to the wall and the golf clubs. Cole scurried to his feet and grabbed a one-wood, refocusing on the fight. The creature now had turned and was facing Cole; the formerly emotionless eyes now carried rage. Anger radiated from the beast, the negative energy it generated was physically palpable.

Pulling back the one-wood, he wanted to swing it with enough power to down the beast, but in that split second, he could see the creature ready itself for the blow. Viewing this teenage monster, with a rod protruding from its belly, Cole knew this was a creature beyond this world. The thing was ready for the fight, and it had the strength and speed to defeat Cole easily, but he had to continue. Swinging with every ounce of strength he could muster, this time he did not aim for its head, but for the knee.

Upon contact there was an audible crack. Cole had swung with all his might and connected with the creature's left knee. The joint gave way to the force of the blow. The pale naked thing released a roar and buckled to the floor, letting go of Brandon.

"RUN!" Cole screamed out.

The young man began to crawl toward the ladder, as Cole pulled back the club for another whack. He could see the beast was laser-focused on its prey, so he stepped forward and once again swung with all his strength. Aiming at the creature's head this time, in hopes to kill it, he gave no pause.

Like a flash and without looking, the creature's left hand caught the one-wood in full swing. It pulled the club from Cole's grasp and flung it across the attic. The thing stood once again. Cole couldn't believe his own eyes. The thing's knee had to be shattered, and the speed at which it moved was inhuman. His mind racing, searching for any strategy to combat such a force, all he could do was watch as it moved toward the boy.

It moved in flickers, like seeing every other frame of a slow-motion scene, but it was so fast. Jerky movements or not, the thing had Brandon by the ankle, and again lifted him off the floor with a single hand.

Cole snatched a putter from the golf bag and strained to think of how to fight such a creature. If he could destroy the mirror, perhaps the monster would have nowhere to go and would disappear. Using both hands, Cole threw the club at the mirror. The putter flipped end over end toward the glass. Anticipating the shatter, Cole watched as the club struck the reflection…but it made not a sound. As if thrown into a still pond, the club disappeared, leaving only ripples in its wake.

"FUCK!" Cole yelled in frustration. The creature still had Brandon and still had its back turned. Cole resorted to primal behavior. Leaping onto the beast's back, wrapping his arm around its throat, he began to try and choke the life out of the thing. Squeezing with everything he had left, Cole allowed murderous rage to drive him. He had never killed anything before, never considered he would, but here he was trying to choke a naked monster to death. Wrapping his legs around the creature and arching his back to increase the pull, he could feel the thing's neck stretching.

He could see the terror in Brandon's eyes as he hung upside down. This young man had seen his father taken, and now he was being abducted by his own evil twin. The boy was screaming a high-pitched wail, so high one might have thought a woman was screaming.

As Cole continued to squeeze the neck of the pasty monster, he thought how different people react to things. No one knows how they will face their fear until they are truly faced with it.

The creature stopped and stood straight, ignoring the clutches Cole was putting on it. He could smell the filth of its matted, greasy hair, its body odor.

Then the damn thing began to turn its head. Like an owl, it turned and was face to face with Cole while its body was still facing forward.

".enim si eH," the creature said in a gravelly voice. Its breath was foul and made Cole gag. Rotted flesh and bad milk, so putrid he almost released the thing just to escape the odor. Jagged teeth and black gums; some of the teeth were broken, and the smell grew in magnitude.

The creature snapped at Cole's face, coming close to biting his nose. Cole leaned back and continued to squeeze, but he could tell it was having no effect. The monster took hold of Cole's hair with its free hand and jerked him full force forward. Head over heels, flipping forward, he was thrown over the creature and onto the floor. He slammed into the attic's wood planks. The top of his head ached immediately from the pulling of his hair; it felt as if his scalp had been torn off. He had landed with such force that it had knocked the wind out of him, and he struggled to take a breath.

Cole staggered to his feet. The creature had turned and was heading for the mirror with the boy in tow. Cole shook his head slightly, in an effort to clear it. He had to act. Barreling forward, Cole lowered his shoulder like a football tackle and launched himself at the beast. The creature was paying him no mind, so it was blindsided. The spear, as it was called when Cole played football, took the trio of them down.

They crashed into a stack of boxes as Cole continued his assault, punching and kicking the thing with all the might he could muster. Rolling on the wooden floor, he threw a flurry of blows. He was very surprised when the creature gave a slight hop and was back on its feet. It looked down at him with those bloodshot eyes and rage like he had never seen. With a half-closed hand, the beast struck Cole on the side of the head.

Cole saw a flash of light and his ear rang. The blow pushed his head down, and it bounced off the hardwood planks. He had been in fights and he had been punched before, but never like that.

The creature plucked Brandon from the floor and tucked him under its arm. Again, Cole struggled to his feet and stared down the beast. "You're not taking him," he stated with conviction.

The creature seemed to understand and stepped forward. Standing in front of him, eye to eye with evil, Cole looked down and saw the handle of the golf club still sticking out of the beast's gut. Taking hold of the handle, he pulled it out. The creature reacted, drawing back to strike a blow, but he knew the thing's speed now and was able to duck the swipe of its claw.

Taking a step to the left, Cole gripped the club like a dagger. Giving another quick move to his left as a feint, he stepped back to the right and lunged, driving the broken club into the eye of the beast, plunging it as deeply as he could. The thin metal tube sank all the way from his hand into the right eye socket. The penetration was so deep, the end of the club came out the back of its head.

Staggering, the beast backed up. It did not go down, and it did not drop Brandon. Cole took hold of the young man's hand and pulled. Brandon grasped back, lifting his head and looking Cole in the eyes. He was holding on for dear life. Cole pulled and pulled, trying to free the boy. The creature's grip was just too strong.

The creature roared, and with its free hand, it jerked the metal tube from its eye socket, throwing it to the floor. It straightened and looked at Cole, one eye filled with rage while the other was an empty, damaged hole. Cole could actually see right through the creature's head; light shone through the hole he had made. The thing stepped forward and roared again, loud and vicious. Cole took a step back.

He looked at the beast and swallowed his fear. "Come on then, come on! Take me, you son of a..." Cole only saw a blur as the creature threw the blow. It struck him in the face, around the left eye. The punch was so strong and so hard, it picked Cole off his feet and sent him spinning in the air. It knocked him back to the hole where the ladder was. Cole fell to the second floor in a clump.

He landed hard. The whole world was fading into a tiny circle just out of reach. He could feel himself going out. The circle was getting smaller and further away. Everything was turning black, and the sounds around him were as if his ears were covered.

"Get up!" a faraway voice commanded. "Go help him!" the voice continued.

He could hear it, but nothing seemed to register. His bell was ringing and the whole world took a back seat to the momentary pause. Cole blinked, blinked again, and the carpet seemed to rush up at him. He realized he was face-down on the hallway floor. Rolling over, he could see Jackie Baker.

"Get up there and help him!!" she demanded.

She was yelling, but Cole could only hear her in one ear. The other just had a constant ring tone, a high-pitched note. Cole sat up, his head pounding. Mrs. Baker stared at him, panic in her face.

He struggled to his feet. His legs were shaky and his balance questionable, but he stood. Shaking his head, he looked up at the hole he had been knocked through. Grabbing hold of the ladder, partly to steady himself, he began to climb. Before Cole could eclipse the threshold, he already knew the boy's fate. The high-pitched screaming was gone. There was no sound at all coming from the attic.

He looked over the edge, but the attic was empty. The uncovered mirror showed the attic as it was; the evil image that had been there was gone. Cole scanned the room, viewing the damage done from the fight with a monster. He shook his head again, partly to allow what had happened to sink in, and to loosen the cobwebs from the blow and fall.

He climbed back down to the second floor. Mrs. Baker's expression altered, from panic and worry, to anger, to sorrow, to despair.

"What did you do? What did you do?" Jackie Baker screamed and slapped him hard across the face. "What have you done? How dare you!" She kept screaming. The woman struck at him again, but Cole blocked the strike and stepped back. "You, you killed my son, my baby boy. You killed him!" she said, advancing and swinging wildly.

Cole didn't know what to say. He took hold of the woman's flailing arms. "It took him. I tried to fight it off…" he attempted to explain.

"Why did you have to come here? You did this. You killed him." She fell to her knees on the hallway floor and began to sob.

Cole looked down and saw a broken human being, the vision of a true victim in every sense of the word. Her men may have been the direct targets, but it was her heart and mind which were crumbling.

"Get out. Get out. Get out!" she began to scream.

Cole backed away, turning to the stairs leading to the first floor. He started down but stopped, feeling guilty about leaving the poor woman in such a way. She continued to scream at him to leave, though, so he continued. Halfway down, he felt his legs begin to shake and then give way. He plopped down on one of the stairs right on his ass. Sliding down a few steps on his backside, Cole leaned back on the stairs. He was beaten and tired, the sound of a screaming woman in one ear and the mind-numbing tone ringing in the other.

Pulling himself up and exiting the Baker home, Cole wobbled to the car and got in. He sat there, looking back at the house, eyeing the attic. He was struck by how ordinary the home seemed. Then the woman's words thundered in his mind: "You killed my son." He started the vehicle. He could only imagine how frightening the creature must have been to Johnny.

CHAPTER 14

His whole body hurt while heading back to the library. The fall had really jarred his bones, and the punch had left his face and head throbbing. Every breath was painful; he might have cracked a few ribs. He had never taken such an ass-kicking in his life. He had learned a great deal, but at the cost of a young man, much like his own son.

He parked and slowly made his way up to the library. Molly and Doris were seated at one of the long wooden tables. Both stood as he approached. "What happened to you?" Molly asked.

"You are going to have to print out some more copies of the story. I forgot the ones I had. Sorry."

"Honey, what happened to you?" Molly asked again.

"Here, sit down." Doris pulled out a chair for him.

Cole plopped down and sighed heavily. "Had a little run-in with one of those things," he said, wincing as Molly poked at his wounds.

"How did you get away from it?" Doris asked.

"Wasn't after me. I met with Jackie Baker and her son, showed her the printouts and asked for any information. She had Brandon show me the mirror. They keep it in the attic. Doris, do you think I could have a glass of water?"

"We need to get you cleaned up. Do you have a first-aid kit?" Molly asked, her voice trailing at the end. "Some of those cuts look pretty deep."

"Cuts? It was rough, but at the time I didn't really notice. Babe, I am really sorry," Cole said, looking into his wife's eyes.

"Sorry for what?"

"For doubting you. There was a while there I didn't really know what to think. I didn't know what to believe. I should have. I do now," he said with compassion.

Molly kissed him on the forehead. "I love you." She turned to Doris. "Where are the restrooms?"

The library was still empty; clearly there was never a big rush in a small-town library. Cole was finally losing the adrenaline buzz and was beginning to feel the pain. He finally noticed the blood and his torn shirt. He had really gone round and round with that beast.

Molly helped him to his feet and took him to the restrooms. "I'll go get the first-aid kit," she told Cole.

In the bathroom, he just leaned against the wall for a long moment. Molly came in and took him by the arm to the sink. "Take off that shirt. Stick your head under the faucet," she ordered him. "Looks like you lost a patch of hair. Got some claw marks up here too," she said as she examined him.

"That thing is fast and so strong. Be glad you didn't tangle with it. It kicked my ass, and good." Cole stuck his head under the running water. "Hope there is some aspirin in that box because my head is killing me. Feels like I been kicked by a mule."

Doris walked in carrying a white box with a large red cross on the front. She set it on the counter and opened it, then stepped back. "Should we be doing this in here?"

All eyes moved to the large mirror which hung over the sink. "She may have a point," Molly said.

Cole looked at his reflection and nodded. "Yeah, why don't we do this out there. Let me wash the blood off and we can go."

He splashed water on his face and chest, rinsing out his shirt as well. "I think I figured out how this works," he said as he left the bathroom.

"What happened at the Bakers'?" Doris asked.

Cole returned to his seat at the long wooden table. Molly went to work on his cuts as he grabbed a bottle of Tylenol from the first-aid box. Dry-swallowing the pills, he gave Doris a look. "Mrs. Baker is a bitter woman and a drunk. 'Course, I can imagine why, given what happened on that Thanksgiving. She reacted to the articles we printed out. I asked her to tell me exactly what had happened and she did. Her husband was carving the turkey and cut himself. As they said grace, the creature appeared and took him. Ouch!" Cole reacted to the disinfectant Molly was applying.

"Shh. Don't be a baby," Molly said.

"Yeah, so anyway, the woman is still suffering. Her depression is obvious. The mirror, the one the thing came from and took her husband into, she kept in the attic, covered up. Ouch! That's enough of that. I'm fine." Cole gave his wife a look.

"You want it to get infected? Stop your crying. You're a big boy, just tell your story and let me do this." She gave Cole a tap on the forehead.

"Florence Nightingale you are not. Mrs. Baker had her son, Brandon, take me up and show it to me. The boy stepped on an exposed nail."

"So, the blood is a trigger? It opens the gate?" Doris asked.

"Yes, I guess so, but not that alone. I was right there at the mirror and the blood was present. I don't think it is just the blood. There is another component. Brandon said, 'God damn,' from the pain. The woman said her husband was saying grace, and Molly, you said Johnny complained about the antiseptic. Did he mention God?" Cole asked his wife.

"'God, Mom, that stings,'" Molly said.

"There's something else bugging me. There was a factory mark on the back of the mirror. I would bet money it was the very same mark as the one in the hotel. I am almost absolutely positive. I can't believe every mirror in America does this."

"So, you think saying 'God' opens the portal?" Molly asked.

Cole tilted his head. "Well, I don't know for sure. Maybe a set of things, a combination of factors. I want to get back to the hotel and check the back of the mirror. It may not be every mirror, but that particular brand."

Doris said, "You may be correct about the mentioning of God. I was reading up on voodoo and curses. Blood is used in summoning spirits, but there is a beckoning that must be performed. You have to call it. It very well may be a combination of factors. Blood is the sacrifice, the mention of God is the beckoner, and the mirror allows the spirit a physical outlet. The mirror is the gate."

"So, the spirit looks like the people it thinks summoned it?" Molly asked.

"This is all just guesswork and speculation. Maybe?" Doris said.

"All I know is the damn thing was stronger than it should be. Stronger than a teenage kid. It was stronger than any man I've ever seen and moved like lightning. Tossed me around like an old rag doll." Cole rubbed his shoulder.

Doris collected a couple of books and returned to the table. "Blood sacrifice has been used worldwide at different periods by a number of different cultures. Voodoo, witchcraft, the Aztecs, early pagan rituals. Even the Bible has the bleeding of livestock. The idea of God as the calling and the creatures being so violent and evil gives me pause. It's a bit strange. It obviously does not bring the spirit of God or any god-like ambassador." She flipped open one of the books.

"I was reading about curses when you came in," she went on. "It is believed that objects or people can be cursed. Like a hex or whatever you might call it. If you say the mark on the back was the same, that could be the mark of the curse or the symbol of a particular spirit."

"I have to get a look at that mirror in our room. Make sure," Cole said.

"Won't the police be looking for us?" Molly asked.

"The police are after you?" Doris asked.

Cole nodded. "They wanted us to come in for questioning. We had to check this out first. They would never believe a monster, spirit or whatever, took our son."

"How are we going to get in there and check it?" Molly asked.

"Well, my love, I don't think we should. I think I had better go alone. If they grab me, at least you can keep looking. While I'm gone, you can continue the search." Cole touched his wife's hand.

"Look at yourself. You went off alone and came back like this. I want to go with you," Molly said firmly.

"No. You stay here and figure out a way to combat this thing. Break this curse or whatever. I will go and check the mirror, get our things and come back."

"Won't we have to be there at that mirror to get Johnny back?" Molly asked.

"Baby, I really don't know. Seems like this thing has been all over. If this is just some sort of portal, Johnny may not be right there. The creature may have taken him somewhere. I don't know. If we have to go back to the hotel, we will."

"You can stay here and we will continue to search while your husband is gone," Doris said.

"Thank you. You've been a great help," Molly told the librarian.

Doris nodded. "This is a terrible thing, and it appears to have been at it a very long time. Never have been a real believer in the supernatural, but I am convinced this is a real situation and we seem to be the only people aware of it." The old librarian paused, looking off at the rows of books. "Something needs to be done. I will help you folks any way I can. We must fight evil at every turn. This has renewed my faith. We must stand together and be strong, it is the only way to destroy such evil."

"Glad to have you on board, Doris Lamb," Cole said. "You have already been invaluable, filling in some rather large gaps for us. I am going to have to ask a favor: I need to borrow your car."

"My car? Why is that?"

"I am sure that Detective Jones put out a watch for our car. Using yours, I may be able to get to the hotel undetected," he explained.

"I still want to come with you," Molly said.

"I know you would, my sweet, but I really think it best you stay here."

"You don't think they will have the room staked out?"

"They might. I'll figure that out when I get there."

Doris walked to the front desk and returned with her keys in hand. "Please be gentle with my car. It was my father's. He bought it before he died, so take care of it, please. It's a dark green Bonneville parked out front, the 1977 boat. I just filled it up, but it drinks gas."

"Thank you, Doris, truly. I will take care of your car."

Molly said, "We will make copies of all that material, just in case they snag you. You can show that old detective this has happened before." Molly and Doris left Cole to himself.

He sat at the reading table, feeling his body ache and his wounds pain him. His heart was heavy and he missed his son so very much. He wondered again how scared Johnny must have been when that creature took him. He remembered the face of Brandon, and his screams of terror. Cole could not imagine where his son or any of the others might be. What might be beyond the mirror. None of this made any logical sense—monsters and dimensions, curses and portals. Many movies and stories involved such things, which he dismissed as pure fiction? This was no movie, this was reality, and how sinister, daunting, and frustrating.

Cole thought of all the scary shows he had seen, ghosts and monsters. Things had seemed just so abstract, as if arguing about God, or aliens. Now here he was trying to figure out how to fight monsters. How could he fight something he didn't understand? He had stepped behind the curtain, and the great Oz was not a man but a great pale beast. The line—there was no such thing, it was a lie now. He had seen it, fought with it, and lost.

He could see the beast, smell its breath, feel the strength and power in its thin and withered body. He had no idea what he was going to do, but he had to do something. Every moment his son was gone was one more moment Johnny was afraid. He could not stand for that. He would march across Hell before he allowed that.

A door shut behind him. Molly approached, papers in hand. She set them on the table and gave him a sad look. "You look exhausted. Maybe you should wait, get a couple hours of sleep."

"Johnny can't afford for us to wait. We have to figure this out, we have to find a way to bring him back. I'm just a little worse for wear is all. I'm fine. Our boy needs us."

"You're right. I can't imagine what he is having to deal with. We need to get our son back. I'll find out what I can."

Doris came in with a couple pieces of paper. "Here you are," she said, handing them to Cole.

Cole stood and gave the old librarian a half-smile. "Thanks." He picked up his wet T-shirt and Doris's car keys and started for the front entrance. "I shouldn't be but a couple of hours. Wait here and I'll be back. If something happens, just find out what you can." He hugged Molly and kissed her passionately on the lips. "I love you."

"I love you too," she whispered.

Cole released her and turned to Doris. He put a hand on her shoulder and said, "Take care of my girl." The two shared a nod and Cole walked on to the door.

CHAPTER 15

The big green boat of a car wasn't hard to spot, parked right out front. He keyed the door and got in. The interior was clean and well kept. It didn't even have a hundred thousand miles on it. Putting the key in the ignition and firing the engine, he could feel and hear the difference from his rental car. He fixed the mirrors, pulled away from the curb, and began his trip back to the hotel.

The car seemed to float as he left Straightsville. He opened it up on the highway. The car leapt forward as he pressed the pedal down. He was careful not to speed, but he liked the power of the big block engine. The two-ton car wouldn't win any races, but it could have run through a brick wall.

As he got closer to the hotel, Cole could feel his nerves begin to tighten. He pulled into a convenience store. Inside, he bought a Coke and a pack of Marlboro cigarettes, then asked the clerk to see the local Yellow Pages. He looked up the Star Bird Inn and jotted down the number. Outside at a pay phone, he popped the tab on the Coke, unwrapped the cigarettes, and dialed the number.

A familiar voice answered. "Star Bird Inn. How may I help you?" Ernest's voice sounded chipper.

"Ernest, it's me, Cole Mason. Can you talk?"

"Yeah, the two detectives came by. Questioned me about you and your wife. I told them what I said I'd say."

Cole looked around and took a swig of his beverage. "Are they still there? Do they have the room staked out?"

"They went up and looked around. I think the big one is parked out front. He was really in a foul mood when they questioned me."

"Okay. Is there a back entrance or something? I need to get back into that hotel room. Can you help me?"

"Sure. In the parking area there is a side door. I can let you in."

Cole thought for a moment, remembering how the parking area was fenced on three sides with only an opening on the street. "Ernest, wait twenty minutes and then come open the door. I'm going to have to scale the fence. That big detective will be looking for me."

"You're probably right. I'll be there, twenty minutes," Ernest confirmed.

"Thanks. I have a lot to tell you when I get there." Cole hung up the phone.

Opening the pack of Marlboros, Cole fired one up and inhaled the delicious flavor. Exhaling a cloud into the air, he allowed the cigarette to calm him. He wasn't going to smoke in Doris's car. The interior was far too nice. Still, he needed a moment to settle and gather his thoughts. He thought about driving by and seeing where the big dumb detective was parked, but he didn't want to risk the son of a bitch recognizing him. After barely finishing half the cigarette, Cole flipped it toward the curb and got behind the wheel.

Cole parked a block down and a block over from the hotel. Giving himself somewhere to escape to, he figured. After locking Doris's Bonneville, he walked at a steady pace toward the hotel parking area. He would have to do this quickly and draw as little attention as possible. Looking up and down the street and through the chain link fence, Cole picked the far corner and gripped the metal. He pulled up, using his feet in the holes, then scurried up and over, minding the three rows of barbed wire at the top.

The fence was pretty tall; as Cole jumped down, the bottom of his feet stung from the impact. He ducked behind a car and scouted his position. Squinting, Cole could see the dumb cop across the street. The white bandages on his nose were like a beacon to be seen for miles. He slipped to the side door, crouched, and waited. As he felt the door begin to open, Cole slipped inside quickly, sliding by Ernest.

"The big dumb cop is across the street," Cole whispered.

"He didn't see you?"

Cole shrugged. "I hope not. He isn't one of the brightest bulbs on the tree. Doesn't seem to be the most observant detective, either."

"What happened to you? Were you in an accident?" Ernest asked.

Cole smiled. "Come on, I'll tell you all about it. I need to see that mirror in our room."

As they rode up in the elevator, Cole told Ernest what he had found out and about his run-in with the creature. Ernest was quiet, listening closely as Cole went on to explain why he had come back to the hotel. Finally, as Cole opened the door to room 411, Ernest asked, "So, you think the mirrors are cursed?"

Cole marched into the room and headed straight for the bathroom. Leaning the mirror forward, he searched for the manufacturer's stamp. "I knew it! I knew they were the same."

The men exchanged a look, and Cole nodded slightly. "So, it's the mirrors?" Ernest asked.

"Yeah, I would say so. The mirror in the Bakers' attic had the same mark," Cole said.

Ernest turned a grey-green color and walked out of the bathroom. Cole followed. The old man sat on the corner of one of the beds. "I feel sick. This is all my fault. You lost your son and it's my fault."

"What are you talking about?"

Ernest Weber raised his head. Tears rolled down his cheeks. "I bought those mirrors. Every mirror in this hotel has that mark. I got a great deal from the company." The old man put his head in his hands. "What have I done?"

"You know who makes these mirrors?"

Ernest nodded. "When we were remodeling, this mirror company offered me a bulk rate, a big discount, and I took it. Thought I was getting a good deal. I have endangered every guest I've ever had."

Cole began to pace the room, pausing to look at the mirror over the dresser. He pulled it away from the wall and searched for the mark. "Every mirror in the hotel?" he asked, and Ernest nodded. "Do you remember the name of the company?"

"I should have the name and address and phone number downstairs."

"This isn't your fault, Ernest. You bought some mirrors for your hotel. You had no way to know. I will get to the bottom of all this. I am one step closer to getting my son back." Cole put a hand on the old man's shoulder. "Let's go."

On their way back down the corridor, Cole looked at the mirrors lining both walls. He couldn't help but think of the monster he had battled, and the likelihood that just such a creature lay in wait within each. He shook his head, trying to expel the thoughts of anger and frustration.

As they stepped out of the elevator into the lobby, Cole found an unwelcome sight: Detectives Jones and Jerkowski were standing at the front desk, both looking at him. Jones grew a wide smile as Detective Jerkowski stepped past him, moving toward Cole at a steady gait.

Hearing the elevator doors closing behind him, Cole took a quick step backward and pushed the button for floor number four. The doors closed between him and the angry cop. "Later," he couldn't resist saying to the red-faced oaf.

"You son of a bitch," Detective Jerkowski snarled as he lunged toward the closing doors.

Exhaling slowly, Cole watched as the dial counted the floors as he ascended. The elevator doors opened, and he began to hurry down the plush hallway. Stopping abruptly, he questioned what he was doing, where he was going. He knew he was only making things worse. As he turned back toward the elevator, the other elevator door opened. There stood Detective Jones.

"What are you doing, Mr. Mason?" the older man said as he stepped out. "Got my goofy-ass partner wanting to call for backup."

Cole just stood there as Jones walked toward him. He wasn't going to run. He needed this man to believe him, to help him.

"Where is your wife, Mr. Mason? Seems you missed our appointment. After I was so nice, too. Now you want to run? Very disappointing."

"Freeze!" ordered an out-of-breath voice. Jerkowski had taken the stairs up the four flights. Now he extended his gun, pointed at Cole.

"Put that away," Jones said. "Mess around and you'll shoot someone." He turned back to Cole and rolled his eyes. "See what you've done. Got the boy all flustered. You really don't want to excite an idiot with a gun."

Cole looked past Jones at the big goof trying to holster his weapon. "Good advice. Thanks."

"You have some explaining to do."

"Yeah, you son of a bitch," Jerkowski added, still half out of breath.

Cole extended his hands slowly, palms up to show they were empty. "Don't panic. I have something to show you." Pulling the printouts from his back pocket, he handed them to Detective Jones.

Jones unfolded the papers and began to read, raising an eyebrow. Furrowing his brow, he focused on what he was reading.

"It's happened before," Cole said.

"Where is your wife, scumbag?" Jerkowski demanded, trying to look over his partner's shoulder.

"I just came from the Bakers' and I saw it. Brandon Baker, that man's son, is now missing as well. It took him right in front of me. This is real, whatever you choose to believe or accept, this is real."

"Another missing person?" Jones said, looking at Cole.

"There is a warrant for your arrest. Put your hands on the wall," Detective Jerkowski said, stepping past his partner.

"Hang on, Jerk, Mr. Mason isn't being a problem. Just relax," Jones said. He held up the papers. "You have a couple of articles. They may describe something similar to your situation, but these are just pieces of paper. You really can't expect me to believe monsters are coming out of the wall, can you?"

Cole tilted his head and gave a shrug.

"Just take it on faith, your word? Turn a blind eye and let you go, and to do what? Let you go monster hunting. And what would my bosses say about that?" Jones continued.

"Well, it would be nice if you actually helped me. Perhaps investigate. Isn't that what a detective does?" Cole asked.

"Don't be a dick," the younger cop said. "Fuck this guy, Shirley. I am taking him in."

"I need to see this through."

"You need shit. Fuck you. I don't give a hang what your story is. Partner, get a grip. We're cops, not ghostbusters."

Jones stepped forward and glared at his partner. "I told you about that, don't call me Shirley." He turned to Cole. "Mr. Mason, he's right. I have a job to do here. You have a warrant for your arrest. We deal in the real world here. What you have is interesting and we will look into it. But the reality is, you don't have any evidence, and that's a problem."

Cole stepped closer to the two detectives. "So, what you are saying is, if I had proof, then you would believe me."

"Sure, you make Bigfoot appear, and he and the Easter Bunny can tell us all about how they took your kid. You sick fuck," Jerkowski said, shaking his head.

"Shut up, Jerk," Jones told his partner.

Cole could feel his frustration building, along with the impatience to find his son. He pulled out a few dollars from his pocket, slipped a single loose, and put the rest back. "Here, Detective Jerkowski."

"Trying to bribe me with a buck?"

The big cop was preoccupied just enough to not notice Cole cock back and swing. A closed fist to the already-broken nose of the big detective dropped the man to his knees. The mushy cartilage reminded Cole of a soft melon or a bag of sand. The cop gripped his nose and tipped forward, curling up in agony. Stepping past Jones and over the big guy on the floor, Cole could see his plan was working. Blood filled the younger detective's hands. He looked up at Jones. The older detective was pointing his gun at him.

"You don't believe me. Hey stupid, what does it say on the back of that dollar? Can you read it or are you too stupid? Perhaps I cracked you so good, you can't see the words."

The big detective shook his head and squinted in pain, spitting blood onto the carpet. "You son of a bitch," he said, coming to one knee. His eyes were filled with tears from the impact to his sinuses.

"I don't think you got the guts. You won't say it. Read the dollar bill," Cole taunted.

"Shut your mouth and turn around. You assaulted my partner," Jones ordered.

"What does it say, Jerk? Read it."

Jerkowski came to his feet and looked at the dollar bill in his hand, then eyed Cole.

"Don't do it, Travis. Don't feed into the bullshit," Jones told his partner.

"What, you believe this guy? Buying into this crap? Fuck this guy. Ain't no ghost gonna save you from me," Jerkowski told Cole.

"So, you a pussy, or a coward, or is there a difference?" Cole continued to taunt.

Looking from Cole to his partner, Detective Jerkowski flipped the dollar to the floor. "In God we trust," he said, looking back at Cole with a hard stare. Advancing toward him, the young detective carried rage in his eyes. "See, no monsters. You are mine."

"Good luck, Detective," Cole said softly. "I am sorry." He turned and ran for the elevator.

The big detective was hot on his heels and took hold of Cole's shirt from behind. "You aren't getting away from me." He jerked Cole back and took hold of him by the shoulders.

In the mirrors along the corridor, Cole could already see the change in the reflection. Everything in the mirrors was becoming dingy and tattered, darker somehow. "Dude, you're so fucked."

Detective Jerkowski punched him in the stomach. The blow bent Cole in half at the waist. "I am really going to enjoy kicking your ass."

A shot reverberated through the corridor, followed closely by three more. The ear-shattering sound in such a confined space gained both men's attention. Down the hallway, Detective Jones was firing into the back of Jerkowski's evil twin. The creature was paying no mind to Jones or the shots ripping through its body; it was focused on Jerkowski.

"What the hell is that?" the young detective yelled.

Cole jerked out of his grasp. "Oh, I think it is going to introduce itself. I think that's your ass. Nice knowing you, cop."

Cole could see the hole from Jones's bullet, but it was bloodless, same as the one in the attic. These things did not bleed. Jerkowski drew his weapon and began to fire at the creature. The thing's jerky motion was hardly interrupted, and it barely showed a reaction to the impact of the rounds or the bullets' penetration. Jones ducked into a doorway. The bullets went right through the creature and he was down range.

"The knees, shoot out its legs," Cole yelled.

Jerkowski adjusted fire and let loose with a barrage of bullets, until the gun emptied. The beast had gone down but had not stopped advancing. It was coming for the big cop, and they all knew it.

The young detective flipped the empty magazine and jammed in a full one. "Goddamn it, won't this thing die?"

That was when the second creature began to emerge from one of the other mirrors. Now there were two of them.

"Jesus Christ, what the hell is this?" Jerkowski cried.

Another face began to push through the glass, birthing from another mirror. "You had better shut up, you'll have an army of those things after you," Cole said.

Three Jerkowski-beasts now occupied the hallway, one crawling ever closer while the other two stood focused on their prey. Jerkowski took aim as the two standing began to move toward him. Like big cats, they lunged, springing off the floor and onto the ceiling. Clawing the plaster, the creatures galloped forward, racing toward Jerkowski.

Cole paused in amazement at the things' agility and speed. They seemed to defy gravity and reason, taking punishment like a cartoon villain and maintaining a singular purpose. It was dreadful.

Jerkowski fired shot after shot, fast as he could pull the trigger, but they were on him. Both creatures pounced, taking the big cop to his back right at Cole's feet.

Jones ran at the pile of Jerkowskis but paused to look at Cole. "Do something!" he demanded.

Cole could only watch and shake his head. He had already battled with the creatures and knew there was little to be done. Jones extended his revolver to the back of one of the creatures and fired into the base of its neck. The bullet ripped through and left a gaping hole where the Adam's apple used to be.

The creature twisted its head like the girl from *The Exorcist*, then spun to face Jones, quick as a flash. Jones looked bug-eyed at the beast before him, knowing the wound he had just inflicted was normally a fatal one. Cole saw the thing draw back and he knew what was coming. He would have warned the older detective, but these things moved with such speed, there was no time.

The punch was a blur, hitting Jones hard and sending him flying. The older man slid on the plush carpet for more than twenty feet. Jerkowski was punching the other one in the face, which seemed to no more than annoy his pasty alter-image. The creature held him off the floor by his throat. As it turned to take him, it tripped over the one crawling on the floor.

So, the creatures did not work together, but neither did they seem to be competing for their prize. The big cop fought, but the grip was more than he could escape from. The thing regained its footing and continued down the hall. Jerkowski was in the clutches of evil and all his efforts were for naught.

Jones held his chest but shakily stood; the want to help his goofy partner was obvious. The lead creature had the big cop held out in front of it, so Jones dared not shoot for fear of hitting Jerkowski. The other two beasts now followed the one as they moved down the corridor toward Jones. The older man charged forward and attacked the thing carrying his underling. Taking another hard blow, this time bouncing the old cop off the ceiling, he lay there, still.

Cole reached the elevator and pressed the button. He saw Jerkowski's gun on the carpet and picked it up before the doors opened. He turned and took aim at the lead creature, targeting the back of its knees. Firing a volley, he saw the knees pop and give way. As the beast dropped the big cop, he heard Jerkowski gasp for breath.

His actions had gained the creatures' attention, but with a ding behind him, Cole stepped into the elevator and pressed the button for the lobby, then turned and threw the pistol down the hall toward Jerkowski. The struggle continued as the doors closed. Falling back onto the little sofa in the corner, Cole thought about what he had done. He had egged the stupid cop on; he knew what was going to happen. He had brought those things out and allowed them to take the man. Nothing about what he had done was right.

CHAPTER 16

The car dropped, the dial moved, and with a ding he was on the first floor. The doors opened to the lobby. Ernest rounded the desk as Cole exited the elevator. The old man carried a look of concern.

"Just had a feeling you would be back around. You are a charmed young man," Ernest said with a smile.

"Is that what you'd call it?" Cole smiled in return.

"Heard some gunshots. Those for you, or...?" The old man allowed the question to hang.

Cole bobbed his head. "Had to introduce the big dumb cop to the mirrors. I don't think they will be doubting me after this." He shrugged and moved toward the desk. "Did you find that address?"

"I was about to go look; the gunplay distracted me. Should be in my office." Ernest rounded the desk and Cole followed. "I think I kept the card, in case I needed more mirrors."

Cole made a face. "More. The place is wall to wall with those damn things."

"It was a very good deal." The old man pulled a stack of business cards from his desk, held by an aged rubber band, which snapped as Ernest pulled it. He handed over half the stack. "Here, this will go faster if we both look."

Cole was still pretty amped up from the business upstairs. His hand shook as he held the first card up. He didn't really want to think about what might be happening up there at that very moment. He was sure that Jerkowski was in deep shit, and like it or not, those things were going to get him. He didn't want to think of the level of responsibility he carried for the whole thing.

Cole exhaled a long breath. He needed a cigarette. Part of him regretted what he had done, but part of him was glad. He had confirmed his theory. He now knew for certain it was the mirrors, and he knew how they worked. He also now knew that more than one beast could emerge at one time. As if one were not enough.

He flipped through the cards. His patience was gone, his nerves were fried and his level of anxiety was ready to boil over. His leg shook; the pain from his earlier encounter was beginning to return. A ding sounded, and both men looked at each other. Someone had come down in the elevator.

Both men began to sort faster, throwing cards onto the desk and going on to the next. Cole leaned back to peek out the doorway and saw Detective Jones stumbling toward the desk. "Here. Keep looking," he told Ernest.

Seeing a stack of fresh towels on a shelf, Cole grabbed a couple, stepped out of the office, and walked around the desk. The detective was bloody and beaten, a large gash at his hairline and number of lumps on his face. Cole handed him the towels. "You look worse for wear."

"You did that. You called on those things. You knew," Jones stammered.

Cole could see claw marks on the detective's chest and pointed them out. "Better put some pressure on those cuts."

"They took him, you son of a bitch. How could you do that?" Jones half pushed Cole away.

"Knock it off. You want to bleed to death?" Cole told the man. He pulled back the towels to take a look. The wounds were fresh and bloody, but not life-threatening. "Some stitches and you'll be fine." Of course, the look of shock on the detective's face was a whole 'nother story. His look of bewilderment and disbelief, coupled with anger and loss.

"How could you do that?"

"Well, you believe me now, don't ya?"

Detective Jones focused on Cole. "You knew they would take him."

"I had that reasonable expectation, yes. Now you can try and explain all this to the powers that be. See how understanding your bosses will be."

"You'll answer for this. You did this."

Cole laughed. "Yeah, bullshit. I tried to tell you. You didn't want to listen. I have to find my son. I give two shits about that big dumb cop. He confirmed for me the process, while proving to you that there really are monsters. Good luck explaining this, Shirley."

Jones gave a hard look at the father of the missing boy. "Don't call me Shirley."

Ernest rounded the desk holding a business card. "I found it. Knew I still had it. Damn, he looks pretty rough."

"Slap of reality." Cole took the card from Ernest. "Thank you. Better call an ambulance for Shirley here."

"I told you not to call me Shirley. And where do you think you are going?" the detective said.

Cole shook his head and again raised his eyebrows. "I told you, I need to find my son. These people know something, and they are going to tell me. Good luck, cop. Maybe next time you won't doubt. Guess we both know there is a much stranger world out there than we figured." He turned the card over to read it.

At the top left, in bold letters, was a symbol: **XX**. Just beside the symbol it read *Walton Mirrors*, with their address and phone number. "Thank you, Ernest." He picked up the phone to call for the ambulance. "Farewell, cop. I got what I came for. Time I get to the bottom of this shit and get my Johnny boy home. Sorry it had to go this way. Now you know, now you can be a cop and do something about it."

"You can't leave, I'm arresting you," Jones said weakly.

Cole stepped around the detective toward the front door. A young couple was just entering. Cole gave a look back at Ernest.

"Sorry folks, we are temporarily closed for remodel. Appreciate you stopping by," the old hotel owner told them.

Cole continued toward the door.

"Stop," Jones yelled. "Stop that man! I am a police detective and that man is under arrest."

Cole met the eyes of the young man and gave a deterrent glare before turning to look at the detective, balancing himself against the front desk. "You can't shut up, can you? Don't know when to stop."

"You are under arrest. Stop him, he is a cop killer."

Cole turned back to the couple and saw the emotions grow on the woman's face. "Do something, James," she said.

"Don't even think about it kid," Cole warned.

"You run and you'll be a cop-killing fugitive," Jones said.

Cole moved toward the door but stopped. "You want to lay this at my feet, after what you have seen? I don't have time for this. You do what you want, say what you want. I'm going to find my son."

He gave the young couple a very serious look, then shook his head. The young man took a step back and lowered his eyes.

"James," the woman said. "This phone has a camera on it. I have your picture and I am calling the police."

Cole advanced. The young man's eyes met Cole's again and he stepped between his girlfriend and Cole. A straight kick right to the man's shin, just below the knee, then a shove. The young man tumbled to the floor and gripped his leg. The young woman stood there in shocked awe, looking from her yelping boyfriend to Cole, as if the whole thing were unbelievable. He snatched the phone from the girl, broke it in half, and dropped it at her feet.

The young woman moved to her hurt boyfriend and Cole moved to the door. He could hear sirens in the distance. He paused to look back at Ernest and Detective Jones. The old hotel owner gave a wave and a nod. The cop was still bitching and complaining.

Cole moved along the street at a brisk pace but didn't want to openly run. He looked at the card once again. *Walton Mirrors, XX*. He looked more closely: the two X's were on top of one another. He slipped the card into his front pocket. The sirens were getting louder; an ambulance sped past two streets over.

He could feel the nerves in his stomach, that unease of a thousand butterflies taking flight all at once with nowhere to go. He turned to see the nosy young woman following him at a distance. He had no time for this. He could hear more sirens in the distance, which he knew weren't ambulances. It was time to pick up the pace; Cole broke into a run. Turning the corner and back past the alley, he sprinted, pausing only to see her jogging after him.

He reached the next block. He could see the Bonneville, and pulled the keys from his pocket. The girl was still coming, but he had created enough distance he figured she wouldn't get the plates. He hopped in, fired up the big engine and pulled the shifter down into drive. As he stomped the gas pedal and turned the wheel, the tires screeched and spun. The cloud of smoke left in his wake from the half-donut he pulled created a smokescreen between him and the nosy girl.

He could see her standing on the corner in his rearview mirror as he made the next right. He needed to get out of town quickly, back to pick up his wife. He mashed down the pedal. The big engine surged forward, and the car swayed from the torque. The vehicle seemed to float as he bounced over the side streets and made his way toward the highway.

Slowing down so as to not draw more attention, Cole made his way back to the state route which would take him to Straightsville. Even if the police arrived and the nosy girl gave a description of the car, he had time.

He drove down a winding, two-lane road, mindful of his speed and the rearview mirror. He was well aware of how out of hand things had gotten, and how any further problems should be avoided if possible. His mind filled with thoughts of his son and Molly, and what he needed to do next. He thought about Ernest and Detective Jones, Jerkowski and the Baker boy. He thought about those creatures, and how afraid Johnny must have been.

Lost in his own thoughts and focused on the road ahead of him, Cole was brought back to the present by the chirp of a siren behind him. A quick glance in the rearview showed the red and blue lights of the police. Cole's mind began to race. Another look, and the cruiser was right on his bumper, the siren on and wailing. A voice announced that he was to pull over immediately.

It was just the one cop, Cole thought, but he knew he couldn't outrun the radio. He peeked back. The cruiser was right on him, and it made him wonder why the man was being so aggressive. Then he remembered that Jones had called him a cop-killer. Cops hate cop-killers; they reason that anyone willing to kill a cop is more dangerous. Cole had never followed the reasoning; a killer is a killer. They just viewed a cop-killer as a greater threat to *them.*

Cole felt a jolt as the cruiser tapped the Bonneville's bumper. A dangerous move at over sixty miles an hour. This really got Cole's attention and focused him on his driving. The voice again commanded him to pull over. He could see the officer in his rearview pointing to the side of the road. He had to do something, and pulling over wasn't it. The time it would take to explain, be hauled down town, deal with the police and see what Jones might say—it was all too much.

A road sign read ten miles to Straightsville. He checked the mirror; the cruiser was still right on his ass. He pressed the brake pedal enough to light up the taillights but not slow down and saw the cop back off slightly. Mashing the gas to the floor, he felt the big engine leap forward and the heavy vehicle seemed to float on the pavement. The speedometer passed seventy, eighty, ninety, one hundred miles per hour.

It wasn't till the next curve in the road that Cole had to slow down. He could hear the tires screech as they tried to hang on to the highway. Stomping the pedal to the floor once again, he glanced in the mirror and saw the cop squealing around the curve right on his ass. The next curve was tighter, and he had to apply the brakes as to not lose control.

He had to lose this cop, but that wasn't going to be easy. Police cars are high-performance, and cops are trained for high-speed pursuits. The further and faster this chase went on, the worse it was for him. This was becoming a real problem. He knew his actions were absolutely criminal in the eyes of the law, but none of that mattered now. All that mattered was Johnny.

A few more curves and then it straightened out. Cole mashed the gas pedal again, trying to gain more speed and more power from the big car. Watching the road, gripping the wheel, checking his speed and his mirrors; Cole was busy, his hands full and his mind racing. This was the kind of moment little boys dream about, scenes from the movies which they can live. As an adult, Cole was scared to death and knew the consequences which would come from his actions.

The police car swerved into the oncoming lane—there were no cars coming, thankfully. Cole could hear the engine of the cruiser rev, growing louder. The cop was making his move. A straight stretch of highway, no cars coming, high speeds. He considered swerving over to cut him off, but quick moves at high speeds could cause real problems. If he clipped the cop, any multitude of things could happen.

Cole had seen enough movies and TV to know the cop was positioning himself to perform the PIT maneuver. He wasn't sure what PIT stood for, but the move was simple: the cop pulls up to the rear wheel and then turns into the suspect's car. By bumping the back portion of the vehicle, it would put the car into a controlled slide, which the cop could power through and maintain control. The result would wreck the suspect's vehicle.

He glanced down at the speedometer—he was going over a hundred miles an hour in a two-ton car. Cole was never a physics major, but mass plus velocity times car crash equals death, or at best being really fucked up. This over-anxious cop was going to get him killed. Losing control at these speeds, in a car that weighed this much, on a road lined with trees—good news would be getting "hurt." He couldn't continue to play these games with this cruiser.

He would have to counter the move. He couldn't allow this cop to bump him or it was over. Fishtailing out of control at a hundred and ten was all bad. Cole checked the driver-side mirror. The police car had pulled up and was in a good position. He had to do something, now.

He let off the gas and pressed the brake pedal, and the cop car shot right past the Bonneville. The cop had been so concentrated on his move, he wasn't paying attention and now was out of position. Cole could see the cop turning his head, watching Cole as he passed. He jammed the accelerator to the floor, and the big engine lunged forward. The Bonneville smashed into the rear of the cruiser.

The policeman had made another mistake: as he passed Cole, he had taken his foot off the gas and now Cole had the momentum he needed. The Bonneville was now pushing the cruiser. Stomping the gas pedal again, he could see they were still over ninety miles an hour. Again, the cop made a mistake, reacting normally but incorrectly: he hit the brakes.

Cole saw the brake lights come on and knew it was over for the cop. He mashed hard on the gas, even though it was all the way on the floor. He could hear the cruiser's brakes on the pavement, trying desperately to take hold, but it was too late. Too much speed, and the weight of the Bonneville created too much force for the cop to do much of anything. The brakes were the wrong move.

He could feel the motion of the cruiser in the wheel of the Bonneville. The cop was losing control. The ass end of the police car began to waver. Cole let off the gas, but only for a moment before jamming the pedal to the floor once again. The impact was subtle but the feel of bumper-on-bumper of the vehicles was substantial. The police car angled left, and again the cop made the mistake of hitting his brakes.

The brake lights lit up and the sound of rubber squealing erupted. The cruiser jogged right and the policeman tried to correct. He was only making things worse. The tail end of the police car jerked more vigorously. Right, then left, back and forth—the car was out of control.

Cole eased off the gas and allowed the cruiser to take its course. He could see the right rear wheel lift off the pavement as the cop continued to try and correct. The cruiser had gone too far, and the inevitable was inevitable. Pressing down on the brake, he backed off and watched. He did not want to get caught up in what was coming.

It happened so fast but seemed to occur in slow motion. As the cop corrected back to the left, the left rear end of the cruiser lifted off the road. The police car went airborne, flipping side over side, until it impacted with the pavement. The crashing sound was enormous. The cruiser bounced and continued to flip, only faster. The momentum tumbled the car high and to the side.

The car flew into the tree-lined roadside, shearing off full-grown trees as it went. Cole could only cringe as the cruiser continued its journey into the trees. A large oak brought the car to a short stop. There was no give in the old oak tree, and the cruiser folded in half.

Cole slowly pulled up to the scene and viewed the pieces of the vehicle leading to the mangled wreckage. It was a horrible scene. The car was ten feet up in the air, smoking and leaking fluids, the metal all bent and torn. Cole could only see the undercarriage of the vehicle; the top of the car was embedded into the trunk of the tree. The bumpers of the cruiser almost were touching around the oak tree.

As he pulled up slowly and off the side of the road, Cole knew the fate of the officer even without seeing the man. Seatbelt, airbag, any safety measure in the world wouldn't make that crash survivable. He didn't want to think about the man behind the wheel, the moments of fear and terror he had just experienced. He didn't want to think of another death as a result of all this.

Looking at the mangled wreckage and where the driver's seat was now part of that old oak tree, he realized he had now killed a policeman. Jerkowski was indirect; this was not. He had not intended for the man to die, but by his actions the man was dead.

Cole could see a bloody hand sticking out of the twisted metal. The sight was traumatic. He thought about how the trooper was going to wreck him, that it would be him dead. He thought about how many mistakes the trained driver had made, and how he was partly at fault.

He then realized that the trooper must have turned in his plate number and called for backup.

He had less than ten miles to go to get to Straightsville. He mashed the gas pedal down once more, only pulling off the main road once he got to the small town. Then he hurried to the library. He could hear sirens and saw flashing lights blur past in the rearview mirror. Such a small town; as soon as the police had the plate and knew it was Doris Lamb's car, they would be at the library.

CHAPTER 17

He parked in front of the library, the tires screeching to a halt. Cole ran up the steps and into the old building. Doris Lamb was at the desk, and Molly was at a reading table with a book open. Both women looked at him as he barged in.

Molly could see right away that something was wrong. "What is it?"

He ran up and hugged his wife. "Grab your things. We have to leave." Then he hurried to the desk. He placed the car keys on the desk, lowered his eyes, and said, "I'm sorry."

The older woman squinted as if in pain. "What happened? Is it bad?" Doris asked hesitantly.

"The front end is dinged up a bit. Not much. But I really feel bad. If there had been any other way…" Cole allowed his thoughts to run. "The police are going to have some questions for you."

"What questions?"

"Yeah, what questions?" Molly echoed.

"I don't have time to explain. We need to go, now." Cole looked at his watch; every moment was extremely valuable. "We have to go, now! Grab your things. I'll explain as we go."

Doris Lamb rounded the desk with her bag and keys in hand.

"What are you doing?" Cole asked.

She stopped and looked Cole directly in the eyes. Her look and tone were serious as she said, "I'm part of this now."

Cole shook his head. "I don't know how this is going to play out. I don't want you in trouble, or possibly hurt."

"You are fighting evil. You are going to need all the help you can get. What kind of person could walk away from doing what is right? So, let's go."

The three hurried from the library. Doris stopped halfway down the steps, looking out at her Pontiac Bonneville. "A little ding?"

"It's fixable. Come on. We need to go," Cole said. Moving to their rental car, he opened the doors for the two women, then rounded the car and slipped behind the wheel.

As he started the car, he asked Molly, "How much cash do you have?" He pulled what he had from his wallet and handed it over to her. "They will track our credit cards if we use them. We have to use cash, and we have a ways to go."

"Sixty-eight dollars and thirty-two cents," Molly said.

Cole looked at the gas gauge and began to figure mileage.

"Where are we going?" Doris asked from the backseat.

"Ohio."

"Ohio?" Molly asked.

"What's in Ohio?" Doris asked.

Cole pulled away from the curb. He pulled the card from his pocket and handed it to his wife. "Thanks to Ernest."

"Ernest?" Doris asked.

Molly handed the card back to Doris. "This is the mark, isn't it?"

Cole nodded as he kept his eyes on the road.

"This could be a conjuring sign," Doris said.

Cole pulled onto the highway and accelerated. "Going to be a real stretch on sixty bucks." As he drove, he told them what had happened at the hotel. He explained how he tested the triggers of the mirrors, how blood and mentioning God brought those unholy beasts forth, and how they claimed the big dumb cop. He told them how more than one ghoulish reflection had come for the cop.

"Did they come from different mirrors?" Doris asked.

"I really didn't notice. I think so, but I couldn't say for absolute sure. Why?"

"If they are doorways, are they to one world or many?" the old librarian asked.

"I don't know." Cole told them the rest, how Detective Jones had called him a cop-killer. He explained about Doris's car and the death of the trooper, that he had actually caused the death of a policeman.

Molly reached over and stroked Cole's arm in a comforting gesture.

They drove in silence for over an hour, each consumed with their own thoughts. Finally, they had to stop and get gas. They all got out as Cole pumped the gas, needing to stretch their legs and use the restroom. Cole had worried about police, but they hadn't seen any the whole way. He would have liked to use side roads, but the highway was better on gas.

Time was also a factor. Johnny had been missing too long; the police would be searching more intensely for Cole and his wife. He had to hurry but keep his head as he rushed. He could not afford to make a mental error. Little sleep, high stress, and dealing with supernatural events—the situation was built for a complicated end.

The trio got back into the car without a word and Cole took them back out onto the interstate. Molly took his hand and gave him an understanding look.

"We will get Johnny back," he told her.

"I know."

Cole thought about what would happen when all was said and done. How he would have to answer for the Baker kid, Jerkowski, and the trooper. Still, he figured it all would be worth it to see his son in Molly's arms again.

"How much further, do you think?" Doris asked from the backseat.

"Cross over into Ohio, then a couple hours, I would guess."

"You know, we should probably do some research on this Walton Mirrors before we just rush in and start dropping accusations," Molly said as she looked out the passenger window.

Cole didn't want to delay, but he knew Molly was the sensible one, most of the time. She would think about things, when he would simply act, or react. "You're probably right. If we walk in telling these people their mirrors have demons in them or are gateways to some dark universe, they'll call the police. Have us all thrown in the loony bin."

Even as he spoke, part of Cole did not want to wait. Every moment he delayed, Johnny was lost. Every moment was another that his son needed him.

"There may be a different circumstance as well," Doris added. "They may know very well that their mirrors do what they do. They may make them to do so. They could be unaware of what is going on, but I would say someone is very aware. I can't imagine why someone would do such a thing, but we had better consider the possibility."

"You think someone at the factory is purposefully doing this?" Molly asked.

Doris leaned forward over the seat. "The curse could have been planted whenever. The current management may not have any idea."

Molly turned in her seat. "It has been going on for so long. It's hard to believe we are the first ones to put this together."

Cole listened, keeping his eyes on the road. They had passed into Ohio, and he felt better about putting some distance between them and the mess he had left in his wake. He had concerns about the mirror and getting Johnny back. Would he have to use the same mirror his son had been taken into? The thought gave him pause and he felt his stomach churn.

"We are going to have to figure this out," he said. "We will probably have to go back and use that mirror in the hotel. I don't know what or where—we just need to get Johnny."

"A trip to the local library may help us," Doris said. "Libraries are wells of information. The local papers may have something on the factory, some history or event which might shine some light on all this."

Walton Mirrors was located in the capital of Ohio, Columbus. The city was in the center of the state, almost two hours from the border. The landscape was flat; farms and chain businesses lined the highway.

Cole suddenly remembered something. "Did you bring the travelers' checks?" he asked Molly.

"I didn't even think of the travelers' checks. They can't track those, can they?" Molly pulled out a plastic-covered checkbook. "At least now we have some money."

By the time they reached Columbus, it was after business hours. They stopped on the outskirts to get gas and a city map. Cole wanted to know where things were and how to get around if need be. He paid with one of the travelers' checks, and felt it was a good omen. They had a resource to use and were ahead of the situation.

Cole looked up the street in the map's directory and turned to the page. It was downtown, west of a river. He looked up the main library. It was on the other side of the Scioto River. They would have to wait until the morning to further their cause. Cole pulled into a moderately priced motel chain and went in, getting one room with two beds.

"I figured we were all exhausted and we didn't need two rooms. Is that okay?" he handed the key over to Molly.

"That's fine," Doris said from the backseat.

In the room, Cole checked the mirrors for the mark but found none. "We should get some food."

"Pizza?" Molly asked.

Doris nodded and sat down on the bed. Molly pulled the Yellow Pages from the drawer. "Who wants what?" After collecting the orders and making the call, Molly hung up and looked at the other two. "Thirty minutes. We should probably have a plan of action for tomorrow."

Cole sat down on the end of the bed, nodding in agreement.

Doris said, "We need to go to the library and do our research. Find out what we can about the company—its history, any strange events, or whatnot."

Cole opened the map to the downtown region of Columbus and laid it on the bed. "Library is here, factory is here. Relatively close. Looks like this Broad Street will take us, and then down to Walton Mirrors. I'm not sure what the research would help us with."

"It might give us the right people to talk with," Doris said. "Like Molly said, we don't want to draw too much attention."

"So, what will we be looking for?" Cole asked.

"I would suspect some kind of event. A fire or deaths, something evil. It's why I think we really need to check. The person or people who opened this door could be long gone, and the current owners may be unaware. A company mark is rather standard. It is reasonable to assume a change in management or ownership may not alter the logo."

"If we do find the person who opened the gate or brought about the curse, then what?" Molly asked. "And what if they are dead, or long gone?"

Doris shrugged. "I am learning this as we go too. I don't have all the answers. Cole, you figured out how the portal works, and that's to our advantage. Now we just have to figure out the rest. We are going to have to go at this carefully."

Then she let out a long sigh and continued, "We also need to see if we can find any instance of someone coming back from the mirror world. If things are only one way, that could be a bad thing."

"Bad?" Cole asked.

"If the gateway is in and not out, we may have to figure how to open the gates from that side, from the other world," she told them.

A knock at the door made everyone pause. Each of them fell immediately silent and looked at the door. They were all on edge. Molly got up and opened it to a man with a satchel of pizzas. He handed over three large boxes and a couple of two-liter bottles of soft drinks. As the door closed, the group relaxed and moved on the pies.

"So, what can we do?" Cole asked, taking a bite.

"And how will we get Johnny back?" Molly added.

Doris put up a hand as she finished a bite of pizza. "If we can find the person who started all of this, they may know how to do everything we need. Certainly, they will know more than I do. If it is a curse, it may bring back those taken if it is broken."

"So, Johnny could just reappear?" Cole asked.

"Cast out of the mirror," Doris said.

"I hope so." Molly took a bite.

Doris wiped her mouth with a napkin. "Logic dictates that if there is a way in, there has to be a way out. We need to be careful, however."

Molly asked, "Careful of what?"

"If we open that door, we don't know what else might come through it. Johnny may return, but if we can't close it or control it... We could open a floodgate, and it could jeopardize the world as we know it."

"Those things are nothing nice," Cole said. "Fast, strong, and as far as I can tell, unstoppable. It seems they are purely goal-oriented, and only want to pull their reflection into the mirror. God only knows what would happen if that wasn't the case."

Doris said, "That's why I was leaning toward this being a curse. Those creatures are single-minded. They don't take anyone else. When the right set of triggers opens the gate, they emerge and snatch and grab. I wonder what might happen if we destroyed the gateway."

"I tried that," Cole said, "when the Baker kid was taken. I threw a golf club at the mirror to break it, but it just went in. It was like liquid, I couldn't break it. I also tried to cover it up; the creature just kept at it. I watched those cops shoot those creatures, and bullets did nothing to stop them. Granted, taking out their legs helped to slow them down, but they kept coming."

"You threw a golf club into the mirror?" Doris asked.

Cole nodded and took another bite of pizza.

"What?" Molly asked.

"If things can go into the mirror that aren't the object of the creature, could a person go in?"

Cole leaned forward on the bed. "So, a person could go in and look around, not have to deal with the beasts."

"I don't know. It would be very risky," Doris said. "Could cause a real problem if the mirrors don't lead anywhere. Even if it does go somewhere else, there are so many factors at work. The gate could close and we may never get it reopened. It's complicated."

"Complicated how?" Molly asked.

The old librarian shrugged and took another bite of pizza. "We are dealing with pure unknowns here. Is time the same in that plane? Are days the same? Minutes, years? Distance? Gravity could be plus or minus. Air quality, water, a million unknowns. We have no way to know. Alternate universe, dimension, or whatever is beyond. Obviously, the rules of this world don't fully apply to those creatures."

They all sat with their thoughts after that, eating in silence for a while. Cole searched his memory of his encounters with the beasts, remembering their movements, the pasty skin, the claw-like fingers. They were beasts, animals which only looked like people. No more human than the image they carried. All rage and anger, along with the singular focus of claiming the prey. Any obstacle was simply forced from its path.

"Entering the mirrors doesn't sound like a good idea," Molly finally stated flatly.

"No. I would certainly recommend another option," Doris agreed.

Cole stood from the bed. "It is an option. Perhaps not an ideal one, but I will get our son back, even if I have to go and get him. I would trek across the fiery plains of Hell, if need be. Whatever it takes. Whatever it takes."

Molly stood and gave Cole a strong hug.

Cole released her and moved to the dresser, pulling a pad of paper from the drawer. "Let's go over what we know. Get this written down, so we can take a look at it." He sat at the room's small table, and they began to go over everything, the whole situation. They talked about the symbols, the creatures, the method of opening the mirrors, and he wrote down every detail.

"We need to know more," Doris said. "We know a lot, more than probably anyone, but we need everything we can."

"Do you really think someone in that factory will know the answers?" Molly asked. "Or some old newspaper?"

Doris Lamb got up and paced the room. "We know how the mirrors work, and we know where they come from. We are working through the who, what, where, when, how, and why. It's the process of solving a mystery."

They used the Yellow Pages again to find the library's hours. It opened at nine in the morning, and they all agreed they should be there then. Cole turned on the television, to see if there was any news about them. They had crossed into another state; it was unlikely the local news would have anything, but he still wanted to check.

Cole lay down on one bed to watch, and Doris lay on the other as Molly went into the bathroom to freshen up. Cole knew he was tired, but sleep overtook him in a rush. He never even noticed Molly coming to bed or the television being turned off.

CHAPTER 18

Cole was exhausted, battered and bruised, stressed out, and his mind was filled with concern for his son. His dreams were occupied by what had happened and what was to come.

Slumber took him into a nightmare, filled with creatures and mirrors. Cole was with his son in a gray world. He beat against the back of a mirror, surrounded by beasts, hundreds or thousands of them. They were encircled and the monsters were slowly closing in. He pulled Johnny into his arms and knew they were in trouble. He could feel the fear, so he leapt into the glass. Breaking through the mirror, he landed in the hotel bathroom. Everyone was there. Johnny ran into his mother's arms as Cole turned to witness the creatures crawling from the mirror. A flood of evil began to emerge from the mirror into their world.

Cole jerked straight up in bed, his eyes wide and sweat pouring from his body. His heart was racing and his breath was quickened, and he could still feel the fear and anxiety from the terrible dream. The short moment of joy at seeing his son was quickly washed away, drowned by the evil and menace of these things. The thought of so many of those beasts, an ocean of angry, primal creatures loose into this world, struck Cole deeply. He sat up and put his feet on the floor.

The dimly lit room gave only shadows and silhouettes, and the sound of traffic leaking through the porous walls. He exhaled a long breath and felt the need of a cigarette. Standing from the bed, Cole looked down at both sleeping women. Neither of them seemed very comfortable. Doris was snoring with a high-pitched wheeze, and Molly turned over with a flop. They too were suffering this ordeal, probably trapped in their own night terrors.

He went to the bathroom, waiting to turn on the light until after he had closed the door. He stripped down and took a shower, wanting to wash away the sweat and fear from his terrible dream. He stood in the spray and wondered what he could use to combat his enemy. Bullets were of no use; the club to the knee had slowed the creature, but far from stopped it. Cole wondered if dismemberment might work, using a sword or an ax. Then he considered fire.

His mind was filled with so much. How his whole world had changed from just days ago. He needed to know more about his foe, but he needed to get Johnny back. Doris was right: they needed to learn more, but there was no time. He couldn't leave his son to suffer in that world, with those things, not one moment longer than he had to.

He turned off the light and stepped back into the motel room, allowing the cool air to embrace his skin. Molly emerged from the darkness as his eyes adjusted, pushing him gently back into the bathroom and closing the door behind them. "You all right?" she whispered.

"Yeah, needed a shower."

"I had a nightmare," Molly confessed. She moved around Cole and sat on the toilet.

Cole heard the trickle of urine hit the surface of the water. "So did I. It was awful."

Molly began to cry. "Are we going to be able to get Johnny back?"

Cole knelt next to his wife and looked her in the eyes. "I will bring him back to us," he said in a stern, confident tone. He knew within himself that his confidence was paper-thin, but his conviction to do so was true and without doubt.

There was a soft knock at the door, and Doris's voice came through just as softly. "Excuse me, I need to use the facilities."

Cole and Molly exchanged smiles and exited the bathroom. Cole clicked on the television set as Doris went into the bathroom. They were all keyed up, and sleep was a struggle. The early morning news was now on. Cole watched as his name scrolled across the bottom of the screen. "Shit."

"What?" Molly asked.

Cole pointed at the screen as he read the words silently. He was wanted in connection with two police officers' deaths, along with their missing son. He had become national news. "We need to go."

"In connection with two officers' deaths?" his wife asked.

Cole shook his head. "It would seem Detective Jones covered his ass. Didn't want to explain the creatures from the mirrors to his superiors or the press."

Doris came out of the bathroom as Molly asked, "What does this mean?"

"Means the heat just went up. We should be ready to go and get to the library as quickly as we can."

"What's going on?" Doris asked.

"Cole is wanted in connection with two cops' deaths?" Molly said, questioning the words again.

"What? How is that?" Doris asked, sounding shocked.

"Just came over the news. The ticker at the bottom had Cole's name and everything," Molly said.

"At least no picture," Cole said. "Of course, the police will have it. We need to get ready." Cole stood up.

"The library doesn't open till nine. Driving around town probably isn't a good idea either," Doris pointed out.

"You're right. I'm thinking." Cole pulled the city map out. He knew he wanted to avoid heading back onto the highway, but Doris was correct about just driving around. Looking closer at the map, Cole pointed at the page. "Broad Street will take us into downtown. We will find somewhere to get breakfast. Some open-twenty-four hours place. We can have coffee and wait."

The trio hurried to collect what little they had and made their way to the car. Cole looked around nervously as he crossed the parking lot. Now he was really on the run. A national fugitive. Cole started the car, headed out of the motel, and made his way to Broad Street.

Downtown, he pulled into a White Castle, choosing a dark parking place and backing into the spot. "This will do," he said. "The food is okay and the coffee is good. We won't look out of place." He walked to the rear of the car and collected some mud, then wiped the handful of wet earth over part of the front license plate.

"What are you doing?" Doris asked.

"In case a cop pulls through, so he can't run the plates."

Molly gave her husband a sideways glance. "Who *are* you?"

Cole shrugged and headed for the entrance, holding the door for the ladies. He could smell onions steaming on the grill.

"Won't the police be looking for us?" Doris asked.

"The locals won't really have any more information than the news did. I can't imagine. We probably have a few hours, at least till the first shift comes on. We should be all right. Besides, they have no idea which direction we went."

They ordered breakfast sandwiches and coffee, and sat by the window so they could watch the car. Doris was the one who asked the question which really hit home. "What are you going to do about those charges? They won't just go away, even if you get your son back."

Cole sipped his coffee. "I know, but one thing at a time."

"We will just tell them. Show them, if need be," Molly said, matter-of-factly.

Cole took his wife's hand and nodded. "That may explain the big cop in the hotel, but the trooper... They will know I hit him, that I ran him off the road. I don't know. I'm not going to worry about that now. We have to get Johnny boy,. That's all that matters."

"If there have ever been extreme circumstances, I would think this would apply. I am in your corner, no matter what," Doris told them both. "Till the end."

Cole gave the woman a warm smile, thinking that, for just being a librarian, she was anything but. "I wish we had more time. I had an idea in the shower. If we could cage or chain one of those things, we could figure out how to kill it."

"That's an interesting idea. What would it do if it couldn't claim its victim?" Doris sipped her coffee.

"You thought of that in the shower?" Molly asked.

Cole nodded. "Bullets and golf clubs don't seem to work. We need to find something else."

"Fire might," Doris said.

"I thought about that. I don't know. These things are tough; it might just run around setting everything else on fire. I was thinking of an ax or a sword. I hit that one in the knee and it went down. Chop one of those fuckers into enough pieces, it might lose interest in snatching someone."

"You would have to be pretty close to use an ax," Molly pointed out.

Cole finished his cup of White Castle coffee and leaned back. "I have the feeling I'm going to have to get up close and very personal with these things to get our Johnny back."

"I don't want you to get hurt," Molly returned.

The group finished their meal and watched the clock, waiting to head to the library. Molly sat up straight, bobbing in her seat. "What about a Taser or tranquilizer? Drug the damn thing."

Cole shook his head. "I can't say these things are even alive. They move around and all, but they don't bleed. I stabbed one, twice, and no blood. And where I hit it, it should have leaked like a rusty bucket. Even when they were shot, just a hole, no blood."

Doris Lamb sat suddenly back in her seat. The blood seemed to drain from her face.

"Are you all right?" Molly asked. "Something bothering you?"

"No, no, it's nothing," Doris deflected.

Cole leaned forward and met the old librarian's eyes. "You thought of something."

Doris finished her coffee, her hand shaking slightly. "We don't know what we are dealing with. I'd really rather not guess."

Cole held his stare and allowed the silence to pressure her into speaking.

She lowered her head a bit and then shook it. "I just had a thought, but there is no validity to it. The creatures have no blood. The trigger is the blood, and the mention of God. My thought was, what if the blood calls them? That is why they come."

"Like vampires or something?" Molly asked.

"They may come for the blood because that is what they lack. The thought frightens me."

Cole nodded and looked out the window at the car. "I get what you are saying."

"What?" Molly asked.

"They take the people for their blood. Drain them. The creature's goal is the blood, not the person," Cole explained.

"So that thing is draining our son?"

"Our boy is alive. I know it in my heart. I will get him back. They take the whole person. They are rough, unstoppable, but they make an effort to take their victims. There is a sense of care involved."

Cole's words comforted everyone's minds, including his own. He wasn't lying: what he said was true. Yet, he also knew—and did not say—that the creatures had some designs on those they took. There was a reason they took them. They could sit there and ponder why forever, and it would do them no good. They needed answers, facts, the real reasons; someone, somewhere, knew and was going to tell him.

"I am sorry, I didn't mean to upset anyone," Doris said.

Molly wiped her eyes. "I'm okay. Just want to get our Johnny back."

"We will get the answers soon enough," Cole said. "Up until this point, we have been speculating, guessing, like blind men in a dark room. We will keep going. I will do whatever it takes."

"It's really hard for me to fathom that no one else has gotten this far, has put this together. It wasn't that hard," Doris pointed out.

"Yeah, that bothers me too." Cole checked the time.

"Who is to say they haven't?" Molly asked.

The comment held the group silent for a long moment. Finally, Doris said, "Do you think others may have figured this out before us? Why wouldn't we know?"

Cole rubbed his eyes and forehead. "We had better tread carefully. We don't know who is involved or what they may do to protect this. Obviously, they are into some pretty heavy shit, the kinds of things that no one knows about. They can create a curse to take random people from almost anywhere. We need to be cautious."

"You think they will kill us or something?" Molly asked.

Doris shifted in her seat. "They use ghouls to snatch people. They may know we are coming. We have no idea what abilities or powers these people may control. We are up against the supernatural."

"Wizards, Merlin, Harry fucking Potter, the Wicked Witch of the West; I don't care who we have to face. We will be careful, but the goal is our son," Cole said.

The "Wicked Witch" comment caused both women to half-smile.

Cole leaned forward. "What Doris said before, about evil. We may be looking at pure evil here. The big and real deal kind, not the evil of men but evil with a capital E. Universal evil, and someone is playing with such things. Toying with people's lives, releasing those things into our world. We are over our heads here, but hopefully we can slip in unnoticed, get Johnny, and then pass this problem on to people better equipped to deal with such things."

"Like who?" Molly asked.

"I don't know. Government, the church, science?" Cole said.

"I get the feeling this is above everyone's head," Doris said.

Cole checked the time again. They still had about a half an hour. He didn't want to be walking around downtown waiting for the library to open. He planned to park in a structure, where it would be less likely the police would notice the vehicle.

"I suspect there will be lots of questions after all this," he said. "It will probably get complicated. I worry about that."

"About what?" Doris asked.

Cole let out a long sigh. "You know how things can get. The police are going to be involved, and that means the government. Anything the government is involved in is always a damn mess. God only knows what they will do when they find out about all this."

"We could go on the computer, the internet. Blow the lid off the whole thing. We can do that while we're at the library." Molly's voice rose with her excitement.

"After," Cole said.

"Why not now?" Doris asked.

Cole furrowed his brow. "We don't really know enough. We don't want to tip our hand, and we don't know who might be monitoring. Who is to say—they may already know all about this. We need to be careful."

A quiet fell over the table again as they waited, each of them deep within their own thoughts. Finally, with the coffee gone and the conversation exhausted, it was time to go. Time to begin, time to face things and get Johnny home.

Cole fired up a Marlboro on their way out. "Make sure you don't leave anything in the car. I doubt they will find it, but take everything with you." He exhaled a cloud of white smoke. "We may not come back to the car, if things get hot."

He opened the passenger doors for them, looking around as he took a drag from his cigarette. He couldn't believe how crazy things had gotten. He was on the run, he had fought monsters, he had lost his son. What a mess things were. Now he was going to dive even deeper down the rabbit hole. Taking a final drag, Cole flipped the butt into the parking lot and got behind the wheel.

They headed down Broad Street into town Columbus, Ohio. "Ever been here before, Doris?" Molly asked the old librarian.

"No. Passed through it once, but never had the pleasure."

Cole saw a sign for mall parking. "A mall. That should give us good cover." He pulled in and worked his way deep into the bowels of the structure. There weren't very many cars in the place; it was still early. He chose a spot between two other cars, figuring they would lend cover to their vehicle. Malls had their own security, so the cops didn't usually check the lots unless they were looking for something specific.

"We should probably get some new clothes while we are here," Cole said. Molly checked the traveler's checks and nodded.

As the elevator rose, everything felt surreal to Cole. How crazy things had been, and yet how mundane it was to be riding in a mall elevator. They found a JCPenney open, having an early bird sale.

"Our luck is changing!" Molly said.

"Be quick and be frugal," Cole told them as they headed to their respective departments.

He picked out a pair of cargo pants and a button-up shirt. In the changing room, he realized he just didn't look at mirrors the same way anymore. In the reflection he saw cuts and scrapes, exhaustion and stress, the lack of sleep, a rough, worn and beaten man.

And then there was the mirror itself, which now carried a much more significant place in his consciousness.

They met up again, paying for their goods and leaving the store. They passed a restroom, and Cole figured it was a good moment to get the necessaries out of the way. "I might be a minute," he told them.

The restroom was clean and smelled of urinal cake. He entered a stall, realizing it had been some time since he last went. As he began to relax, a cramp confirmed this. Allowing the pain to run its course, Cole released a sigh and felt much better.

Someone else entered, whistling a tune as he went into the stall next to his. A newspaper hit the floor: the *USA Today*, he could see from under the metal partition. He couldn't help but wonder if he had made the national news.

He heard the man work his belt and drop trou. As he took his seat, Cole heard the echo of a loud, moist fart. He could see the man reach down and take up the paper. The sound of rustling and unfolding, along with another juicy release.

Again the paper hit the floor. Cole guessed the man had taken out the sports section. "Say, mind if I check out that front page?" he asked. He watched as the man picked up the paper and held it under the metal wall. "Thanks."

There was blood in the headlines, but nothing to do with him. Papers always had bloody ledes: death sells. People have a macabre sense. It was page three that caught his attention. A small picture of his family, with the caption, "Child Missing, Man Wanted for Questioning." The article was a work of fiction. It said he was a suspect in the disappearance of his son, that he had killed two police officers and kidnapped a librarian.

Seeing the words in black and white made Cole feel like a notorious outlaw. Sitting there in a mall toilet taking a shit was America's most wanted. The urge to complete his task had subsided. Folding the paper, Cole handed it back under the wall. Wiping himself, he exited the metal box and washed his hands.

How quickly his life had gone into a tailspin. The whole situation had gone from bad to worse, and wasn't looking to get any better. They had learned a great deal in a short time, but he was now in the papers. It would be only a matter of time before this was all over, one way or another.

Molly and Doris were waiting for him in their new clothes. "Don't you look spiffy," Molly told her husband.

"Thanks. We need to get going." He took his wife by the arm.

"What's wrong?"

Cole looked around, paranoid but trying to hide it. "We made the papers. Oh, by the way, Doris, I have kidnapped you."

"You have?" She sounded puzzled.

He told them about the paper, then checked his map as they headed for the mall exit.

"You are in a lot of trouble, aren't you?" Doris asked.

"It would seem so."

"I could call them, explain everything."

Cole smiled. "Thank you, Doris. The time will come for that, but right now, we need to stick to the plan. Besides, you haven't actually witnessed anything. They will ask you to verify what we claim. Plus, they will track your call, find our location."

"Why didn't that cop back up your story?" Molly wondered.

"He knew."

"Knew what?" Doris asked.

Cole said, "He knew no one would believe him. It was just easier to point to me and let me try and explain."

They walked, crossing a number of streets as they made their way through the city. Soon they turned a corner and saw a large stone building at the end of the street. It was beautiful, gray with large columns, a very traditional style of American-imitating-ancient architecture. The street dead-ended into a large grassy yard in front of the building. It was a very nice scene, with blue sky above to accent the whole thing.

The sidewalk cut through the green grass up to the main entrance. The building was a number of stories tall, very impressive in its size. Cole led them to the two massive doors, pulling the right one open for the ladies. The library seemed even bigger on the inside than out.

Doris marched straight to the information desk and asked for the archives. The young woman behind the desk pointed them in the proper direction, and Doris led the way.

Cole could see Doris's confidence grow as they found themselves in an arena she was familiar with. As he looked at the expanse around them, an idea struck.

"Hey, hold up." The women stopped and turned to look at him. "This is going to take a while," he told them. "There is a lot of information to go through and find. While you two get started, I'll go check out the factory."

"We should stay together," Molly said.

"I agree, I don't think that is wise," Doris added.

Cole shrugged. "Just a look around, is all."

"What will that accomplish?" Molly asked.

"Look, honestly, I don't want to walk in there with the two of you with no idea about what we are walking into, without any lay of the land. That would leave me vulnerable."

"I don't like the idea of splitting up," Doris said. "You ran into trouble last time. Still, we do have a lot to do, and having a sense of the place and the people is not a bad idea. I will say, be very careful. Be aware of what you say, do and observe. You don't want to give anything away."

"I appreciate the concern, and I will watch my ass."

Molly hugged Cole hard and squeezed him tight.

"I won't be gone long. It's just over the river. Besides, these people are readers; they might recognize me from the paper. It will take me a couple hours is all." He kissed his wife. "If you go anywhere, leave word with the lady at the desk. Use the name Jack Smith, in case they read the paper and remember my name. Okay?"

Both women nodded agreement.

"I'll be fine. No worries," Cole said over his shoulder as he headed for the main door. There, he glanced back, watching as the two women walked off to do their research. He pushed open the big front door and felt the warmth of the day press against his face. Pulling the map from his pocket, he checked his best route to the factory. The street they had used earlier, Broad Street, seemed like the best place to start. After a couple of blocks of walking, he had broken a sweat, but he had a ways to go and kept his pace.

CHAPTER 19

After crossing a number of streets, Cole saw the Ohio Capitol off to his left, as the heat of the day really began to blaze. The concrete, steel, windows and exhaust of downtown seemed only to make the world hotter. The city had come to life; people moved about, occupied by their lives and what they were doing. Most folks were well dressed, but Cole saw the one thing he really disliked: women in skirts and tennis shoes. He understood the reason, and that they would put their high heels on at work, but it was ugly nonetheless.

Traffic had also increased, with buses, cars and cabs. Cole kept his pace, thinking how the whole world had become like a hive of bees, everyone with their tasks, doing their little part to make the big machine function. Consumed, oblivious, self-involved, alone in their individual worlds. His thoughts moved to his own situation and how easily it was for people to not believe, to not care, to not want to know or get involved.

Cole had to acknowledge that he had been thrown into this situation, and that he had doubts and questions. He could not look for help from others; this was something he was going to have to deal with on his own. Doris Lamb was a very special woman, and her diving into the mess of their lives was singular in kindness. The police were being no help. As he crossed the next street, his mind stirred with so many thoughts.

He thought of Detective Jones, of how he had seen, he knew, and he passed the buck. *How could he have done that?* Cole wondered. He started across a bridge, checked his map, and pressed on. Stopping halfway across, he looked down at the brown water. A smell rose from the dirty liquid and filled his nostrils. As Cole looked back at Columbus, he saw a Midwestern city. A few tall buildings, and a lot of people trying to be like someone else.

The river wasn't very wide, so the walk was short. On the far side of the bridge, a sign had been spray-painted: "Welcome to the Bottoms." Cole pondered *the bottom of what?,* and then he looked around at the condition of things. The nice buildings were gone, as were the clean streets and the sense of safety. Houses were run-down, in need of paint; most had dirt yards or weeds knee-high.

Cole turned the next corner, walking on. Then he saw the two letters over-lapped, the same symbol as on the mirrors. There was a building with the letter **W** over the letter **M**, making an **XX**. Next to the **XX** read "Walton Mirrors" in old, weather-beaten letters. The building was also old and worn, one of a thousand factories like this throughout the Midwest. Yet he knew there was something very different about this particular factory. This place produced more than just mirrors: this place produced evil, and someone inside knew it.

Wiping the sweat from his brow, he continued toward the factory. He had anticipated this, but as he came closer and prepared to walk in, he knew he had to be very careful. He hadn't really come up with a good cover story to explain why he was there. Nerves grew within him, an uneasy feeling in the pit of his stomach. As he took hold the handle of the door, Cole released a sigh and paused to breathe.

Looking at the **XX** painted on the glass door, Cole realized he had grown a great distaste for the mark. The very sight of it caused his temper to flare and his pulse to increase. He had to maintain and control his actions. Who-ever these people were, they didn't know he was coming, and they had no clue what for.

A very lovely young lady sat behind a large reception desk as Cole en-tered the offices. The cool air felt good after his long hike. The girl held up a finger as she spoke on the phone, signaling to Cole to hold on. He could see the large mirror behind her on the wall. It had to be eight feet by eight feet, with that damn mark engraved right in the middle. The front of the desk had another mirror with the company name engraved, "Walton Mirrors".

Cole noticed some pictures on the side wall and moved over to look at them. They were old, most of them black and white. Pictures of the factory and workers, furnaces and molten glass. Then, right in the center of all the pictures was a smiling man. The placard beneath read, "Richard Walton Se-nior, founder, 1919." Cole looked closer. The man was young, not more than just a boy, and he was smiling a genuine smile.

That was when Cole noticed something else. The building was exactly the same as it was when he walked in, except...

"Welcome to Walton Mirrors. Sorry for your delay, may I help you?"

The young lady's voice grabbed Cole's attention. He turned away from the wall of pictures and gave her a smile.

"Good day," he said. "I'm here to look at mirrors and talk business. Got a big hotel I am renovating, and a friend of mine urged me to come and talk with you folks. So, here I am."

"I will have a sales representative come right out. Would you like a water or coffee?"

"Water."

She pulled a cold bottle of water from a small refrigerator under the coffee pot and handed it to Cole. Moving back around the front desk, she picked up the phone and dialed.

Cole returned to the pictures on the wall and opened his water. The cold liquid tasted so good. He had not realized how thirsty he was. The walk had been really long.

He looked closer at the founder's picture, wanting to double-check what he had seen. Behind the smiling young man was the name of the company in big block letters. Yet, it wasn't the same as today. There was no symbol, no mark. "Walton Glass and Mirror Works" was all it read. This was a significant difference.

"That is my great-great-grandfather. Been a family-owned business since 1919." A voice from behind again disrupted Cole's thoughts.

Turning, Cole saw a young man, barely into his twenties. Tall and muscular, probably six-four and a couple hundred pounds. He was a pretty boy, a jock type, one of those clichés from the movies.

"Came over from the old country," the young man continued. He extended his hand and shook Cole's firmly. "I am Tommy Walton. How can we help you today?"

"I am beginning a remodel of a hotel, and a friend in the business pointed me in y'all's direction," Cole bullshitted. "Said he got a real good deal from you, buying direct. I was in the area and thought I would come in and see for myself, check it out. I really love the mirrors he has and am interested in the process. Thought maybe I could get a tour, some history behind the place, pick up some talking points for the guests. Mirrors bring depth to a room, and I am planning on making them a centerpiece for my décor. Having a good story behind them would be a plus."

"How many pieces are we talking about?"

"That depends on the break and what kind of discount you'll give me," Cole said, seeing the dollar signs behind the kid's eyes.

Cole took a step toward the receptionist's desk and fingered the engraving in the glass. "You can do this kind of work? 'Cause I like this. Price is not really an object."

"Absolutely, anything you want." The salesman salivated at the opening.

"I noticed in the picture that the name has changed somewhat."

The young man nodded. "My great-grandpa wanted to specialize in just mirrors."

Cole nodded in return. "Well, that insignia is very interesting. Almost looks like two X's. Any significance beyond the initials?"

The salesman shook his head. "Not that I know of. Great-grandpa came up with it, far as I know. Been there long as I can remember. We put it on every mirror."

Cole stepped back and looked around the room. "I am interested in the process. To be honest, I have no idea what goes into making a mirror."

Tommy Walton smiled. "I guess I can give you the nickel tour, before we head up to the office."

Cole followed the young man down a hallway to a door marked, "FACTORY: EMPLOYEES ONLY." As Walton opened and held the door, Cole could hear the sounds of manufacturing. The heat of the day again pressed itself to his face, and the smell of something burning filled his nostrils.

They stood on a small landing with a few steps leading down to the factory floor. People were busy, wearing goggles and ear protection, safety helmets and gloves. "We really shouldn't be out here. Stay close and don't touch anything," Walton yelled above the noise.

Cole saw piles of sand and a large furnace. The heat coming from it was intense, even at a distance. Large vats poured molten liquid onto some flat surface, which workers sprayed with hoses. Steam rolled off the liquid, like an eerie fog.

"Here is a question for you," Tommy yelled. "Glass: do you think it is a solid, liquid, or gas?"

Cole leaned in to have the salesman repeat himself, then shrugged. "It's made out of sand. Sand is a crystal, right? I would guess a solid."

Tommy shook his head. "Glass is a very dense liquid. The molecules in glass never totally solidify. This is why over time a window distorts. They will even fall from their panes after decades. The whole thing is a very technical process."

Looking up, Cole could see large windows overlooking the factory floor. He figured those must be the offices. He felt a tug on his arm; Tommy Walton was motioning for them to go back inside. As the door closed behind them, the sound of silence returned.

"I didn't know that about glass: that it remains a liquid. Now that you mention it, I have seen old houses with warped windows, and really old places where the windows are all gone. I thought kids had broken them out." Cole couldn't help but to think of the mirror in the attic, how he threw a golf club through it and it rippled like the surface of a pond.

Tommy nodded. "Let's head into my office. Easier to talk in here than out there."

A very old man in a very nice suit walked into the hallway. He was shorter than Tommy by a lot and slightly hunched over, but he seemed in pretty good shape for a man his age. "Tommy, come here," the old man commanded.

"Excuse me a moment." The young man quickly moved to the old man. He nodded a great deal and then motioned at Cole.

After a minute, Tommy returned with a little of the bounce in his step removed.

"Problem?" Cole asked.

"That's my grandfather. Just reminding me I am not supposed to take people on the factory floor. It's dangerous. Lawsuits and that sort of thing. He is an overly cautious man."

The old man lingered in the hall, eyeing the two of them. Cole saw this as an opportunity. Advancing past the young Walton, he extended a hand. "I am sorry, sir. It is all my fault and I apologize. I am looking to make a large purchase and was interested in the process. Tommy was just making the customer happy."

"I am Elliot Walton," the old man said, shaking Cole's hand. "Can't be too careful, you know."

"I understand. I must say, I am very impressed with your operation. You must produce a great number of mirrors."

"Over six hundred thousand last year," Tommy interjected.

"So, it was your father who started all this? The pictures out front?"

The old man shook his head. "No, it was my grandfather who founded the company. My father saved it."

"Saved it?" Cole asked.

"The Depression. The company almost fell, almost went under entirely. Dad kept it running, even made it grow during the worst economic period of our nation," the old man said with pride.

Cole furrowed his brow but nodded. "Wow, that's incredible. Impressive. Times were really tough back then. Sounds like a very driven man."

"Yes, he is. That's why I am named after him." The young salesman again jumped into the conversation.

"All this wouldn't be here if it weren't for my father," Elliot Walton said. "Pulled this company out of the red in the heart of the disaster and flourished. An American success story. A true businessman, but with the sense of the working class."

"I am glad I had a chance to meet you. I am sorry for going on the factory floor. It was a pleasure."

Cole followed Tommy down the hallway toward his office. "Have a seat," Tommy said, walking around behind his desk.

"Sounds like your great-grandpa is a hell of a man," Cole said. "He must have some stories, huh?"

"He is a real hoot. You should hear some of them."

"Oh, I would love to. He is still around too, then?"

Tommy nodded. "Ninety-eight years old, and still comes in to work every day. Checks the books, oversees the day's numbers. Sometimes I think he is a thousand years old, not almost a hundred. The old guy looks rough, but he goes strong. He is really incredible. Three years ago, on his birthday, he arm-wrestled me. I was twenty, but he won. People thought I threw it, I didn't. It's freakish."

Cole's eyebrows raised at the comment, as he nodded along, interested.

"He's been doing this since he was a kid. A very serious man. He never jokes." Tommy went on.

"Well, at ninety-eight years old, the arm-wrestling thing sounds incredible," Cole said.

"Yeah, well, when he was around my age, he burned his hand. Grabbed one of the vats. As a kid, I was always afraid of it," Tommy confessed. "Melted flesh, scared the crap out of me. He would reach out at you and wow, it would freak me out. It was a thing."

Cole didn't really know how to respond, so he just nodded again.

"Anyway, down to business. Sizes, shapes, how many you'll need, and I'll see what you're looking at." Tommy Walton found his way back to his salesman role.

"Right, ah, well, like I said, we're just getting started. I don't have the blueprints with me. Say three hundred rooms, bathroom and bedroom, bar and restaurant, lobby and public restrooms. My friend actually has mirrors in the hallways of his hotel. Large rectangular ones in nice frames. You do provide the frames too, correct?" Cole improvised.

"Oh, of course. I didn't show you but off to the right of our docks, we have a wood and metal shop. Can make any kind of frames you'd like. Of course, the more elaborate, the more expensive. Yet at this number, I am sure we can work something out." Tommy winked.

The young man began to write down numbers, talking as he went. "Three hundred rooms, two mirrors in each room, that's six hundred. If you go standard size, chrome framing. Do you want the public restrooms the same style? And what of employee restrooms?"

"Yes," Cole lied.

Tommy Walton continued to calculate. "Three per, eighteen. Employee, figure a couple. Twenty-three. Shipping and tax. Now, we do also have different styles and engravings we can do."

The price he quoted was large, but Cole didn't know what almost a thousand mirrors should be. From what it sounded like, it was a good deal. The game of business was one of feints and tells, need and supply, excess and necessity. Some people enjoyed the dance; Cole was not one of those people. He hated the haggle and the gouge, the predatory behavior of screwing over the other guy. Fair business was a thing of the past.

"Like I said, price really isn't an issue," Cole said, maintaining the ruse. "I want quality."

"That is all we produce here, sir," Tommy Walton returned. "Our standards are the highest in the industry. 'Quality at a reasonable price' has been our motto since we opened. Great-grandpa says he wants a Walton Mirror in every home in America. The only way to do that is to offer quality at a price people can afford."

"Every home in America. That is very ambitious," Cole said, thinking how dangerous it would be to have these cursed-ass mirrors in every home.

"We will need some lead time for any special orders. We keep a number of standard sizes in stock, but at that volume, we'll have to punch up production."

"Like I said, this is the preliminary stage. Once I know, I will give you plenty of time and notice," Cole assured him.

"Great. Why don't I take you to our show room and give you a few ideas? You may see a few different options you might like."

The young man stood up, and Cole rose too, following him down the hall and down a few stairs further back into the office area, finally coming to a set of beautiful wooden double doors. Tommy Walton turned, making sure he had Cole's full attention before opening them.

As the doors swung wide and Tommy stepped out of the way, the reveal was breathtaking. A room full of mirrors. Mirrors everywhere; on the walls, standing, on easels, on the ceiling, even the floor was polished to shine a reflection. The sight turned Cole's guts into a knot. So many evil creations made him so uneasy, he had to remember to breathe. As Tommy walked in and turned to look at him, waving him to enter, the lump in Cole's throat was unswallowable.

The kid doesn't know, Cole thought. No way he could and walk into a room like that so casually. The young Walton was oblivious. Cole braced himself, then stepped into the room slowly, eyeing his reflections in various mirrors, the haunting memories of the last few days flooding his mind. He looked down at his arm; it was covered in goosebumps. Cole shivered.

"We call this our Hall of Mirrors," Tommy said, with some dramatic flair.

Cole had to swallow hard and clear his throat to overcome the apple-sized lump that lingered there. "I can see why," he forced out.

Tommy Walton walked over to a particular mirror propped up on an easel. "This is our standard model. The one I quoted you." He waved his hand in front of the thing like a Price is Right girl.

Cole nodded and stepped forward, seeing his reflection in the dozens of mirrors. "Nice," He uttered, feeling totally uncomfortable and on edge.

"Tommy." A voice came from the doorway.

A tall man in his early fifties stood in the room's entrance. "Excuse me," Tommy said, moving past Cole. "I have to see about something, but since you were curious as to the process, this is the man to tell you all about it."

The well-dressed man closed the doors behind him and stepped toward Cole. "Good day to you, sir. I am Franklin Walton, Tommy's father—family business." He extended his hand. "He won't be but a few minutes. So, you are curious about the process? Allow me to give you a quick lesson."

"That would be great, thank you."

"First, you have to focus on the glass. Used to be we would polish metal and use those for our reflection. Glass has come a long way through the years. The ancient Egyptians treasured glass. In fact, most of the fancy jewelry you have seen from that period is glass, not gems."

Cole furrowed his brow. "So, all that priceless jewelry, necklaces and headpieces were just glass?"

Franklin Walton nodded. "Colored glass. Historians estimate glass has been around since about 400 B.C. It has always been difficult to produce, especially colored glass."

"Your son said glass is a liquid, but doesn't glass come from sand, and isn't sand crystals, a solid?" Cole asked.

Franklin smiled. "You are full of good questions. Silica. Silica is like sand, true enough. Did you see the factory floor?" Cole nodded. "We use tank furnaces to heat the silica, moltenize it. Adding a flux of sodium oxide, or salt, which if left as such is called water glass. Water glass will actually dissolve in water. So, we have to use a stabilizer. Then we float it."

Cole was listening intently. "You float it?"

"As we moltenize or heat these ingredients, we also melt down tin."

"Tin?" Cole asked.

The man smiled again. "Yes, tin. We pour both onto a flat surface together. As both cool, the glass comes to the top and is flat and smooth. It's kind of like grease in your dish water. The grease floats atop the water. Glass does the same with tin. Came up with that in the fifties, and they call it float glass," Franklin Walton said, a little smugly.

Cole could tell the man really knew his business. Still, he couldn't get past the uneasy feeling in his gut, and the lump in his throat persisted. Cole walked over to some of the different mirrors and looked closely at them. "Why are some of these different colors? Some are really clear, while these others look bronzed, or antique."

"That's the backing we use. The backing is what gives a mirror its reflective quality. Without a backing, a mirror would be just a pane of glass, a window. The clear ones, as you called them, have an aluminum backing. We also use aluminum as a stabilizer, so it has a dual purpose, and is standard in the industry. The bronze look is not bronze but copper. The copper gives an antique-y quality. Some customers like that," Frank Walton said with an air of satisfaction.

"Real nice, quality work, and you seem to really know your stuff," Cole complimented the man.

The double doors opened and Tommy Walton entered the hall of mirrors. "Sorry about that. Did the old man talk your ear off?"

"He was very helpful and knowledgeable. I really appreciate all he had to say," Cole said, giving the father a wink and a nod, then extending a hand for him to shake. "I believe I have what I came for. I will be in touch, or have my contractor place an order. The price sounds reasonable, and I really like that copper look," he said, continuing with his ruse.

"The copper backing is a little bit more on the price than what I quoted you," Tommy said. "Of course, with your volume, we may be able to work something out."

"I will get with my contractor and figure it all out. You run a fair shop here, gentlemen, and it is nice to see. I can see why you have stayed in business so long."

"Quality at a reasonable price," Frank quoted the company motto.

Cole made his way toward the double doors, accompanied by the two Waltons.

"Allow me to show you out," Tommy said.

"A pleasure to meet you, Mr. Walton," Cole said, and both men thanked him. Cole gave a final nod to the older man and followed Tommy out.

The young receptionist was on the phone again as the two of them reached the entrance. "You have been most helpful. I'll be in touch soon," Cole said to Tommy, shaking his hand.

"We look forward to your business, Mr.—I'm sorry, I didn't get your last name."

The moment almost caught Cole off-guard. "Jack, Jack Jones." He spouted the first fake name to pop into his head. Giving a nod, Cole opened the door and stepped back out into the heat of the day.

CHAPTER 20

As he walked away from the factory, Cole looked at the two letters overlapped on the side of the building and felt the anger swell within him once again. These people had a hand in his son being kidnapped by those creatures. They were going to answer for that. He remembered the picture of the smiling young man in the picture, proud of his business, and he felt disgust.

He was glad to be out of that place. The whole time he had been uneasy; now, even in the heat, it was a relief. There was no way these people could be clueless about what their mirrors were. He had never been so nervous as he was in that god-awful room with all the mirrors. He felt like a cat in a clock factory. Now he had seen the source, but what to do?

He walked, looking around at the poor living conditions that surrounded the factory as he thought about what he had learned. He recalled the pictures, and how the mark had come about later. Something had changed, and that mark, that symbol, became the emblem of the company. This would mean the elder Walton had changed it. The smiling young man who grew a company in the worst economic times in history.

Cole thought about the story Tommy had told, the man's ninety-fifth birthday. He was going to have to have a little talk with the old man. That old man was the one who was going to give him some goddamn answers.

Back on Broad Street, Cole walked east. His temper had risen with the heat of the day. The sweat dripping from his face only made Cole that much more irritated. He stopped again on the bridge, feeling the breeze coming off the water. The air stank from the brown river, but the movement of air felt good. Looking back toward the mirror factory, he knew he was going to have some real problems.

He figured the great-great-grandpa of young Tommy Walton knew what was going on. Pulling answers out of a very old man was going to have its own issues, but he was going to have to get to him and deal with the rest. He pondered who else might know. It didn't seem that Tommy knew; he wasn't bright enough to really fake much of anything.

This had been going on for decades, at least since World War II. The old man knew, and he surely would have warned those he loved. They might not know all the details, but they had almost certainly been told not to mention God in front of those mirrors.

Cole continued his hot walk. His mind switched gears to his police problem, as he watched a city police car pass by. His situation did not lend itself to patience. He needed to get answers and produce a solution for getting Johnny back. He did not have one more day to find his son; he had to find him now.

As he trekked on, he hoped the women had found some good information, something helpful. Yet he could not imagine what that possibly could be. This was something that was going to have to be dealt with, and not with a gentle hand. This was demons or dimensions; whatever the case, the Walton family wasn't going to give up their secrets easily.

The police would soon enough figure out he had gone, left the state. Another night in a hotel only increased the risk of someone recognizing him. Johnny needed him and couldn't wait any longer. He turned south toward the main library, pondering how to get the Waltons to talk, or even acknowledge that they knew. How would he get his son back? Cole's mind swirled with thoughts, questions, and doubts. The heat of the day and the stress had delivered a major headache, now throbbing at Cole's temples.

The cuts on his face burned with his own sweat, and his body hurt from all the walking. The beatings he had taken were adding up. Turning the corner to see the large building filled with books, Cole smiled. He needed a cool drink and the air conditioning would be a godsend.

His mind flashed to the mirror in the attic and how the golf club flew into it. What Tommy had said about glass being a liquid spun in the back of his skull. It all meant something, but he couldn't put his finger on it. There was a significance to the liquid aspect, the reflections, the mention of God. Cole shook his head in an attempt to shake loose the answers, but nothing doing.

He had much to tell Molly and Doris. He hoped they had much to tell him, that they had found a solution. He looked up at the large columns of the building, feeling fatigue, the ache in his bones. As he climbed the steps, he knew any research they may have found would simply be an added nail in the coffin. He knew what he needed to do.

Time was not on his side; so many factors were pushing for an immediate solution. Johnny needed him, the police were hunting for him, and he needed to stop this from happening again. As rushed as he felt, Cole knew he needed to focus. When you hurry, you make mistakes.

Grabbing the library door and pulling it open, he felt the cool air escaping and stepped quickly inside. He paused just inside the door, taking a moment to refresh himself, holding a deep breath of the environmentally controlled air in his lungs. He knew he had already made a number of mistakes. His actions had put him and the two ladies in the news.

As he walked toward the information desk, he wondered if he could have done things different, made different choices, had different reactions. But it was pointless to think such thoughts. What was done was done. This was where he was, and forward was the only way to go. *If ifs and buts were candy and nuts, we would all have a merry Christmas.*

"Any messages for a Jack Smith?" Cole asked the clerk at the desk.

The older gentleman looked at a couple of papers. "Your party has gone to the third floor."

"Thanks."

Cole took an elevator to the third floor. He thought about the Star Bird Inn and Ernest, wondering how his new friend was handling things. No doubt the police had asked their questions and probably tore the fourth floor apart. Cops probably dragged Ernest downtown, locked him in the interrogation room.

Another reception desk, manned by an older woman. A set of doors lay beyond her. She gave him a strong stare as he approached, so he smiled. "Hi. Downstairs told me my friends are up here."

"These are reserved books. They are not for loan," she said, flatly.

"I just need to get my friends," Cole explained.

The older woman nodded him along. Walking through glass doors marked "reserved", he began to look for Doris and his wife. In a reading area, he saw them at a table with a stack of books. Both women were engrossed in their reading as he approached. "Ladies."

They both looked up and Molly smiled at him. "I love you," she said softly.

"I love you too."

Doris collected up the books and walked a stack over to the book return cart. As she returned, she smiled at them. "You are a lovely couple."

They blushed in unison.

Cole said, "We should go. We can go get something to eat, and talk."

The trio headed out the glass doors and down the elevator. As they walked to the main exit, Cole stopped a young person and asked if there was anywhere close to get a bite to eat. He was directed to a bar and grill a few blocks away.

They exited the library and were met with the heavy air and heat of the day. They walked west, then north, making their way back to Broad Street. "Guy said there is a bar that has good burgers down this alley." Cole led the way. "I figure a little more out of the way is better than a chain restaurant."

As he opened the door, a cold blast of air struck them and they all released a sigh of relief. The place was fairly empty; a couple of people at the bar and two tables with couples at each. Cole led them to a table in the back and waited till both were seated. "Cool, quiet, just what we needed. I'll get us menus and drinks; what would you like?"

"Iced tea, unsweetened," Doris requested.

"That sounds good, I'll have an Arnold Palmer," Molly told Cole.

Cole nodded. He had never been a fan of ice tea or lemonade. The only lemonade he could stand was schnapps, because it was so sweet. He approached the bartender. "Grill hot?" he asked.

"You bet. What can I get you folks?"

"Couple menus, an unsweetened ice tea, an Arnold Palmer, and a draft, whatever is cold."

The barkeep handed over menus. "I'll bring over the drinks and get your order."

Cole brought the plastic-covered menus to the table and slid into the booth beside his wife. They each perused the selection. After a minute, the bartender came with a tray of drinks and a pad. "Decided yet?"

Cole wasted no time taking a sip of his beer. The cold liquid granted him the realization of just how dry his throat had become. Doris ordered a Reuben sandwich, while Molly ordered a hamburger with avocado and guacamole. He had a mushroom and Swiss burger and onion rings. After the bartender left, Cole said, "The Walton family. What did you find out?"

Doris said, "We did a search. Found the website and some news coverage. Most of it was the company doing goodwill and the building becoming a historical site." She paused to sip her tea. "The original owner left the business to his two sons. Not long after that, one had an accident and died. Fell into one of the factory furnaces. Rough way to go, if you ask me."

"That's when the company changed to Walton Mirrors and adopted the symbol," Molly added.

Doris nodded. "Over the years there have been a couple of accidents, but nothing really putting them in the headlines. Curiously, most of the accidents resulted in no bodies being found. That furnace has claimed five people. They have done very well over the years, even when times were tough and the industry was down."

"So, one of the brothers, the owner's son, fell into the furnace. That is interesting," Cole said.

"No bodies, yet five, or six including the son, die?" Molly said. "Do you think that's what started it all? The son?"

"Something happened," Cole said. "But they aren't just going to tell us the family secrets. What else did you find out?"

"The symbol, I tried to see if it had some special significance," Doris said. "Perhaps voodoo, or some occult mark of some kind. Nothing. W is the twenty-third letter of the alphabet, and the chemical symbol for tungsten, which is a rare metallic element used in filaments. It is seventy-fourth on the periodic table of elements. W is the letter which represents watt, width, and west." Doris ran down the research.

Cole drank from his beer and listened intently.

"M. The thirteenth letter of the alphabet. The Roman numeral signifying a thousand. Represents the symbol for Mass, Medium, Meter, and Minor. I really couldn't see a connection between the two. So, I checked the letter X. Twenty-fourth letter, Roman numeral for ten, one of two of the chromosomes in the body and a very popular mark with pirates." Doris gave a smile at her own joke. "But I couldn't find any reason those particular letters would be important here."

The bartender arrived with their sandwiches and asked if they would like refills on their drinks. They were all thirsty and were quick to say yes. Cole didn't realize how hungry he was until he took that first bite.

"Tell him what we learned about curses," Molly said, covering her mouth to speak.

Doris chewed quickly and then began. "If it is a curse, whoever placed it can remove it. Yet we did not find anything on mirrors except urban legend." She paused while the fresh drinks arrived, then went on. "These mirrors are in the White House, or at least they were. It was in an article about the company. LBJ put them in. Whether they are still there or not, I don't know."

"Have to admit, it would be interesting to see the Secret Service react to monsters," Cole said with a smile.

"People would know then, wouldn't they?" Molly smiled as well.

"Maybe," Doris said. "What did you find at the factory?" she asked before taking another bite of her rueben.

Cole washed down a mouthful of burger with a deep swig of his draft beer, then wiped his lips with his napkin. "I met a number of the Walton clan. Toured the facility, and learned more about mirror making than I ever wanted to know. The company was started in 1919 by the eldest Walton. They have a bunch of old photos on the wall in the lobby. I noticed the name used to be Walton Mirror and Glass Works. I asked why they had changed it. The details were a little glossed over, but it was that brother, Tommy Walton Sr. His namesake and great-grandson explained that he wanted to specialize in just mirrors. I suspect there is much more to it." Cole took another bite.

"You spoke with them? How did they seem?" Molly asked.

"Like business people. Normal. This has been going on so long, they probably don't think about it." Cole sipped his beer.

"So, the great-grandfather, is he dead or alive?" Doris asked.

"Alive. Ninety-eight years old. Comes into check the books every day." He told them about the arm-wrestling on the man's ninety-fifty birthday.

"That's strange. What could that mean?" Molly asked.

Doris wiped her mouth. "He could be drawing power from the curse, or he is possessed, or something of the sort."

"I also met an Elliot Walton, as well as Franklin and Tommy," Cole told them. "Grandfather, father and son. Didn't get to see the old man, but of the three generations I bumped into, they didn't seem to be icons of evil or Adolf Hitler, Dracula, or the Creature from the Black Lagoon. Yet the place had a very strange vibe. Especially when they took me to what they called the Hall of Mirrors, their showroom of different mirrors. Freaked me out."

Molly raised a hand to pause the conversation while she chewed. "You were in a room full of those things? No doubt you got a strange feeling. How could they not know? They have got to know."

"What else did you learn?" Doris asked.

Cole picked up his draft beer and tapped the top of the glass with his finger, making it ring. "Glass is a liquid," he said with a smile.

"Glass is a what?" Doris asked.

"The kid's dad, Frank, said glass is not a solid but a very dense liquid. Something about how the molecules never solidify. He seemed to know what he was talking about."

"What does that mean?" Molly asked.

Cole shrugged. "I don't know what it means, but after I tried to break the mirror when that thing took the kid and the golf club disappeared like I had thrown it into a pond, it just struck me as curious. There may be something to the fact that it is not a solid but seems to be. Some kind of properties which allow this to happen. It just seemed odd, and I thought it might be relevant."

"The real question is, what are we going to do now?" Doris said.

Molly nodded. "We really haven't found the answer yet. Have we?"

Cole downed the rest of his beer and set the glass on the table. "We found the source. There is something to this old man, Thomas Walton. His company pulled a U-turn in the heart of the Depression and has made money ever since. The kid said they put out six hundred thousand mirrors last year alone. Said the old man's goal was to put one of these mirrors in every home in America. We have to do something."

"What do you mean?" Doris asked, giving Cole a sideways look.

"Well, we can't allow this to go on. Somewhere out there, today or tomorrow, sometime, someone else is going to get taken. We need to shine a light on this thing and get these mirrors out of people's homes. Make sure not another one of those fucking mirrors leaves that factory." Cole spoke with more aggression.

Molly took hold of her husband's arm. "What about Johnny?"

"We know who has the answer. We just need to get it out of him."

"Is that all?" Doris asked. "And how do you plan to do that?"

Cole tilted his head. "I haven't figured everything out yet. Some of the details are still a little fuzzy, but a plan is coming together." He smiled.

"If the old man does know," Molly said, "he isn't going to just tell us how to get our son back. He certainly isn't going to watch us destroy his whole business and cause a national panic over what kind of mirror people have in their homes."

"And that is the rub. I have to figure out how to make him talk."

"You are in enough trouble already," Doris pointed out. "One call to the police and we will all be explaining this for the next week to come."

Cole nodded and gobbled up his last bite of burger. He knew it wasn't going to be easy. Things were probably going to get messy. At this point, he was already in trouble. He wasn't concerned if he had to get his hands dirty. He was going to have to deal with the authorities at some point, but not until he got his son back. *Whatever it takes*, he thought. *No matter what.*

"You have that look. We have to be careful, I can't lose you too," Molly said with concern, and began to cry.

Cole hugged his wife. "It's going to be okay."

"Promise."

"Baby... I sure do hope so, but I can't really promise. Most of this isn't just up to me. Our son will be back in your arms. I'll promise you that, or I will die trying," Cole assured her. He wiped the tears from her eyes and kissed her softly on the lips. "I love you."

Molly nodded and swiped at the tears with her napkin.

"We need to go back to the car," Cole said. "We will park and watch for the old man to show up at the factory, to count his money."

"Do you think that is safe?" Doris asked.

"Better that than the three of us standing out there on a street corner. Besides, the neighborhood is not so good." He slid out of the booth and picked up the check. Walking up to the bar, he said to the bartender, "Settling up."

"Everything good?"

"Real good, thank you."

CHAPTER 21

T he heat once again met them at the door, like a wall. The smell in the alley was more noticeable than when they had gone in, but they walked through it. Now that their bellies were full and throats were quenched, the conversation resumed.

"Doris, I think you should go back to the library," Cole suggested. "Begin sending this story out over the internet. That way people will know. Contact newspapers, the Secret Service, FBI, whoever you can think. That way, whatever happened, we are covered."

"You really think we should split up?" she asked.

Cole tilted his head. "You are our insurance, just in case. I also want you to do something very important. You need to email Walton Mirrors. Send the same message as you do to everyone else, explaining the details and how it works, the name and location of the company. But, you need to send this email at a very specific time. How late is the library open? The factory closes at six; that's got to be when the old man shows up to count his money."

"Most coffee bars have internet," Molly said. "Probably be easier to cover our tracks. Send the emails and then just wait for us. Plus, a café would be open much later."

"That's a perfect idea," Doris agreed.

"Ohio State University is around here somewhere," Cole said. "They should have what we need there." Cole took a step away from the ladies and addressed a stranger walking toward them on the street. "Pardon me, could you tell me how to get to the OSU campus?"

"Right up High Street, not more than a mile or so," the man said.

"That was a real good idea, Moll. Doris can hang out, drink coffee, wait, and no one will look twice."

"Except I am an old woman in a college coffee shop," Doris pointed out.

They walked back to the mall parking garage and the car. Cole was cautious, looking carefully at every car around for police. After deciding it was safe, they got in and headed out of the mall.

Doris asked, "What time do you want me to email Walton Mirrors?"

"Well, let's say seven thirty. An hour and a half after the place closes. Plenty of time, I would think," Cole said.

They headed north on High Street. Cole's mind was filled with thoughts of how he would get the old man to talk. Having Doris email was simply a ploy to push the old man past his secret. If he knew it was out, knew everyone now knew, trying to keep it became irrelevant.

"I really don't like the idea of splitting up," Doris said from the backseat. "I understand it, but I can't say that I like it. A lot could go wrong."

"Well, I've been thinking about that too. I think you both should wait at the coffee shop for me. Safer," Cole said.

"No way!" Molly insisted.

"Honey, I know you want to come along, but I really think it's best if you don't."

Molly took hold of his arm. "No," she said sternly. "I am coming with you and that's final."

"Look, I don't know how these people might react. I can bet it isn't going to be positive." He paused to look his wife in the eye. "Plus, I don't know what I may have to do."

"Exactly why you need someone to watch your back. Besides, do you think there is anything I wouldn't do to get our son back? They will talk, or I will make them." Molly's voice had an edge he had not heard before.

"I can move faster on my own. And I won't have to worry about you."

Molly sighed. "This isn't a debate. I am going."

"If you go…"

"I *am* going! That's final." Molly cut him short.

Cole pulled into the turn lane and depressed his blinker. "Fine, but you wait in the car. This is non-negotiable. In the car. You see trouble, you call the police and we let the authorities figure it all out." Cole shot a glare at his wife.

"Now I know why I never got married," Doris joked.

Cole made his turn and gave a glance at the old librarian in the rearview mirror. "There we go. Says 'internet' in the window."

Cole pulled in front of the café and parked. Turning in his seat, he looked the old woman in the eye. "Doris, we really owe you. I can't thank you enough. You believed us and have helped us, more than I can ever express.

This is not over, and with all hopes, we will be back to get you before seven thirty. If not, don't forget. Right at seven thirty, send the email. Put our story out there and shout it at the mountaintops of the computer range."

He paused for a moment. "I would add a disclaimer when you post the news. We don't want stupid kids trying it for shits and giggles. You know how kids can be." Cole took her hand in his. "If trouble finds us, you are who will save us. You are our voice. We fight this evil together, but I know that you want to face it with us. This makes your task harder than ours, but so much more valuable. Once this is over, you will get to meet our son and we will tell him it was you who saved him. Doris, without you we would not be here. Thank you."

Doris leaned up and hugged Cole over the seat. Molly joined the embrace, and both women began to cry. "You two be very careful. I will be here waiting. Get in and get out. I don't know how you will get the man to talk, but believe that such evil will defend itself. Be ready and keep the strength of your love for your son deep inside your hearts. Don't risk yourselves; this evil will be brought into the light. It can not survive there, the truth will destroy it."

Doris pulled away and got out of the car. Molly rolled down her window and Cole handed her some cash. "We will be back, don't worry," he told her. Doris took the money and pushed it into her handbag. As she walked toward the door of the coffee shop, she turned and gave them a look of caring and concern.

"She is a good lady," Molly said.

"Yes, she is. I really wish you would stay here with her. Molly, I love you, and this could be dangerous." Cole tried to dissuade his wife one last time, but he could see by her expression she wasn't having it.

Cole backed out of the space and made a right onto High Street. He checked the clock on the car radio; they had a bit of time to kill. "We need to make a stop, pick up a few supplies."

"Do we have enough money?" Molly asked.

"We're done hiding now. We can use the credit card, let the cops know where we are. By the time they come around, it will all be over."

"What kind of supplies do we need?"

Cole shrugged. "Not exactly sure yet. I am kind of figuring it out as I go."

Traffic was slow-moving as they continued south. He saw the sign for a surplus store and pulled in. He had thought of trying to get a gun, but it didn't seem that bullets had the desired effect on what he was fighting. Besides, a gun would probably only increase his problems.

"Are we going camping or dressing up in World War II uniforms?" Molly asked.

Cole looked around at the flags and uniforms, medals and patches. "If you are going to fight evil, this is the place to do it," he said with a wink.

"You think you're funny, don't you?" Molly smirked.

The two of them walked through the aisles of canteens, tents, belts and uniforms. "I think we need a cart."

"Really, we need that much stuff?"

Again he shrugged. "I don't know, but I don't feel like carrying around a bunch of stuff."

Cole watched as Molly trotted off to get a cart. He loved his wife deeply and hated they were having to deal with such craziness. He moved to the side of the store, which had a number of display cases containing an assortment of knives.

"Something particular?" a man in fatigues said as he approached.

"Just looking for something big."

The man moved behind the cases and opened one. "This is our deluxe survival knife. A twelve-inch blade, serrated across the top, comes with a compass in the butt of the handle, matches, fishing gear, laser-etched edge and sheath. You have probably seen it in a couple of movies."

"Not big enough," Cole said.

The man nodded and put the large knife back into the case. "This is the best of the best. A Case brand, Double X, Bowie knife. Sixteen-inch blade, reinforced guard across the top edge of the blade to prevent breakage in battle. The hilt is larger, to protect the hand, and the blade has a blood groove."

"What's a blood groove?" Molly asked as she came up next to Cole.

"It's so if you stick it in someone, the blood has a way of escaping. If the blade is flush, the wound seals around the blade and the person won't bleed out as quickly. That little groove allows the blood to run out, so the person will bleed to death faster," Cole told his wife.

"That's right. Now, this being a Case knife, it is a bit more expensive, but you can't buy any better," the salesman said flatly.

Cole knew the man was correct, the Case Double X was top quality in craftsmanship. Still, something large was needed to battle the creatures from the mirror. "Anything bigger?" he asked.

"Bigger?" Molly questioned.

The salesman nodded. "Have some machetes over there. That's about the largest we carry. Sounds like you want a sword."

"Do you have swords?" Cole asked. The salesman shook his head. "Okay, I'll take the Case Bowie. Do you have straight razors?"

The clerk moved down the display and pulled out a number of different straight razors. "This has a mother of pearl handle. This one has a rare ivory handle, recovered from a Japanese soldier during World War II. This one here is a modern take, with a locking blade and rubberized handle. This is more of a weapon than a shaving device. Laser edge, medical steel. It is a long scalpel. Mother's little helper, is what we call it."

Cole nodded. "I'll take that too. The ivory and the lock blade."

"All right, sir, you seem to be a man who knows what he wants. Can I help you find anything else?"

Cole looked over his shoulder. "Do you have flares, or a flare gun?"

"No flare guns, but we have a variety of flares."

The clerk collected the two straight razors and the Bowie, putting them behind the counter. "Let me show you what we have." He led them down an aisle. "Here are the machetes." The clerk pulled one from the bin and unsheathed it. "It's a mass-produced item, but it could hack down a tree. Definitely will keep an edge," he said with a smile.

Cole took the long-bladed weapon and examined it. It was big, but the handle was short, one-handed. Still, he figured it couldn't hurt and tossed it in the cart. They came to the end of the row and turned down the next.

"We have a couple different brands of flares. Some burn longer than others, some burn hotter. The blue are hot, the red are long. These are the simplest: twist the cap, pull the pin, and fire. They have a long burn and are reliable. These blue ones will even work underwater."

Cole threw a package of each into the cart. "Duct tape, a duffel bag, starter fluid," Cole spoke his mental list out loud. He contemplated what else he might need. He considered asking the man about guns, but didn't want to drop any bigger red flags than he already was. People could be crooked;

easy enough to sell him a gun and then turn around and turn him in to the police for some brownie points. There was no honor among thieves; the underworld was not a place built on trust.

Cole could tell the clerk was one of those types of people, the underworld type. Gun dealer, drug pusher, pimp, robber, all-around dirtbag. They all worked around the police; the cops use them and they use the police. A dirty pool type of game of mutual benefit, where no one wins. The underbelly of society was a lose-lose situation.

Here Cole was in his Dockers pants, with his pretty wife. A stranger in a strange land. Making the wrong request of this guy would fire off warning flares and red flags would go up. Such a simple scumbag would begin to try and think, scheme. Best to keep the simpleton in the dark and get what he could in a legit way.

Cole moved to the clothing. His Dockers pants had to go. He pulled a pair of black cargo pants from the rack and looked for a black T-shirt. A pair of black combat boots and he was ready for a strange night out. Molly waved a roll of duct tape at him as she threw it into the cart. Returning to the clerk, Cole asked, "Baseball bats, or something, you know, stick…" He allowed the comment to linger uncompleted.

"Got nightsticks. Seem to work for the police," the clerk said with a smile.

Following the clerk, Cole saw a pair of lead-lined gloves and tossed them into the cart. Arriving at the bin of nightsticks, Cole picked one up. Had he been fighting a normal man, the stick would be more than effective, but these were not normal men. One of those creatures would shrug off a blow from one of these sticks like a twig had struck them. A bat at least had some weight.

"Ah, that's okay. These are a little light for what I need."

"They can put a man down and out easy enough. The light weight makes it manageable to swing. They handle better than a bat would."

"All right, put one in there. Never know."

Heading to the register, the clerk began to ring them up. Cole noticed the Zippo lighter display and pointed at one of them as well. Handing over his credit card, Cole waited, hoping the police hadn't thought to freeze his accounts.

"Appreciate you folks coming in today," the clerk said, clearly pleased with making a sale.

Cole pulled out his Marlboro cigarettes and fired his new Zippo lighter. The flame was large and tall. He lit his smoke and snapped the lighter closed with the trademark sound. *What a simple and quality device*, Cole thought.

Letting his wife into the car, Cole put the duffel bag into the backseat. He knew by using his credit card the police would track them quickly. Hopping behind the driver's seat, he fired the engine and pulled away from the store. He looked at the clock; they were timing this perfect. They should arrive at the mirror factory before five and be able to keep an eye out for the old man.

As they crossed the bridge, Cole was glad to be in the air-conditioned car and not sweating through his shirt and smelling that stinky water.

"Look, a pirate ship," Molly said, breaking into his thoughts.

Cole leaned forward and looked back at the eastern shore of the foul river. Lo and behold, a masted ship was at a dock. "Columbus; must be some sort of replica of one of his ships. Can you imagine crossing the Atlantic in that? Don't look that big sitting in a river."

"Smarty pants."

The two shared a smile as he continued toward the factory, cutting down the side streets. Soon he pulled up to the curb and put the car into park. "There it is."

"I see it. That damn mark." Molly shook her head. "What are we going to do?"

"*We* aren't going to do anything. *You* are going to wait right here." Cole got out of the car and retrieved the bag from the backseat. Pulling out the cargo pants, he quickly changed next to the car and slipped into his combat boots. He fed the belt through the loops, then placed the big Bowie knife on his hip.

"You just going to waltz in there looking like Rambo?" Molly said.

"No, I don't have the headband, jeez." Cole returned her sarcastic tone.

"That's not all you're missing." Molly gave him a suggestive look.

Cole looked his wife in the eye. "Hey, better watch it." He slid back behind the wheel. "Here." He handed over one of the straight razors. "Mother's little helper."

Molly took it and looked at her husband with concern.

"Put that in your pocket. If you have to use it, quick slicing motions. Keep your hand moving; that little sucker will cut to the bone." Cole nodded at the ivory-handled weapon.

"You really expect me to cut someone?" Molly asked.

"If it comes to it, you had better. Besides, that is why you need to stay in the car."

Cole pulled his pack of Marlboro from his pocket and fired one up with his new Zippo. He checked his watch and looked out at the factory.

"Are you going to make a mess in there?" Molly asked.

Cole looked his wife in the eye, pouted, and then smiled. "I am going to find out how to get our son back. I'll do whatever it takes. I have a sneaking suspicion these men, this family, aren't going to want to cooperate. I may need to convince them. Motivate them."

"So, what are the flares for?"

Shrugging, he gave her a sideways look. "The flares are to protect the next man's son. It is time the Walton Mirror company had a fire sale. They just don't know it yet."

"So even if they tell you what you want to know, you are going to burn them out?" she asked.

He nodded. "I can't allow this to continue. Those mirrors have to go."

"Won't that destroy any evidence we could use against these people?"

"Honey, the evidence is everywhere. Every mirror they have ever made holds the evidence. I am just going to make sure they never make another one."

"You think a little lighter fluid and a bunch of flares are going to take care of that?" Molly asked in a doubtful voice.

Cole mashed out his cigarette butt in the ashtray, shaking his head. "I learned something today from the Waltons. They talked about the backings on their mirrors, that they use aluminum on some and copper on others. Each gives a different look."

"So?" Molly said, furrowing her brow.

"God bless PBS. I watched a show they had on about the *Hindenburg*."

"So?" Molly became impatient.

Cole smiled at his wife. She could be very insistent when she was irritated. "So, the *Hindenburg* was a zeppelin back in the day. The famous one that burned up."

"I know what the *Hindenburg* was." She continued to be short with her husband.

He went on. "Well, had you watched the show, you would know they used powdered aluminum and powdered copper to cover the outside of the balloons. Lightweight and more durable than anything else. What they didn't know was, they had discovered thermite."

"And what is thermite?"

"Combining those two in powdered form makes for a very flammable concoction. All it takes is a spark, or in the *Hindenburg*'s case, lightning. That mix will burn until it is gone, a hot flame, and nothing will put it out till it burns out. I am just going to borrow some of theirs and see what happens."

Molly shook her head. "I never knew you knew so much about arson," she said with one raised eyebrow. "You had better be careful in there, playing with fire. I don't want to be married to a crispy bit. Freddy Kruger, or the like."

"Yes, Mother," he said in a smartass tone.

Molly smacked his arm. "I am serious. You be careful, got it?"

Cole nodded but kept his gaze on the factory. It was a bit after five. A fancy Cadillac drove right past them and pulled up to the factory, parking in front. A very old man got out. As he walked around the vehicle, though, he didn't move like a broken-down old man.

"That's him, isn't it?" Molly asked.

Cole nodded. "Yeah, that would be my guess." He turned in his seat and kissed Molly passionately. "It's time. Stay here, no matter what. If I'm not back in one hour, go back to the coffee house and get Doris. Then, go to the police. Make sure she sends that email."

"What is so important about that email?"

"I hope nothing. It is just to show them other people know. Once the cat is out of the bag, they may feel differently. They might make a mistake."

Cole got out of the car and closed the door. Molly slid behind the wheel and lowered the window. "Be careful, get the answers, and come back to me."

"I will." He leaned in and kissed her on the lips. "I love you."

CHAPTER 22

He walked toward the factory, pausing once to look back at his wife. He wondered if he would ever see her again. There was a good possibility things could go very wrong. He pushed the thought from his mind, though the nervous shake in his legs reminded him of how on edge he really was.

He crossed the street, looking around as he moved up next to the fancy Cadillac. He pulled out the big Bowie knife and pressed it firmly into the rear tire, hearing the hiss of air escaping. Cole pulled the blade from the rubber and moved to the front tire, doing the same. "In case you thought of leaving before we have had a chance to talk," Cole said quietly.

Sliding the large Bowie knife back into its sheath on his belt, Cole moved up next to the building. He needed to make a stealthy entrance, but the side of the building had no doors or windows. At the corner, he could see the gravel lot and the dock area, which he had seen from inside. The back door would be his point of entry, he decided.

The dock doors were still open, no doubt to allow heat out and fresh air in. Staying close to the building and ducking below the dock's edge, Cole made his way to the furthest door. Peeking over the edge and into the factory, he could see workers cleaning up and turning off equipment. Timing his move as to not be seen would be the trick. If someone spotted him, the game would be over before it had begun.

He waited and watched, his whole body a loaded spring of nervous energy. The moment arrived. No one was looking. Quickly he pushed himself up and over the dock wall and hurried into the warehouse. Moving into the shadows, Cole hunkered down and waited to hear an alarm or yelling. Moving next to some boxes of mirrors waiting to be shipped, he watched as the employees clocked out and began to leave for the day.

Sweat ran down his face as he maintained cover. He listened intently as the sounds of the factory fell silent. The dock doors were closed and the lights turned off. The lack of outside air immediately increased the temperature and the stuffiness. All grew still, but Cole stayed in his hiding place until he was sure all were gone. Moving carefully around the crated mirrors, he crab-crawled deeper into the factory.

He could feel the heat from the furnaces, a radiating force of hot. Sweat now dripped from his nose and his clothes were soaked through. As he searched the darkness, Cole realized what he had forgotten to purchase: a flashlight.

He waited, allowing his eyes to adjust. The factory had more light than it first appeared. The windows from the offices illuminated the rafters and cast long shadows across the floor. Cole knelt and opened his bag, pulling out his gloves. The powdered lead across the knuckles made them heavy, but Cole knew if he hit someone with them, it would be like a blackjack. An added bonus over just protecting his hands.

He began his search for where they kept the powdered aluminum and copper. Figuring it had to be near the end of the production line, that's where he started. He found a locked cage, which had large cylinders inside marked with capital letters. AL, NA, CU were stamped on different cardboard barrels. The cage was locked with a padlock and a sign read, "Flammable".

Cole began to look for something to break the lock, but knew he had to be quiet. Moving toward the line where the mirrors were produced, he remembered they made their own frames and that some were metal. Keeping a cautious eye, he headed to the framing area and found a large set of metal cutters. Moving back in the shadows, Cole placed the lock in the teeth of the cutter and squeezed the handles together. Surprisingly, the padlock snapped with little effort.

Laying the cutters on the floor and removing the lock, he opened the cage and slipped inside. One of the lids on the cylinders was open. Pulling it off, he reached in and pulled out a fist full of powder. The initials on the barrels were the elemental symbols for each ingredient. The fine granules ran through his fingers like sand. This was going to be one hell of a fire. Twelve cans of aluminum and ten of copper—this stuff would burn through the foundation.

Inside the cage was a dolly, and a bucket and scooper for each of the elements. Just what he needed. He looked up at the office windows, checking to make sure no one was watching, Cole took to his work. He needed to mix the aluminum and the copper, he couldn't just pour them side by side. He couldn't afford any mistakes. Once he started this, there would be no do-overs.

Pulling the scoop from the half-empty aluminum barrel, he moved to the copper cylinder and was surprised at the weight. It was much heavier than he expected or liked. Moving the barrels closer together, Cole scooped out some of the aluminum into the buckets, then scooped some of the copper into the aluminum cylinder, mixing them.

The process took time and was more work than he'd anticipated. Working as fast as he could, while being quiet as a church mouse, Cole wheeled out the mixture as he finished each one. As he began to spread his mixture, he moved past the furnaces and noticed they were natural gas burners. An idea struck him like lightning. Finding the pilot light, Cole extinguished it, and turned the gas on full throttle. The two large furnaces would be like bombs once they were filled with gas.

Going back to his mixture, Cole used the scoop to spread the fiery concoction all over the factory floor, leaving a nice pile on each of the furnaces. Taking one of the barrels, he moved to the steps Tommy had brought him down when they toured the place. The door led to the offices.

Cole had left a trail for the thermite to follow, a powdery mixture of potential destruction. The incendiary power of thermite was impressive, or so he had seen on TV. It would not be like black powder, like some fuse burning; this was like brimstone. Once on fire, it would burn, and burn hot until it was gone.

He wished he had brought a bottle of water; sweat now dripped from his elbow. He could feel the soggy bottom of his underpants and knew he was risking a serious case of monkey butt. He also needed a cigarette something fierce. Stopping to take a deep breath, Cole knew where he needed to go next. The lion's den, the offices, to get the answers he needed to retrieve his son.

He headed back toward the dock doors, far enough away from all the thermite he had spread. Taking off his gloves, he fired up a smoke. The furnaces needed time to fill, and he needed a last smoke to settle his nerves. Covering the flame of his new Zippo lighter, he inhaled deeply and enjoyed the flavor of the Marlboro. As he held the deep drag, he thought how crazy everything had become. His whole world was upside down. Here he was seriously breaking the law, wanted for murder, among other things.

Shaking his head, Cole knew he needed to focus. He couldn't afford a lapse in concentration or judgment, couldn't allow his emotions to wiggle into his mind. The anger and frustration would cloud his senses and could lead to mistakes. Looking around the factory and puffing on his cigarette, he was confident the fire would go well, once it got started. He put the cigarette out and began to question the best way to start his blaze. Once those furnaces blew, anyone close would be killed. *Hell, they might blow up the whole building*, Cole thought.

Cole took another canister of his mixed thermite and headed to the entrance of the office area. Leaving the barrel on the landing, he quietly, slowly opened the door, listening intently. He figured the receptionist would be gone, but he couldn't afford to be wrong. Any alarm to his presence would ruin his plan. Moving down the little hallway, Cole peeked into the lobby. No one was around and the lights were off. They would be upstairs, probably counting their money.

Cole returned to the barrel. Using the dolly, he wheeled it into the office area. Scooping a trail of thermite from the factory floor into the lobby and up to the stairs, Cole knew he was creating a very dangerous situation. Reaching the top of the stairs, he stayed low and peeked over the landing. The hallway was empty and the doors were closed. He moved back down the stairs, pausing to look out the front window at where Molly was waiting in the car.

He could only hope all of this would work out, that he could force these people to cooperate. Taking a breath of the air-conditioned air, he returned to his task. Putting the duffel bag over his shoulder, he picked up the half-empty barrel of powder and quietly moved up the stairs. Using the scoop, he spread his concoction everywhere.

As he opened one of the double doors to the Hall of Mirrors, he froze. He heard something. Some sort of rhythmic sound, over and over, and some kind of smacking sound. He opened the door just enough to see inside, using the mirrors to see different angles around the room. Catching some movement, he focused and could see the back of young Tommy's head.

Quietly, Cole slipped inside and stepped behind a mirror. Now with a better view, Cole could see that Tommy had his shirt off and his pants were down around his ankles. He leaned to the side. Now he could also see the receptionist bent over in front of Tommy. He was giving her his all, and the smacking sound was flesh on flesh. The young Walton pounded away at the pretty secretary as he admired himself in the mirrors. Cole could also hear the soft grunts of the girl with each thrust of Tommy. *Perks of the job*, he thought.

He slipped back out into the hallway, wondering what to do. Once they were finished, the girl would most likely leave, surely noticing the powder everywhere. He didn't want to interrupt the two kids, but it seemed he would have to. He entered the Hall of Mirrors again. The two were still at it, Tommy preoccupied by himself, and the girl with a better view of her feet than anything else.

Cole closed the door slowly and quietly. He was going to have to do this quick and silent. He moved right at the couple; Tommy wasn't aware of Cole until he was almost on top of them. Pulling from the girl and removing his hands from her hips, he turned. "What the hell?"

Cole threw one blow with all his might and struck the kid on the chin. The blow pushed Tommy back, knocking both him and the girl to the floor. Cole stepped forward over Tommy. The kid was not knocked out, but his bell was ringing. Pulling back to deliver another blow, Cole gave the girl a quick glance.

"Hey, what the fuck?" the receptionist yelled.

"Shut the fuck up!" Cole hissed. "Not one word. Got it?" He punched Tommy in the face repeatedly with short, quick blows.

With fear in her eyes, she pulled her skirt down, trying to cover up. As Cole pulled the big Bowie knife from his belt, her eyes grew even wider.

"Stay quiet and you won't get hurt," he told her. "Roll over on your belly. Now!" Cole ordered the girl. He pulled the duct tape from the bag and quickly covered her mouth, then secured her hands and feet. Then he taped up Tommy Walton.

Cole shook his head at himself. He had really stepped over a line. Returning to the dolly, he began to throw the powdery mixture around the Hall of Mirrors. Wheeling the dolly past the couple on the floor, Cole ran a trail from the doors to the back of the room, then left the canister in the middle of the room. He took a flare from the bag and stood it unlit in the powder.

Kneeling next to the couple, he met both of their eyes. Cole started with the girl. "I am going to talk and you are going to listen. Do what I say and you'll be fine. You aren't part of this; just in the wrong place, wrong time. You work for monsters. When this is over, you'll go free and you will find out why this happened. You will find a new job."

He stood and nodded at her; she nodded in return. "You'll be fine." Giving a wry smile, he eyed the woman up and down. "Nice tits, by the way."

The young woman rolled her eyes and squirmed a bit in an attempt to get more comfortable.

Moving over to Tommy, Cole knelt beside him. "Now, you I am expecting some cooperation from. Don't know if you are in on all of this or not, so I have to assume you are. I am going to ask the questions and you will answer me. Got it? No screaming, no bullshit. Understand?"

Tommy Walton nodded. His bloody face leaked slowly from his nose, mouth and a cut above his eye.

"Good. How many people are left in the building?"

"My dad, grandpa, and great-grandpa Walton. Why are you…" the kid began to ask, but Cole put a finger to his lips and shook his head.

"Where are they?"

"Great-grandpa's office. Last office, end of the hall. We don't have any cash here."

Cole pointed the finger at him and again shook his head. He replaced the tape over Tommy's mouth and helped the pair to their feet. "Okay kiddies, going on a field trip. Down the hall and to Grandpa's office we go. Remember, no running in the halls, and let's keep it quiet. Don't want to disturb the other children."

He pulled the nightstick from the bag and showed it to them. "Fall out of line, you get a bonk on the head. Yes?" Cole wiggled the stick. "Slow and easy, okay kids? I have really had a rough couple of days, and as much as I don't want to beat your asses, well, I will. At this point, I just don't have anything else to lose."

Going to the double doors, Cole peeked out and then waved the couple on. "Let's stay together now." Throwing the duffel bag over his shoulder, he followed the two out of the Hall of Mirrors, and began down the hall. As they moved slowly forward, Cole rested the nightstick on Tommy's shoulder as a reminder. As they reached the last office door, Cole could hear voices. Then there was something else, a clicking sound.

CHAPTER 23

The distinct sound of a hammer being drawn back on a gun is something a person just learns, and knows. Hearing that sound made Cole's guts drop. "Easy does it there, smartass," the voice of Detective Jones whispered in his ear.

"Ah, fuck," Cole muttered.

"Oh, that's right. Figured out where you were headed, now didn't I?" Jones whispered again.

Cole had not turned around, hadn't moved. The trio stood stone still. The receptionist started to look, but Cole used the nightstick to ease her chin back facing the office door. "You know, you kind of remind me of Nancy Drew. I think it is the man boobs," Cole said snarkily.

"Still got jokes, even with a gun to your head. You are a cop-killer. I could put one in the back of your skull right now and call it a day. Be a hero. Think that's funny?"

"Yeah, I do. I've seen you shoot. Even at this range, I figure I have a better than good chance you'll miss." Cole couldn't help but smile. "Look, Jones, the answers are right beyond this door. You saw what we are dealing with. I am going to get my son back, and that's that. If you want to shoot me, that's what you are going to have to do." Cole turned and looked the detective in the eye. "Let's end this and then you can have your man. No trouble."

"Let's see who is behind door number one," Detective Jones said.

"Your Monty Hall sucks," Cole said flatly. Stepping between the couple, he opened the door and allowed it to swing wide open, then motioned the two young people to step inside. He followed them into the office, with Jones coming up the rear, his gun still pointed at Cole's back.

An old and feeble-looking man sat behind a large desk, with name plate reading 'Thomas Walton'. Cole recognized Frank Walton standing by the desk, and another man was seated in front of the desk.

Cole scanned the room. A very large antique-looking mirror hung from the wall. The walls were done in walnut panel, creating a very dark space.

The chairs were dark leather and the desk was also walnut. The whole place looked like something out of an old movie. An old light in the ceiling and two small lamps on each corner of the giant desk were the only light, and the walls seemed to absorb even that. This office looked and felt like the man behind the desk, old and creepy.

"What the hell is all this?" Elliot Walton demanded. Tommy mumbled from the tape over his mouth, trying to talk.

"Gentlemen, I am Detective Jones. I have been in pursuit of this suspect and tracked him to your factory here," Jones said to the men.

"This guy was here earlier, looking to purchase mirrors," Frank Walton said.

"Casing the place," Jones said.

The old man, Thomas Walton, squinted and leaned back in his chair. "I saw this man on the news. Seems he murdered a police officer. Why haven't you put him in cuffs, Detective? Taken him away to jail? Why do you barge into my office with a murderer?"

"I just caught the man, right outside your door. He had these two people tied up, and I would assume you would have liked to know a crime has been committed on your property. I will also need to take statements, call in the local authorities, take photos. This is a crime scene."

Frank Walton approached his son and removed the tape from his mouth. "They know each other," Tommy said. "That asshole hit me and was spreading some stuff all over. Dumped a bunch of powdery shit all over the Hall."

The young receptionist began to squirm, wanting free.

Cole gave Jones a look. "Don't panic," he said and stepped toward the girl, pulling the tape from her mouth with a quick jerk. Then he grabbed her by the arm and turned her to face Jones, pulling the Bowie knife from its sheath.

"Hey, goddamn it!" Jones yelled.

Cole cut the tape on the girl's hands and slid the big knife back into the sheath.

The receptionist turned to Cole and slapped him hard across the face. "You son of a bitch."

Cole eyed the girl. Nodding and rubbing his cheek, he winked at her and gave a half smile.

"Why don't we allow the young people to go? They have been involved enough. I am sure they will be available when the time comes," Thomas Walton said from behind his desk, as if he ran the show.

Cole and the detective exchanged a look, and Cole nodded.

"You kids go on home. We'll see you tomorrow." Elliot Walton spoke up.

"I wouldn't bet on that," Cole uttered.

The couple moved to the door of the office, then turned, checking to make sure it was all right to leave. They closed the door behind them and were gone.

"Detective, do you have identification?" Thomas Walton asked.

Jones pulled his wallet from his hip pocket and tossed it on the big walnut desk. Cole could see the hand Tommy had mentioned. It was seriously burned, but functional. The old man examined the badge. "I see that you are not from Ohio. Doesn't that create a jurisdictional issue?" The old man extended the wallet with his burned hand.

"I tracked him here," Jones said. "Like a slow chase of sorts, shouldn't be a problem. My authority isn't in question."

"Well, I just ask because, from what I saw on the news, this is serious. Cop-killer, fugitive, and yet I don't see any backup?"

"I was following a hunch and I was right. I don't need backup."

It wasn't until Jones had taken back his wallet and slipped into his pocket that he saw the old man was now holding a gun. "Why don't you just set that pistol on the desk? Slow and easy, copper," Thomas Walton ordered.

"Grandpa, what are you doing?" Frank Walton asked, confused.

Jones laid the weapon on the desk and took a full step back, now standing next to Cole. The two exchanged a look, and Cole shrugged. "Thanks for the help," Cole said, sarcastically.

"You may be a cop, but you are out of your yard and no one knows you are here," Thomas Walton said. "Elliot, take the gun if you would. This cop came for the same reason as this guy. They have stumbled onto the family secret. You are going to wish you had left well enough alone."

"Gave up your gun," Cole said. "Thought cops didn't do that? Smooth, real smooth."

"Give me a break, will ya?"

"Both of you, shut up," Elliot Walton ordered.

"What are we doing?" Frank asked. "This man broke in here. He is wanted. Why don't we let the police handle this?"

"He must have cuffs on him, and the other one has duct tape. Secure them, Franklin," the old man ordered. Thomas waved the gun between Frank and Jones with a relaxed manner, but his eyes were serious. "Do it!" he commanded.

Frank moved behind them and found Detective Jones's handcuffs, then secured the detective's hands behind his back. Moving to Cole's bag, he found the tape. "He has road flares and lighter fluid in here," he announced.

"Planning a fire?" Thomas asked.

Frank taped Cole's hands behind his back and gave a nod to the old man.

"Set them down," Thomas instructed.

Cole smiled as he took his seat. "He may have come alone, but I didn't. People know I am here and what you people are doing with these mirrors."

Elliot Walton moved Detective Jones around the leather chair and pushed him into it. "What is he talking about?" Frank asked.

The old man looked Cole in the eye. "You have been a bad boy. Did you really think you could destroy all of this?"

"You are finished. By tomorrow, everyone is going to know and they will be coming with questions for you. People know, and they know I am here, right now." Cole looked at Jones. "He's a cop. He will be missed. Won't take people a stretch to put him and me together here. This is over. Tell me how to get my son back." Cole returned the old man's look.

The office door opened, which drew everyone's attention. In walked Molly and young Tommy Walton. Cole's heart sank; all he could think was, *Damn it.* Tommy gave Molly a shove into the room.

"Watch it, kid," Cole said, with absolute seriousness.

"Who do we have here? Guess we found who knew you were here, didn't we?" the old man said with a shitty smile.

"Sorry, baby," Molly said. "I saw that cop creep in and thought you might need some help." She moved between the two leather chairs in front of the desk and looked down at her husband. "Sorry," she whispered.

"It's okay. sweetheart. Very brave. I told you, stay in the car no matter what, but it's okay. Actually, you are just in time to hear this old piece of crap tell us how to get our Johnny back. Go ahead, you son of a bitch." Cole turned his gaze to Thomas Walton.

"You are pretty ballsy for a man in your position. You'd better be more concerned about what I am going to do with you."

"Seems to me you have some explaining to do, and we are all anxious to hear all about it. Besides, you need to practice. I told you: this time tomorrow, you'll be front page news and doing the explaining to government officials."

"What, did you mail a letter? Come on, this isn't the movies. You had your wife as backup. Now she is in here with you. Don't play games with me, boy."

"Who you callin' *boy,* you twisted old fuck? Had you read the paper, you would know it isn't just my wife and me. Dumbass."

"What are we going to do, Dad?" Elliot asked.

The old man looked closely at Cole. "We could stage a gun battle between these two. The wife got hit in the crossfire. They all killed each other. We could say he was ranting, talking crazy, about demons and whatnot."

"Are you talking about killing these people?" Frank asked. "Why don't we just call the police? They all broke in here."

Thomas looked at his grandson and great-grandson and tried to smile, then shook his head. "No police. Not yet. I guess this is overdue: it's time the two of you know your family history. Frank, you have always been such a kind-hearted soul. Time to grow up and deal with the real world."

The old man turned back to Cole. "It was only a matter of time till someone came to call, and here you are. Son got took, huh? Now you want answers." Thomas Walton gave a creepy smile.

"Know what family history?" Frank interrupted.

"Are we really talking about killing these people?" Tommy Walton asked, with a hint of enthusiasm.

Thomas slapped his hand down on the desk hard. "Listen up! Family first. This company has kept all of us rich and worry-free, and we will protect our livelihood. What this man—or whoever he has out there—says, no one will believe. Ghost stories, folklore, myth—no one will believe. Especially if these people vanish. There may be some questions, but that's all."

"Are you stupid?" Cole asked. "People will be dumb enough to try it. Plus, I have someone contacting the kind of people who will be *very* interested in all this kind of stuff. CIA, NSA, DOD. This is over, old man. You're done. Covering it up won't do it. However, I will offer you a deal."

"You really think you are in any position to make a deal?" Elliot asked smugly.

"How do you think the Department of Defense will treat you fellas? They are going to want answers, and they won't just go away," Cole said.

"Why does it seem that these people know more about this than we do?" Frank asked the patriarch. "Family first? Seems that Tommy and I have been left in the dark. I want an explanation."

"We didn't tell you in order to protect you," Elliot said to his son.

Cole scoffed and shook his head. "Bullshit."

"Shut up, you!" Elliot demanded.

Cole looked at the Waltons. "Wonder what kind of mirrors y'all have in your houses. Hell, the kid was just down getting his rocks off in a room full of those damn things. 'Protect them'… Please," he said with disgust.

"What is he talking about?" Frank asked.

"See, old man? You have some explaining to do. You are only digging your own hole deeper. Tell me how to get my son back. He is only eight years old. Whatever you have done here, you can't justify one moment of his suffering. Your family, your success, your livelihood—he's a little boy."

"You knew about this? You do this on purpose?" Detective Jones asked.

"Elliot, tape their mouths shut," the old man said. "They have nothing to say here. I am afraid they will all have to go."

"You're going to kill us?" Molly asked in a high-pitched voice.

CHAPTER 24

Thomas Walton smiled his evil smile. "You killed yourselves the moment you thought you could attempt to damage my business. This is my life and it is protected by the most powerful. You brought this to my doorstep, and now you will pay the price. I shall sweep you away." His tone was void of inflection.

Elliot Walton proceeded to place tape over their mouths.

"Grandpa, what is all of this?" Frank asked. "The one guy is a cop. No doubt his car is out there. People are going to wonder. There will be questions."

"And what about the other person this guy mentioned?" Tommy asked.

The old man stared at Cole. "It's a bluff. Besides, no one believes such things. The bodies are easy enough: the two large furnaces downstairs will do the trick. Ashes to ashes. The cars we can just drive down the street. The kids from the Bottoms will steal them and strip them down. No problem." Thomas Walton once again grinned his sinister smile.

"You had better tell us this family history. Burning bodies and all, 'cause I have a problem," Frank told the old man.

Thomas stood from his big leather chair and walked around the walnut desk. He stood in front of Cole and glared at him before slapping him hard across the face.

The old burned-up hand felt like it was made of lead. He had been punched and it hadn't hurt as much as this senior citizen's slap. Then the mangled fingers reached out and took hold of Cole's face, squeezing it hard. Thomas leaned in, and Cole could feel the heat from his breath.

"You. You thought you could come here and destroy me. Get answers. Find your brat. You thought you would force me. Manipulate the situation. You have no idea, sir, none. You have stepped into the darkness and you shall be consumed." Thomas Walton pushed Cole's face away.

Then he walked back behind his desk. "So, you want to know? Fine, it is your legacy. Frank, Tommy, pay attention. You both know the story of my father, and how he came to this country and opened the factory in 1919. The roaring twenties rolled in and were just that. People wanted fancy things and business was good. He was a good man, fair, and a true craftsman. All this you already know."

Sitting down, he looked around at their faces. "When he died, he left this company to my brother and me. Richard had grown up in this building. He knew all the workers, every machine. He too was a craftsman.

"I had gone off to university, a college man. Father wanted me to learn business, economics, accounting. That would be my role in the family business, so that when the time came, Richard and I could handle both sides of the business." Thomas pulled a bottle of Blue Label from his desk drawer, followed by a glass.

He poured a healthy amount, drank deeply, and closed his eyes as he swallowed. "In 1929, the Depression began. Stocks crashed, banks closed, unemployment skyrocketed. At first, we were all right. Family business; we had invested back into the company and had little debt to speak of. Those furnaces had shorted our capital, and the number of employees was rather high. Still, we were in relatively good shape compared to the rest of the world."

He paused to take another drink. "Times got tough, the Depression went on, and by 1931 our father passed away. Richard and I had a real problem." He poured more scotch into the glass. "It was right here in this office where we had our last fight. Richard was an idealist. The company was slipping, product was suffering, people couldn't afford bread. We began to build debt and couldn't afford quality materials. Richard sold his car, furniture from his home, took home the same pay as the lowest of our employees. He expected me to do the same, to sacrifice and hope times would improve."

Thomas scoffed, then sipped. "I knew better. The Depression was just getting started and I knew it was only going to get worse. We needed to sell, get what we could while we could. Trying to hang onto the company would only drag us both down with it, and we would have nothing. I can still hear him, so loyal to the workers, to Father's ways, our responsibilities. Fool. My suggestion to sell was taken like a personal insult."

"You wanted to sell out? All these years you talked of our loyalty to this company and you wanted to sell?" Frank asked with disgust.

"Believe me, it was the correct choice. It was only 1931. Things did get worse, years of decline and poverty. We would never had survived."

"If you wanted to sell, why are we still in business?" Tommy asked.

The old man emptied his glass with a gulp and glared at Cole. "It was late one night, just the two of us right here. We argued again, very heated. I told him half of the company was mine, that I had the right to sell. Richard flew into a rage. He knew he couldn't buy me out, and that anyone else would want to dismantle the factory. Granted, I knew anyone who could buy me out wouldn't pay the true value, but at that point, some was better than none.

"Over the years, Richard and I had fought. Over toys, girls, whatever else. We hadn't thrown blows at each other for years. This was different, though; we were men, each with cause and purpose, reasons." Thomas Walton refilled the glass and returned the bottle to the drawer.

"All his anger and frustration boiled to the surface. His desire to keep the company and help the workers drove him, devout in principle. His passion had become rage. I had never seen my brother in such a state, filled with hate toward me. We fought, exchanged blows and broke things. He was older, bigger than I was. I found myself in a real struggle. Not only did he have size, but he was fighting for a cause, his dedication to the business and the employees. It wasn't going well for me."

The old man paused to take a drink. "I tried to get away. Threw lamps and chairs, tried to run, but he had me and beat me. He pounded on me till I swore I would never sell." Thomas looked around the office. "This is where the story takes a very strange turn. I knew that Richard couldn't be reasoned with. Had I not promised never to sell, he would have beaten me to death."

He picked up the gun from his desk and admired it. "This was my father's gun. It has been in this desk since 1919. Once Richard had stopped his assault, I seized the opportunity and rounded the desk. I knew I was right, and I wasn't going to allow my brother to ruin us both. I couldn't beat any sense into him, and neither of us was going to change our minds."

Taking a large swallow, the old man closed his eyes again as the scotch poured down his gullet. "Richard didn't like me pulling a gun on him. His rage bloomed again, and he resumed his aggression. I tried to keep the desk between us, I begged him to stop. He would have none of it. He told me he would kill me, that the company would never leave the family. He said I would have to kill him, that only over his dead body would I sell the company. He shamed me as a Judas, taking pence for my legacy. He charged me from right there."

MIRRORS

The old man gulped down the last of the glass. "I shot him. I killed Richard right here in this room." Thomas threw the glass against the far wall, smashing it into pieces.

Molly jumped at the sound; everyone was quiet, uneasy. Hearing the old man just confess to murder, to killing his own brother, disgusted Cole even more.

Thomas Walton stood from his chair and rounded the desk, this time moving behind Cole, but still visible in the mirror. Cole watched the man very carefully. He could see in the man's eyes that he was reliving the moment.

"His blood sprayed that mirror, Father's first. My brother dropped like a stone, leaving me to stand here and view myself. The reflection of my sin in the mirror made by our father's hand. The smoking gun, the blood on my face, on the glass. That's when I noticed that the blood on the mirror was being absorbed, melting right into the glass. The room changed. I changed; what I saw was colorless and dingy."

The old man shuddered. "The room grew hot like a fever, and there was a smell of old death and the bowels of the Earth. My skin crawled and my stomach turned over. I watched as the mirror began to swirl within itself, like a great whirlpool."

The man's voice quivered. "As if from a pool or through a doorway, out came a man; or what I thought was a man. The mirror rippled behind him as he stepped down and viewed the bloody scene. It was no man. Eyes void, black as the darkest night, sockets of nothingness. His hair was black as ink, long and flowing. He was finely dressed, and I must say he was the most handsome creature I had ever seen. Not that I find men attractive.

"Tall and slim, but with obvious strength and power. He stepped around Richard's body, pausing for a passing look, careful not to get anything on his shoes." The old man walked back around his desk again and sat, then pulled the bottle out and refilled his glass once again.

"You're saying a man stepped out of that mirror?" Frank asked. "What was he, the Devil?"

"Yes, yes he was. His voice boomed, echoed off these walls. Even over the ringing in my ears from the gun shot. I have never heard anything more clearly. He spoke softly and effortlessly, but his resonance was incredible. His voice was like nothing you can imagine."

"What did he say?" Tommy asked with excitement.

Thomas looked at the mirror. "He called me Cain, as if what I had done was some how humorous to him. Explained he had a solution to my problem and would help me. He understood what I had done, respected it, and sought to assist me, that was why he had come. Said how Richard's murderous rage had drawn his attention, but seeing my defense of myself, he had to do the right thing. Since Richard and I were the only ones there, who would believe I had defended myself?"

"The Devil had to do the right thing?" Cole shook his head at the comment.

"You made a deal with the Devil?" Frank asked. "You really expect us to believe this? I have heard of better plots in dime novels. Dad, do you believe this?"

Elliot held up his hand. "Just listen, son. Your grandpa isn't making this up."

Taking another swig from his glass, Thomas continued. "He said he knew the company was in trouble. He knew the country was in trouble. Told me I was correct about times to come being tough. He said he could help. He said he could ensure I would always be well off and no trouble would come from what had just happened."

"So the Devil didn't make you do it, but he helped cover it up?" Detective Jones mocked.

"I was young, afraid, and in shock. His request was not such a tall order, so what could it hurt? He wanted a mark placed on every mirror, a specific mark. Told me to strive to place a mirror with his mark in every home in the United States. He instructed me to burn my brother's body, and to say he must have run off. He told me as long as I did what he said, all would be well. I agreed, and we shook hands." He held out the burned hand and looked Cole in the eye.

"I had never felt such a pain in my whole life. A pain so deep, as if he branded my very soul. That smile and laugh will haunt me to the grave. His laugh vibrated the very walls, and shook me to the bones. Those black eyes glared into mine as he told me if I tried to break the deal, I would suffer in this life and after. Said if I honored it I would live well and long, which I have."

MIRRORS

The old man finished his glass and allowed a long pause. "Then he turned, with that raven-black hair, and returned from whence he came. A ripple in the glass and he was gone. I did as he said, and it was as he said it would be."

"So, now what?" Frank asked.

CHAPTER 25

Thomas leaned forward, returning to the present. "Tommy, collect their car keys, drive the cars a few blocks away, and leave them. Elliot, take them down to the furnaces and clean it up. It will all work out, just as before."

"Grandpa, you expect us to just murder these people?" Frank asked.

"Yes. Franklin, you have had an easy ride up until now. It's time you earn your place. This is a family business and will all be yours one day. If you are going to dine with the Devil, you should bring a long spoon."

"What the hell does that mean?" Frank asked. "This was your deal, not mine, not my son's. We are Christian men. We do not do the bidding of Satan, we will not be in league with the Devil."

"You have already reaped the fruits, my boy. Benefited from my labors and the deal of your blood. You will do as you are told, without debate." The old man slapped his hand hard on his desk. "Family first! Now, do as you are told!"

Elliot moved to his son's side and placed a hand on his shoulder. "It will be fine. We just have to protect what is ours. Don't give it another thought."

Cole could feel the tension in the room tighten. He knew the conflict of being confronted with something so hard to believe. He also had yet to get the answer he was there for.

Frank Walton tugged on Cole's arm for him to stand up. Tommy was frisking Detective Jones, and Elliot had the detective's gun trained on them. The old man stared at Cole with hate-filled eyes.

"Frank, you go and do what needs done," the old man said. "Be the example for Tommy. Have faith that we are watched over, protected. We will talk about it more once this thing is done."

Frank guided Cole toward the office door and opened it. He led the way; the three captives followed, Elliot in the rear. Frank opened the door to the stairway which led down to the factory floor. "Be easy," Elliot said from behind them.

Cole could see Molly trying to pull something from her back pocket, but her jeans were pretty tight. Granted, her ass did look good in them jeans. Cole wasn't afraid, or even really nervous. The old man's story had done a number of things for him. He now knew they were dealing with true and pure evil. He knew the old man was a twisted, sick fucker who murdered his own brother over money. Ironically, he had kept the company which he had killed to get rid of. He now knew there was a Devil, Satan himself, the real deal. This naturally meant to Cole there had to be a God. If one played a part in the world, then so did the other.

If the Devil could make deals with murderous greedy sons of bitches, then God would look out for the good guys. He also figured he had better start going to church. Getting a confirmation, such as it was—better safe than sorry.

He watched Molly pull the mother-of-pearl-handled razor from her back pocket and open it. She was trying to cut her hands free. Frank stopped to check the progress of everyone. This was Cole's chance. He turned to face Elliot as he reached back to take the razor from Molly's hands.

"Turn around and get moving," Elliot ordered, pointing the gun at Cole's head. "Move it!"

But Elliot made the mistake of moving with them as he guided them toward the furnaces. This allowed Cole to just turn with him, keeping his hands obscured as he cut at the duct tape. His hands finally freed, Cole maintained the illusion of being bound. The group moved closer to the furnaces; Cole saw Frank Walton look up at the window above the factory. The old man was watching.

"On your knees, cop!" Elliot ordered and pushed Jones to the ground. His hands still cuffed behind him, the detective landed hard on his knees and rolled onto his side. Jones looked at Cole, his eyes filled with fear and anger. With his mouth taped, his pleas for mercy were muffled.

Cole gave the man a wink, causing the detective to double take.

"I'll fire up the furnace," Frank said as his father leveled the gun at Shirley Jones's head.

Cole ripped the tape off his own mouth and said, "I wouldn't do that." Elliot turned, swinging the gun in Cole's direction. Cole gave a quick swipe of the razor across the wrist of the seventy-year-old man. Elliot dropped the gun, clenching his cut. Cole followed with a straight left to Elliot's nose. He still was wearing the powdered lead gloves and they gave weight and force to his blow. Elliot Walton fell backward, already unconscious, landing hard and flat on his back.

Cole picked up the gun. "Get away from that furnace, Frank. Your dad over here needs your help." He stepped toward Molly; she turned around so Cole could cut the tape on her wrists.

She pulled the tape from her lips. "Really is Mother's Little Helper, huh?"

Cole smiled. "Why don't you give Shirley a hand with those cuffs?" Jones shot him a disgusted look. "Yes, I called you Shirley. Just saved your life, so don't go givin' me the stink eye."

Molly pulled the tape from Detective Jones's mouth. Frank moved to his injured, elderly father. The old man was still down, leaking from his wounds. Cole had no doubt he'd busted the man's beak. He smiled, thinking, *Two broke noses in as many days, a trend of sorts.* He hadn't reconfigured faces like this since his bad-boy high school days.

"Damn it, you people," Jones said, rubbing his mouth where the tape had been. "I'll tell ya. Mr. and Mrs. Mason, you have truly dragged me through a pile of shit. I regret the day our paths ever crossed."

"I wasn't going to say anything, but since you brought it up, do you smell that? Did you poop?" Cole raised an eyebrow at Jones. "Gun to your head make you crap your pants?" Cole laughed.

"I keep telling you, nobody likes a smartass, and I mean nobody," Jones returned.

Cole looked at Frank and Elliot on the floor. "Wrap your shirt around the wound. Don't want the old fuck to bleed to death."

"That kid got my keys. The cuff key was on it," Jones said.

Cole rolled his eyes, walked over to Molly, and handed her the gun. "If you have to, in the legs. I need them alive." Then he headed into the darkness of the factory.

He moved quickly back to the cutters he had used to cut the padlock and collected them, pausing to look up at the office windows. The old man was still there, watching, waiting. He must have seen what had happened. Even if his sight was shit, he had to be wondering what was going on. Cole knew he was going to have to make the old bastard talk, but how was the question. The old man still had a gun, and from his story, he wasn't afraid to use it.

Returning to the scene, Cole had to pause. Molly, standing there holding a gun on two old men. One shirtless, holding his father's bleeding arm; Detective Jones standing there with his arms pinned behind him, looking very helpless. This vacation had really taken a turn.

Cole rejoined the group. Stepping up in front of Jones, Cole held up the cutter and raised both eyebrows. "Jewelry removal."

"Thanks," Jones said, turning around. "Let me get to a phone. I'll have a hundred cops here in ten minutes. Send these twisted fuckers, Devil-worshipping, murderous sickos to the goddamn electric chair."

Cole stopped, holding Jones still with the cuffs. "Oh, I don't think so. I came here for an answer, which I haven't gotten yet. You and a bunch of cops in here—no, no. Too much explaining for me to do, and these fuckers will just lawyer up. I need to know how to get my son back."

"I will tell them. I'll back you up," Jones told Cole.

"Yeah, I appreciate that, and I am going to need that once this is all over. *After*. The old man up there isn't going to talk to the police. He's old as dirt anyway; he will take what he knows to the grave. Him and that one…" Cole pointed at Elliot. "They knew about all this. He has to be seventy. Sending them to prison won't do much good. I am here for my son. I am going to put an end to this once and for all. You can help me, or you can sit it out, but I have work to do and can't be restricted by the laws of men." Cole cut the cuffs and stood in front of the detective.

"As you heard and have seen, this is a fight against the darkest of evil. We cannot comply with the rules and reasons of men. This is the big game. Gods and Devils. This ends now. I *will* get my Johnny back," Cole said with determination.

He looked up at the office windows again; the old man was no longer looking down on them. *He better not have tried to run away*, Cole thought, turning back to the two Waltons and ordering them to get up.

"You broke his nose," Frank said with concern.

"That seems to be a thing with you, huh? Busting noses," Jones said.

Cole smiled. "So, you going to help?"

The detective nodded. "Yeah, figure I better see this through. I have been behind on this thing since the beginning. Guess I can explain all this once it's done. What can I do?"

"Molly, give the detective back his gun. Now, let's go get this done. Go up and see to this old man." Cole pulled Frank to his feet, then headed to the far door, not up the stairs they had come down.

"Why are we going this way?" Molly asked.

"I have a plan coming together. Plus, I don't want that old son of a bitch up there waiting for us with his pistol," Cole explained.

Molly nodded.

"Honey, I want you to stay back," Cole went on. "To be safe. Stay behind Detective Jones. I don't know what is going to happen. I want you safe."

Molly gave him a soft kiss upon the cheek and they shared a slight smile.

Cole opened the door into the hallway, looking in at the lobby. He knew Tommy was still creeping around somewhere. Cole led the way, followed by Elliot, Franklin, the detective and then Molly. He saw no one, and the lights were off. As he started up the stairs, he watched the top tread for any sign of movement, listening for any sound. He had no gun but was ready to move quickly if need be. He still had his knives, but if the old man started shooting, it might be all she wrote.

Cole advanced quickly, taking steps two at a time. The group was still at the bottom of the stairs; Thomas Walton's office door was closed. "Come on," Cole said down the stairs. Elliot climbed the steps, looking pale and gasping for air.

Cole moved down the hall and stopped at the double doors of the Hall of Mirrors. He went inside, accompanied only by his reflection, once again disturbed by the presence of them. He pulled one of the smaller displays and rejoined the group, now in the hallway.

"What are you going to do with that?" Jones asked.

"Here, take this and be careful." He handed the mirror to Molly, then moved to Frank, took his hand, and turned it palm up. "I am a palm reader. I see…you are going to bleed." He ran the straight razor over his hand. The cut wasn't bad, but it did bleed. "Oh, I also see you have money coming." Cole slapped a dollar bill into his hand.

Frank gripped his hand and gave Cole a horrified look. "Why did you cut me?"

"Your life line was a little too long, I need to remedy that. Ask me another fucking question."

MIRRORS

Cole could feel his heart pounding, and sweat at his brow and on his upper lip. His nerves were pins and needles; his anxiety was heightened beyond what it had ever been before. Arriving at Thomas Walton's door, Cole turned the knob and pushed Elliot and Frank inside.

CHAPTER 26

The old man was seated behind his desk, looking smug. The group entered and filled in behind Frank and Elliot. "Where is Tommy?" "I sent him to get rid of your cars," the old man told him. "Guess if you want something done correctly, one must do it oneself. Can barely rely on any of you to do anything beyond the simplest of tasks."

"I am bleeding," Elliot said.

"Shut up. Useless. How I have carried this family, and look at the two of you. And you people, what do you want?" Thomas said venomously.

"Don't blame them, you old coot," Cole said. "This is all your doing. You're disappointed they didn't kill us; probably not the stance to take in this moment. There is something really wrong with you." Cole advanced toward the desk.

Reaching across the desk, Cole plucked up the bottle of Blue Label Scotch and swigged a large gulp, then handed the bottle to Jones.

"Hey!" the old man protested.

"Hey, what? You drunk asshole. You've had enough. Kiss my ass." Cole pulled his cigarettes from his pocket and placed one between his lips, then pulled out his lighter, flipped it open and lit his smoke. Sitting in one of the chairs, he inhaled deeply and watched the cherry glow red hot. Cole and the old man locked eyes once again.

"There is no smoking in my office," Thomas Walton commanded.

Cole again inhaled, then exhaled a large plume of smoke. "And yet, there is. What, you think I give a shit about the Devil-worshipping ass-clown getting lung cancer? You fuck. Worried about secondhand smoke, you arrogant ass. How about you stop being a smoking Nazi and fuck off." He puffed the cigarette and blew smoke across the desk in a defiant gesture.

"Your husband really has a way with words. I think he has some anger issues, but a real poet, to be sure," Detective Jones said to Molly.

Molly smiled. "It's a real gift. He almost had a career in greeting cards. 'It's your fucking birthday, you old shit-bag.' Just ahead of its time."

Cole gave a glare around the edge of the chair at the two. Molly shrugged and smiled.

"Okay, enough of this crap," Cole said. "I came for answers and you are going to give them to me."

"Answers to what? I told you what happened. You heard the story, that's it," Thomas Walton said with disgust.

Cole squinted at the old man behind the desk. His patience had run its course and he was done playing around. "The mirrors? The mark? Explain it," he demanded, feeling his face flush and grow hot.

"The Devil said make mirrors with the mark on them. I don't know what you mean. I wasn't going to ask Satan to explain himself to me, especially over the body of my brother. You keep asking for answers; well, I don't have any. You keep talking about your son; he isn't here. I don't even know how you found out about all this."

"Right. Do I look stupid to you? You were going to kill three people, burn us up in your furnace. Not the first time for you. Smells like bullshit to me."

"He said the mirrors would have power, that they would benefit his cause. What do I know? It was a five-minute conversation, almost eighty years ago."

"Oh yeah, I can see how the Angel of Darkness appearing before you and giving you orders might slip your mind, be a little foggy and vague. Please. All those little details just fade with time. Sure."

"Look, you young punk, he said, I did, and that's that. Whatever happened with your brat, that's your problem. Take it up with the man upstairs, or down, whichever. It's got nothing to do with me or my family."

"Nothing to do with your family?" Molly said. She leaned the mirror against the wall and stepped forward. "This is all because of you. Now you play stupid, you son of a bitch."

"No worries, my dear," said Cole. "He is going to tell us everything we need to know."

The old man made a face. "Am I? And how do you see that? I don't know anything."

"You sound like a broken record, old man," Cole said, shaking his head.

"Can my father please sit down?" Frank cut in. "He needs medical attention. He is losing a lot of blood." Frank tried to hold his father up.

Cole shrugged. "He's not leaking that bad. He's got another couple hours before he passes out, so shut up already." Granted, he could see the fellow was getting pale.

Focusing back on Thomas, Cole could tell the son of a bitch wasn't going to cooperate. He was going to have to move on with the plan. He stood and began to move about the room, meeting each person's eyes in turn. He could see that Molly was still agitated by what the old man had said.

Detective Jones gave him a questioning look. Cole returned the look with a quick wink and a half-smile. Franklin had fear in his eyes, along with concern for his father. Elliot held his wound and focused on staying conscious; pain lived in his eyes, with dread behind them. Thomas's eyes followed Cole as he moved. They were dulled with time and alcohol, and carried a glaze.

"Last chance, old man. Time to spill the beans or face the music." Cole met the man's glare with a hateful one of his own. Nearing the windows, Cole looked down into the dark factory. "I have nothing to lose, so speak up."

"I have nothing to tell you. What, you want to try and hurt me? Well, good luck. Punk."

Cole just looked at the old bastard and shook his head. What a clusterfuck this man had made of things, his evil deed spreading into so many lives. How could he be so detached?

"I have to sit down," Elliot muttered.

"Just move over there. You're in the way." Cole pointed at a spot, then turned to Franklin. "Say, do me a favor." Then he paused to look at the old man. "Last chance."

"What's that?" Franklin asked.

Cole watched Thomas Walton carefully as he spoke to Franklin. "The thing I gave you, after cutting you. What does it say on the back?"

Franklin pulled the bloody dollar up and turned it over. "Says, in God we..."

The old man pushed back from his desk and grabbed his gun, raising it toward Cole's face. Cole dodged to the left as he saw the muzzle flash and felt the heat from the burning gun powder. The projectile zinged as it zipped past. In a fluid motion, pure reaction, Cole swooped his right hand and took hold of the old man's wrist. He could feel the strength in the man as the gun fired again, and then again.

CHAPTER 27

C ole smashed the right hand of Thomas Walton on the walnut desk and followed up with a left-handed punch. The powdered lead glove landed solid on the old man's ear. The gun fired a final shot and then dropped to the floor. Cole moved quickly to take possession of the weapon, looking to make sure Molly was all right.

She had moved to the windows and was holding her ears, but she appeared to be fine. Cole's attention was drawn to the mirror she had leaned against the wall. The reflection had changed. The office looked dirty and ancient. Then Cole saw the image of Frank Walton begin to emerge.

Detective Jones was just standing, like a statue made of stone, frozen. Then Cole noticed the bloody circle growing on his stomach, and that he had dropped his gun to the floor. He had been hit. Belly wound, no less. Jones dropped hard on his ass, still looking straight ahead.

Molly pointed behind him. Cole turned quickly, fearing the old man had recovered and was trying something. Such was not the case. The first mirror, the big one made by the original Walton, was swirling; blood had spattered onto the glass. Slowly, the blood was absorbed, soaked right into the mirror.

Glancing back, Cole saw Elliot slumped out on the floor. Thomas had shot his own son. Frank cradled his father, screaming, looking from his dead father to the pale twin which was crawling from the mirror against the wall. The blood drained from Frank Walton's face and his screams silenced, even though he continued in terror.

The creature slithered out and stood, focusing on its prey, Franklin. Laying his father's head upon the floor, Frank came to his feet and backed away. Cole knew what was coming. Moving in that jerky manner and with the speed it had, Frank was gone, he just didn't know it yet.

Cole looked back at the large mirror. The swirl seemed to pulse, and then there was something in the center. Then Cole witnessed the strangest of things. The most beautiful blonde he had ever seen in his life appeared and stepped through the frame.

Long golden hair, flowing and shining as if ablaze. Large, firm breasts, hidden only by a rebel flag handkerchief. High-heeled boots which went to her thighs, milky white thighs, Cole noticed. She wore a denim skirt, which barely covered a thing. The woman was sexy, seductive, and truly beautiful. A face of an angel. Then Cole noticed the eyes. As she stepped firmly onto the floor and looked up, her eyes were solid black. Void, they were pits of darkness. Sockets of nothingness. Cole instantly knew who this lovely was.

"Doesn't this look like fun? Hope I'm not late," she said with a booming voice and wry smile.

The old man was right, it was like nothing he had ever heard before. The damn thing smiled a wicked smile and looked toward the other mirror. Cole turned to see Frank Walton vanish. The glass rippled, then went still.

"Here I am again, and there doesn't seem to be a lot of change happening. You killed another family member, Thomas? Guess it doesn't pay to be related to you." The woman laughed.

The sound the woman released was eerie, and it itched Cole to his soul. The shiver which ran up his back was so deep it rattled his very vertebrae.

"Iblis, these people look to destroy our work. They caused me to kill my son. Strike them down, I beg of you." Thomas Walton was on his knees behind the desk.

"Shut up, old man. This is just who I wanted to talk to," Cole said, taking a step forward. "You seem a bit frilly to be the Prince of Darkness. You look more like a streetwalker from Alabama. Guess it fits—a big-titted blonde as the devil. Who would have guessed it?"

"You dare address me? I find your tone to lack the respect that I command." The voice exploded in the office and was not feminine in any way.

"Perhaps those big double D's under your chin don't exactly spell R.E.S.P.E.C.T.," Cole said with a shitty grin.

Molly had moved to his side and gripped his arm. He could see the fear in her eyes. "It's okay, baby. We will be just fine," Cole assured her.

"Bold words, human," the Devil said. "You expected horns and a pitchfork, a tail? Here, maybe this will be more to your liking." The Devil began to change right before their eyes.

The golden hair became streaked with coal black from roots to tip until it was as black as a raven's wing. The large breasts sunk into its chest, and it grew in height. The beast's clothes changed. The face became manly with a day's growth of beard. The she-bitch had become a man, a large man, dressed in a fine dark grey suit. Cole had to admit, the Devil was as handsome as he had been beautiful.

"Strike them down, my lord. They aim to destroy us," Thomas Walton pleaded.

"Nothing can destroy me, slave," Satan said in that humongous voice.

Cole tilted his head and shrugged. "Well, you aren't exactly flying around Heaven anymore, now are you?" Molly squeezed his arm to caution him.

The Devil took a couple of steps into the room, around the desk. He looked at the bodies on the floor and then at Cole. Those blackened sockets were an eerie sight, to be certain. "Ah, you have sass. Weak, pitiful, little man. What do you know? Talking monkey." Satan's words pained Cole's ears.

"Just what I have read. It's never fun to be tossed out of a place, is it? I've been kicked out of a few bars in my day; but kicked out of Heaven..." Cole raised an eyebrow. "Wow, that's got to sting. I kind of get the whole *you're pissed off* angle now. Got some hurt feelings there, do ya?" Cole said with a frown.

The Devil smiled a large, perfect smile, straight white teeth. "Hmm. You have fire in you, I like that. You have no idea of the insult I suffered. I am first, before all things. There was God, then there was me. I shaped the universe and placed every star in the sky. I am the light. The first footprint on this stinking planet was mine. Then, as some kind of afterthought, humans. Expect me to bow to the likes of you—ha! Share my home—ha! Please. I would not have such disrespect and hatred had it not been earned and deserved. You flesh puppets, talking monkeys, placed in Eden all safe and sound. Ha. How easily you fell to temptation, bending to your wants and greed. My stand was righteous and so my power is great. Your fall was shameful, and so you are sheep."

Satan stepped close to Cole, his body so near they almost touched. Cole felt the invasion of personal space but did not move. As if in a whisper but with that impossible booming voice, the Devil continued. "I was not cast from Heaven. Ignorant. My disgust was recognized and my opinion valued. Humans have no right to Heaven. You are your souls. You are weak and easily swayed, vain and stupid, with no real faith, dedication or loyalty. A bargain was struck and I was given a new task. It's so easy." Satan smiled.

Cole smelled the hot breath of the beast and felt his stomach turn. The reek was disgusting, but Cole did not flinch or waver. He stared into the black emptiness of the Devil's eyes and held his faith close to his heart.

Satan nodded toward Thomas Walton. "Look how weak. Cain. Killed his own brother for greed's sake. Now he falls to his knees to me. Man bows to me." The monster grinned an evil grin.

"I am not on my knees," Cole pointed out.

"Not yet. You too want something, I can smell your desperation, monkey. Want has a distinctive scent. I can smell it a mile away. That's how it works, sassy. This is my job. Every day I show my maker how wrong he was to favor the likes of you. Adam, Eve, from the very first of your kind, you have failed." He laughed and stepped back toward the desk.

"You cannot claim the innocent." Molly finally found her voice.

"Ah, it speaks. A tainted soul. I can see your sins; how dare you speak of innocence to me?" The Devil glared with those black eyes at Molly.

"Our son is innocent. Give him back to us," Molly demanded.

Cole turned and gave his wife a strong look. He had not wanted to tip their hand, but now the cat was out of the bag.

"See, now we come to the meat of it. Want. Told you I can smell it. Ah, yes, little Johnny Mason. Found his way into one of my mirrors, did he? That's too bad. Oh, and right in front of you. Bad mommy," the Devil mocked, laughing again.

"Molly, go check on Detective Jones. Leave this to me," Cole said.

The echoes of Satan's laughter lingered in the room, resonating.

"How can you claim people? A boy? These cursed mirrors of yours, it's not right. You have rules, I know you do. You are not free to do whatever you want. So, you tempt people; my son was not tempted."

"You aren't just a sassy monkey, you're smart too. There are rules to our game. You humans are what we play with, like toys. You learned how the mirrors work, not overly complicated. You should already know the wrong of your son." The Devil gave a wide smile.

Cole knew but recognized a baited comment.

"What did little Johnny say?" Satan asked.

"I know what he said, and I know what he would say to you right now. 'Kiss my ass, you ugly son of a bitch,'" Cole baited in return.

"Ugly?!" the Devil roared. "You dare to call me ugly!"

Cole nodded. "That's right. Like a fancy shithouse. Fresh coat of paint don't keep the inside from smelling like shit. The funny thing is, take a look into your precious mirror. There is a man staring back at you. You can take on any image, and you want to look like us, hmm?" Cole sniffed the air. "Hey, I can smell want too. Somebody wishes they were human." He smiled. "You want to be like us, we stupid humans. The favorite, the favored. You were first, we were last, and we all know you save the best for last. Your jealousy is transparent. Call me weak, but I wouldn't want to be you for shit. You have longed to be me since creation. To have a soul, to love, to be loved, to feel joy. All you have is your games, and it's a game you can't win. You will never fill your hunger, your anger. You call humans weak? I stand here and pity you. You are sad and broken, worthless."

Satan walked around the desk to Thomas Walton. He carried a smile but it was sinister, watching Cole as he moved. The Devil motioned for his slave to stand. "I think the smart monkey is trying to get an emotional reaction from me. You have no idea what you have stumbled into. You carry the false notion that somehow you are safe, protected from me. Your confidence is only ignorance."

"Grant me the strength, the power, my lord, I will punish them. Please," Thomas begged. "Allow me to kill them for you. Allow me to prove my worth to you."

"Hush, slave! You bring me to this mess. How long you have reaped the rewards, felt my generosity. Bathed in wealth and good fortune. You failed me. Spread the tale of our agreement, as if to justify your doings."

"But, Iblis. Master. I have been loyal. I have done as you asked of me. Give me the chance, I will remove these people from your presence."

With the back of his left hand, Satan slapped the old man hard across the face, sending him flying over the large walnut desk and crashing into the chair Cole had been sitting in. Blisters formed on the man's cheek, burnt by the touch of the Devil. The beast rounded the desk with speed and grace. The dark angel had a definite quality, but evil; the feeling of doom surrounded him. Just to be near him caused Cole's stomach to turn and his skin to crawl.

"Slave, your payment is due. Time to show sassy monkey reality," the Devil said. "Stand and deliver."

Thomas Walton struggled to his feet. The flesh on his face was burned badly, and his knees shook visibly. The old man swallowed hard as the Devil walked up to face him. With his thumb, forefinger and middle finger, the Devil plunged his hand into Thomas's chest. Cole was not two feet away, but saw no wound or any blood. Pulling his hand back, Satan held what looked to be a large black marshmallow. The old man fell to his hands and knees, heaving. Satan held what was in his hand up so that Cole could see it.

"A blackened soul, my favorite," Satan said and lifted it to his lips. Those straight white teeth were gone, replaced by jagged, pointed teeth and large fangs. He bit into the soul like an apple, chewing, feasting; the Devil devoured his prize. Shoving the rest of it into his mouth hungrily, he made a sound of pleasure.

The creature again focused on the old man still on his hands and knees. Taking a step back, Satan kicked Thomas Walton in the rib cage. The kick was so powerful, Cole heard the bones break on impact. The old man's body flew through the air and smashed the office windows, landing halfway across the factory below.

The sound of shattering glass filled the office as the Devil turned and faced Cole. "Afraid yet?" Satan raised an eyebrow and wiped his mouth with his sleeve. "Seems you have grown quiet. Nothing smart to say?"

Cole looked around and shrugged. "Well, if you didn't bring enough for the whole class... Rude. Oh, by the way, you have a little bit of evil soul right in the corner of your mouth." Cole motioned.

Satan laughed with that booming voice. "That's sassy. I like that. Now, why don't we talk? Talk seriously. You want your little boy back. Little Johnny. I can give you that. A snap of my fingers and all is right with the world." He gave a sinister smile. The Devil moved to Cole's right. He moving like a snake, smooth and effortlessly. "Let me help you. Be the big hero. Sacrifice yourself for love." Satan leaned in close. "Let your wife do it. She already feels guilty, for losing him. You're a smart monkey. Let her give up her soul. No worries for you. I'll talk her into it, easy. She is weak, she is a woman. I've got some experience with this. Eve turned so quick, easy. Have to admit, it wasn't even a challenge," the Devil whispered to Cole and then leaned back, smiling with those pearly whites, giving a slow and purposeful wink.

Cole thought of the saying, 'the cat who ate the canary.' The evil radiated from the beast and made him shudder. "You have nothing for us. I'll get my son back. You and your bag of tricks, your games. I said I pity you. You've shown your true colors. You are the beast and my pity is gone. Thanks for stopping by. You had your dinner, now beat it. Soup kitchen is closed. You prey on the weak, the needy, and the stupid. Look into my eyes, fallen angel. This is a man, and I am telling you to be gone."

"How dare you!" Satan's voice exploded and rattled the very walls.

Cole stepped forward, face to face with Satan. "I am man. You are not. My standing is not in question; you are the one who hides in the shadows. Fallen from grace. Your jealousy and pride; you are shamed, not me."

"You do not know your place, human! I can see your sin too. You are already mine," the Devil stated in the most evil voice known.

"I don't think so. You lie, cheat, try to play lawyer ball with people's souls, this technicality or that. I'm not buying. You can go now, we have other things to attend to."

"You think that you can order me? Talk down to me? Hmm... Well, we shall see what fabric you are made of." Satan stepped around Cole.

Cole moved toward Molly, who was still tending to Detective Jones. The man's belly wound was bloody and leaking onto the floor. She was on her knees and had his head propped up.

The Devil passed right by them and walked to the door. Cole stood between Satan and Molly, watching his every move. He turned and looked at Cole with those black, lifeless sockets, holding up his hand. Cole watched as his fingernails grew. Satan turned and jabbed his fingertips into the door and jerked his hand away, leaving the nails embedded in the dark wood.

Satan turned again and showed Cole his fingernails grown long once again, like claws. As he plunged his fingers into the door once more, Cole saw that he was driving them from the door into the frame.

"No escape for you, sassy monkey," the Devil said, nailing the door closed again. He laughed his booming laugh, hurting everyone's ears. Then he picked up the duffel bag Cole had brought. "I can be clever too." He raised an eyebrow. "So, what do we have here?" he said, opening the bag.

The Devil drew out a flare, pulled the pin, and lit the stick. With a flash, the flare ignited and red-hot flames shot forth. Smoke and the stink of sulfur filled the room. A wide wicked smile filled the Devil's face. "Smells like home." He laughed.

Casually the walking beast tossed the flare across the office, out through the broken windows he had sent Thomas Walton flying through. "You are right, it is time for me to go. So sorry I can't stay and watch you burn, we can talk about it later. I have a prior engagement. How I would enjoy smelling your wife burn, but work calls. You are a sassy one. Stay strong, and you might want to say a little prayer. Never too late, right? I'll be seeing you real soon." Satan laughed so loud it sounded like the roar of a thousand lions.

He slithered around the walnut desk, then paused. "If you do get to Heaven, mention my name. You'll get a good seat. Fools." He looked Cole in the eye. "Last chance, monkey. Let's make a deal." He raised an eyebrow. "Well, how about one last zinger for the road? Come on, sassy."

Cole watched as the Devil's feet floated off the floor and his body moved toward the mirror. Cole flipped him the bird and shook his head.

"Oh, come now, you can do better than that. You have been so brave. Don't lose that spunk now, monkey boy."

Cole had plenty of comments running through his mind, but he wasn't going to give the Devil the satisfaction. He just smiled and moved to the broken window, looking out at the factory. The flare had done exactly what he had intended it to do. The thermite was raging and the flames were growing high, quickly. The fire was headed for the tank furnaces and dread filled Cole's heart. Looking back, he watched as the Devil stepped into the mirror and vanished, his laughter lingering.

CHAPTER 28

G et Jones away from the windows, back behind the desk," Cole told Molly. Running to the door, Cole examined what the Devil had done. Indeed, he had nailed the door closed with his fingernails. Pulling the Bowie knife from his belt, he tried to pick away at them, but they were like stone. He moved to the wood of the frame and tried to pry them loose. The nails were so deep. He had driven them into the very walls. Cole knew they didn't have time to free themselves.

Stepping back, Cole put his heel to the door, kicking hard, but the wood was solid and sturdy. He would have struggled to get through the damn thing with a chainsaw. The sound of fire filled Cole's ears, coming from the broken windows— pops and cracks, along with the whoosh of flame. The smell of smoke and a growing heat filled his nose.

Molly was dragging Jones across the floor, his moans of pain now replacing the faint sounds of the Devil's laughter. Cole pushed the Bowie knife back into its sheath and surveyed the room. Searching the office for something, anything.

"What are we going to do?" Molly yelled over the growing roar coming from downstairs.

Cole could hear the panic in his wife's voice. He too was becoming alarmed, but he tried to keep his head. He had to do something. His plan had gone to shit, a real backfire. Of course, he had not expected to face down the Devil himself. Who plans for that? Molly and Detective Jones were both looking at him with fear in their eyes. He scanned the room again, looking for any opening.

Jones's gun was on the floor, next to the blood which had left his body. Cole had an idea. He picked it up, turned and fired the pistol at the center of the door, shooting and shooting until the gun emptied and the slide was locked open.

"What the hell are you doing?" Molly yelled.

"Can't open the door, maybe we can go through it." He tossed the gun on the floor, pulled the big knife from his belt and went to stabbing at the bullet holes. The opening didn't have to be large, just enough to squeeze out of. Cole worked feverishly, knowing time was not on his side. Strike after strike, pulling the splinters from the old, thick, wood door, Cole hurried to make their escape. Smoke was rolling in the broken widow and the temperature of the room had increased dramatically. Cole used his fists, the lead gloves protecting his knuckles, giving his blows power. Stepping back, he again kicked at the door, stomping hard. Finally, his boot smashed through. The hole was just big enough to get his head through.

Cole turned, ready to tell Molly to come on, when he heard the whooshing sound. It was as if the air had caught fire and then there was the explosion. The windows shattered in unison. The force of the blast picked up Cole and slammed him against the wall. Glass and wood, metal and fire filled the room. One of the tank furnaces had blown.

Perhaps three seconds passed; it was hard for Cole to really have any sense of the moments between one explosion and the other furnace erupting. The sound was deafening, and the force of the blast shook the whole building. The office ceiling danced with flames as the natural gas burned and searched for its own escape. The heat was intense, Cole could feel his face burning. Plaster fell from the ceiling and the edges of the windows burned.

Then the fire seemed to draw back, as if the building inhaled. Cole rolled onto his side and looked around. He was deaf, the ringing in his ears constant. Faintly, he heard other explosions, or felt them, he couldn't be certain. Shaking his head in an attempt to clear his scrambled mind, he moved to his hands and knees. He tried to collect himself, thinking how glad he was he had been wrong about the furnaces. He had thought they would bring down the whole building. Cole tried to stand, but he was shaky. The blast had really rattled him, and his senses were fried.

Along the factory wall of windows, he could see flames licking into the room through holes in the glass. The office was rubble, charred and burning areas, smoke everywhere, parts of the ceiling missing. "We have to get out of here!" Cole yelled.

He stumbled over to Jones and Molly, but he could tell they couldn't hear him; the blast had deafened them all. Cole looked at the hole he had made in the door, but there were flames beyond. The thermite he had poured in the hallway had ignited, and now, there was no escape.

They were trapped. Any route of escape was now aflame. He had imprisoned himself and his wife in a fiery tomb. Unintentionally, he had sealed their fates. He had killed them.

Molly reached out and touched his shoulder. She was saying something, and coughing because of the thick smoke. "What do we do?"

Cole lowered his eyes and shook his head.

Detective Shirley Jones gripped Cole's arm. Watching his lips, a bit of blood at the corners, Cole tried to make out what he was saying. "You need to save your son. I'm sorry for how I acted. Forgive me. You are good people. I have been jaded far too long. Use the mirror. I'll open it for you."

Cole looked over. Miraculously, the mirror Molly had leaned against the wall was intact, looking clean and clear as new. The reflection showed the devastation of the office and his own eyes staring back at him.

"You can't. Those things will take you," Molly said.

Jones took Molly's hand and gave a weak smile. "I am already dead. Just a matter of when and how."

Cole could see the tears swell in Molly's eyes. She was a compassionate human being. Emotional and caring, even for a stranger. Her heart was a big part of why Cole loved her as much as he did.

Cole felt admiration for the detective and what he was suggesting. The man was willing to sacrifice himself to give them a chance.

The keg of thermite in the Hall of Mirrors exploded and shook the building.

"Hurry, there is no time," Jones said. "No time to delay or debate. You need to go. Get ready."

Cole scanned the room one more time as Molly gave Jones a hug. The mirror the Devil had come from, the first mirror made in this factory, still stood in pristine condition. He picked up a lamp that had fallen from the walnut desk and heaved it at the mirror. He could see his action in the reflection, and as the lamp flew through the air, he saw his own smile.

The glass fractured, shattering into a million pieces. Cole thought of the old wives' tale of seven years bad luck, but figured his luck couldn't get much worse. Then Cole thought that the Devil would never enter this world through that door ever again. That particular mirror had cast its last image.

Cole moved to his wife's side and took her hand. They walked to the mirror they had brought in. Cole gave Shirley Jones a respectful nod, and waited.

The heat from the fire in the factory was intense. The smoke was thick and visibility was bad. Yet, Cole could see the detective on the floor, saw his mouth make the words. Cole looked at the mirror; the reflection of the room was chaos, but it changed, got even worse. The surface of the glass liquefied, and the creature began to emerge.

"Once it is out, you go in. Got it?" Cole said to Molly.

"What about you?" she cried.

"I'll be right behind you," Cole screamed over the roar of the fire.

The creature was out, standing, beginning its walk toward Jones. Molly stepped closer to the mirror and looked at Cole. He nodded for her to go ahead. She stepped her foot into the glass; it moved like water, like dipping her toe in a pool. Bending to fit, Molly stepped inside. As if she walked behind a waterfall, Cole struggled to make out her figure. Then her head popped back through and her hand waved him inside. Cole held up his index finger, to signal her to wait.

Turning, he pulled the machete from his hip and advanced on the creature from behind. It had almost reached Detective Jones. Cole pulled the large blade back and swung as hard as he could. With one heavy swipe, Cole cleaved the head off the shoulders of the beast. It bounced and rolled across the floor. Cole couldn't help but think of how many movies he had seen that happen in and how crazy it had just been to have done it for real. No blood squirting or anything like that; in fact, the body started grabbing for its head.

Cole pulled back and took another swipe, this one at the knee. The creature's body toppled over as it lost its leg. "Oh, no you don't, you son of a bitch," Cole told the dismembered creature. He kicked the body hard and it flopped over. He snatched up the head, and the damn thing snapped at him. Cole stepped closer to the mirror. Holding the head from the side, he drop-kicked it like a football, punting the head through the broken windows and out into the burning factory.

As Cole stepped into the mirror, he gave a last look at Jones. The cop was giving him a thumbs-up sign. Cole nodded and winked, then ducked into the mirror and was gone.

Jones watched as Cole Mason vanished into the liquid. He smiled as he thought of the happenings over the last couple days. The creature that had come for him was lost without its head, crawling around and feeling for anything. The flames were at the door, in the window, and the smoke gagged Jones. He tried to stay low to the floor and take a breath, but he choked nonetheless.

Jones could feel his world fading. He could only hope that he had done enough. He began to pray silently, not wanting to invite another monster from the mirror. The pain in his wound was now gone. He could tell that death was close. His body struggled, fought to live, but his spirit was finished. He was done. With a gasp, he sucked in his last breath and his heart finally stopped. As he lay there, eyes wide open, the room became engulfed in flames, then was overtaken: the walnut desk, the walls and floor, along with the bodies of the dead were all burning.

Tommy Walton got into the Masons' rental car and put the key into the ignition. A large explosion shook the ground, and he could see dark black smoke billow out of the factory. He stared out at the building. The thick cloud floated skyward, and he could see that a chunk of the building was missing. Flames licked out of the hole. Tommy shook his head in disbelief. He had just been right there.

Sitting there in shock, he wasn't sure what he should do. Something had obviously gone very wrong and now the whole building seemed to be in flames. No one could survive that. Another explosion, and a fresh, large plume belched forth into the sky. Tommy's heart raced and his bowels turned. Getting out of the Masons' car, he ran to his own.

Sweating and out of breath, the young man climbed behind the wheel of his car and fired the engine. Squealing the tires, he made haste to get away from the scene. His only thought was to go home and pretend he had never been there. As he drove, he pulled out his cell phone and called the receptionist. He had to cover his bases, and she knew all about what had happened. They needed to have the same story. She answered, and Tommy talked fast. He explained about the fire, and that they were to say they had left together and knew nothing about any of it. She agreed.

Doris Lamb sat in front of a computer screen typing out the information about the mirrors, the company, the creatures and how it all worked. She sipped her coffee and read over what she had written. She went on to explain the history and the actions Cole Mason and his wife had taken. She made certain to paint them in a heroic light.

Keeping her eye on the clock, knowing she had a very specific time to send the email, she worked and drank her coffee, waiting. She couldn't help but wonder how things were going. Doris liked the Masons and sympathized about their child. What a crazy situation to find yourself in, to try and deal with and explain. The loss of a child was so horrifying, but then to have to explain and be questioned, doubted and accused? Cole was a good man, and now he was wanted by police. She shook her head, wondering how it would all work out.

She continued to type, going over the details of what they had learned. The time was growing closer. She was growing more nervous, anxious for some news. She wanted to see Cole and Molly walk in with their little boy in their arms; the longer she waited, the deeper her dread. She ordered another coffee, though she knew it was not going to help with her nerves. Then she began to send the message.

She had collected the email addresses for the different groups where she was planning to send the information. She watched the clock; it was almost time. The girl brought her coffee, and the aroma was strong. Doris looked around. None of these people had a clue at the evil which lurked in their world. This had gone on since before World War II, and the public was oblivious. She was going to change that.

Seven thirty; Doris began to send emails. Walton Mirrors was first. She felt in her heart that she was fighting evil, and that only by shining a light on it, the light of truth, could it be vanquished. News organizations, law enforcement, police, FBI, CIA, and the National Security Agency, along with the Department of Defense and the White House. She wanted as many people as she could to know.

As each moment ticked by, Doris couldn't help but worry. Sipping her coffee, she looked at the young people around her. What an amazing world they lived in. The computer age, communication and information flowing around the globe in a matter of minutes. Five hundred years ago, the world knew nothing of this entire continent. Now they could view the world from space. Truly amazing.

Doris began to ponder many things, allowing her mind to wander. Here she was, a book person, devoted to knowledge and the written word, a librarian. Yet, the world was changing. Few people came to the library to check out books anymore. The passion to find a lost treasure, a volume that speaks to your soul, the story you just can't put down, that you long for it never to end. She could remember as a little girl walking into the library with all those books. Exploring the rows, understanding the work and experience that it took to create those novels.

How she enjoyed the different images, smells, feelings from all those books. Some were so very plain; others with beautiful artwork or pictures. Some were old and dusty, with mildew on the pages; others new and crisp, the spines never broken. The right book could make you laugh or cry, happy or sad, fill you with pride or sorrow. Pictures painted with words. Doris knew that the written word was what made human beings civilized. From the Egyptians to the Constitution, history was passed down page by page.

Doris was proud of what she did, what she was, proud of her library. An entire building devoted to learning and her passion, built with bricks of words. The modern people, the computer screens; the words were there but not to stay. They existed like a whisper on the wind, heard only for a moment and then gone. A generation without substance, no solid foundation, only speed, convenience, and instant gratification. The patience and stillness to curl up with a good book was gone, treasured only by a few. A society which loses its literature loses its soul.

It was now eight o'clock and her dread increased. No arrival, no word, nothing. She couldn't help but think something was wrong. Worry had settled in her bones. Another half an hour passed. She became more and more anxious. Finally, she had to figure out what to do next. Going to the phone, Doris hesitantly called the Columbus police department's non-emergency number. Cole was a wanted man and she did not want to hinder his plan, but an hour had gone, and Doris just knew his plan had taken a bad turn.

When the operator came on the line, Doris explained who she was, what the situation was, and requested that police be sent to the Walton Mirror factory. The operator was polite and assured her that help would be sent. She told

Doris to stay where she was, that a car would come to take her statement.

Not five minutes later, a police cruiser pulled up, lights flashing and siren blaring. She had not expected such a speedy response, or such a loud one. She looked out the window as the car screeched to a halt. Another cruiser zoomed in, followed by another. The police exited their cars with guns drawn, at the ready. They made their assault on the coffee shop as if attacking it, covering one another as they moved. Doris felt alarmed at the response, her heart thundering in her chest.

She advanced toward the police slowly, with her hands raised. "I am the one who called. I am Doris Lamb," she told them. The police ordered her to turn and put her hands on her head. They cuffed her and asked where Cole Mason was. Doris told them he had gone to the factory. They hurried her outside and into one of the cruisers. An officer got in and they pulled out of the parking lot at speed. Doris was afraid; she had never been in the back of a police car, or in cuffs. She felt very small and had no idea what was ahead.

Ernest Weber walked in the front doors of the Star Bird Inn. The police had kept him and questioned him for over twelve hours. First detectives, and then the FBI. What did he know? Where had the Masons gone? Had he seen the death of Detective Jerkowski? They had made him feel as if he had done something wrong, as if he were guilty of something or complicit in some crime. Cops were always that way, pushy and accusative. They applied pressure using threats and fear, good cop/bad cop, isolation and lies. Authority always went about it the same way: Romans, Spanish, English, Nazis, cops.

Ernest locked the front doors behind him. His beautiful hotel was closed. What a terrible mess had come; he had put cursed mirrors in his hotel and brought evil into his home. He could only hope that Mr. Mason had found his answers, found a way to retrieve his son. He walked around the front desk and back to his office. Ernest couldn't help feeling a sense of responsibility for what had happened. This was his hotel, and that family had come here on vacation. They didn't deserve what had happened.

He picked up a bat he kept next to the door for protection and walked back around the front desk. Ernest remembered the smile of the little boy, how he had wanted to go swimming in his pool and was so excited. He had purchased so many of these damn mirrors. They were all over his hotel. He had thought he had gotten a good deal, but what he got was wrong, was evil.

Ernest stood in the lobby, looking at his own reflection in the large mirror on the wall. He would do his part to ensure nothing like this ever happened again. Swinging the bat at his own image in the glass, he shattered the mirror. Shining glass rained to the floor. Ernest moved on into the bar. Sounds of glass breaking filled the emptiness of the hotel. Swing after swing, and Ernest felt better with every mirror he destroyed.

The old wives' tale of seven years bad luck for breaking a mirror came to his mind. He smiled to himself in the women's bathroom mirror as he smashed it to bits. The bad luck had already come. If the tale was true, after this day he would have bad luck for a hundred hundred years. He did not fear such reprisal. What he was ridding his hotel of was evil, demons, bad. He didn't see his actions as destruction, more of an exorcism.

Floor to floor, room to room, Ernest made his way, bat in hand, smashing every mirror in his hotel. Down each hallway, he swung the wooden Louisville Slugger as he passed each mirror hanging from the walls.

It wasn't until the fourth floor that Ernest felt an eerie chill. The creatures had exited these mirrors. They had used these mirrors to claim a man, the big detective.

He gripped the bat with both hands and swung hard at the first mirror, striking it with such force that he broke the plaster of the wall behind it. Ernest could feel his efforts in his arms and shoulders. He had avoided such labor since his days as a younger man. He entered and smashed the mirrors in the first ten rooms with little thought and no hesitation. He had found a good rhythm from the other three floors, but now he found himself at the door of room 411.

Sliding his master key into the lock, Ernest pushed the door wide open. The Masons' bags were still on the floor, just as they had left them. The old hotel owner felt very uneasy as he entered the room. He could still see the little boy's smiling face in his mind's eye. Stepping into the room, he looked around. How could this have happened? He poked the bat into the mirror above the dresser, and the shards of glass fell onto the wood. Then he focused on the bathroom.

He stood there, looking at his reflection in the bathroom mirror propped up against the wall. He couldn't help but think of all the time and effort, the care he had put into his hotel. Ernest knew why: he loved his wife, and the hotel was a reflection of that love. She was so lovely to him, so his hotel had to be beautiful. She was classy and so too was his hotel. The mirrors enraged him for disgracing her memory, her image which was the Star Bird.

Ernest pulled the bat back, ready to give a full swing through the cursed mirror, then stopped. *What if this is the boy's only exit, his only way out?* he thought. He could not destroy the only chance the boy had. He lowered the bat. Ernest hoped that Mr. Mason had found the key, that somewhere, the Masons were all together again. But he could not risk the chance. He set the bat on the sink and picked up the mirror.

He carried it out of the bathroom, back to the elevator, down through the lobby, through the kitchen, and into the basement, where they kept dry goods and extra whatnots. He had thought of turning it into a laundry at some point, but it needed a lot of work. He had spent a lot of money, and his nest egg was getting smaller by the day. The basement had an old root cellar and that's where Ernest put the mirror. No one went in there; it was empty, with dirt walls and a locked door.

Ernest promised himself he would come down once a day to knock on the cellar door, just in case. Honestly, he didn't like the thought of even one of those mirrors being in his hotel, but as he leaned on the locked door, he reassured himself that at least it was locked up.

Ernest Weber headed back up to room 411. He had many more mirrors to break, and he didn't want to wait another minute.

CHAPTER 29

It was six days after the factory fire.

Tommy Walton received a call from investigators to come to the factory. He had already been questioned by police, but that was right after everything. He had stuck to his story, and the receptionist had confirmed it. Now almost a week later, Tommy was nervous to come down and answer any further questions.

Police, the fire department and the FBI were all there and all wanted to talk with him. The factory had burned to the foundation. The fire department and arson investigator said they had found some bones, but the blaze was so hot, any identification would be impossible. The investigator was actually surprised they had found anything at all.

The police detective acknowledged that there were no witnesses. In that neighborhood, Tommy wasn't surprised. The detective asked who was there when he had left; the same questions he had been asked and had answered that first night. They were trying to figure it all out, but Tommy wanted nothing to do with any of it. He may have been young, but he wasn't stupid. He kept his answers short and vague.

He told them again that his great-grandfather, grandfather, and father were all there when he left. He was no actor, but he played the role well enough. A well-dressed woman joined the conversation, asking about the chemicals. Tommy explained that everything was always locked and double checked. "Safety first," he told them with a smile.

The woman was no cop or fire person; his questioning look made her introduce herself. She was from the insurance company. She represented the money. Tommy didn't want to seem eager. He told them how he was sure his family had been killed in the fire, since he hadn't heard from any of them and some crazy man had been placed there.

The FBI man produced a driver's license photo of the man who had caught him with the receptionist. The Fed asked if he had seen this man before. Tommy gave them the story of how he had come in asking about mirrors and how they were made. Said how he even gave the guy a tour of the factory, because he thought the man was a potential customer. Again, putting on an act, getting upset. He asked the FBI man if that was the man who killed his family.

The Feds kept rather tight-lipped, simply saying something about an open investigation. He did say the man in question was wanted in connection with other serious crimes, and that this company appeared to be part of his obsession. The police detective offered up that the man was on the run for killing two police officers. The FBI agent asked if there was any more Tommy could remember. Tommy again didn't want to be any more involved than need be and said nothing more.

The well-dressed woman took Tommy by the arm and walked him away from the group. She explained that her company carried the insurance on the factory, as well as the life insurance policies on his family. Once the official cause of death was determined and certified, he would become a very rich man. He was the sole living beneficiary, and the policies covered arson and accidental death, which doubled the policy. Murder fell under this clause, so Tommy was looking at multiple millions of dollars.

Doris Lamb awoke strapped to a bed. Everything she could see was white. The walls, the ceiling, the sheets, all bright white. Her head felt like lead, thick and heavy, dull. After her eyes focused, she followed the tube which was taped to her arm up to a plastic bag hanging from a metal pole. She tried to pull her arm up, and could now see the restraints. The brown leather stood out in all the white, the buckles cinched around her wrists and ankles. She searched her memory for what had happened, where she was, how she came to be in such straits.

The police had taken her into custody, and she had been questioned by detectives for hours. They were trying to determine her involvement with Cole and the mirrors. Other men came, all of them tie-wearing slick-talkers. They had her emails, and questioned if she was kidnapped or planned the whole thing. At some point they told her about the fire and said Cole was most likely dead. A casualty of his misdeeds, they had said.

Doris tried to defend Cole, giving his reasons for his actions. She pointed to the emails and expressed the genuine nature and factual essence of what was said. They didn't believe her, didn't want to hear any tall tales of demons or evil. The attitude of the detectives was less than understanding or cooperative.

Then the FBI showed up. Same suit-and-tie types, just nicer cheap suits. They seemed to know everything. Their questions were different than those of the detectives; they didn't seem to care so much about Cole. They wanted to know where she had gotten the information about the mirrors.

At some point the FBI had a doctor come in to check on her. She remembered the man didn't seem like a real doctor; he didn't have a caring feeling to him. A doctor usually carries a compassionate thread in their being, yet this man had no such fiber. He asked about the mirrors as he examined her. He asked whether she believed creatures could come out and take people. He asked about evil, and the things she mentioned in her email.

He was leading her down a path she did not want to go. She remembered being very uncomfortable and becoming irritated. She remembered becoming vocal, and that's when he called in the FBI guys and they gave her a shot. She had struggled, screamed for help, for a lawyer, but they gave it to her anyway and her world faded away.

Now she found herself strapped to a bed. A nurse entered her room, dressed in all white. Doris had never been a fan of white, and this place overdid it by far.

"You're awake. Good. How do you feel?" the nurse asked.

"Where am I?" Doris demanded.

The nurse smiled a generic smile. "You are in a hospital. You are safe, hon." She spoke in a very calm tone.

"Where?" Doris repeated.

Another smile. "You're in Washington," she said with a tilt of her head.

Doris looked at the woman, puzzled. The stupid little white hat on her head, the gold name tag. "Washington State?"

"No, sweetie, DC," the nurse answered.

"DC!? Why am I tied to this bed? What kind of hospital is this? Who brought me here?" Doris became more agitated, the stress audible in her voice.

The nurse patted Doris on the leg. "Stay calm. We had to put the restraints on because when you came in, well, you were a little combative. You are here for observation. You need some help, hon. You have been through a trauma and become delirious. Are you feeling better? No more monsters?"

Doris Lamb began to put the picture together. This was a nut house; they thought that she was crazy. Why would they bring her to Washington, DC?

In walked two men, one of whom she recognized from the police station. He was an FBI agent. The other man had on a lab coat, and must be the doctor. They excused the nurse and advanced to the sides of Doris's bed.

"Awake finally, hm?" the man in the lab coat said.

"I would like to speak with my attorney. You can't just keep me here, like this," Doris said with true irritation.

"You are here to stay, Doris. Can't have you out in the world spreading rumors, frightening the good people of the nation. Stirring the pot," the FBI agent said, looking Doris in the eye.

The doctor added, "We're afraid you are paranoid, delusional, a danger to yourself and to others. No lawyers, no phones; we have a court order from a judge, and you are now under our care. Doris, you might as well get comfortable and forget all that nonsense. Stay calm and quiet and your time here will be smooth. Fight with us, and you will stay in a medicated haze for the rest of your life." The doctor in the lab coat smiled.

"You want the secret for yourselves, is that it? Lock me away in here and label me crazy. Close the door on the truth."

The agent nodded. "No family, no real friends, just a small-town librarian. No one is even going to notice you're gone. It's the big picture, Doris. Sorry. We already sent in a lovely young woman to replace you at your library."

Ernest Weber sat in his room watching the news. The top story covered Cole Mason and his wife. The picture they painted was not a pretty one. They listed charges of killing two police officers, perhaps a third, and three prominent businessmen, as well as arson, kidnapping, fleeing apprehension. The anchorman said authorities believed Mason to be dead, along with his wife and son. Authorities were withholding details because the case was still active and open.

Ernest clicked off the television set in disgust. Fifteen seconds of nothing, bullshit and lies, deception. None of what was said was the man he knew. A man dedicated to finding his son. Not a word about the mirrors, or the factory being makers of evil. Perhaps he should invite the news people down, give the public a real show. He could imagine the anchorman with his perfect hair and bleached teeth, trying to fight off one of those creatures. "Talk about action news," Ernest said to himself.

"Excuse me?" a voice said, startling Ernest.

"How did you get in here? We are closed. We have been closed for a week." Ernest turned to see two men.

"FBI, sir. I'm Agent Smith. We have a few follow-up questions with regard to the Mason case. The man that stayed here with his family." The man flashed an identification.

"I know who Cole Mason is. You still haven't answered my question: how did you get in here? The doors are locked."

"We can see that you've been doing some redecorating. A lot of broken glass. They say to break a mirror is seven years bad luck." The other agent looked around the lobby.

Ernest was getting a strange feeling from the two men. He knew he had locked the door, and Feds don't break and enter. "Yeah, well... What questions did you have? As you can see, I have a lot of cleaning up to do."

"We are curious about these mirrors," the second agent said. "Are they all destroyed? We were sent down to investigate some rather interesting claims, involving these mirrors."

Bells and whistles sounded in Ernest's mind. Something was amiss. These two were not FBI, or at least not local field agents. This load of crap they were pushing was even less believable than they were. Ernest could tell these two were up to no good. "Will the two of you excuse me for just a second? I have something on in the kitchen and I don't want it to burn. Be right back."

"It will wait. Answer the question," Agent Smith softly demanded.

Ernest eyed the two men and shook his head. "So, that's it then, is it? 'Agent Smith, FBI'? Please, the two of you won't win any awards for acting. I know bullshit when I hear it. I broke all the mirrors. I destroyed them. Whatever you are looking for is gone. Breaking in here, into my hotel. There is nothing left. So, beat it. Best you fellas leave those mirrors alone. You really don't want to deal with what's on the other side."

"How old are you, Pops?" Agent Smith asked.

"I am sixty-two. Why, you writing a book?" Ernest returned.

The man in the suit shook his head. "Not a book, your obituary." He grabbed hold of Ernest and put his arm around the old man's neck, then pulled a syringe from his pocket.

Ernest struggled to get free, clawing at the man's arm choking him. He wiggled, squirmed, and twisted, stomping on the man's feet and scratching at him.

"Hold him. Hold him still. We don't want to leave a bruise."

The agent behind him kicked out his feet from under him and sent Ernest to the ground. He fell flat on his back with the agent holding his shoulders, but at least Ernest could breathe again.

"You sons of bitches. What the hell is this? Kill an old man. FBI, my ass," Ernest said, still trying to fight.

Agent Smith straddled Ernest and pushed his arm out flat on the floor. The other man quickly stuck the needle into his arm and plunged it, injecting Ernest.

Both men stood and looked down at Ernest Weber.

As he lay there on his back, his chest grew tight and his left arm went numb. He was having trouble breathing, he began to gasp. He was having a heart attack. They had injected something into him, to kill him, something to cause a heart attack. They were making this look like natural causes. He looked up at the men, feeling the darkness of death folding over him, covering him, encompassing him.

They just stood there, waiting, watching him. Ernest felt the pain in his chest spike, like a coiled snake crushing his heart. Then, it stopped and he felt the last beat. It was the final moment, the threshold. He could still see, but it was as if someone was dimming the lights. He was fading away. He couldn't take a breath, he couldn't move, he couldn't even blink. His final thought was of his birth, and how none of us ever really know the beginning, a memory none of us keep. Our first breath. What a significant moment and none of us are truly aware.

How very aware he was now, in this final moment. The end of his life had not eluded him. He was present for his death.

Ernest Weber died of a heart attack on the floor of the Star Bird Inn, so the paper would say.

CHAPTER 30

ix months after the factory fire.
Tommy Walton, or as he was now calling himself, Thomas Walton, pulled up in his brand-new silver Corvette. The insurance money had come through and tomorrow was the ribbon-cutting on the brand-new factory. Young Thomas Walton had decided to relocate the factory. The old neighborhood was less than nice and not safe, so a fresh start seemed appropriate. He had decided to invest the money back into the business; he knew the ins and outs of the mirror business and he knew the history.

The insurance on the factory more than covered the cost of building and equipping a new facility. Great-grandpa had over-insured; he must have feared someone would eventually come to call. The life insurance was the same, and he had received triple because of the murder. Looking at his new factory, Tommy smiled. The large symbol on the side of the building, which he had thought tacky for so many years, now was all his.

XX

Walton Mirrors meant just him now. Sole owner of a multi-million-dollar business. The new factory, shiny and clean, exactly as he had commissioned it to be. Four large tank furnaces, enclosed in fire-resistant walls, float tanks and cutting areas for each tank. The factory was five times larger than the original. He had innovations come to him. He planned to cover some mirrors with a thin transparent layer of plexiglass for safety. Shatterproof, while maintaining quality of image.

He thought of allowing a minimal space between the mirror and the plexi and inserting phosphorus gas. By running an electrical current through the gas, you could get a fluorescent light. It would be a mirror which illuminates a room, or has a light built into it. The idea had some ironing out, but Tommy could see it as a wave of the future. No more nightlights in the bathroom. A soft blue glow from his mirror would light your way.

He thought of a glow-in-the-dark type of substance which could light a room. Applying it to windows, they could gain energy by day and glow at night. He also thought of mirrored windows for your home. You could see out but no one could see in. Thomas was now the boss, and it excited him. Orders had already been rolling in, the phones and computer had anxious customers waiting. All he had to do was open the doors.

He wanted a Walton Mirror in every home in the world. As he sat behind his large glass desk, he thought about his family. He thought about the story, the deal with the Devil. He hadn't seen any devil, and business was better than ever. Big contracts lay in the future, and this was his doing, not anyone or anything else.

Still, Tommy worried about the man who had come and burned the place to the foundation. He believed the stories; he had come out of nowhere. He didn't want some nut destroying his factory. He took precautions, safety, security, every instance he could think of. He did not want to look a gift horse in the mouth, so questioning things took a back seat. He was about to be richer than he had already become. Devil or no, money talks.

The nurse in her all-white uniform entered Doris Lamb's room. Her white shoes squeaked on the well-polished floor as she walked. She carried a tray of food; it was time for Doris Lamb's feeding. Doris sat in a wheelchair, a strap around her belly to keep her from falling out. Her head was cocked to one side and her eyes were unfocused, just staring off into nothing. Her hair had begun to grow back, but the woman still looked like she had just joined the army. The stubble was still very short and could not hide the scar.

The doctor had tried medication, increased dosages, varied treatments. The nurse had had to administer them, even though Doris Lamb didn't seem crazy to her. It was not her place to question the doctor. Many patients didn't want to take their medications. Doris had begged her, but the nurse watched as the old woman slipped deeper and deeper into confusion and aggressive behavior. The nurse knew something was wrong, but insanity didn't seem to be the issue, even if her stories seemed crazy.

The doctor moved onto electroshock therapy. The nurse had to assist, and she hated it. She had to strap the almost coma-like woman into a chair, put a rubber mouthpiece in her mouth, attach the harness to her head and watch as the doctor attached electrodes to her temples. Running electricity through a person's brain is monstrous. Watching the old woman convulse, shake and flop, as the voltage pulsed through her. It was medieval.

She watched as each jolt caused the woman to spit, grip the chair, wet herself and even defecate. The treatment seemed more like torture than anything else. She had seen far worse patients not be treated in such fashion. It was when she was ordered to prepare Doris for surgery that she had to speak up. She approached the Chief of Medicine about Doris Lamb's treatment.

As with all doctors and bosses, they did not like to be questioned, especially by their subordinates. The chief marched her right back to the doctor and they both proceeded to read her the riot act. The dressing-down was serious and direct, with a warning of her to do her job or she would not have a job, anywhere. They spoke of insubordination and disrespect.

The nurse had gone back and shaved Doris's head. The lobotomy was an extreme measure by any standard. The doctor removed Doris Lamb's frontal lobe, cutting away part of her brain. Vegetablized her. The poor woman now couldn't walk, talk, feed herself, or use the bathroom. Doris Lamb was alive, but who she had been was gone. She was only a shell of a human now. No memories, no personality, no thoughts. Having a heartbeat may technically determine life, but Doris Lamb was dead to the world, dead within herself. She had been a woman, now she was a turnip.

The Star Bird Inn had gone up on auction soon after the death of owner/ operator Ernest Weber. Victim of a massive heart attack, the man had passed in the hotel he loved and cared for. The new owners were a wealthy couple from New England, looking to invest their money and retire with an income. The Star Bird had a class and potential the couple saw immediately.

Touring their purchase, the couple couldn't help but question why all the mirrors had been broken. They thought perhaps kids, but nothing else was messed up. No spray paint or beer cans, and the windows hadn't been broken. Just every mirror, in every room, every bathroom, all the hallways. It was very puzzling, but the couple could imagine the look with all the mirrors. Most of the frames still hung in place.

The rooms were simple but elegant, and the couple had visions of making the hotel more an upper-class type of place. A known chef, a wine cellar, a spa, all top quality. They wanted the hotel to draw clients by its service and standards of care and detail. They knew it would take some doing and some investment, but the fact that the previous owner had died and not gone out of business was a good sign.

CHAPTER 31

Wright-Patterson Air Force Base; Dayton, Ohio.

Ron Farr was a scientist, not a soldier, and he felt uneasy when he took the job with the air force. He felt even more uneasy as he checked in with security to enter the base. They had offered good money and good benefits; with a family, such was important to Ron. Growing up in the Northwest, in Oregon, he never imagined working for the military in the Midwest. His parents had been hippies and his wife was a progressive, a nature lover, and a liberal thinker. Not exactly a tree-hugger, but he did have a picture of her actually hugging a tree.

They had never been east of the Mississippi River, but now found themselves moving to Ohio. The air force offered on-base housing, but his wife did not want the kids growing up seeing men with guns all around the house. They had only been in Dayton a week; this was Ron's first day on the job. The security made him uneasy, but he was excited and anxious to dive into a project. Ron really wasn't clear as to what exactly his job was to be. They had been very vague on details.

The air force had recruited him from his education and experience: a PhD in quantum physics and molecular science from Stanford University. He had written a thesis on dimensional theory and a second thesis on quarks. Ron Farr had seen his future more in academia, a professor or researcher, a grant to study or experiment. He was very surprised when he was approached by the air force. He couldn't imagine why the US Air Force would need a scientist in molecular science and quantum physics; NASA maybe, but not the air force.

The wife was surprised as well, and news of relocating took some convincing. The very first night they arrived, his wife watched the local news with disgust. Crime was all they talked about. Ron had tried to comfort her, but the truth was, she moved for him. She would never have lived in Dayton, Ohio, or had any dealings with the military had she not been a good wife.

The truth also was, he had taken the job for her, and his family. It was the money and the insurance. The job itself had been light on detail for security purposes. He had to take extensive security protocols and checks to arrive at the needed clearance. He was given three polygraph tests and asked very personal and uncomfortable questions.

Now, as he was given directions by the armed air force guard, he parked and headed into his new top-secret job in a top-secret facility. He had heard the stories of this air base, that the alien autopsies had been performed here after Roswell. He couldn't help but allow his imagination to wander; after all, his field of study was quantum physics. Of course, he dismissed it, thinking aliens are not part of reality.

He was met at the door by a captain, who introduced himself and checked Ron's identification. The captain led Ron into the lobby, where both had to sign in and show their IDs to an armed soldier. They were then buzzed into the facility. It was very quiet and very clean, Ron thought as he followed the captain down a hallway. They stopped at a door and the captain punched in a code on a keypad. The door buzzed and he opened it. "Please wait here," the captain instructed.

The room contained a table and four chairs. Ron was struck as to why they would keep such a room so secure: there was nothing in it. As the captain closed the door behind him, Ron saw there was no knob on the inside. The security wasn't to keep people out but to keep people or a person, which was him at the moment, in. He had expected a level of security and paranoia, being a military base and all, but he didn't like being locked in a room.

He sat down and waited patiently. About twenty minutes passed before the door buzzed and in walked two older men. One was in plain clothes and the other in uniform. Ron stood as the two men entered and extended their hands.

"Good morning. Sorry for your wait." the plain-clothed man said, shaking Ron's hand.

"Morning," the officer said as he shook Ron's hand.

"Please sit." The plain-clothed man motioned to the seat.

Ron sat back down and eyed the two men as they sat across from him. The uniformed man placed a file in front of him.

"I am sure you are anxious to get started," the plain-clothed man said with a nod.

"Sir, I am a little in the dark. What exactly was I hired to do here?"

The man smiled and nodded. "Yes, there are certain security protocols. What we work on here is highly sensitive material, and secrecy and security come first. You understand?"

Ron nodded and smiled as he continued to listen.

"That's why we are here; to go over some of the rules."

Ron noticed the camera in the corner of the room. It felt like someone were watching him. Both of these men seemed like very serious people.

"Allow me to introduce myself, and the general here. I am Dr. Todd Bull. I will be your supervisor and head your department. This is General Jefferson. He is our military oversight. I am your boss, the general is my boss, and the President is his. You and I are civilians under government contract with the Department of Defense. You break the rules here, you won't go to prison. It is considered treason. They still shoot traitors. You will be held at the highest level of accountability. Do you understand?"

The word lingered in Ron's mind. "Shot?" he repeated.

"That's correct," General Jefferson said. "What we work on is top, top secret. National security and the safety of this country and all of its people are not to be compromised. We have rules, and these rules do not bend, for anyone. This is a dark operation. The order is a standing one. You talk about what you do outside this facility, try and take anything from this facility, bring anything or anyone into this facility, that is treason." His tone was flat yet ominous.

"Ron, we aren't trying to frighten you," Dr. Bull said, "but you do need to fully understand the seriousness of this place and what we do. Imagine the Manhattan Project, the level of security and seriousness that project carried. This is more serious and more dangerous. Those scientists were locked inside that base. We are allowing you to go home, live a quiet life with your family. We will provide a cover story, but you can't tell them or anyone of what you are really doing. Once you see what we are working on, you'll understand."

"So, you expect me to lie to my wife?"

The general shook his head slightly and eyed Ron across the table. "I expect you to say you are sorry for wasting our time and take a pass on this job. Go on with your life and build a better toaster, or whatever it is you think you can do. I have little give-a-fuck and no expectations of you. What I can guarantee is, if you do take this position, your country will be better off. I can also guarantee if you do tell your wife, the nation will seal the leak of information permanently. By not telling your wife, you would be protecting her—protecting her from knowing something that could get her killed."

"Okay, now you are threatening my wife? What the hell is this?" Ron Farr said angrily and stood.

"Ron, Ron." Dr. Bull waved Ron back to his seat. "These are not threats. There are just certain realities with this type of material. If China knew what we have, or Russia, or the Middle East. What do you think they would do to your family? We won't put you or anyone else here at risk like that, understand?"

The man gave a slight smile. "Only you will know. Only you *can* know. We need you and believe you will be a valuable asset. This is a leap of faith. Believe when I tell you, you want to say yes. We need to believe you can keep a secret. I think you can, I think after you see what it is we are working on, you will understand and be fully on team."

"Gentlemen, I can keep a secret, and I even understand the need of security, but threats I do not like. I accept the position. Obviously, this is important. You mentioned the Manhattan Project, and this alarms me. Before I go any further, I must ask, if you are building weapons here, you can count me out. I want no part in killing people. This is military, but in my view, the military should be defensive. I won't work on the next bomb."

"It's not a bomb," Dr. Bull assured him. "Ron, this is the very beginning of a whole new world. The military is part of this, because they discovered it. We aren't building weapons."

"So, you on team?" General Jefferson asked.

"Yes. What is a dark operation?" Ron asked.

The general smiled. "To put it in perspective, the President doesn't know exactly what we do here. Besides a handful of people outside this facility, no one knows what we do here."

"We have an unlimited budget, total focus on one task, ultra-modern equipment, and the very best in their fields to work the solutions," Dr. Bull said. "Yet, we are ghosts. No congressional committee is going to come in and want a tour or answers, or pull our funding. I am sure you've heard the stories of this place. Aliens? Yeah, well, that's nothing compared to this."

"So, that alien stuff was true?" Ron looked at both men closely.

Dr. Bull just shrugged, as if saying that he didn't really know. The general looked Ron directly in the eyes and said, "Didn't I just explain the rules to you? Well, they are across the board. Classified top secret is not talked about."

There were papers to sign and identification tags were handed over. A bit of small talk was exchanged, but the interview was over. The three men shook hands, and the general gave a wave at the camera. Moments later the captain opened the door from the outside, and the three stepped into the hallway. The general walked off down the hall and left the men standing in front of the door.

"Well, Ron, why don't I show you what we are really dealing with?" Dr. Bull said, motioning down the hall.

Dr. Bull, the captain and Ron Farr walked down the hall and around a couple of corners, until they approached another desk with an armed soldier. The sentry checked each of their identification carefully, looking at each man then back at the cards.

"Please place your hand on the scanner," the sentry said. Ron saw the device on the desk. Each in turn placed their hand on the scanner. The guard then punched in a series of numbers on a pad, and a set of doors opened to reveal an elevator. The three men entered and the doors joined behind them.

"Lots of security, huh?" Ron said.

"You'll get used to it," Dr. Bull said.

The elevator had no buttons, no numbers for floors; it was simply a big metal box which began to drop. Ron wasn't sure how far down they went, but they had been on the first floor of the building and the ride took every bit of two minutes.

"We work underground? How deep is this?" Ron had to ask.

"Not claustrophobic, are you?" the captain asked.

Dr. Bull smiled. "You can't even tell, once we are down there."

The elevator stopped and the doors opened. There stood another armed soldier at the ready. This time it was IDs, hand scans, and an retinal scan. Dr. Bull told Ron the security protocols were done from this position on. Anything beyond this point was absolutely top secret at the highest level.

The soldier opened a vault-like door and the men proceeded inside, where they found more soldiers. "Welcome to your new place of employment. I am sure you are anxious to see what you'll be dealing with. Thank you, captain. Ron will you come with me." Dr. Bull dismissed their escort and started down one of the hallways.

"I'll show you your office and those things later. First, I want to show you the main attraction, get your impression of the situation." Dr. Bull led him to another elevator. "The area we are headed is the most secure. It's where the experiments are conducted."

"Experiments?"

"You'll see."

The men entered the elevator and waited in silence. As the doors opened, two guards with rifles stood at each side. "Please remove any metal from your person," one soldier said, and pointed to a small table.

"Lose anything metal. Put it in the basket," Dr. Bull said.

As they stepped forward into the hall and a tunnel-like entrance, Ron could hear the sound of a machine, a loud knocking sound. "We do this coming and going," Dr. Bull said. "It's perfectly safe, like a MRI. Just makes sure your heart is beating and blood is flowing. Come on."

They turned the corner and the room opened up. There were people moving about in lab coats and carrying clipboards.

As they moved into the laboratory, Ron noticed very thick glass-walled chambers. Those in the room were observing the chambers and writing on their clipboards. From his angle, Ron couldn't see what it was they were observing.

"Let's go introduce you," Dr. Bull said, putting a hand on Ron's elbow.

The group did not turn their attention from their task. As they approached the scientists, Ron could see inside the chamber. There stood a naked man, a very strange and sickly-looking man.

"Had you been here yesterday, you really would have gotten the full show. Ron, what can you tell me about alternate universes? The multiverse? Dimensionary concepts?"

"There are theories. Some say there are different planes of existence. Hawking described a multiverse when he theorized about time travel. Space and time are both manmade measurements, speed and molecular cohesion. It is complicated. Why?" Ron asked.

"Yes, but is it a 3-D world or do we only perceive it to be? Length, width, depth; does speed factor in, what other factors are at play? Solidity, liquid, gases? Do you see that mirror behind the creature?" Dr. Bull asked.

"Yes. Creature? Why do you call that man a creature?"

"Oh, that is what it is. That creature came out of that mirror. That's why you are here. Our task is to solve this question." Dr. Bull paused.

"Came out of that mirror? What do you mean?" Ron asked, puzzled.

Dr. Bull nodded and motioned with his head. "Come with me, I'll show you." He led Ron beyond the rows of glass chambers into an office. Turning on a television screen, Dr. Bull pressed a button and the screen began to show the experiment. A man stood inside the chamber. It appeared he had something in his hand, a knife maybe. It appeared that he cut himself and said something, then rushed out of the chamber.

Watching the creature crawl out of the mirror made Ron think of some sort of illusion or magic trick. Dr. Bull turned off the screen and looked at Ron. "Well, what do you think?"

Ron Farr furrowed his brow. "So, this creature, as you called it, just emerged from the mirror? What does it want? Does it communicate? Is this for real?"

"This was video of our first one. We have determined these creatures are violent, aggressive, and myopic in task. They come to retrieve their mirror image. They are almost unstoppable. This is very real, and you have been brought here to figure out how the mirror works, where those things come from, and whatever other questions which are bound to come up." Dr. Bull shrugged slightly.

"Why me?"

"Your field of study. You are young, open-minded, and a problem solver. This is going to take time to figure out. We know some, but to truly discover the technology, to use it for our own purposes, it could take decades."

Ron squinted at the man. "What do we know?"

"There are triggers. We know how to activate the mirrors and bring out the creatures."

"Where do these mirrors come from? We have gained this information through these experiments?"

Dr. Bull tilted his head. "Most of what we know has come from these experiments, but also some private field research. Let's just say the details are limited. People have had to deal with these things. Now we have to figure this out and protect people."

Ron looked around the room and shook his head. "I didn't think this was what I would be working on."

Dr. Bull smiled and nodded. "It's a big step. Everything is on the secure server. Let me show you to your office. It is a lot to absorb your first day. Ease into it, but I need you to roll with this. Look over the material and develop a hypothesis. I would like an initial report by Friday. Broad strokes. Ideas on the creature, the mirrors, how you think they function, where the energy source might come from, and the possible properties at work."

"By Friday? Will I be able to analyze the creatures, the mirrors?"

No. You will have to learn the proper protocols first. I want a first impression. Sometime a fresh look at something can spark some good insights, or thoughts we may have overlooked," Dr. Bull said.

"You realize I would be simply guessing. Without any real contact or analysis, I will be shooting in the dark."

Dr. Bull smiled. "Yes, but it would be an educated guess. That's why you are here. Ron, this is new territory for all of us. Those creatures are not of this world. This is significant. This will change science forever, answers to questions man has had since the beginning. Where do we come from? Why are we here?" He put a hand on Ron's shoulder. "We are *all* guessing at this point. I'm not looking for you to be right or wrong. Just give us directions to look. We are going to discover the answers together. This is our baby. Sure, the military sees a new world, new threats, and unstoppable soldiers. Imagine what might lie beyond that threshold. What is in that other dimension could help mankind for centuries to come."

"You realize what jumped out of that mirror doesn't seem to be friendly," Ron pointed out. "That's not a good sign. We open a door which we can't close, that could spell disaster for mankind. It was the reflection of that man which emerged. If it is an alternate universe, a mirror of our world, only with different properties, they could be as anxious as we to better themselves from our world."

Dr. Bull pulled back his hand and moved toward the door. "That's why we had better be very cautious. That is why we are all here. Why we will take our time and make damn sure we can protect this world from that one." He nodded for Ron to follow him and the two men exited the office.

They stood and observed the creature beyond the thick glass partition. Ron was amazed and somewhat frightened by the being trapped inside the chamber. "What are you going to do with it?" Ron asked.

A woman scientist in a lab coat gave him a glance. "See what it takes to kill it," she said emotionlessly.

Ron looked at the creature more closely and began to question such tactics. Just killing the thing seemed wasteful. That was when the creature lunged at the glass and struck with such force it shook. Ron took a number of steps back, as did the others. "Is that going to hold it?" Ron asked. The thing had bounced off and shook its head. It lunged once again, with even more force than before. The thick glass shuddered and it seemed the whole chamber shook.

"Gas it," Dr. Bull said. One of the other scientists pushed a button. A thick cloud of some kind of gas was released. Ron Farr watched as the chamber was filled with the white smoke and the pale monster seemed to disappear into it. Then it flung itself at the glass wall once again, with even more intensity than before. The gas didn't seem to affect the creature. "That is incredible," Dr. Bull said. "Zyklon B, a full canister of Zyklon B, and it is fine. There is enough poisonous gas in that room to kill a thousand people. This thing is as strong as ever."

Dr. Bull approached the glass and the controls. "We will deflate the room. See if this thing can go without air altogether." Dr. Bull pushed another button.

Ron watched as the cloud of gas and, apparently, the air, was sucked out of the room. No effect on the creature.

Dr. Bull nodded. "Interesting."

Ron didn't find it interesting, he found it very alarming.

"Call in the team, I want to avoid frying it. We want a good specimen to examine," Dr. Bull told one of the other scientists.

He moved over next to Ron. "These things are tough. There is a copy of a report on your desk. An initial report, our findings and some information from a group of civilians who had to deal with these things."

"Civilians?"

Dr. Bull nodded. "They posted the information on the internet. Luckily, we scrubbed it before too many people read it. Could have been a real disaster. We used a lot of their discoveries to go by."

"How did they stop the thing?" Ron asked.

"They didn't. The creature took who it was after," Dr. Bull said somberly.

Another thunderous collision sounded, which again startled Ron. The creature was growing more and more enraged. Ron was really beginning to question the integrity of the chamber. A group of soldiers arrived, in full riot gear and armed.

"Are you going to shoot it?" Ron asked.

"Bullets don't work either," Dr. Bull said over his shoulder as he moved toward the soldiers. "Gentlemen, the creature in there may look like a frail and weakly man, but you will quickly learn that is not the case. I need you to go in and restrain it. Bullets may slow it down, but they won't stop the creature. Get it down, get it restrained and get out."

The creature slammed into the glass again. This gained the full attention of the six soldiers who had just been ordered to go into the chamber with it. They all had looks of surprise and concern. Ron Farr was impressed with the level of momentum the creature could generate and the sheer force with which struck the glass. He thought he would not want to go into that chamber.

"Let me put the air back into the room. You guys can't work in a vacuum," Dr. Bull said, moving to the controls.

The comment got a couple reactions from the soldiers. These were tough men, trained killers, but they were uneasy at the task ahead. They bunched together and made a plan of attack, then moved to the side of the chamber. Ron could see a series of chamber doors. For security purposes, one had to go through a series of smaller chambers to enter. The soldiers waited as the final glass panel between them and the creature began to open.

"Where is the person you used to draw the creature out?" Ron asked.

"Why?" Dr. Bull asked in return.

Ron nodded toward the glass. "Look at that thing. It is watching the team. Why not distract it?"

It was too late; the soldiers had entered the main chamber. They rushed the creature in a blitz attack. The glass panel behind them closed as they charged forward. One soldier went high, another low, and still another went for an arm.

The creature moved; with barely a hop, it sprung straight up and with a flip in mid-air it bounced off the ceiling, then off the far wall. It moved like lightning. It was so quick, its movements were almost a blur.

The bounce off the wall put the creature to one side of the group. With one swat of its hand, a soldier flew to the other side of the chamber. One of the larger soldiers tried to jump on its back, but the damn thing jumped and smashed the man against the ceiling. As the creature landed on its feet, the large soldier landed in a clump.

"You better get that guy out of there. You better get them all out of there and just fire the room," Ron suggested.

Dr. Bull grabbed the phone and yelled into it, then went to an intercom and told the soldiers to back off and move toward the door. The order was really after the fact; the soldiers had already begun to back away from the creature.

The creature's attention shifted. Ron hadn't noticed the man enter, but the creature was now laser-focused through the glass. Just as Ron turned to really look at the man, the creature slammed into the glass harder than it had before. Ron could see the supports for the glass wall stress from the impact.

"Get them out of there!" Ron yelled. The creature was now fixated on the man just a few feet from Ron. It was the reflection, the double, the trigger which brought the creature from the mirror. Ron could see the thing trying to figure out the obstacle, the obstruction between it and its prey.

Ron realized the creature had been slamming the glass in a primitive testing process, a trial and error. It was classic animal behavior. As Ron was watching the pale beast, it made a quick move, jumping up on the back wall of the chamber, using it as a platform to push off from. It lunged, flying through the air at the front wall of glass, at its mirror image, the man.

Ron took a number of steps back. The damn thing was using all of its body weight and all the force it could generate to try and break through the glass. From the last hit, Ron had seen the support on the floor stress, and he knew it would be a matter of time before they finally gave. The soldiers were finally making it out of the chamber, but it was too late.

The creature impacted the glass and the bottom support snapped, breaking loose. Dr. Bull had been correct: the glass was strong enough, but what held the glass in place was not. The thick sheet slid out and collapsed on top of the crea-ture. It had to weigh a ton, Ron thought. Moving further back, he watched as the creature, no longer behind glass but under it, began to wiggle out from underneath.

The thing slipped out from under and sprang on top of a desk. The man who had come in just stared at the creature, frozen with fear. He stood there, open-mouthed, terror across his face. Ron could only watch in pure amazement and surprise.

A gun shot cracked in the room. One of the soldiers had stepped from the chamber and fired a shot, hitting the creature in the back. The creature glanced over its shoulder at the soldier, gauging the threat, then refocused on its target and leapt forward. One magnificent leap and it had its prey. It threw the man, its mirror image, over its shoulder, like he was a bag of potatoes. Pivoting, it turned back toward the chamber and bounded back past everyone. It was so quick; from the moment it had broken out of the chamber till this very moment was maybe a minute, two tops.

A ripple in the mirror at the back of the chamber and both the man and the creature were gone.

All went eerily quiet, as everyone stood and stared at the mirror. Ron almost had overlooked the reflective piece of glass in the back of the chamber, but now it stood out as a solitary invader to their world. The creature was gone; the only evidence of it was the destruction left behind. The man was gone as well. Ron suddenly questioned the wisdom of taking this position.

He was fairly certain that the man who had been taken didn't expect what happened to happen. His drive into work most likely did not involve thinking he would be abducted by his creepy reflection from an alternate dimension.

Dr. Bull shook his head and sat on the edge of a desk. The soldiers moved from the chamber and gathered together, confused and disheartened. The other scientists were as he was, frozen in shock. This was the worst first day on the job, ever.

They all now had a very good idea of the power they were dealing with. They had lost one of their own. Ron hadn't met the man, but witnessing the fear and the brutality of his abduction, he felt a personal connection. He had never seen anything like that, and the reality of being there didn't make it any more or less unbelievable.

"Is everyone all right?" Dr. Bull stammered.

"What the hell was that?" one of the soldiers said.

Dr. Bull leaned up from the desk. "You men will be debriefed. Go and get checked out. This was a terrible error. We have a lot of work yet to do. Everyone, please take a few moments and then fill out an after action report. We want to evaluate the events."

It was a good couple of hours before the confusion and calamity of the event finally simmered down. Ron had gone off with one of the other scientists to his office, not remembering where it was after all the excitement. He took a few minutes to collect himself, then dove into the file on his desk. He wanted to know as much as he could.

The information in the file was very illuminating. He read over it three times before a fellow scientist came to collect him for a debrief.

He was escorted to a conference room. Dr. Bull sat at the head of the table and six other people, all in lab coats, surrounded it. His escort pointed out a chair and they both sat down.

"Thank you for joining us. This is Dr. Ron Farr, our dimensionary expert. Eventful first day," Dr. Bull said with a raised eyebrow. "I am very upset by the happenings and the loss of Dr. Dunkirk. James was a good man. Such an oversight can not be repeated. We lost James Dunkirk, and I am going to have to explain that to a lot of people, and especially to his family. This is unacceptable. This was a valuable lesson learned, a tragic lesson, but valuable. I think now we all see what we are dealing with and the seriousness of our responsibilities."

Ron was surprised at the calmness of the meeting. The fact was, a creature from some other world had just taken a human being, right in front of them all. The military couldn't stop it, had seemed helpless in comparison. He thought they might be more upset. Especially after losing a member of their team.

"James was a good man and we all should take a moment to appreciate his sacrifice. I do not mean to seem cold or unfeeling, but he, as we all do, knew the risks here. Now, why don't we go over what we have learned. Address what happened." Dr. Bull began the meeting.

Ron Farr listened as the talk bounced around the table. One scientist, who must have majored in the obvious, suggested better reinforcements for the chamber. What changes could be made were discussed. Another scientist brought up the control of the creature. Ron just listened as he sat there, looking from person to person.

"You are awfully quiet, Ron," Dr. Bull said after a while. "Jump in, give us your thoughts. It's why you are here."

Ron saw no reason not to speak candidly. "My opinion? Seems like kids at Christmas, with a new toy you all want to play with but don't know how it works. I didn't know James, but I am certain he is disappointed with how things went. Whatever the plan was, what I just saw was a monumental failure."

"James volunteered, and knew the risk of opening the mirror," Dr. Bull said. "This is a learning process; there will be more failures than successes in the beginning. Do you have any real suggestions to better the experiment, or did the event just rattle you to project your fear into snarky comments?"

"The creature adapted," Ron said. "It used momentum and defended itself. As primal and simple as it is, having what seems to be only one objective, it did use logical thought. It figured out how to achieve its purpose. Any creature that comes out of there will do the very same. We have to better anticipate, be much better prepared, if we decide to open the mirror again."

"Such as?" Dr. Bull asked.

Ron shrugged. "Perhaps fill the chamber with water, so it can't gain the force it needs or use other forms of deterrence. Does it have to be a human target? Granted, to activate the mirror it must speak of God, so perhaps use a parrot?"

"Hadn't thought of that. Would a bird emerge? That's an interesting thought," Dr. Bull said.

"I would worry about the water. What if it just ran into the mirror?" one of the other scientists hypothesized.

"Can we remove the mirror?" Ron asked.

Dr. Bull nodded and looked around the table. "See people, this is what fresh eyes can do. A new perspective. Dr. Farr, glad to have you with us."

Ron wasn't too sure how he felt about his new situation. Yet he realized he was in it now and was going to have to make it work. He knew one thing for damn sure: he did not want one of those things after him.

CHAPTER 32

One year later...

O Time passes and memories fade, things become routine. Ron Farr was now a valued and experienced member of the research team at Wright-Patterson Air Force Base. He had come to know a great deal more of the story and the cover-up involved with the mirrors. He had learned a great deal more of the mirrors themselves. Ron had not forgotten his very first day of work and the dramatic loss of one of the team.

Ron had not forgotten his first night home after work either. His wife had questions, and Ron was not the type to lie to his wife. Not wanting to involve their children, he asked her to wait till they were in bed and then they could talk about it. He sat her down and told her he could not discuss his work with her, not now and not ever. She did not like the sound of such a situation and got upset. He explained that it was national security and part of the contract. Still, she was angry.

Ron had to beg her to understand, told her how important his work would be. Tried to explain that the importance was why it was so secret. He said it was just part of the job. It took some doing and a long night of talk, but in the end, she allowed her love for her husband to overcome her anger.

She never asked about it again. Not a "how was your day", or "what did you do at work today", or even "rough day at the office?" She never asked, and Ron was grateful for that. The kids from time to time would inquire, but Ron could go into some scientific talk and they would quickly let it go. Home life was good; it was work which troubled Ron's mind, troubled his conscience. Aspects of what he had learned made him feel soiled down to his very soul.

Dr. Todd Bull had come to count on Ron, to confide in him, and he moved Ron up. Ron was made lead researcher, and with the title came a lot of responsibilities. People wanted progress, results, and Ron had more questions than answers. This led him to begin to try and solve them, and this was where he began to learn the treachery and lengths his employer, the federal government, would go to keep it all secret.

The email in the report he had read on his very first day was from a woman, Doris Lamb. She'd had direct knowledge of the mirrors and Ron wanted to speak with her.

Dr. Bull had not wanted to go into it with Ron; he avoided the subject a number of times. Finally, Ron cornered his boss and demanded a direct answer. Dr. Bull reminded Ron as to the level of security involved in this project. He informed Ron that great effort had been taken to silence those who could compromise that level of secrecy. The email she had sent to so many was clamped down. The law enforcement agencies were easy enough, but the news people had to be ordered to bury the story.

Being news people, they had argued the public had a right to know, but national security trumps the freedom of information. As for the woman, Dr. Bull explained she had to be institutionalized and was now in a vegetative state. Ron asked about the Mason family and was told they were missing but presumed dead. His boss talked about the factory fire and that the family who had made the mirrors was dead.

Ron was no naïve child, or some kind of rube; he knew cover-ups happened, that people don't just disappear. The team had made advances and developed ways of opening the mirrors and maintaining the creatures. They conducted their experiments and the creatures were incredible: super strong, virtually unstoppable. Dismemberment and fire seemed to work best to hinder their singular purpose.

They didn't need to breathe and they had no blood, so cold and gas didn't affect them. The beasts were not the focus for Ron; he needed to get at the mirrors. They now had five open mirrors, but the creatures were a problem and had to be dealt with first.

Today was a big day for the team: they were going to send in a robot into one of the open mirrors. The robot had all the latest technical devices and would send a signal back, hopefully giving the research team their first look into the world beyond.

The plan was to send it in, gain information, and bring it back out. The robot had sensors and soil sample devices; it was very similar to the probes NASA had sent to Mars. The team had tried a robot once before, but no information had come back. The million-dollar robot went into the mirror and vanished. Nothing. That was it.

The use of the robot had been Dr. Bull's idea, and Ron had thought it a very good one. When nothing was retrieved, the idea took a back burner. Ron came up with the suggestion of using a lifeline, to use a cable that would remain attached to the robot that the information could come through. Also, the cable could be used to pull the robot back if need be. The idea took some convincing for the general; even if they'd had an unlimited budget, which they didn't, he wasn't going to throw good money after bad. Ron could understand that, but the data needed to be had. It was a sound idea and Dr. Bull backed him.

Today was the day to test Ron's idea and with all hopes gain the insight as well as hard data of what they were really dealing with. They had moved the creatures into solid concrete bunkers and now observed them via video surveillance cameras. The robot had been introduced through a small panel. The creature paid it less mind than the hole it had emerged from. The mirror had been placed in front of a ramp, prior to activation, and all was ready.

Ron walked into the control room. The other scientists and crew needed to run the robot were already ready. Monitors showed the scene, the room from different angles, from the robot, every possible view. Dials and buttons, lights and indicators—Ron was amazed by the amount of equipment that was in use. Dr. Bull entered with the general; of course they had come for the show. "We ready to go?" Dr. Bull asked Ron.

"Yes, sir, ready."

"Is it going to work this time?" the general spoke up, irritably.

Dr. Bull nodded. "We are confident that it will, sir."

Ron knew the real answer was that they didn't know, but no one was going to tell the general that. "Okay, people, let's do this," he said. "Are the recording devices functioning? No mistakes, people."

"Don't want someone saying they forgot to put a tape in the machine, now do we?" the general said with a little chuckle.

"Move ahead slow. Don't want Stanley to notice the robot, Ron voiced.

"Stanley? You named the creature Stanley?" the General questioned. Dr. Bull nodded to the General and gave a slight shrug. "Where did you come up with that?"

"That would be me, sir," one of the scientists spoke up. The general no doubt noticed the scientist looked exactly like the creature.

"Dr. Stan Burrows, our bio-engineer, General," Dr. Bull introduced.

"Start up the ramp, easy. Don't want that cable moving too much. Let's distract Stanley, throw up the picture and spray the mist," Ron ordered.

The general drew closer and watched the monitor. "What are they spraying?"

"Dr. Burrows's blood into the air. Just a small amount, but it really distracts the creature," Dr. Bull explained.

The general nodded and watched as an image of Dr. Burrows appeared on the wall.

"All right, here we go, ladies and gentlemen. All systems green. Move the robot into the mirror. Break the plane," Ron ordered. His heart beat with excitement and nervousness, thump after thump. All eyes were glued to the monitors. The tension in the control room was thick. The view of the mirror grew closer and closer. "Easy now," Ron said. This was the moment. The threshold to a new world.

As the robot moved through the mirror, passing beyond the liquefied glass, the monitors went dark. In that moment, Ron's heart sank. "Use the night vision lens," he said. He had been concerned, thinking if it was an alternate universe, a robot from that world might roll into the room here, in place of the one they were sending into the other universe. As Ron waited for the night vision to come on, he checked the monitor in the room. Stanley was focused on the image of Dr. Burrows, and there were no other robots in the room. The cable extended into the mirror. All seemed to be going as planned.

As the picture on the screen became a green image and focused, Ron could tell immediately it was not a mirror universe to our own. The robot was not in a room at all, it was outside. "Hold it right there," Ron said. "Don't move it. Let us get our bearings. We don't want to draw attention if there are other creatures about."

"Look, is that a foundation? As if the room was there but now isn't?" Dr. Burrows pointed out.

It was true. It looked as if a room had been there, but all that was left was one row of cinderblocks at ground level.

"Is it night?" a voice asked.

The overhead view showed clouds, and it was very dark, but considering the pale condition the creatures emerged in, Ron had to assume there was little to no sunlight to be had. Ron looked closely; the clouds were thick and ominous, like storm clouds here, but he saw no lightning or rain.

"Put the rear camera up on the big screen," Ron ordered. One of the team punched a button and the view was on the large monitor. "Look at that. No mirror, no nothing. You can see the cable and it just stops. As if it hangs in mid-air. No wonder no one comes out of these things. They can't find an exit."

"Look closer, there is a distortion. Looks like heatwaves or vapors or something. Almost can't see it but it's there," Dr. Bull pointed out.

"Punch up the front view. Does any one see anything moving?" Ron asked. Everyone in the room leaned in a little closer.

"Is that a tree in the distance?" a female voice asked.

Ron moved closer to the large monitor. "No grass. Looks like stripped earth. Streaks in the ground. If there is no grass, there can't be a tree." Still, the closer he looked, it did appear to be a tree. "Zoom on that, that, tree," Ron ordered. It had no leaves, but the very dead tree had some branches and a trunk.

The team and crew, along with Dr. Bull and the general, all just watched the monitors, their eyes moving from one to the next. All were silent, concentrating, thinking. "Does anyone see any movement?" Ron finally asked, but a pin could have crushed the silence.

"Move slowly, forward. Get a soil sample, that dirt looks crazy. And collect an air quality test as well." Ron continued to run the experiment.

"Where are those creatures?" The general asked the question they all were wondering.

"Move to the edge of the foundation and scan," Ron instructed. *Those things should be everywhere, this isn't making any sense,* he thought. A parallel or reflective dimension would have made more sense, considering the creatures which emerge were identical to the individuals who triggered the mirrors. They kept watching the monitors. The robot stopped, the picture shuddered, and then the camera began to pan to the right.

"There is nothing here. Where the hell is this and why the hell aren't those creatures around?" the general asked.

"Okay, let's move back and anchor. Prepare to fire the rocket," Ron said.

"Rocket? What rocket?" the general asked.

"It is a reconnaissance drone rocket," Ron told him. "We fire it and it sends an aerial overview, photographs and mapping back to the robot and on to us. This should give us a larger picture of the area we are dealing with. Landscape, terrain, occupants, landmarks, water, possible areas of interest."

"Good idea."

"We are in position and ready," one of the crew members said.

Ron paused and checked each monitor. "All systems ready? We only have one of these. Let's get this right. Fire the rocket when ready."

The overhead view lit up with fire. The main monitor showed the view and information from the rocket.

"We are green," a crew member said. "At one hundred feet, five hundred… a thousand feet. All systems green. Two thousand feet. Pitching and beginning arch. Three thousand feet."

"What's the range?" the general asked.

"The recon rocket goes up about a mile, then deploys a parachute, continuing to scan and deliver information on descent, sir," Dr. Bull chimed in.

The camera shook and the crew member continued with the status report. "Five thousand feet. Detachment of fuel cell and we have deployment of chute. Green. Green across the board."

The rocket landed and still nothing stood out. Nothing seemed to move. The entire area seemed dead. Ron had expected something.

"Okay, let's pull the robot back, slowly. Let's get Stanley distracted and get this locked down," Dr. Todd Bull said. "There is a lot of information to go over and a lot of questions to ponder. Good work, people. Professional job. I am proud of your efforts today. General, I can't explain the lack of movement, but we will. This is a big step, but it is just our first step into this world."

The general addressed the room. "I am very happy with the experiment. Good work, team. We all know this is a process. What you've done here today is important. We will find the creatures, and we will get to the bottom of all our questions. I am impressed with what you've done here today and looking forward to reading the report."

"Ron, why don't you accompany the general and me. Debrief the experiment," Dr. Bull said.

The three left the control room and headed to Dr. Bull's office. No words were exchanged until the door was closed behind them. The general now spoke in a displeased tone. "That footage concerns me, and it's going to concern others. Where were those things? I didn't see shit but a dead tree. I have one of those in my backyard, for Christ's sake. We have been at this for a while, gentlemen. We have made some progress, but I don't hear a lot of answers."

Ron knew he needed to spin the situation, put a positive outlook on the experiment. "General, we need to evaluate the footage and the samples. I was as surprised as you that we didn't see those creatures, but that's a good thing. Can you imagine a million of them waiting on the other side of the glass? You want to walk through that mirror and be surrounded by those creatures, or a dead tree?"

Ron could see his tactic was working. "The tree shows that at some point life was sustainable. The soil produced life. You are a military man, so you look for threats, enemies, targets, advantages, strategy. We are scientists, and we see a whole new world, General, which seem to be empty. This could solve lots of problems."

"Like what?"

"We all report to somebody, don't we? Imagine if there is oil there. Imagine how the powers that be would like a whole new world of untapped resources. Hell, if we only used it as a dump, it would pay for all this and then some."

"There is no evidence of oil," the general stated.

"There is no evidence there *isn't* oil there either," Dr. Bull pointed out.

The general nodded. "This was a good step. We have gained entry and discovered no resistance. Further investigation and research will have to continue to determine the full potential of this…" he paused. "What is this? What is this called?"

Ron tilted his head. "Let's call it an alternate dimension. Being that there were no creatures, this could be a gateway to multiple dimensions."

"Is there any evidence to support that?" the general asked.

"No, that's why I said *could*. One thing for certain, those creatures come from somewhere."

The meeting lasted a while longer, and Ron believed he had turned the general's mood toward the positive. Ron needed to get back and begin going over the material. He knew reports would need to be done.

Returning to the control room, he had expected his team to be busy, but when he got there, his team seemed anxious and excited. "Sir, you have got to see this," Dr. Burrows said, rushing to meet him at the door.

"Run that again. You aren't going to believe this," Burrows said, excited. The tech punched up the video on the main monitor. "Okay, run it. This is on descent, four thousand feet. There, look right there. Three figures."

"Freeze that!" Ron commanded.

"Wait, it gets better," Burrows said.

"Three thousand feet," the tech said.

Ron moved closer to the screen. "Wait, go back. They are going to go out of frame. Can't believe we missed that." Ron shook his head.

"That's not the best part. Fast forward after the landing," Dr. Burrows instructed the tech.

"There is more?"

"You left after it landed, we all started to shut it down. Here, stop the image. We were just pulling the robot out but the rocket was still sending an image. We only have a couple seconds but look, go slow motion," Burrows ordered the tech. Ron watched the screen, tilted angle, half of the view obstructed by dirt. The rocket had landed and fallen over.

Ron strained to see, looking for any little thing in the background. All of a sudden, the whole picture moved and a giant face filled the screen, so close it was out of focus and all blurry. The rocket's autofocus adjusted and a little boy's face, smiling, filled the monitor. Ron knew he had seen that face before. He just knew it. Johnny Mason; the little boy who had gone missing. Then the screen went black.

"What? That's all we have? Run it back," Ron instructed.

"We can't believe it either. Did you see his eyes, that smile? That was no creature. That was a little boy," Burrows said excitedly.

Questions swirled in Ron Farr's mind. How did he get there? Was he alone? How did he survive? Ron's brain ached with thought. "Go back, back to the descent. Those images. Blow that up, close up, zoom in."

The tech punched keys on his computer and the image enlarged. Click after click, the image filled the screen.

"Clean it up. I want clear," Ron instructed. He moved right in front of the screen, looking closely. A small person in front, the little boy, Johnny. Two images walked behind, close together. Ron put his face almost to the screen. It appeared they were holding hands.

CHAPTER 33

The year was 2009. Patty Johnson sped down an on-ramp. She was late for work. Trying to make up time, she pressed on the accelerator and tried to apply her eye makeup in the rearview mirror. There was a light sprinkle of rain; she turned on the windshield wipers to clear her view of the road. Driving down the ramp and onto the freeway, she came up behind a slow-moving tractor trailer in the merge lane. Patty signaled and sped around the trucker, the pressure of air shaking her car. Driving the freeway always made Patty nervous. Had she not been running late, she would have taken surface streets.

The rain picked up and she increased the speed of her wipers. A flash of lightning lit up the sky in front of her, followed by the crack of thunder. Patty didn't much care for driving in the rain. She gave up on her makeup, wanting to focus on the road. She hated to be late and checked her speed. Pressing a little more on the gas, she figured she had new tires, all-wheel drive, a newer car; a little rain shouldn't be a problem.

The raindrops got bigger, splashing off the freeway and pelting the car hard. She looked at the clock on the radio. She only had ten minutes to get to work or she would be late and be in trouble. Pushing just a little more on the accelerator, Patty gripped the wheel with both hands. She turned the wipers up to full speed and focused on the road.

Her cell phone rang, just as a small deer came from the right side of the road. A little hop from the berm and it landed right in front of her car. It had appeared quickly, but Patty saw it and changed lanes to avoid it. The car began to hydroplane, continuing its path across the road. Patty gripped the wheel, turning to correct but it was still sliding. She applied the brake on the water-covered road.

Turning the wheel more and pushing harder on the brake, she got closer to the side of the road and the grass. The car finally began to react and straighten, but her right rear wheel caught the edge of the road and jerked the back of the car. Grass and mud flew everywhere and the car was sliding again. Patty's heart raced as she tried to correct the other way. She was losing control, then she was out of control. Her new tires dug into the wet earth and her nice new car flipped into the air.

There was an explosion in her face. The airbag. She felt the seatbelt cut into her shoulder and her arms flew every which way. She hit her head on the roof, then pitched forward and then slammed back in her seat. The world outside tumbled past, topsy turvy. Then the car impacted with the ground again. Flip after flip, mud flying, metal bending, plastic and glass breaking, her car came apart around her.

It was a magnificent crash. When the car finally came to rest in the mud, Patty was dizzy and banged up pretty bad. The cabin of the car was smashed and she hurt all over. Her legs were pinned, or at least it felt that way. Her face hurt and her mouth was full of blood. She had about bit her tongue in half. The car had landed on all fours but the roof was caved in; she was smashed down against the seat. The rearview mirror was on the floorboards, and she could see she was missing teeth. She was a bloody mess, cut, broken nose, busted teeth, half-bit tongue.

"This is Road Star, satellite monitoring system. We have been alerted to your airbag deployment. Do you need assistance?" a voice sounded in the car.

"I have been in an accident. Please help me. I am hurt," Patty said, lisping badly.

"We have your location. We will dispatch an ambulance immediately. Are you alone or are there other occupants?"

"It's just me. I am really hurt. Knocked my tooth out and I'm bleeding. Oh my God, I think my legs are broken. I smell gas. Get me out of here. Oh no, what is that. Help me!" Patty screamed. "HELP ME!"

"Help is coming. Just remain calm, they are on the way."

"That's not right, no! What the hell. STOP! NO! There is something. HELP! HELP ME, PLEASE. AAAHHH!" Patty's voice was filled with terror and then all was silent.

"Ma'am? Miss Johnson? Please stay on the line. Make a sound if you aren't able to speak. Are you there? Miss Johnson? Is there someone there?" the voice asked.

The Road Star operator stayed on the line until emergency responders arrived. There was no Patty Johnson, just two legs smashed under the dash, a lot of blood and a mangled car. The call was recorded and is one more mystery in a world full of them.

— ABOUT THE AUTHOR —

Phillip A. Weaver was born in Raleigh, North Carolina, but he was raised in Montana, on the grounds of the state mental institution at Warm Springs. Phillip is the son of a PhD in psychology and a nurse. He moved to Ohio to attend college and be near family. Phillip was incarcerated in 1996 for attempted murder with no witnesses, no motive, and no direct evidence. Twenty-one years granted Phillip the opportunity to produce numerous handwritten manuscripts; he hopes you enjoy this one. Mr. Weaver still lives in Ohio with his wife Joyce, their two dogs, and a skinny, elderly cat.

www.ingramcontent.com/pod-product-compliance
Lightning Source LLC
Chambersburg PA
CBHW030108260626
47156CB00008B/2574